THE VOYAGE OF
THE SABLE KEECH

Neal Asher was born in Billericay, Essex, and still lives
nearby. He started writing SF and fantasy at the age of
sixteen, and has since had many stories published. His
previous full-length novels have been *Gridlinked*, *The
Skinner*, *The Line of Polity*, *Cowl* and *Brass Man*.

NEAL ASHER

THE VOYAGE OF
THE SABLE KEECH

TOR

First published 2006 by Tor

First published in paperback 2006 by Tor
an imprint of Pan Macmillan Ltd
Pan Macmillan, 20 New Wharf Road, London N1 9RR
Basingstoke and Oxford
Associated companies throughout the world
www.panmacmillan.com

ISBN-13: 978-0-330-41160-8
ISBN-10: 0-330-41160-8

1 3 5 7 9 8 6 4 2

A CIP catalogue record for this book is available from
the British Library.

Typeset by IntypeLibra Limited, London
Printed and bound in Great Britain by
Mackays of Chatham plc, Chatham, Kent

To Paul, Martin and Bob Asher,
for being my brothers

Acknowledgements

Cheers and best wishes to everyone involved in bringing this book to the shelves, including my wife Caroline, my parents Bill and Hazel, and those working at Macmillan and elsewhere: Peter Lavery, who should write a book himself about matters editorial, Rebecca Saunders, John Jarrold, Steve Rawlings, Jon Mitchell, Chantal Noel, Neil Lang, Chloe Brighton, Keith Starkey and many others besides. If I've not listed your name it's not because I don't appreciate your work, but probably because I don't know about it and because remembering names is assigned to that small portion of my brain labelled 'real life'.

Prologue

Seeing the creature loom out of the underwater gloom, Vrell immediately recognized it from the bio-files concerning this planet's fauna. The humans called it a molly carp – the second part of its name resulting from its huge main body resembling a Terran fish called a carp. However, rather than use its tail for propulsion, this creature towed itself along the seabed with masses of belly tentacles. Now, it drew to a halt, those same tentacles winding together to form one trunk, so it came to stand like some strange fleshy tree. Perhaps this was some form of camouflage? No, the trunk twisted, turning the utterly level carp body towards Vrell, and thick lips drew back from a mass of translucent teeth.

Vrell felt his guts shrink with fear. Those few weapons he had retained were useless here, as they had been specifically designed for land warfare. Moreover, the natural cowardice of Prador adulthood – which he had only recently attained – had been exacerbated by many recent attempts on his life. He kept moving further down into the depths, his beacon return telling him that his father's ship was not far away. The carp eagerly closed in and began to circle him, observing. Perhaps it was curious about this potential dinner.

Vrell now surmised that his father, Ebulan, had been verging on senility, of which his venture to this hostile world had been just one sign. The war against mankind had been over for most of Ebulan's lifetime and now trade and better relations were growing between the Prador and the humans. Because of atrocities Ebulan, with the connivance of certain humans, had committed here during that long-ago war – the coring of humans to use as Prador slaves – his fortunes in the Kingdom had recently been on the wane. However, coming here in an attempt to wipe out the Old Captains – ancient sea captains who were the only remaining survivors of the coring trade and therefore actual witnesses to Ebulan's crimes – had been futile. Vrell, being an adolescent rigidly under the control of his father's pheromones, had no say in the matter, and nearly died as a result. During those same events Ebulan's spaceship had been knocked out of the sky by some missile, and it seemed likely that all those aboard were dead. Vrell assumed himself the only survivor – and maybe not even that for much longer.

The bottom here was a sloping stone slab crawling with leeches. Vrell skirted the occasional clusters of spiral-shelled hammer whelks, knowing that a concerted attack from them would be enough to crack his shell. The frog whelks he encountered quickly scattered, perhaps thinking him some new kind of glister – a creature he resembled only in that he possessed an exoskeleton and a similar number of legs. Vrell saw the vague shape of his father's crashed spaceship ahead of him, picked out by the glow of still-burning internal fires, when the molly carp finally attacked.

It came in fast and low, clamping its thick-lipped mouth on his damaged claw. It rolled over, its tentacles starring around it. Vrell tried to spin over as well, but was not fast enough. The monster tore Vrell's claw away from his body, gristle and tendons ripping out of his carapace and his green blood squirting into the water. The pain of that would have been more than enough, but while he was on his back, struggling to right himself, leeches attached themselves to the wound and began eating their way in. His bubbling scream echoed into the depths as he finally righted himself and forced himself onwards. He turned one palp eye and watched the molly carp champing down on his claw, crushing the shell as easily as chalk and sucking out the meat. He could feel the leeches simultaneously working their way into his carapace, chewing into his flesh, but could do nothing about that without the surgical tools stored inside the ship. Once it finished the claw, the carp tilted its head like a diner appreciating a particularly tasty starter, then it came after Vrell again.

The molly carp hit his side, flipping him over again, bowed itself down over him and snatched away one leg. Vrell dragged himself away on his back, as the carp made a half-hearted attempt to pin him down with its tentacles. Almost the instant he was upright again, another leech attached to this new wound, and also began boring its way in.

As the Prador struggled on, the carp paused to run its recent prize back and forth in its mouth like a toothpick. Vrell screeched and bubbled as it finally snapped this down and surged towards him again. Ahead, the edge of

Father's ship loomed like a cliff, and in that cliff Vrell spotted an open triangular port. The carp hit him again, took away one of his remaining two manipulatory limbs, and mashed it up in a cloud of green blood. Leeches now ribboned the surrounding water. Vrell hit the lower lip of the port and scrabbled to pull himself inside, but the carp clamped its mouth on the Prador's carapace edge, and began to drag him out. Vrell turned both his eye-palps to triangulate, then kicked back with one sharp leg, piercing one of the creature's eyes. The carp released him, drew back, then jerked forwards again to close its mouth on that same leg. Luckily it slipped at the last, and took off only the foot as Vrell lurched inside, reaching out with his remaining claw for the door controls. They were dead, however – there was no safety here.

Vrell sculled hard for the far wall of the chamber as the carp nosed inside after him. He noted, along the side wall, four empty clamps which had contained his father's activated war drones. He was now in the drone cache. There were spare drone shells left in another two clamps, but they contained no minds so could offer no help. The control and backup mind would be here somewhere, but somnolent. He reached an airlock, jammed his claw into the pit control and began pumping the hydraulic opener. Slowly the lock door eased up, releasing air that rose in wide flat bubbles to silver the ceiling. These distracted the carp. It rose up high on its tentacles, sucked in a bubble and blew it out again. Then it returned its attention to the panicking Prador.

The door was open nearly wide enough. Vrell jammed himself underneath it and tried to heave it up further. He felt the carp bite on the rear of his carapace, and shell cracking with an agonizing underwater thump. But the attacker's teeth then slipped and the Prador propelled himself into the lock beyond. The molly carp itself was too big to follow, but still probed after him. Through a haze of pain, Vrell pumped the door shut, hoping to sever some of the creature's tentacles, but the molly carp withdrew them just before the lock closed.

When the seal on the inner door broke, water quickly drained into the ship. Intermittently issuing bubbling groans, Vrell continued working the hydraulic door mechanism until he could follow the water into the dank corridors. His father, he felt sure, was dead, but he had no intention of finding out for sure just then. He could feel that the three leeches inside his carapace had finished feeding – probably sated on the flesh they had already eaten as they bored their way in – but they were shifting about and the pain was still intense. He could do no more than keep dragging himself along the corridor on his three remaining legs, unable to even swat away the ship lice that dropped on him from above to graze around the edges of his wounds.

One of Father's human blanks lay in the corridor, cut in half and burned down to bone in places, but still moving weakly. Suddenly, despite his pain, Vrell felt the hard clamp of hunger. He had not eaten in many days, and his recent transformation into an adult had sapped his energy. With his remaining claw he snipped away one of the blank's arms, held it up to his mandibles, and began stripping cooked flesh away from the bone. He was about to move on, but realized the arm had not sated him, so he then picked up the remaining torso. Soon he had finished that and, feeling more energized, began eyeing the blank's severed hips and legs. But then the leeches started moving inside his carapace again and, hissing like a leaky air compressor, he lurched onwards.

The chamber he sought was open. Here a Prador second-child – one of Vrell's own siblings – lay in the corner with all its legs folded underneath it. Vrell prodded it with a claw and it moved sluggishly.

'Attend me,' he hissed in the Prador tongue.

Suddenly the youngster was up on its legs and brandishing its claws threateningly.

'Not Father!' it bubbled.

Knowledge, long ignored as irrelevant during Vrell's enslavement to his father's pheromones, suddenly became relevant. This second-child would still be similarly enslaved, and to it Vrell was only a competing adult. It would attack him if it considered him vulnerable, or else escape if it could. Vrell reached over to a nearby rack and inserted his claw into a large triclaw extension, then quickly turned and brought it down hard. The polished steel smashed through the second-child's legs on one side and knocked it flat to the ground. As it tried to rise again, Vrell hit it once more, this time pulping its remaining legs. He then opened the metal claw and used it to tear off the younger Prador's claws, before turning round and closing the door manually. He did not want further interruptions from any more of his kin.

'Not Father,' the second-child protested from the floor. Vrell considered finishing it off, but there might be things to learn from it, so he ignored it for the present and studied the tools available to him.

The extension he held was too large, so he returned it to the rack and took up the smallest one he could find. He would have liked to use an anaesthetic on himself, but then he would be unable to feel what he was grasping. He dipped the triclaw in a tub of sterilizing grease, closed it, then placed it against the gory hole where the two leeches had entered at the joint of his missing claw. There must be no further delay, as they could start feeding again at any moment. He eased the claw inside himself, tracking the path of one leech by just how much it hurt him. The path curved round, very near a major ganglion, and he adjusted the joints in the extension to follow. There was no doubt when he tracked down the leech, for it thrashed inside him and began chewing to escape. Vrell opened the claw, shoved it even deeper, closed it and pulled.

Vrell knew how humans, subjected to a sufficient level of pain, could lose consciousness. He had seen this many times and learnt the various techniques for preventing it happening. No such luxury was available to himself. He shrieked as he tore the leech out, hissed at it when he held it up before him, all bloody and writhing, its tubular thread-cutting mouth still seeking blindly for flesh. He dropped the vile thing down by the grease tub, picked up the tub itself and crushed the creature to slurry with it. Then he went after the other two.

When the last leech was nothing but a stain on the floor, Vrell swapped the triclaw for a large-bore injector. He fed this inside himself and pumped the leech-made cavities full of collagen foam and growth promoter. Into the cracks in the rear of his carapace he injected quickset porcelain. This done, he found carapace patches of a sufficient size, and stuck them over his other wounds. Now he felt utterly exhausted and was beginning to settle down to rest when that hard clamp of hunger returned with renewed intensity. Any kind of meat would do, but fortuitously Prador had a particular relish for the meat of their own kind. Vrell decided his hunger more important than any information he might obtain, so settled down by the carapace of his sibling, broke it open with the large triclaw, and began eating the contents.

'Father,' the Prador second-child kept repeating. 'Father. Father.' Until Vrell devoured *its* major ganglion.

Somewhere a reactor was still functioning, for at last, after days of searching, Vrell managed to find a power source for the bank of hexagonal screens before him. He reinserted his remaining hand into a console pit and called up the ship's diagnostic programs. Studying the Prador glyphs scrolling down before him, he soon saw that the missile that had brought down this same ship had penetrated the hull very near to his father's – Ebulan's – sanctum. That area was now sealed behind airtight doors – the ship's system reacting to the damage as it would out in space, though the closed-off area was now flooded with water rather than open to vacuum. Repair mesh had grown across the upper hole punched through the hull, and breach sealant had been pumped between these mesh layers and there crystallized. But where the missile had exploded from the lower hull, the mesh had failed to connect up, so no breach sealant had subsequently been pumped in.

Vrell decided that for now, whatever repairs he must make, he would approach them from inside the ship. Only when he had accomplished as many of those as feasible would he venture outside, and only then if absolutely necessary. But those repairs must be made, for he needed access to Ebulan's sanctum, where the ship's centralized controls were located. There were also the adjacent storerooms to consider, where thrall and control units were stored. But even inside the ship he must once again enter the water. He shuddered at the thought. Now being an adult he would not regrow his limbs, and could afford to lose no more. However, this venture was unavoidable if he were to survive.

Checking screens, he found two sets of doubled blast doors, one of them accessible from this side of the ship, so he could enter that area without flooding any more of the vessel. He checked the codes for each of those doors and memorized them, then swung away to find the required tools. Luckily, he had entered the ship on the engine side, where most of the maintenance and repair equipment was stored. He soon found a molecular plasticizer, a multipurpose welder and cutter, and a couple of hull-metal sheets which he loaded onto his back. Hopefully there was sufficient hull metal remaining around the breach that he could form back into place, and these two sheets would be all he needed. But if that were not so, then he would just have to make more than one trip, or as many as would be required. He felt a sudden flash of uncharacteristic irritation about that, then wondered why.

Vrell had never expected this to be easy, but the potential benefits were huge. He could return to the Prador Kingdom, inherit his father's wealth, his father's property, wives. Strangely, that last thought did not hold its earlier appeal. Vrell shook himself and continued with his task, hanging the equipment on his weapons harness. He next went to one of the many armouries to find a rail-gun that operated underwater, then as an afterthought added a water gun – a device that sucked in water and spat it out in a superheated stream. He would have added more weapons, but possessed only one working claw and one hand to hold them.

The first blast door slid up to reveal a stretch of corridor, empty but for one human hand which Vrell absent-mindedly picked up and ate. As the second door slid up he held his breath which, being Prador, he could do for about a day. Water began to squirt in under pressure, then roared in carrying detritus with it. Soon submerged, Vrell saw he was surrounded by leeches, and though they thumped ineffectually against his now sealed shell, he still used the water gun to explode them into black gobbets of boiled flesh. Moving into his father's section of the ship, he immediately saw that something strange had happened here.

Someone had cut through the door to Father's private sanctum. Vrell peered inside, observing a multitude of leeches and whelks, and a couple of glisters clinging to the ceiling. It took him a moment to discern human bones on the floor, a shell cutter lying nearby, and pieces of his father's carapace scattered all around the room. Vrell stared, and stared, then abruptly understood. As well as the physical attack on his ship, Vrell's father had been assailed by a viral program. Something obviously had suborned Ebulan's human blanks and used them to attack him.

He also noted the crushed remnants of juvenile Prador carapaces scattered here and there. Ebulan must have killed them first, believing there to be a betrayal from within. The surviving one Vrell had found must have been unable to move from the hospital area when it was summoned. Vrell turned away to be about his task, then swung back as the glisters dropped from the ceiling and sculled towards him. He fired the rail-gun, shattering them and turning the water within the sanctum cloudy. Leeches and whelks quickly moved in to clear up the mess, as they must have earlier cleaned the flesh from the human bones and the meat out of his father's carapace. Vrell hoped Father had taken a long time to die.

The hole was large, and the surrounding area had been subjected to a plasma fire – little remaining but warped and melted metal. As he hoped, the hull metal was broken open here, and bent down in large jagged sheets. Repair mesh had extruded from the layers, forming a crumpled tangle in the dark waters below, but it had been unable to connect. He spent hours cutting it away with the welder's plasma setting, then watched it sink to the sea floor five metres below, where it stirred up silt and sent scuttling the razored disks of prill. Then he set to work with the plasticizer, softening the hull metal, hauling it into place and reversing that effect to harden it again. Mesh immediately began to extrude, but there were still some larger holes to deal with. Roughly cutting up the sheets he had brought, he manoeuvred them into position and began to weld. Many hours later he finished and, satisfied the mesh would fill the remaining holes, decided to return to the unflooded section.

Vrell felt tired as he scrambled through the darkness to the blast doors. His sealed wounds were now aching and itching, and there seemed a pressure in them. His tough Prador body was almost immune to any kind of infection, but he was beginning to wonder if he might have picked up some alien bug. He was also, he knew, suffering from oxygen deprivation.

The first door opened and he scrambled inside. He then approached the control panel and tried to get a pump working to extract the water, but it just would not respond. Angry, he slammed his claw against the wall beside the panel, and was surprised to see he had left a dent. Suddenly, the area of flesh underneath the patch over where he had lost his claw began to really hurt. Never mind the water, then. He input the code to open the second blast door. Nothing happened for a moment, then his father's ident glyph appeared on the hexagonal screen. Vrell realized he had walked into one of the automatic code-change traps his father had spread throughout his ship. The doors now would not open unless an override was sent from Ebulan's sanctum.

Vrell lost it then, smashing the panel and screen with his claw. This exacerbated the pain radiating from underneath his patches. His legs folded underneath him and he sank to the floor. It was no use; he was finished. Sudden weariness washed over him and he began to drift in and out of consciousness. In one lucid moment he realized this was the result of anoxia, but he was unable to do anything about it. He was going to suffocate in here. Blackness swamped his senses.

Time passed, a very great deal of time.

'This has to be the most alien skyscape I've seen, yet humans created it,' said Janer.

He had seen many unusual worlds during his indenture and subsequent voluntary service to the hive mind. Here, strange weather patterns, due to the atmosphere's odd gas mix and aerial algae, divided the sky with cloud layers in varying shades of blue and green like vast floating isles. And now, at sunset, a backdrop of half the sky was a veined explosion of indigo, gold and ruby. The sky alone would have been enough, but there were snairls here as well.

'Genfactoring was at its height when humans first came here,' the mind observed.

It spoke to him through the hivelink in his right ear. Two hornets, which were akin to two synapses in the hive mind and were also one facet of its disperse sensorium, rested in the transparent skin-stick box formed to his shoulder. He eyed them, noting the circuit patterns on their thoraxes and abdomens. He had only recently learnt that rather than decoration those patterns were the exterior evidence of the nanocircuitry linking synapse to synapse by radio, rather than by slow pheromonal transfer of thoughts as had originally been the case, for the hive minds had not been averse to benefiting from human technology. Though for humans it had been a shock to discover that they shared Earth with hive intelligences carried by hornet swarms – a fact impossible to accept for some. Even after long familiarity Janer still found the concept problematic.

Janer returned his attention to the spectacular sky, reached out and wiped condensation from the curving transparent shell before him, beyond which he observed a translucent bladder trailing tentacles, swept past by an errant wind.

'That was one of the earliest adaptations,' the mind commented.

Janer nodded. He knew this world's history. When humans first came here the place had been choking on its own aerial algae, the ecosystem teetering on the edge of catastrophe since a volcanic eruption had provided a huge food resource for those floating diatoms, thus causing their population to explode. Computer models predicted as a consequence the extinction of all other life here within five thousand years.

'Introduced to feed on the algae – an adaptation from the Portuguese man-of-war jellyfish.' Janer pointed past the creature to a circling flock of rooks in the distance. 'And they were introduced to feed on them when *their* population exploded. But in the end they weren't enough to keep the algal population down. I know what happened here. If you recollect, I was required by you to research the history of this place when I first came here indentured to you.'

'Of course I recollect. The capacity to forget is a purely human trait.'

Janer snorted and peered through the clouds. *There*: three huge life forms. Many creatures had been introduced here: alien, Terran, and adaptations of both. The one that had averted the ecological catastrophe was a splicing of humble snails, those same floating jellyfish and a couple of alien forms. The result was snairls.

Floating amid the slate clouds were three behemoth spiral shells like fairy towers. These supported huge grey-and-white snail bodies that probed the air with glistening antlers in search of rich masses of the algae on which the creatures fed.

Snairls hatched from eggs the size of footballs, dropping from the sky like jelly hail. They fed on the thick ground-slicks of dying algae, growing aerogel shells that they filled with helium. By the time they were the size of cows, they achieved buoyancy, and left the ground for richer fields. The genetic manipulation might have stopped with them had it not become a part of the very culture of this place. But here the rulers of humanity were the CGs – Chief Geneticists – and the manipulation continued. Some centuries past, a CG adapted humans to live in the slimy arteries and cysts inside snairl bodies. Now these people sailed the skies in their strange craft, trading genfactored artefacts. They were a long-lived people whose span was delimited by the life of their host. Janer turned away from his viewpoint within Upper Shell to observe the gas bags behind him, and to remember.

He had lived with the crew of this very snairl, the Graaf, and been aboard when it mated with another of its kind, and then died. He had seen the crew die inside it, and a lover die, and been saved from death himself by the hornets he then carried. The fleshy body of the Graaf had long since decayed and dropped away. Now this shell was ballasted, and driven through the sky by motorized screws attached to the huge shell he stood inside. It was also the home to hornets. Thousands of nests occupied Lower Shell – ballast being shed as they increased in number. This shell had seemed a safe haven to this particular hive mind. Other minds occupied other shells. But for the indigent and barely human population, this world belonged to the hornets. It was, inevitably, called Hive.

'How many shells now?' Janer asked.

'One hundred and twenty – all minds older than myself.'

Janer winced. It was well to be reminded that this particular mind – the youngest – had been around for about ten thousand years. There were many more even older ones: strange minds seemingly incapable of communicating with humans, or perhaps just disinclined.

'Most older minds still keep to Earth, though,' he observed.

'It's what they know, though to me Earth seems more alien than other worlds I've visited.'

'Yes, we saw many together.' Janer was starting to get irritated. Over the last few hours the mind had just been rambling: it wasn't getting to the point. The mind must have sensed this, again causing him to wonder just how close the hivelink keyed in to his thoughts.

'You are independently wealthy,' it said.

'Certainly, and all due to you. But it wasn't my fault you didn't establish nests on Spatterjay. Is that what this is all about? Is that why you called me here?'

'Spatterjay,' the mind repeated.

In the background of that word arose an angry buzzing. Janer knew it to be mere theatre, since individual hornets might buzz, but the mind itself was a disperse and not easily definable entity, and it certainly did not make any noise it did not want to. He considered the strange and lethal world just named.

Second on Janer's list of weird places he had visited was Spatterjay. A virus there toughened human bodies to nigh indestructibility, and there were people sailing the seas of that world, Old Captains, who had lived perhaps a thousand years. A strange place. A place where the most valuable commodity for the Hoopers – as the people there were called – was death. Death came in the form of a poison obtained at great risk from sea-going leeches the size of whales. Sprine, they called it. Sprine was what this hive mind had once paid him to obtain for it, so it could adapt its hornets to carry the stuff in their stings and thus become the ruler of that world. Their mission had failed.

'I do hope you're not expecting to get your money back,' said Janer, eyeing the hornets on his shoulder –

which gave him at least something to address. 'The Earth Central ruling was not open to interpretation. I did what you asked of me, even though I only did it so we could finally kill that damned skinner creature. And you were warned that your actions, though they might not be illegal under human law, would nevertheless not be tolerated.'

'I do not want my money back,' the mind sulked.

'Then what do you want?'

'Many people infect themselves with immortality,' the mind told him.

Ah . . .

'Yes,' Janer agreed, 'Spatterjay has become a big attraction for Polity citizens. We live in an age when you can choose your route to eternal youth, and some of those choices become quite esoteric.' Janer mulled that over. In the Polity, that political unit ruled by artificial intelligences and now spread across a considerable portion of the galaxy, death could quite often just be a matter of choice. 'Are you going after the sprine again?' he added. He studied the circular leech scar on the back of his hand through which he had been infected with the Spatterjay virus. Soon, before that virus started breaking down inside him and causing him some major problems, he would have to return to Spatterjay for reinfection. It was thus he himself had been infected with immortality.

'I am not.'

'I'm glad to hear it. For I suspect that, if you were to try, this partial home of yours might end up subject to an accidental meteor strike. Polity AIs tend to get a little tetchy when their warnings aren't heeded.'

'But someone else is,' the mind added.

*

'Due to the lower gravity here and some minor tinkering with the trees' genome, our redwoods can grow half a kilometre tall,' explained Hannister, the tour guide. 'They reach maturity very quickly – a hundred years – and that is when they are harvested.' She turned from gazing up at the forest giants to survey her party.

Three were not easily identifiable. They were clad in grey enviro-suits, their faces concealed by domino masks. Two of them also wore short hooded flak jackets, while the other wore a tighter-fitting long black coat, which was also hooded. There seemed something unsavoury about them. The rest of the party consisted of a cat-adapt, an ophidapt, and five standard-format humans. The little girl, who was clearly the apple of her parents' eye while an all-round pain in the arse to everyone else, was the first to pipe up.

'But surely that's not ecologically sound,' she said in a kid's voice seeming to contain a hint of fingernails on blackboard.

'That would be the case if they were part of the local ecology, but they are not. Firstly the biota here is incapable of breaking down that quantity of cellulose, secondly, a falling mature tree often takes others down with it, and thirdly they are a valuable resource to the economy here.'

'You make money out of them,' said the girl.

Hannister hated talking to children, which made her particularly unsuited to this job. She turned to the rest. 'Harvesting is also necessary because once the trees reach maturity they begin to produce viable seed. We do not want any of that seed germinating outside the plantations.'

'Because a competitor might acquire seed or saplings,' said the girl.

Hannister frowned at her, then decided it was about time she checked her aug. Her augmentation – a piece of computer hardware that nestled behind her ear and linked into both her brain and into vast informational networks – displayed some text in her visual cortex:

Smila Pottifor, 8 years solstan, Solsystem Abraxis Station . . .

She did not need to go any further. For a moment she thought the girl might be one of those people who preferred perpetual childhood to perpetual adulthood.

'Are we to proceed to a harvesting now?' hissed the masked individual in the black coat.

Hannister finally soft-linked to his ident and auged again:

Taylor Bloc, reification incept special request Anubis Arisen, Klader Alpha—

Reif?

Hannister suddenly felt her mouth go dry. She was not entirely clear about the details. On some world it had been fashionable to reanimate murder victims, using implanted technology, and send them after the murderers. These reanimations had possessed no intelligence, merely rough memcordings from their dead minds and programs to follow. In later years, as memcording from dead brains was perfected, people could live again. Some of them chose to live on in their own corpses – some cult had arisen out of it all. Reifications were high-tech zombies. Hannister felt it all very well for her to be showing around adapted humans, and brats, but she was not sure how she felt about acting as a tour guide to the dead. It was then she recognized a slight whiff of spoilt meat and realized it had been in the air all along.

'*Drave, do you know there are reifications in my group?*' she sent.

Drave replied: '*Yes, I do, and, being as they are buying a whole tree from us, I suggest you treat them with the utmost consideration.*'

'Shall we move on?' said Hannister, smiling.

They rode up on a supervisor's platform to observe the harvesting. Other platforms, holding other tour groups, hovered in the forest nearby. Hannister gazed at the arboreal giants all around and felt a familiar loosening in her chest. They were awesome, and she was part of all this. Glancing back to her group she felt a flash of irritation. The tourists were surrounded by all this yet they were waiting to be entertained. She stooped and opened the locker to one side of the platform's control column and began passing round disposable image intensifiers, glad they would not be returned because no way was she again handling the ones the reifs took.

'Here comes the stripper,' Hannister said, raising her intensifier to her eyes.

The drone dropping out of the lemon-stained sky bore the appearance of a giant horse fly, though it lacked wings. It homed in on the tree like that same insect sniffing bare skin, landed hard, low on the trunk, driving in the piton feet of its lower four legs. Its forelimbs remained free, and at the tips of them something glittered and blurred into motion – chainglass saws.

'This design of drone is optimum for the task. We've learnt that over the years,' Hannister told them.

'Why chainglass?' asked one of the normal humans.

'Any kind of directed energy is a fire risk, and not

very efficient. Chainglass cuts clean, keeps its edge for a very long time, and is cheap to replace.'

The drone began climbing, its pace constant as it reached and severed each branch close to the trunk, though its course necessarily spiralled to take it to every branch. Sawdust snowed down, coating both the drone and the ground below. Falling branches slammed into it, but it continued inexorably. Quickly reaching a point where the trunk was no wider than the branches sprouting from it, the drone cut around twice, and the upper section of the tree toppled. Hannister glanced down to watch treaded handlers with large spidery claws coming in to take up great piles of branches and cart them away for processing into paper. Another device sucked up the fallen sawdust. Nothing was wasted.

The drone then descended to the ground and waited, as around it the handlers soon cleared away all the remaining rubbish.

'Now the carrier.' Hannister pointed.

The machine now descending from the sky was a hundred-metre grey cylinder with fins down its entire length on one side, to cool its heavy-duty gravmotors, and with wide pincer clamps down the other side. It was utterly functional. It dropped parallel to the trunk, and closed its three clamps on the wood. Immediately the horse fly began cutting, two fountains of sawdust spraying from where its forelimbs entered the tree's bole. The tree tottered, and they all heard the humming of the carrier's gravmotors as it took up nearly a thousand tonnes weight of wood. Slowly, tree and carrier rose into the sky.

'Now it goes to the sawmill, to be cut up – usually into all sorts of wooden shapes already designated by the numerous customers who have bought the tree. Probably, that trunk will be turned into many thousands of items of furniture, planking, panelling, grips for knives or guns, wooden dice or toys. Not one cubic centimetre of wood will be wasted,' said Hannister.

'That is not precisely the case here.'

Hannister glanced round, auging at the same time. Taylor Bloc, the one who had spoken, removed his mask with a slight sucking sound and pulled back his hood to observe her. She bit down on the gasp. One side of the reification's face was worn down to bone, his teeth exposed on that side in a perpetual grin. In that same side's eye-socket, surprisingly, there remained an apparently alive but unlidded eye. The revealed skull above was translucent, showing liquid movement and the occasional glint of optics. The other side of his skull was clad in grey wrinkled skin, and his other brown eye retained its eyelid. Strangely, the reif seemed to be wearing silver spectacles – something Hannister had only ever seen in historical entertainments. She realized her mistake when a fine mist sprayed from the frames to moisten his eyeballs. From the spectacles themselves, where they hooked behind the ragged ear on the left side of his head, a pipe ran down, stapled to his neck, and into the collar of his envirosuit. He shrugged, as if accepting that he was hideous. Probably because of the spectacle-frame irrigator, he seemed to Hannister horribly, almost supernaturally, studious.

After a couple of attempts at speaking, she managed, 'What is the case here, then?'

'Nothing will be wasted, as you say, but your sawmill will cut whole from this trunk a ship's keel and, from the remainder, its ribs and many other necessary items. The hull planking for our project we will obtain from yan-wood and peartrunk trees.'

'Ship?'

'On *Sable Keech* I will bring my kind to the Little Flint. Some of them, if they are worthy, will become the Arisen, as did he for whom the ship will be named.'

'Right, right okay,' Hannister just let that lunacy go and instead eyed the little girl called Smile, who was holding her nose. 'Let's move on, shall we?'

1

Spatterjay Virus:
many questions surround this virus and its relationship with the leeches, and few of them can be answered. There is little fossil evidence of leeches, for obvious reasons, and that of viral growth in other life forms tells us only when it began to appear, and then only to the nearest hundred million years. Genetic archaeology is also of little use, since the virus is an eclectic collector of Spatterjay's equivalent of DNA from the planet's biosphere.

Terran viruses, upon entering a cell, propagate from it and destroy it in the process. The Spatterjay virus roots in it and grows as a fibre to other cells, gradually networking the host body in a fibrous mass. These cells are then maintained perpetually. But the virus also engineers the DNA. Should the animal be damaged, or its environment change, the virus will alter its host to the optimum for survival in those circumstances. An animal can have its head cut off and yet not die; the virus will stimulate it to grow the necessities of survival. The usual result of this is the body growing a leech's plug-cutting mouth, probably because the bulk of additional DNA the virus carries is of the leech, its original host. In this manner the virally infected prey become a perpetually reusable food resource for the leeches themselves. So it would seem that when the virus appeared, the leeches swiftly took advantage of it.

Humans, being ill-suited to Spatterjay's biosphere, are quickly adapted by the virus, unless they take preventive measures. Hoopers stave off the 'change' by eating Terran foods which, lacking in nutrition for the virus, very much slow its growth. Drugs such as Intertox also inhibit it. Without these, humans can change into chimerical creatures that are a random combination of Spatterjay animals. Evolutionary effects of the virus on native life are most ably demonstrated in teleost forms such as the turbul –

Ambel listened to the wind in the sail and wondered if the rhinoworm steaks the creature had just eaten might be on the turn. The veined pink sheets of the living sail's wings were spread in the spars of the *Treader*, stiffened by its spines and ropes of muscle. It gripped wood with numerous spidery claws at the ends of these spines, and its neck was wound once around the mast, its crocodilian head poised a couple of metres above the deck. It looked contemplative as it turned the mast on the static spar, thus turning the other two masts via mechanisms in the body of the ship. Or perhaps that look was dyspepsia?

'You all right there, sail?' he asked.

The sail turned its demonic red eyes towards him. 'I'm fine,' it grated. 'And the name is Gale . . . catcher?' It shook its head. Obviously it still could not grasp the new name issued to it by the Boss. But then, barring the Boss himself, it had, like all the other sails, borne for many years the name Windcatcher. Centuries ago these huge batlike creatures of this world had possessed enough intelligence to learn human language and make themselves useful to humans by actually taking the place of fabric sails on ocean-going ships, thus benefiting from food supplied by the humans, but the concept of names ever evaded them. Now, one very intelligent sail was changing all that. Their wages had changed too.

'Don't seem right,' Peck muttered from just behind Ambel's left shoulder.

'I think I warned you, Peck,' said Ambel mildly.

'Sorry,' said the ship's mechanic.

Ambel glanced at him. The man's appearance was unchanged: bald head, weird green eyes the hue of the sky above them, the long hide coat he preferred, and filthy canvas trousers, but in other ways he just got stranger as he got older. His latest odd habit was to quietly creep up behind people to abruptly issue his gripes. It was annoying for many, which was why Ambel had given him a warning earlier. The Captain himself was past such little irritations. You don't recover from being a stripped fish and still allow someone like Peck to get under your skin, so to speak.

'Go and grease your ratchets,' Ambel added, then returned his attention to the sail. 'Your name, if you recollect, is Gale*grabber*.'

The sail blinked at him, and mumbled in a decidedly Peckish way.

Ambel let that go. 'How far to Olian's, do you think?' he asked instead.

The sail lifted its head higher, until it was almost past its own body, peered into the distance for a while, then returned to Ambel's level.

'Twenty-two point six five kilometres.'

Ambel eyed the creature then turned to head back

to his cabin. Could not remember its own name, yet Galegrabber had a mind like a computer when it came to anything involving figures. But then maybe the small black aug attached behind its ear hole was configured for that. Ambel opened his cabin door and stepped inside.

After they had dragged the *Treader* out of the jungle on the Skinner's Island, where it had been thrown by the massive explosion intended to kill all the Old Captains – being witnesses to the Prador Ebulan's long-ago crimes – it had taken Ambel a few years to lose the creepy feeling he got every time he entered his own cabin. His sea chest was still there against the wall, a little battered but intact. However, that chest no longer contained anything nasty. The living Skinner's head, which once resided in a box inside the chest, was dead along with the rest of the monster the erstwhile pirate Jay Hoop had become.

Ambel sighed and dropped into his reinforced chair. So many events back then, but already they were being buried under the trammelling years. It was the understanding that this was always the way of things that he tried to impart to Erlin, to help her through her crisis of ennui – something all those who might live forever faced at about their two hundredth year. He hoped to have succeeded, hoped she would not kill herself out of boredom. He still loved her, though considered her rather impetuous and inclined to drama. Youngsters.

Her recent expedition was a further sign of what Ambel considered her immaturity. He had dropped her off on an island where ostensibly she intended to study some of the local homicidal molluscs, but really she 'needed to think'. Maybe she intended to kill herself, but if that was her intention Ambel would not stop her – he didn't have the right – and probably could not anyway if her intention was serious. He would find out soon enough. After making a deposit at Olian's, he was going back for her. She had been on that island for about a year, so her supplies of dome-grown food must be running out, and he didn't want to risk her turning into another skinner. Shaking his head he turned to his charts.

An hour later there came a recognizably tuneful knock at his cabin door.

'What is it, Sprout?' he asked.

There was a pause while Sprout, not the sharpest gut-knife in the box, tried to figure out how Ambel knew who was knocking. Then the man said, 'Comin' up on the island now, Captain.'

Ambel stepped back out of his cabin, glanced at Sprout – a short thickset man with dyed purple hair tied in a ponytail; lip ring, nose ring and ring in his left ear all joined by a chain; and wearing a long brown leather coat over his canvas Hooper clothing. Sprout also wore an aug, which accounted for his facial mutilations and the dye job. He had found the look on some historical site, and been much attracted to it. He was not the only one either: body piercing was becoming quite the fashion amongst the younger Hoopers. Ambel felt that wasn't healthy for a people whose relationship with pain was questionable at best. He now turned his attention to Olian Tay's island.

Some years ago the approach here had been difficult because of the packetworm reefs surrounding it. Now channels had been cut through many of them, large bubble-metal jetties extended from the beaches and smaller pearwood jetties branched off from those. Many Hooper ships and boats were moored here and, as the

Treader drew in, Hoopers waved and called from their decks. Ambel smelt the tobacco smoke before he spotted Captain Sprage on the deck of the *Vengeance*, chair tilted back and pipe firmly clamped in his mouth. Sprage nodded and Ambel raised a hand. They had a history together, but then so did most Old Captains, most of them having lived for over five centuries in this same area of the same world. Ambel saw a new Captain, Lember, who at one time had been Sprage's bosun. He saw Cormarel and Tranbit. The first of these Captains was unnaturally tall and long-limbed due to a lack of dome-grown food in his past, resulting in a near skinner-like transformation, and the last, a squat wide man with red skin in which the blue leech scars seemed to gleam like silver. Utterly different in appearance, yet the firmest of friends. Many other Hoopers unloaded cargoes, loaded supplies, chatted, worked on their ships, sat on the jetties fishing for boxies and swearing at their bait, or gathered in groups to crack open barrels of sea-cane rum. Ambel smelt roasting glister, and heard the thumping of hammer whelks trying to escape the cauldrons in which they were being boiled. He eyed someone searing turbul steaks on a hotplate, then caught the eye-watering stench of someone emptying a slops bucket over a ship's side.

And the *Treader* drew in to dock.

The gleaming metal nautilus, three metres in diameter, its grasping tentacles neatly folded and its head withdrawn inside, was a drone shell. A bubble-metal framework held it upright, and it had been carefully wrapped in translucent shockfoam sheeting. Studying the spaceship's manifest, Captain Ron wondered why anyone had bothered with the wrapping, since the damned thing was made of a highly advanced ceramal and diamond fibre composite, and plated with nanochain chromium. Working with a sledge-hammer for the next decade, Ron would hardly manage to scratch its surface, and the Old Captain could do more damage with his fists than any normal human could do with such a hammer.

'Who's it for?' he asked casually.

'The Warden,' Forlam replied.

'Ah . . . figures,' said Ron.

Ron was built like a piece of earth-moving equipment: slabs of muscle shifted underneath his silk shirt, his hands were like spades, his legs pillars, and he stood solid as a boulder. Unlike Ron, Forlam possessed a head of hair, and was wiry. He was as tough as seasoned oak, and wore the expression of someone perpetually on the edge of needing cerebral adjustment or confinement to an asylum. Both men bore a slight blue tint to their skins. Both men were covered with circular scars, though in Ron's case there were so many that he appeared mottled, almost scaly.

'Not our most unusual cargo,' Forlam added.

Ron eyed him. 'We have a *usual* cargo?'

Forlam gave a wincing shrug.

Since Ron had taken on the Captaincy of the *Gurnard* they had visited many worlds inside and outside the Polity, and hauled everything from components for the Cassius Dyson sphere to genfactored replacement bodies in the shape of mythical beasts. Ron's particular favourite had been the live cargo of a creature called a 'gabbleduck', which had been restrained by composite chains equally as strong as the material in this drone shell, to prevent it breaking free and eating the crew. All it had done though was sit in the hold: a huge pyramid of flesh with too many arms, topped with a domed head wrapped in a tiara of greenish eyes and sporting a large duck bill, eating the food provided and speaking non-sense that always seemed on the edge of making sense. Ron knew there was a lot more oddities for him to see and other interesting cargoes to haul, but it felt good to be going home. He moved on down the hold with Forlam trailing behind him.

'What else have we got here?' he asked, eyeing his notescreen manifest.

'A really big lump of wood,' replied Forlam. 'I think you'll know what it is as soon as you see it.'

'I'll be buggered,' Ron later said, while eyeing the huge ship's keel they had transported to Spatterjay.

By all Polity definitions Taylor Bloc knew he was an AI: the memcording of the man running entirely in crystal. That cyber mechanisms moved his dead and chemically preserved body was irrelevant for definition. But he retained his flesh, his skeleton, and his own peculiar belief in resurrection. Bloc's beliefs ran contrary to those of *others* and, as always, *they* were trying to thwart him. He was angry, he was always angry.

In the embarkation lounge on Coram, the moon of Spatterjay, he walked jerkily around a bumbling beetle-bot that was meticulously polishing the floor, and stepped into a private conferencing booth, where he removed his mask and slid back his hood.

'I must speak to the Warden,' he said succinctly, as soon as he saw that the privacy field had come on.

'Hello, dead man,' said a submind.

Bloc was momentarily taken aback. After a pause he went on, 'I said, I want to speak to the Warden.'

'Can do, but I warn you he's not the soul of patience nowadays – not that he ever was.'

'Okay, I've got it now, Seven. What do you want, Bloc?'

'I've been informed that my cargo is not to be delivered to its intended destination.'

'Yeah, no shit?' replied a bored voice.

'That is breach of contract.'

'Spatterjay is not a Polity world, reif. You don't talk to me, you talk to the Boss.'

'Boss?' Bloc paused, then continued regardless, 'The agreement was that we would lay the keel on Chel – the Embassy Island.' He blinked and his spectacle irrigator started working. He shut it down and his constant internal diagnosticer immediately threw up the message in his visual cortex: IRRIG @@#* SHUT??DOWN. Such corruptions were the inevitable result of the additional hardware his dead body now contained, but still it took him a moment to register what the Warden said next.

'What?'

'I said: have you got that in writing?' the Warden repeated.

'I can send you the package right now.'

'I mean, have you got that in writing on paper signed by both parties?'

'Paper?'

'That's how it's done down on the surface. Now, why don't you get yourself and your friends down there – you're stinking up my base.'

Bloc took a step back. No AI had ever spoken to him

like that before, though admittedly his experience of them was deliberately limited, as there were certain things about himself, and his companions, best kept secret from the artificial intelligences that ruled the Human Polity.

'I am not . . . stinking,' he said carefully. 'My anosmic receptors are the most advanced, and I would have detected—'

'Too late, Blocky boy. Old Sniper ain't got much of an attention span.'

'Sniper?'

The conferencing booth shut down and the privacy field turned off. Bloc stepped out backwards, then turned to his two companions. 'We have to speak to the "Boss" apparently,' he said.

Aesop replied, 'That means we have to go down to the surface and take a ride on a ferry.'

'Ferry?' Bloc repeated.

'No antigravity transport is allowed on the surface,' Aesop continued. He and Bones remained securely masked and hooded, as Bloc had decided that to be best. Although he felt their kind should not have to hide themselves from the rest of humanity, the appearance of his two reified companions tended to draw more unwanted attention than even he himself.

'No AG transport,' Bloc repeated stupidly.

Aesop and Bones obeyed orders and provided information when it was lacking, but they were never solicitous in such service. Aesop said flatly, 'If you recollect, that is why we chose to build a ship, for the mass transportation of reifications and amniotic tanks. It is also to be a monument to the Arisen One, and yourself of course.'

IRRIG. WARN: CELLULAR DAMAGE IMMINENT

Bloc turned his irrigator back on. He eyed his two companions through the spray, and his mind started working properly again.

'Thank you, Aesop, I recollect precisely,' he said, and began leading the way to where the planetary shuttles docked. He showed no sign of his earlier confusion, and now showed none of his present chagrin, which was easy enough when you were dead. But something was wrong. That glitch with his irrigator warning was a familiar one, but his memory lapse was something new, for Bloc's memory had been perfect for two hundred years, ever since Bones and Aesop had murdered him back on his home world.

As the door to the coldsleep coffin crumped open before him, and as the feeling began painfully returning to his limbs, Janer told himself, 'Never again.'

The mind had not wanted him to come here via the runcible for three good reasons. Something he was carrying came under the weapons proscription – which prevented travellers carrying arms above a certain power level through that same matter transmitter. Secondly, the ruler of Spatterjay might object to him coming here with hornets, and so block him. And, lastly, the mind did not want any Polity AIs nosing in on its business, since this was a private matter between hive minds.

'You brought them buggers back with you?' said a familiar voice.

'Ron? Captain Ron?'

Establishing control over his limbs, Janer took a shaky step from the cold coffin. Cryogenic Storage was a chamber ringed with upright coffins similar to his own.

The Old Captain was stooping over one of the cryocases stacked haphazardly in the centre of the room. He appeared little different to how Janer remembered him: bald-headed, leech-scarred and massive. He stood upright and grinned.

'What the hell are you doing aboard?' Janer asked.

'I'm the Captain.'

'I know that, but why are you aboard this old lugger?'

'I'm the Captain of this old lugger.'

As far as Janer understood it, captaining a sailing vessel on the surface of Spatterjay did not qualify one to run a spaceship. Numerous questions came to mind, but all he managed was, 'Uh?'

'Been looking around for a few years,' Ron added unhelpfully.

Janer turned to a nearby dispenser and took from it a disposable coverall. He then punched in for a hot coffee before donning the garment. This gave him time to get his thoughts in order. After sipping coffee he couched his question.

'How come you have the know-how to run one of these?' He gestured about him with the cup, spilling coffee.

'Oh, I learnt all this stuff years ago, just never had the money to buy passage off-planet. But things have changed under the Boss, and now Hoopers can afford more than their next sack of dome-grown grub.'

Years ago.

Of course, that was it about the Old Captains: they were *old*. Ron had lived on Spatterjay for a very long time. Knowledge had always been accessible to him, if the means of employing it had not, since this world had been visited by space travellers for long before the runcible was set up here over two centuries ago. How much knowledge could you pack into your skull over such a period of time? Maybe, to Ron, the complexities of space travel were not too much of a bother. Then Janer remembered something else: Ron had fought in the Prador War. Perhaps he had known how to run spaceships even before coming here, the best part of a thousand years ago.

'You've been on a trade route between here and somewhere else?' Janer asked.

'Nah, more of a circuit.' He beckoned to Janer. 'Come on.'

'And it's brought you back here?'

'No, lad. I arranged it like that.'

'Why?'

Ron glanced at him. 'I want to go home. Still got a mug down there with my name on it, and I got a ten-year thirst on me.'

Janer felt his head twinge almost warningly. He remembered drinking seacane rum – well, remembered starting to drink it. After a certain point things had become rather fuzzy.

He paused at the door, gesturing back to the cryo-cases. 'The hornets . . .'

'They'll be fine. I'll bring 'em down with the cargo I have to deliver. And you can come down with me too. You're our only human passenger.'

Janer didn't respond to the slight query in the Captain's voice.

Ron added, 'Don't get many passengers, not inside the runcible network.'

Janer didn't rise to that either.

★

Only when Erlin moved the underwater remote eye, for a better view of the colony, was it attacked by leeches that had soon forgotten the device was no source of meat, so she was glad to have found this rocky marine peak to which it could cling with its three sharp legs. Not that leeches could damage the device, but when they swarmed they did tend to block her view of the ostensible reason for her being here.

The whelks were all of a similar size and bore near-identical shell markings. Each spiral shell was about half a metre from base to tip, pyramidal, and glittering with whorls of iridescence. Sitting in the mouth of her temporary home – it was Polity technology: the kind that could be inflated in minutes and, when ballasted, stood as solid and impenetrable as a stone house – Erlin gazed at the image on her fold-up screen, remaining perplexed and fed up. These molluscs were neither frog nor hammer whelks, and were actually quite boring. Her gaze wandered from the screen. Boredom, if she was to acquire that 'long habit of living' to which Ambel often referred, was something she must avoid. She felt the black pit of ennui at her core, robbing her of volition and threatening to spill out. With almost a physical wrench she forced her attention back to the screen.

She had expected to move the eye, following the whelks' migration around the island or deeper into the ocean, but they remained exactly in the same location. She had expected to see a lot more activity than this. Other whelk species were always hunting for food or trying very hard not to become food, and even though they were the sexually immature version of a larger deep-sea whelk, they manoeuvred in elaborate social pecking orders. The only sign of movement from these creatures was when small leeches, glisters or prill came too close. Then they snapped out squidlike tentacles to drag those creatures down and eat them. That was all they did: fed and sat and grew. She closed down the screen. The damned things had done nothing else for a whole year, which was why Erlin had tried to occupy herself with other studies on the island.

When she had arrived, the leech population was low and no individual leech longer than her finger. It seemed some event had denuded the island of anything larger than this prior to her arrival. Now those fingerlings were about the size of her arm, though there were fewer of them, and they fed upon small heirodonts creeping through the vegetation (she could hear their screams in the night). There had once been big heirodonts here, too – their bones were mounded on the beach, so obviously the same event that had cleared this place of bigger leeches had done for them as well, though why their bones were piled up she did not know. It frustrated her that she could not put together all the pieces of the puzzle: the leeches, the bones, the shattered peartrunk trees on either side of a lane of destruction driven over the middle of the island. Maybe some kind of storm? Maybe some kind of outside interference by humans, or even by the Warden? Whatever, she certainly intended to solve at least one puzzle before Ambel returned for her. And to do so she only needed to risk her life.

Erlin did not like invasive studies, but it was time for her to discover what was going on with that colony of whelks. Her various scans had been inconclusive, but then her equipment here was limited. She needed one of those creatures here, on the surgical table she had erected in her abode, so she could dissect it to divine the function of its parts. She opened up the screen again.

The camera had moved. It had been doing that a lot lately. Maybe an earth tremor, though she had felt none, or maybe it was malfunctioning. Making adjustments she brought the colony back into view. It seemed closer now, which was ridiculous. She closed up the screen, stood and, stepping back inside, placed the device on a rough table she had fashioned from peartrunk wood. From her sea chest she removed her diving suit and donned it. The thing was heavy – two layers of mono-filament fabric sandwiching ceramal chain mail – but it was what you needed if you ever wanted to take a swim here and remain intact. Her haemolung breather would give her three hours underwater before its cells of artificial haemoglobin became overloaded. More than enough time, now she had resolved the difficulty in get-ting one of the creatures ashore. To that end she had made some additions to her harpoon gun. Now, when the barbed point penetrated shell and delivered the spe-cially tailored nerve agent, airbags would inflate on the haft, dragging the chosen whelk to the surface. Then all she had to do was drag it ashore. Picking up her equip-ment she headed off.

The beach here was stony, consisting of agates, rounded nodules of rose quartz and bullets of chert. At the tide line she donned the haemolung, mask and flippers, took up her harpoon gun and, without more ado, entered the waves. Immediately leeches started to thud into her, their grinding tubular mouthparts trying to penetrate her suit. She ignored them, kept going till submerged. In a short while the attacks ceased; each nearby leech having ascertained that she must be a large crustacean like a glister.

Ten metres out, the bottom dropped sharply. She sculled slowly down into the murk, soon locating the peak to which her camera eye clung. Circling this she spotted an iridescent gleam to the gutlike rolls of stone which she had not noticed before. Soon she was above the whelks – out of tentacle range. Something shifted, a current shoved her sideways. Earth tremor? No, just the current. She aimed down at one of the whelks and fired. The harpoon chopped into its shell and the airbags expanded. Trailing a cloud of yellow ichor the creature rose to the surface with its tentacles clenched up inside it, the nerve agent having done its work. Erlin rose with it and swam quickly ashore, towing it behind by the harpoon's monofilament. After detaching the harpoon's barb, she rolled the creature through the shallows to the beach. A momentary pang of guilt touched her, but she dismissed it. These were primitive molluscs of a kind she had been eating, nicely broiled and dunked in spiced vinegar, for years.

Once ashore she stooped and picked up the mollusc, acknowledging to herself that without the changes the Spatterjay virus had wrought in her body, the creature would be too heavy to manage. Back in her abode she dumped it on the surgical table, then began removing her gear. From the sea she heard a huge splash, and peering out observed a disturbance in the water above the colony. Glisters probably – on tasting the ichor in the water. Returning to the table she placed a camera eye over it before getting to work. She used her vibroscalpel to slice from tip to base around the shell, then her Hooper muscles to pull the two halves apart. The shell, she saw, was surprisingly thin. The creature inside was octupoidal, and opening it up she saw it also possessed much the same anatomy as a frog whelk. Another huge splash from outside. Erlin stepped over and flipped up her screen, but it showed nothing but underwater murk. She returned to her dissection.

The creature seemed ill-formed – soft and immature – and she could not find its nascent sexual organs. That was very odd as, being this size, it should at least be approaching adulthood. Perhaps she had stumbled on an aberrant colony of mutants. Or perhaps these were whelks affected by some agent, some pollutant. It had happened on Earth a long time ago: creatures similar to this changing their sexual characteristics because of pollution by human birth-control chemicals or antifouling paints on boats. Some there now were also genfactored to grow simply as meat and so did not require sex organs. But here the process could not have been initiated by humans; there just were not enough of them, and their society was not sufficiently industrialized to affect their environment. Maybe some connection with whatever had happened here on this island? Erlin allowed her attention to stray back to her screen, and for a moment just could not fathom what she was seeing. Then the view came clear. She was now looking at her own dwelling, viewed from a point out at sea and some metres above the water.

Erlin stepped to the doorway and gaped. A year of navel-gazing had obviously rotted her brain. The tip of an enormous pyramidal spiral shell was now two metres above the waves, her camera eye still clinging in place on its tip. Of course, frog and hammer whelks were adolescent by the time they reached the size of the one on the table, which it now appeared was the juvenile of a very different and much larger species. She had not been studying a colony, but a brood of creatures that were a magnitude larger than the oldest whelk of the other kind.

And now the mother whelk was coming ashore after one of her missing offspring.

2

Frog Whelk:
this whelk's cartoonish appearance belies its voracity. Its shell is much like that of a Terran whelk, and it has a single powerful foot that can launch it long distances when on land (there is nowhere on Spatterjay safe from these creatures). But seeing a flock of these creatures with their stalked eyes extended can be an amusing sight. The complex grinding and slicing mouth which it can extrude from underneath is not so amusing however. The adult whelks are large and dangerous, but are not often seen, as they inhabit the deep ocean trenches. After mating, the female lays a cluster of eggs which float slowly to the surface to hatch. The young whelks, no larger than the tip of a finger, which survive to reach an island's shallows herd together for protection from larger predators, but they also hunt in packs. As they grow, they begin moving out of the shallows and down to the trenches. Very few survive the journey there through the awaiting pods of glisters and packs of hammer whelks, fewer still survive the attentions of their much larger kin: Whelkus titanicus –

Sprout and two others leapt ashore to wrap kelp-fibre ropes around gleaming bubble-metal bollards. Anne and Boris shortly joined them, hauling on the ropes to bring the *Treader* up against the jetty, while the three youngsters – not yet as strong as the two older crew and incapable of such a feat – took up the slack and finally tied

off the ropes. Grumbling to himself, Peck lowered the
gangplank, then stood staring suspiciously inshore. Peck
had a bit of a thing about islands, but then some particularly horrible things had happened to him on one particular island. Carrying a box hung by a strap from his
shoulder, Ambel slapped Peck on the shoulder and
stepped past him.

'Come on, Peck. The only skinners here are fish skinners,' he said.

Ambel then turned to peer up at Galegrabber, who
was waiting expectantly. He reached into his pocket and
took out a roll of notes, unfolded a couple and eyed the
picture of a sail's head on them, before holding them up.
Galegrabber reached down a spider claw, delicately took
the notes then secreted them somewhere about its person.

'That completes this contract,' said Ambel. 'But we'll
be sailing again,' Ambel gazed towards the lemon-yellow
sun nestling in jade clouds on the horizon, 'in the morning, so if you want to take on some more work . . .' The
Captain shrugged.

The sail swung its head round to stare out to sea,
where rhinoworms were exuberantly hunting whelks and
leeches amid the remaining reefs. 'I'll grab a bite and get
back to you.'

The creature now released its spiderclaw holds in the
spars, drew in its veined translucent wings and, like a
giant spider tangled in sheets of pink cloth, hauled itself
to the masthead. There, with a dull thumping, it spread
its wings again and launched into the sky. Ambel turned
to the gangplank and stepped down.

Ten years ago, Olian Tay had lived alone on this island
in her tower, adding to her black museum and research-

ing the past crimes of the Eight – Jay Hoop and his pirate crew who, based here on Spatterjay, had terrorized this sector of space for nearly two centuries, before moving on to kidnapping and coring humans to sell to the Prador during that long-ago war. Some years ago she had expected to make a small fortune on Earth by displaying two items that had come into her possession, but before she could commit herself to the journey, things changed very rapidly on Spatterjay.

The increasing influx of Polity citizens in search of novel immortality brought with it a flood of wealth. Windcheater, the brightest of the living sails, had risen to power because he was both politically adept and financially acute. He knew the old currency of Spatterjay, based only on equivalency, needed to be replaced with currency based on something of genuine value to the larger human population. Gems there were aplenty, but to Hoopers, who until recent years despised personal decoration, they were worth only as much as they could be sold for to a Polity citizen. Polity citizens, moreover, being able to obtain manufactured diamonds, rubies, emeralds and many others, were only interested in rarities: unique gems like some types of fossilized wood or opalized skulls, of which the supply was limited. Windcheater toyed briefly with basing a currency on artefacts remaining from the time of the Eight but, again, not enough of them were available. Then he had his brilliant idea.

The immortal and practically indestructible Hoopers valued one thing above anything else, something they rarely used yet always coveted: the poison sprine and the quick (though messy) death it could impart. Windcheater based his new currency on sprine. The fifty New Skind

banknote thus promised to pay the bearer one death
measure of sprine. But where to keep the gathered sprine
safe from nefarious Hoopers, and from those that might
want to control Hoopers? Olian Tay made her fortune
because she was the only individual on the planet with a
secure vault, around which she established Olian's: the
first planetary bank of Spatterjay.

Strolling along the walkway leading from the jetties
into the island, Ambel gazed ahead at cleared dingle and
the new structures built there and being built. Olian's
tower stood at the centre of this, but now a long low
building led to it. Anyone coming to the bank must now
enter through her museum and get to know something
of Spatterjay's past.

'I'll bugger off now,' said Peck. 'Any chance I can
have mine now?'

Ambel nodded, took out his cash roll and counted
out Peck's wages. 'Any of the rest of you?' Sild and
Sprout took their payments, as did other crew members;
only Anne and Boris stayed with Ambel to enter the
museum. Over his shoulder Ambel told those departing,
'First thing in the morning. No excuses.'

The life-size and lifelike statue just inside the door
was the reason Peck did not enjoy this place. The
Skinner loomed four metres tall over the entryway: his
skin was blue, he was famine thin and possessed spidery
grasping hands. His head was monstrous: hoglike and
bony under taut-stretched parchment skin. The Skinner,
which had lived up to its name in Peck's case. Ambel
moved on, viewing display cases containing skeletons
with spider thralls attached at the backs of their necks,
or with skulls open to show deeper thralls installed after
coring to replace the human brain removed. Other skele-

tons were weirdly distorted, showing the initial stages of viral mutation which if it had been allowed to go on long enough would have resulted in the statue by the door. There were slave collars, weapons, mounds of personal belongings – all that remained of the millions of humans who had been processed here nearly a millennium ago. He came eventually to single cases containing models of the infamous Eight: the Talsca twins, Jay Hoop as he had looked before his transformation into the Skinner . . . and Ambel himself when he had been Balem Gosk, before the Old Captains threw him into the sea to lose most of his body and, throughout an eternity of agony, his mind as well. Two models only were missing from the set.

Chainglass pillars on either side of the bank's entrance contained Rebecca Frisk and David Grenant, but these were the real thing: unable to die because of their tough Hooper bodies, unable to live because of their imprisonment and lack of nutrition and oxygen. Olian, on special occasions, fed them small supplies of both so that they could then hammer at the impenetrable walls of their containers and mouth screams through the preserving fluid in which they floated.

In the bank foyer, Olian Tay sat behind her desk working a console and screen. Two large Hoopers and two large skinless Golem stood to either side of her. The Hoopers eyed Ambel warily, knowing that if he caused any problems the four of them might not be enough to restrain him. Ambel studied the Golem, which stood there like silver skeletons. They were products of Polity technology: androids manufactured by Cybercorp, and here deliberately lacking their syntheflesh coverings so as to appear more threatening. He was not going to be a problem, though. With Boris and Anne standing at each shoulder, he took the seat opposite Olian and placed his box on the table.

'Captain Ambel,' began Olian, 'always a pleasure. How is the lovely Erlin, and how is your crew?' Before he could answer she went on. 'And how is Crewman Peck?' She repeatedly offered Peck a job in her museum as a guide and as an exhibit himself, he being the last victim to be skinned by the monstrosity back in the museum. Peck said the very idea gave him the willies, so it was not just the statue by the entryway keeping him away from here.

'Peck is . . . Peck, and all the rest are fine,' Ambel replied, opening his box.

Inside, two chainglass bottles nestled in kelp cotton. They contained rhombic ruby crystals. Ambel handled the bottles with care as he took them out and placed them on the table. Olian slid on a pair of surgical gloves, then a mask and goggles, before pulling over a set of scales. Though a Polity citizen, she had long been infected with the same virus as all Hoopers. Ambel leant back as she tipped crystals into the scales and weighed them.

'I make that about four hundred and seventy-three grams. The Spatterjay measure is three hundred and twelve thanons, fifteen sear and twenty itch. Do you agree?'

Ambel nodded – he had weighed the stuff himself about five times.

'A profitable trip. Anyone get hurt?'

'Not by the leeches.' Ambel gestured with a thumb over his shoulder. 'Boris managed to cut off Crewman Sallow's hand, but luckily it fell inside the giant leech we were cutting open, and we were able to retrieve it. Sallow's as good as new now.'

'So that's three thousand one hundred and twenty New Skind, fifteen shligs and twenty pennies.' Olian nodded to one of the Golem, who departed. She sat back. 'Our rate is five per cent, as always, but you can keep the money here on account at three per cent interest, or we have some other interesting deals.'

Ambel started to fidget and scan around the room.

Olian continued, 'You can buy share options in Artefact Trade Inc., or Island Jewels have an interesting . . .'

Ambel completely lost interest and the rest of her speech became just a background mutter to him. Once the Golem brought his money, Ambel thanked Olian and made his escape. What need did he have of accounts and investments? He would buy supplies, buy new rope and wood for repairs, maybe some Polity toys. But very soon he would be back out on the open ocean, where the Skind in your pocket meant less than the wind in your hair.

Below a low bloom of pastel green cloud spreading across the emerald sky, Windcheater the sail drifted on thermals high above the ferry. This was the only powered vessel he allowed on the seas of Spatterjay. He had lifted the design of the boat via his aug from historical records maintained in cyberspace – liking it because it ran counter to all the Polity's present discrete technologies. It was in fact a Mississippi riverboat, though driven by a fusion-powered electric motor with a guaranteed life-span of two hundred years. Windcheater liked to choose the technologies employed here, preferring his world not to be absorbed into the homogeneous Polity.

Gazing down he noticed that some rhinoworms were following the ferry, no doubt snapping up other creatures the big water wheels stunned in their leviathan progress. He watched as one of his own kind in turn snapped up a rhinoworm and flew off with the creature writhing in its jaws. He focused on the decks, but the people there were unclear, so he routed visual reception through his aug and in it magnified and cleaned up the image. The individual standing in the bows, clad in a long black coat, had to be the reification. Windcheater growled. No doubt Taylor Bloc had come to complain about interference in his plans. The sail now lifted his head and peered towards the ferry's destination.

The Big Flint – a giant column of flint rearing a kilometre out of the sea – was wreathed in scaffolding which supported platforms, stairways, the oblate forms of easy-to-manufacture habitats, and communication arrays keeping the inhabitants here in contact with the Polity's AI networks. Hoopers and some Polity citizens occupied those habitats, but his own kind kept to the platforms and the flat top of the Flint. Windcheater had briefly tried out enclosed residences for himself and his kind, but the resultant claustrophobia for flying creatures accustomed to living in the open had been difficult to overcome. At some point he intended to obtain Polity shimmer-shields because, that phobia aside, he had never enjoyed some of the weather the planet threw at the Big Flint.

'I take it the *Gurnard* has arrived?' he queried through his aug.

'It's in orbit, and Taylor Bloc's cargo is being shuttled

down to Mortuary Island,' Sniper, the de facto Warden, instantly replied.

Windcheater banked, feeling the warm air rushing over his wing surfaces, found a thermal to take him higher.

'What about the reifications?'

'I've put out a call to those in the Dome. They'll be shuttled to the island. I'll also lay on a special shuttle for those yet to tranship, to take them direct. It's about damned time. I'm getting an average of one complaint every few minutes and the air is none too sweet up here.'

Windcheater growled agreement. He understood reifications trying to ascertain why the nanochanger technology that could resurrect them had only worked on Spatterjay. But their deification of Sable Keech into the 'Arisen One', and their aim to journey to the Little Flint, where he had first employed his changer, and there attempt their own resurrection, stank of religion. Keech himself, before returning to the Polity and his beloved profession of hunting down criminals, had warned Windcheater not to let something like that get established here, as excising such was as difficult as getting rid of a bait-worm infestation. However, reifications were very often wealthy, by dint of having been around for a long time, and though Windcheater, Boss of Spatterjay, did not want them on his world, he did rather like their money.

'By the way,' Sniper added, 'are you also aware that a large number of those reifs are not dead at all.'

'You're talking about the Batian mercenaries?'

'Ah, so you are aware.'

'Security for Lineworld Development's investment in Bloc's enterprise, and probably what Lineworld will use to steal that enterprise from him. I don't know if Bloc is aware of them, nor do I care.'

'Might get nasty,' said Sniper with relish. 'Many of the reifications are Kladites – Bloc's little army.'

'It might.' Windcheater gave an aerial shrug – that wasn't his problem.

Sniper did not want to be Warden, but such was his age and the sheer bulk of his experience, it had been unavoidable. Having sacrificed his old drone body to knock a Prador spaceship out of the sky before its owner used the vessel's weapons to fry a Convocation of Old Captains, he had uploaded to the other Warden's crystal and displaced that entity into storage. To relinquish control back to the original Warden required his being loaded to some other form of storage, and Sniper had thought about that long and hard. Over the last ten years, various drone bodies had been offered to him by the sector AI, all of which were better than his original in all but one respect: their armour and weapons. The sector AI had obviously wanted a less troublesome Sniper: a nicely castrated facsimile easier to control. But Sniper was a war drone, first, foremost and always.

Obtaining the body he wanted took years, and used up a substantial portion of his personal fortune. His search for a manufacturer capable of building to his specifications was blocked by the sector AI at every turn. Then, when he did find a manufacturer, on the fringe of the Polity, he discovered that the drone body he sought came under Polity weapons proscription, and so could not be transported by runcible or by any Polity vessel. But there were many free traders working those fringes, and he used one of them instead. And now, at last, his new body was here.

'Looks like you'll soon have your job back,' the war drone informed the entity crammed to one side of the space he occupied.

The original Warden muttered something foul. Its language had been deteriorating lately, probably because of its close proximity to Sniper. The war drone grinned inwardly, then directly picked up the feed from cameras aimed at the spaceport on Coram, the moon of Spatterjay. His view was distant; the port itself did not really come under Polity jurisdiction and so no permanent cameras were established there. He magnified the image and tracked back and forth across the crowded population of mostly privately owned ships. These were of every imaginable design: utile ovoids, sharkish vessels, multispherical – up to decasphere ships – a replica of an ancient passenger aeroplane, deltawings, and even a replica of Nelson's *Victory*. The grabship from the *Gurnard* rested amid these like some blunt tail-less scorpion skulking from the light, though what it now held in its claws gleamed. Impatient with this view, Sniper sent out one of his drones.

'Two, go take a look at my delivery for me, will you?'

The drone, a little cranky ever since occupying an enforcer shell on the planet below during the same battle in which Sniper had brought down the Prador ship, now resided in a body the shape of an iron turbot a metre long. It had been sloping about the concourse waiting for Sniper's attention to roam elsewhere so it could go off and moonlight in one of the bars as a vending tray.

'Sure thing, Warden,' it said without much enthusiasm.

Tracking it with pinhead cameras in the concourse, Sniper watched it shoot out through a shimmer-shield port in the glass roof, briefly ignite a small fusion drive it should not have possessed, then coast over to the spaceport. He then lightly touched its mind and peered out through its eyes. Dropping down through the diamond fibre rigging of the *Victory*, it then grav-planed a few metres above the plascrete towards the grabship. Now Sniper could see the ship had released its gleaming cargo, and that a big man in a big spacesuit was driving a handler dray towards the precious load.

'Is that you, Ron?' Sniper sent, after probing for the suit's com frequency.

'It certainly is, Warden,' replied the Old Captain.

'I hadn't expected to see you back here so soon.'

'Nowhere is there anything like the seacane rum of home.'

Through the eyes of the turbot drone, Sniper watched while Captain Ron brought the dray in close, picked up the framework containing the shining nautiloid drone shell, then took it towards the cargo sheds on one side of the moon base. Seeing where the man was heading, Sniper suddenly realized how he himself could speed things up considerably.

'Ron, don't take the shell to the cargo sheds. There's a clear area over to the left of the base, as you face it. The drone just above you will lead you there.'

Captain Ron looked up, nodded, then drove the handler after the drone as it turned and slowly led the way to the area Sniper indicated. While this was happening, Sniper began scanning through the systems he controlled. Yes, if he wished, he could transmit himself directly into the drone shell with it located anywhere up to a hundred thousand kilometres away, but there were losses that last time, when he had transmitted himself up here to the Warden – about two per cent he estimated. Bringing the shell in via the cargo sheds would take time, as there was a lot of stuff going through there. But he did not need to do either.

As many Polity citizens had discovered ten years ago, when the Prador ship had revealed itself and begun its attack, this base was surrounded by powerful armament. The particular weapon that interested Sniper was a projector for electronic warfare, but not just the kind that knocked out systems with an EM pulse. This projector also transmitted kill programs, viruses and worms, and all the destructive cornucopia that had been evolving from the beginning of the information age. He tracked the system, shutting off all the alarms and disconnecting it from the rest of the weapons that could rise out of the ground in a concerted response to a threat, then he activated it.

'Well bugger me,' said Ron.

Ahead of the Captain, precisely in the centre of the level area, the ground erupted and out of it rose a column topped by the blockish structure of an emitter array, enclosed in armour. It rose twenty metres into vacuum, then the end split and opened like a tulip bud, to reveal the array itself. Sniper began drawing in his awareness from the numerous systems he controlled. He shut down the runcible, but it would not be off for long – only two people would find themselves stepping out on the wrong world, and only a further two would have their journey away from here delayed. The bandwidth, to the electronic warfare weapon, was necessarily wide; wide enough to take semi-sentient killer programs, and wide enough for Sniper. He probed ahead first to check the receptivity of the drone shell, and the shell then activated dormant power sources.

'It might be an idea for you to just drop the shell there and move back, Ron.'

'Yeah, it might at that.'

Sniper noticed how the Captain was peering at the signs of movement from the nautiloid's silver tentacles, and the occasional glimmer of lights from optic ports in the head. The man lowered it in its framework, released it, then put his handler dray hard in reverse.

Sniper was now ready, but one thing remained for him to do. He quickly found a link that he, out of a sense of propriety, did not often use. Suddenly he was gazing out across blue sea to an island where self-inflating habitats had been landed, and where robots had built jetties and other structures. The eyes from which he gazed he knew were turquoise, and set in the head of a floating iron seahorse.

'How goes it, Thirteen?'

'Fair,' replied this one of the old Warden's subminds, SM13.

'Perhaps you'll soon think things better than fair. I've just transferred funds to pay off the last of your indenture. You are now a free drone.'

'Um,' said the SM, 'I really wanted to do that myself.'

'Ah, but the old Warden will shortly be back in control, and he might be a bit tetchy. Best it be done now.'

'I see . . . Your shell arrived?'

'Certainly did,' Sniper replied, then cut the connection.

Nothing else remained now. It had been an interesting ten years acting as Spatterjay's Warden: watching Windcheater's rise to power and the changes the sail Boss wrought on the surface. But time and again he had wanted actually to be there, and been hard pressed not to take over some of the various drones scattered about the planet. Now he could get back into the game.

'It's all yours, Warden,' he said, and began transmitting all that he was down the optic and 3-con linkages to the transmitters on the weapon. He grew less, felt displacement and the division of self. As he went he could feel the Warden coming out of storage and unfolding itself to reoccupy abandoned spaces.

Hiatus.

Sniper expanded within the drone shell, checking out the systems at his disposal as he shrugged himself into his new body. He began running diagnostics, started the fusion reactor which until then had been in stasis. He opened crystalline orange eyes, probed his surroundings with radar, a laser-bounce spectrometer, many other instruments. Ultrasound, infrasound and sonar would have to wait for a more suitable environment. He extruded his two long spatulate tentacles and ran them through the stony dust before him, then reached back and tore away protective wrapping and the encaging framework. Engaging gravmotors, he shrugged away the last of his packaging.

'A very fine swan,' he stated, then turned on his fusion engines and hurtled up over the moon base and round the moon itself. He checked his weapons carousel, selected a low-yield missile, targeted a boulder on the moon's surface and spat down the black cylinder. The rock blew apart in a candent explosion, hurling pieces of itself out into space. Sniper selected in turn a laser, particle beam, then an APW, and converted each fragment in turn to vapour.

'Now we're cooking!'

The blue and gold orb of Spatterjay rose above the rocky horizon. He adjusted his course towards it, and accelerated.

Coming out on deck with Bones trailing behind him, Aesop eyed the long pink serpents thrashing in the sea, often lifting their rhinoceros heads out of the waves with mouths crammed full of squirming leeches. He then turned his attention to the beach, and saw that what he had at first taken to be flocks of gulls were in fact clusters of off-white spiral shells. Frog whelks. It seemed such an innocuous name for creatures that would happily chew down to the bone anyone who set foot on the beach. Thankfully an enclosed walkway led across that shore from the jetty the ferry was now coming alongside.

Aesop walked along the deck to where Taylor Bloc stood watching – bare of mask and hood.

'What do you think the response will be?' Aesop asked.

Bloc paused before replying, probably wondering if he was prepared to permit such familiarity from one of his slaves, then said, 'Whatever it may be, we will still get established on this world and the ship will be built.'

And how so very much did Taylor Bloc want that ship built. It had taken some time in the early years for Aesop to figure the reif out, simply because there was little facial expression to read. But now he was certain of what drove Bloc. Few sentient reifs had any belief in the tenets of the Cult of Anubis Arisen, as most of them became too old and experienced to be taken in by it all, yet many of them remained the way they were out of long habit. Bloc did believe in resurrection through the flesh, but his real aim in bringing reified people here was for one purpose only – adulation – though as a corollary he had become a leader of what some described as 'the militant dead'. Bloc also became very annoyed whenever he was thwarted, which was happening right now. Certainly the relocation was a result of machinations by Lineworld Developments, for the more cash it was necessary for the company to inject, the greater would be their percentage of the eventual take, and cash injection beyond a certain level meant they could also take control of the entire project.

'Of course, relocating the enterprise away from what passes as civilization here, though initially costly, does provide other advantages,' Bloc added.

Aesop knew what that meant. 'But to both sides,' he suggested.

'I have one advantage of which Lineworld Developments could not conceive.'

Aesop made no reply to that. Despite all his years of experience Bloc had still yet to learn that you could not coerce people into adulation, that it was not something you gained through intimidation and murder. Aesop knew that, for he had made a profession of such.

Crewmen, big heavy individuals with skin distinctively leech-scarred and bluish, threw ropes to others of similar stripe down on the jetty. Aesop watched with interest as the second group began hauling on the ropes. He had heard about this sort of thing but thought the stories exaggerated. However, as the ferry moved sideways up against the pearwood platform, he had to make some rapid reassessments. Perhaps Bloc's hiring of so many Hooper crewmen had not been such a good idea.

As the three of them disembarked, Aesop noted that other ferry passengers were keeping their distance. Bloc was beginning to reek, but no doubt wanted to get this meeting out of the way before he again used his cleansing unit. Or perhaps he was just getting careless. Aesop had noticed Bloc behaving rather oddly lately – perhaps it was the pressure. As he stepped onto the jetty, he turned and saw one of the Hoopers kick something squealing into the water. The woman grinned at him.

'Don't worry,' she said. 'We only get one or two up on the jetty.'

Aesop made no response but to follow Bloc on into the enclosed walkway. There he saw numerous stalked eyes, sticking up from the gathering of shells on the beach, turning to track the progress of the passengers. He controlled himself when a couple of those shells launched into the air and crashed against the mesh before falling back down onto the beach again. A screech from a man nearby told him that others had not been quite so prepared for this.

'Have either of you had any odd messages from your internal diagnostics yet?' Bloc asked.

'I've yet to be bitten by a leech,' Aesop replied.

Bones made no sound – his reply by other means.

'Viral infection can be caused by other media,' Bloc stated.

That required no response, so Aesop gave none.

It was the general opinion of those who had investigated the matter that Keech's success with the nanofactory changer had been due in part to his being infected by the Spatterjay virus. There were other elements to take into account though, like him being shot, his use of Intertox inhibitors, and the delay before he got himself into a jury-rigged tank containing sterilized seawater. It was all very risky, and not something Aesop would have countenanced had he the choice. He kept himself well dosed with inhibitors to prevent viral infection, and just hoped. Too little was known about the damned virus. Bloc probably looked forward to his first 'outside parameter function' message from his internal hardware, which would tell him he was infected.

They mounted an enclosed stairway spiralling up the side of the Flint and began to climb. Other passengers were soon wheezing after only a few flights. Aesop, Bones and Bloc, clumping along behind the main crowd, did not wheeze, of course, did not breathe at all.

At the first platform, most of the ferry passengers left the stairwell to enter some kind of market. Aesop gazed out at the various stalls, many of them stacked with souvenirs: reproduction thrall units, slave collars, figurines of the Eight, variously sized models of the Skinner and other examples of the planet's weird life forms, whelk shells, heirodont mandibles or their bones made into Hooper scrimshaw. Other stalls carried the usual cheaply produced items found in markets all across the Polity: ceramal cutlery, chainglass knives that would keep their edge for decades, image intensifiers, enviro boots and suits, augs . . . The list just went on and on. A couple of stalls carried terrariums and aquariums, and those who spent their money there would afterwards require medical attention. Here, in this market, you could buy everything from scratch-resistant sunglasses to the leech bite that would impart immortality, even if that could be obtained for nothing anywhere else on

Spatterjay. Those tourists who bought it here showed their timidity or stupidity.

By the time they had passed another two platforms, the three were alone on the stair leading up. Eventually they stepped out on the top of the Big Flint where Aesop studied his surroundings. Ten years ago Keech stood up here, but things had certainly changed since then.

Some sails were huddled in a mass: large pinkish baggy bodies, long necks hooking above them, terminating in crocodilian heads. Other sails were scattered separately about on the top of the Flint or out on the bubble-metal platform ringing it. Some operated cowled machines Aesop could not identify, until stepping close to one with its weather shield open to find the sail working, with its big spider hands, a touch console and screen inside. Satellite dishes were positioned further out on the platform; cables snaked across the stone. None of the sails paid the three much attention.

'We are here to see Windcheater,' Bloc announced.

Abruptly a number of heads swung towards them. Then the crowd of sails parted and a larger, more aggressive-looking creature mooched over towards them. This was definitely Windcheater – Aesop recognized him from the files he had been instructed to study.

'Yes,' said the sail.

'You're Windcheater?'

The sail did not reply.

'Are you Windcheater?' Bloc tried again.

'Evidently.'

Bloc said, 'You've relocated us. We had an agreement.'

'Yes.'

'This is unacceptable. You can't go back on your word.'

The sail arched its neck to bring its head down level with Bloc. 'You paid me so you could come here and build a ship to sail your pilgrims to the Little Flint. The plans you submitted were for you to launch it from the Chel Island, but I did not agree to them. I don't want you people that close to me. Now bugger off.' The sail began to turn away.

'What about the sails for our ship?' Bloc quickly asked. 'You agreed to that. It's part of your law that no ship can sail without at least one of your kind aboard.'

'You'll get your sails,' Windcheater told him.

'There's an economic reason for you moving us, isn't there?' Bloc suggested.

Aesop was impressed: Taylor Bloc was not normally so restrained.

Showing more interest than heretofore, the sail swung back. 'For example?'

'Because no more are being produced, there's only a limited number of reifications who can come here for either a cure or their physical destruction by the virus, so eventually pilgrimages by those you find distasteful will dwindle. So afterwards you'll get yourself a piece of civilization established on another island.'

'Smart dead man,' said the sail.

Aesop felt like laughing, but had lost that ability long ago. Nothing about the additional costs and a probable takeover by Lineworld. Windcheater had clearly been paid to relocate them. However, Bloc was only going through the motions. He had obviously decided on his course now.

The sail Huff had been informed by humans, AIs and Windcheater that he remembered his name because he was brighter than the average sail, for a certain horrible reason. When the Batian mercenary Shib had stapled Huff's neck to the mast of Captain Drum's ship, the *Ahab*, and when Jay Hoop's lunatic wife Rebecca Frisk had subsequently cooked Huff's skull with a laser, his brain had then regrown without the usual hard wiring. Puff, it was supposed, remembered her name for similar reasons, telling Huff she only vaguely recollected the heirodont that had clamped its jaws on her skull when she had peered over the edge of the Little Flint to see about snapping up one of the hammer whelks nestling down there. Huff speculated that a similar happenstance had resulted in Windcheater's enhanced intelligence, perhaps when the planet had been ruled by the Eight, who had taken as much pleasure in hunting indigenes as those humans who escaped from the coring facility. Windcheater was not telling. However, no such drastic damage had resulted in the cerebral rewiring of the third sail, nor was likely to. Huff now eyed their companion.

Zephyr was as big as Windcheater, and no heirodont's jaws carried the muscle to crush his ceramal skull, and no one would be stapling him to a mast. His tough carbon polymer skin was the hue of blued steel. His teeth were chainglass and his bones were composite-reinforced bubble-metal. In his chest he carried two state-of-the-art fusion reactors, which drove his carbon-fibre muscles and powered his crystal brain and formidable sense array. His eyes were gleaming emeralds. Zephyr had very little to fear, being a Golem sail.

Huff and Puff's partnership had lasted for ten years, from when they discovered much in common with each other and little with their fellows. Zephyr, when he arrived here less than a year ago, had been much less coherent than he was now. Windcheater had treated him with suspicion; the response of other sails had been confusion. Huff and Puff, however, adopted him as an outcast like themselves. They showed him their world, talked and flew with him. In a short time they became fascinated by the Golem sail's strange combination of hard-headed wisdom and not quite sane pronouncements on life and death. They argued and flew, learnt, and thus became even more distant from their fellows. When he volunteered the three of them for a task other sails wanted no part of, he became the leader and they the followers.

'I think I see it now,' said Huff.

'You do,' Zephyr replied. 'And now we need to go faster.' The Golem sail accelerated.

Huff and Puff looked at each other questioningly, then grabbed air to catch up with their companion.

'What's the hurry?' Puff complained. 'The money's the same either way and there's no way they'll be sailing without us.'

Zephyr glanced aside. 'I will see the soulless sail.'

'And . . . ?' said Huff.

Zephyr's voice changed to more normal tones, as if the Golem sail now assumed a prosaic guise. 'Beyond the reason that will soon become evident to you, we have reason to get this part over with as quickly as possible.' Zephyr held up the harness he clasped in one claw. 'We might not be within the Polity, but this Warden will take a dim view of what we're about if he catches us. From what I've been told he doesn't put much credence in the rules and regulations supposedly governing his status.'

'What might he do?' Puff asked.

Huff had a damned good idea; he had been in the middle of the events that resulted in the new Warden. He still remembered the taste of the human heads he had bitten off just before the *Ahab* sank and the device inside it detonated. And later he had been high in the sky watching when the war drone Sniper, who was now the Warden, had come down like a hammer on that Prador ship.

'It is this way,' said Zephyr. 'The new Warden would try not to endanger any innocent Polity citizen, but it might be possible to identify us by a chemical analysis of the ash floating on the sea. I do not choose Death. I refuse it.'

'But you are a Polity citizen,' Huff pointed out.

Zephyr exposed his chainglass teeth so they glinted in the sunset light. 'But not innocent; and that I'm not an ignorant native makes me doubly culpable.'

'No forgiveness then,' asked Puff.

'Outmoded concept of human law. We are all responsible for our actions.' Zephyr pointed ahead with one long metallic talon. 'Do you see now?'

Huff and Puff peered ahead.

'Oh, one of *them*,' said Huff.

3

Putrephallus Weed:
phallic in shape and stinking like rotten corpses, this is not a
plant xenobotanists much enjoy studying. They grow from
a large seed, throwing up in only a few days a two-metre-tall
green phallic stalk, and spreading catch leaves low to the
ground. The tips turn red as they ripen, attracting the lung
birds to eat them, gain some nutrition from the outer fruiting
body, then vomit up the inner pollen sack. This usually hap-
pens in another stand of the same plants, perhaps caused by
some kind of pheromonal trigger. The pollen sacks splash on
the ground, spraying liquid pollen over the catch leaves and
entering their central stigma. The seeds then developing are
raised up in the tips of yet more phallic growth, are eaten by
the lung birds, then vomited up at other locations. Lung birds,
perhaps gratefully so, are also the main pollinators of the sea
lily –

His room already booked and hotel code key to hand,
Bloc strode into the hotel ignoring the dubious looks
cast in his direction. His suitcase, walking on four spidery legs, had to scuttle to keep up with him. Usually he
used a hover trunk to transport his belongings, but had

purchased this semi-AI luggage thinking Windcheater's proscription covered all forms of anti-gravity. It annoyed him to now discover the ruling applied only to privately owned transportation for people and cargoes that could be moved by sailing ship but, even then, reasonable requests might be granted. Windcheater simply did not want the skies crowded with AG scooters and cars, and did not want the sail and Hooper monopoly of sea transportation undermined.

Taylor Bloc entered the elevator, a couple stepping in behind him, then quickly stepping out again while staring at him accusingly. It was long past time for Bloc to use his cleansing unit and related equipment. He stepped out on the relevant floor, moved quickly to his room, and there ordered his suitcase up on the bed and open, while he shed his coat and envirosuit, followed by an underlying noxmol suit. This particular garment consisted of a porous inner layer, a layer of activated carbon wool through which air was cycled, finally exiting through micron filters at his shoulders, and an outer, impenetrable layer of monofabric. Shedding that he then inspected his absorbent under suit, which was stained and stinking. He stripped it off, balled it, and threw it into the disposal unit. Then walked over to the wardrobe mirror to give himself a visual inspection.

He was a corpse, grey and wrinkled. His death had been hard, and though they had done their best to put him back together during the reification process, their work had been, so to speak, cut out for them. His genitals were gone. They had never been able to find them, though he had later learnt, to his disgust, what had happened to them, and consequently something of one of his killer's appetites. His broken or severed bones, the reifiers bone-welded and clamped, while installing the joint motors. His organs and muscles had been meticulously returned and connected up with balm pipes. Cell welding, carbon-fibre mesh, collagen foam and even stitching had all been used. Much of his seared skin had been useless, hence his appearance now: muscles visible in their wash of dirty blue balm under translucent syntheskin.

Bloc inspected his front, noting the growth of some sort of mould at the join between synthetic and real skin at his waist. He took a hand mirror out of his suitcase, then turned slowly, observing himself in the now doubled reflection from the wardrobe mirror. Ah, there was the main reason for the multitude of error messages flashing up in his visual cortex: underneath syntheskin covering his lower back, a wriggling colony of small green maggots. They had to be some tough alien strain, since the insecticides in the balm washing round inside him was proof against all Terran infestations. But he had dealt with such problems before and knew the routine. First, though, his exterior.

From his case Bloc removed a flat square bottle of a green jelly and a long-handled soft brush, and took them with him to the bathroom. Here he found, as requested, the shower had the facility to mix additives. He uncapped the bottle, pressed it into the receiver, and turned on the shower. The water turned green with the addition of a powerful concentrate of antivirabact and insecticides. The water that ran down the drain was not such a pleasant colour, though. Now using the brush he worked over his entire body, cleaned away the mould and eyed some of the green maggots wriggling down the waste. After his shower he used the air dryer, as employing a towel might have rubbed away more than just moisture.

Returning to his bedroom, Bloc took a handful of elasticizer cream from a tub in his case, and rubbed it into all his grey skin. Sitting on a towel on the bed, he then took out his cleansing unit. This device was encased in brushed aluminium, circular, twenty centimetres across and ten deep. It was a more modern version of the device Sable Keech had once used in this very hotel, but then Keech's reification did predate his own by about five hundred years. The two tubes he uncoiled from a hatch in the side, he plugged straight into sockets below his armpit. The device started cycling immediately, pumping out filthy grey-blue balm, filtering it and adjusting its chemical composition back to optimum and pumping it back in like liquid sapphire. He would empty the device's sump sometime later. Now for the maggots.

Bloc pulled out a flat square box of the same brushed aluminium as his cleanser, opened it, and scooped out a handful of small silvery objects. To the naked eye they looked nothing much, but magnification revealed them as small metal beetles, scarabs, with their legs folded close. He placed them against his skin below the maggot infestation, waited a moment, then took his hand away. They were all gone; burrowing through the joint to hunt down their prey.

While he waited for the various processes to complete, Bloc pulled his noxmol suit closer with his foot, stooped and picked it up. He opened the top pocket and removed from it a lozenge of golden metal with attached neck chain. This was what it was all about.

The nanofactory changer was the creation of a brilliant scientist, resulting from her research into an alien technology that had caused some problems for the Polity a few centuries back. It was packed with Von Neumann nano- and micromachines, and as such was capable of reproducing itself. All that was needed was another case built to specifications stored in its memory – a case packed with the base elements required to build its complex guto. The two cases were then connected, submerged in a zero-G tank of water containing metal salts, nanoscopic gold particles and free droplets of liquid mercury, which then had a huge electric charge put across it. Bloc had seen this done. When the process completed, the two now identical nanofactories rested in a Gordian tangle of strange nanocircuitry which rapidly began to fall apart. The whole process defied analysis even by AI, for, following twisted Heisenbergian principles, it broke down if any kind of scan was used to study it. The nanofactories themselves were the same: a scan of the case resulted in processes activating inside it, which in turn resulted in the case ending up full of either metallic sludge or dangerous nanomachines that not even the dead would want in their bodies.

The first nanofactory changer had been given to the Cult of Anubis Arisen – their shot at resurrection. It had never worked: of the first three reifs to use it, two had come close to life before collapsing to sludge, and the third was now an exhibit in a museum on Klader. He was subsequently named the bone man. Over the years many others had taken the chance, and none had succeeded. The tales of what had happened to them were all grotesque: there was the reif who nearly made it, but as his blood began to circulate he sprouted hands all over his body before falling into a pile of those members;

there was the one whose head turned into a single glistening eye; and another in whom the process generated so much heat that he simply exploded. Sable Keech, during his relentless pursuit of the Eight, had never learnt of this history. But then he had never been a member of the Cult, which was something Cult members had never publicized. Bloc only learnt the truth when he bought out what remained of the Cult, and transformed it to his own purposes. Where Keech had obtained his changer, no one knew. His use of it, even in extremity, obtained from his ignorance of what it might do to him. Yet he had succeeded: it had resurrected him. He was the Arisen One. It somewhat annoyed Bloc that, having returned to life, Keech had then returned to his old existence as a policeman – such a prosaic denouement.

Bloc replaced the device in his suit's pocket, unplugged his cleansing unit, then looked down at the towel behind him. The beetles were marching out in a neat line, stacking dead maggots before returning to the hole in his back. They were not finished yet. He would wait with the patience of a corpse.

Sitting alfresco at the Baitman, sipping a tin mug of rum, Janer wondered if it was true they made the stuff by straining rocket fuel through a bag of seacane. It certainly seemed that those Hoopers who smoked were wary of lighting their pipes or cigars in the proximity of their drinks. He scanned around. These outside tables – a new addition since he was last here – were mostly occupied, as from them it was easy to see the raised platform nearby over the heads of the growing crowd. Evening was now closing in and electric streetlights –

another addition – were coming on and igniting all with lurid greenish light. Forlam, sitting in one of the three seats around the table, had not taken his avid gaze away from that platform since they arrived. The other seat was empty, but the large tin mug before it engraved with the word 'Ron' was enough to deter any of the surrounding Hoopers from sitting there. Janer remembered a conversation with Keech in this very street. '*He, I would guess, is an Old Captain, and has authority by dint of the simple fact that he can tear your arms off.*' Janer had just met Captain Ron for the first time.

'I didn't know you did this sort of thing here,' Janer said conversationally.

It was the hive mind that responded: '*It was going to happen to Captain Ambel.*'

Forlam said nothing, just kept on staring.

Janer nodded. Of course, had the Convocation of Old Captains found Ambel guilty, the sentence would have been death, though the method different. He looked up as the crowd parted and Ron came through to reclaim his seat.

'What's happening?' Forlam asked, licking his lips.

Ron eyed him. 'Two lads off the *Vignette*, they slipped some sprine into a fellow crewman's tea after a fight over money. Can't say I'm surprised. Convocation sentenced 'em to the same end.'

'Convocation?' Janer peered around. 'Where are the rest of the Old Captains?'

Ron glanced at him. 'Seems we've entered our technological age. Not sure I like that.'

The hive mind chipped in with, '*All the Captains now use holographic conferencing links for Convocation. They now only meet physically if the matter is really serious.*'

How serious was 'really serious', Janer wondered.

'Why aren't you surprised?' he asked.

'The *Vignette*, bad ship, and Captain Orbus . . .' Ron trailed off into an embarrassed silence.

The three returned their attention to the platform as the first of the Hooper crewmen was dragged up onto it, fighting all the way despite the ceramal band around his body to which his wrist manacles were secured, and the manacles around his ankles. The man was naked, and by the look of him Janer reckoned him to be a Hooper of about a hundred and fifty years. Those wrestling with him attached a chain from the band to one of the two heavy iron posts protruding from the platform.

'Fucking bastards!' the man yelled. 'He was squeaky weed-head slobber-arse!' Released, he yanked at his chain, glared around.

The second man walked calmly onto the platform. His expression contained some of the craziness Janer had seen only recently in Forlam's expression. He stood meekly as they attached him to his post. When the platform was clear but for these two, an Old Captain stepped up and stood with his back to the abusive Hooper.

'Orbus,' Ron muttered. 'There won't be any fancy speeches.'

'Well, you know the decision,' the Captain said, 'and it's my job to deal with my crewmen.'

He pulled on a set of gauntlets, drew a dagger from the sheath at his wide belt, and inspected the blade. Before the Hooper behind him could react he turned fast and drove the dagger into the man's guts, withdrew it, then stepped away from him. The man grimaced, did not bleed.

'Sprine on the blade,' Forlam informed Janer irrelevantly. Janer realized it had to be that. Stabbing a Hooper with a clean blade would not kill him, only irritate him.

Orbus returned the dagger to its sheath, rattled it up and down for a moment then took it out for his inspection again. The second Hooper was watching his companion when the dagger, more sprine on it from the sheath, went into him. He oomphed, turned to Orbus with an expression of hurt accusation.

'You could have let me watch,' he complained.

'Now,' Forlam whispered.

The skin around the first Hooper's stab wound turned yellow, that stain spreading. He started to shake, froth bubbling from his mouth. The crack of one of the manacles snapping was audible from where Janer sat, but the man only raised his free hand to wipe his lips. The second man was going the same way. Now the first one's eyes rolled up into his head and he issued a long-drawn-out groan. A split appeared in his torso and black liquid began to run out. Other body splits appeared; more liquid poured onto the platform. Then he really began to come apart. One of his biceps departed his arm bone. His guts began to bubble out of the first split. The victim started to sink down, still coming apart. What remained was a steaming pile of separated bone, flesh and organs, as if the man had been slow pressure-cooked for a day. The second man reached similar pilehood shortly after him. Janer gulped some rum. 'I nearly gave you the power to do that,' he said, peering down at the encased hornets on his shoulder.

Ron and Forlam glanced at him, saw who he was addressing, then returned their attention to the platform, where a group of Hoopers had climbed up with shovels, buckets and mops.

'*If you recollect, you did give it to me, but then Captain Ambel took it away again. But be assured, in my possession such power would have been rarely used. What one of the older minds might do with it, even I am loath to speculate.*'

'What are they like then, these older minds?'

'*Unfathomable,*' was all the reply the hive mind offered.

Janer returned to easy conversation with his two human companions, as the rum began to work its familiar magic on him. At one point he commented, 'They showed little fear.'

'Hoopers don't fear a quick death,' Ron replied.

'Do they fear anything?'

'Oh yes, *young* Hoopers fear falling into the sea and not dying.'

'Old Captains?'

'What young Hoopers fear, plus the fate they avoided when Jay Hoop was in control here: they fear and hate the prospect of coring or having a thrall implanted,' Ron explained.

'Still . . . it was all such a long time ago.'

'Never underestimate how Old Captains feel about that,' Ron warned.

Seemingly without transition thereafter, they were sitting in twilight reliving old battles. Janer asked Ron if he knew what Keech was now doing.

'Last I heard, he's back on Klader working for the Polity monitor force,' the Captain replied.

'Still a policeman?' Janer asked incredulously.

Ron eyed him. 'Seven hundred years being dead didn't put him off, so what do you think?'

Thereafter Janer and Ron became intent on extracting from Forlam the truth about what he had done with a certain female Batian mercenary. The other tables were empty now and no one objected when someone brought a chair to their table and joined them. Janer studied the dark-browed Hooper, trying to figure what it was about him – something out of kilter.

'I want to join your crew,' said the man to Ron.

'And you are?'

'Isis Wade.'

'What experience do you have, Wade?' Ron asked genially. Janer had lost count of the refills now.

'As much experience as I want or need,' Wade replied.

Ah, that's it, Janer thought. The man was dark, his skin was patterned with leech scars, and he moved with that Hooper rolling gait. But Janer could see the difference. It was in the minutiae: mannerisms, exactitude of speech, how precisely soiled was his clothing, how his breathing was not quite in synch with his speech and movement – and probably also in things below conscious perception, like pheromones. Now why would a Golem android want to join Ron's crew, and, for that matter, the Captain's crew on what vessel? Ron was not returning to the *Gurnard*, and his own sailing ship had ended up at the bottom of the sea ten years ago.

Janer lost track of their conversation for a while, then came back to hear Ron saying, 'Okay, you're on. One like you might be useful.'

'When does she sail?' Wade asked.

Ron replied, 'They've got some of your kind working day and night on her, so not long. I'm getting some others together, but most are already on contract.'

'What are you talking about?' Janer asked.

Ron eyed him. 'Why, we're talking about the *Sable Keech*. What else?'

A skirt of warty flesh, hard as stone, oozed up the beach, and a long tentacle uncoiled from it. Erlin glanced back at the dismembered whelk on her surgical table and guessed the monstrous mollusc rising out of the sea was not looking for explanations. Its shell, encrusted with flatweed and alive with small prill, was the size of a large house. It rose up on a mound of flesh and in that mound two eyes blinked open, then everted from the main body on stalks thick as her leg. More tentacles unrolled up the beach, then a longer one with a wide flat end snapped back behind the rising shell then slammed forward and down exploding a shrapnel of stones in every direction. The tentacle tip rested momentarily a few metres from her door before the creature drew it back again. It was coming on rapidly, having now risen over the underwater ledge. Erlin dived aside as the pillar of stony flesh slammed down where she had just been standing. Rolling to her feet, she saw the tentacle slide quickly inside her house. There it paused, and a deep bass groaning issued from the monster. As the tentacle withdrew, a second one of the same type hammered down, and Erlin stared aghast at her home of a year. She had hoped to dive back inside, retrieve some weapon, but the dwelling now looked like a simnel cake that someone had smacked squarely with a lead bar. She glanced back towards the sea, and the two eyes pivoted towards her. She ran inland.

Stupid stupid stupid. What catastrophe had denuded this island of large animals? What had smashed peartrunk trees and driven a lane through the island's central jungle? Well, her answer was coming after her now, by the tonne.

As she neared the island's centre she looked back to see the monster revealed in all its glory, ploughing up the lane it had made before her arrival here. Sunset light glinted on a shell similar to that of its young, just rougher, older, and a lot lot bigger. Its visible body, stretching out below that shell, resembled that of an octopus, though the eyes extruded on stalks, the tentacles were without suckers, and the skirt between them extended further from the body itself than it did on the Terran cephalopod. Its upper surfaces were warty and a greyish purple, whilst its under surfaces were almost white – a pastel lavender shade. Had she not been running for her life, Erlin would have been fascinated.

She turned abruptly to her right and entered the dingle. A few hundred metres inwards, the island rose to a rocky peak which the monster might not be able to reach. Immediately, as she ran into the gloom, a leech the size of her arm dropped on her head and attempted to slide down round her neck like a feather boa. She grabbed it and flung it aside as its bubbling and churning tube mouth groped for her cheek. Other leeches fell around her in an awful fleshy rain, but she was moving too fast now to allow any of them an opportunity to feed. She crashed into a stand of putrephallus, held her breath going through it, and for as long as she could after departing the other side. Even so, when she did take a breath, she nearly vomited at the stench.

Now a slope lay before her, thick with bubbleweed. She skirted this, knowing that running up a slope this covered was almost impossible, as the weed bursting underfoot would turn the surface almost frictionless.

She mounted a stone ridge snaking down the slope, and ran up that, slipping once and banging her knee, then again as she departed it at the top. From down below she heard the creature's crashing commotion as it entered the dingle. Glancing back she saw it wrench from the ground the peartrunk tree from which the leeches had been falling, lift it ten metres into the air, then hurl it. The tree crashed into the slope below her. Leeches, pieces of wood and sods of bubbleweed rained past her. She fell flat to avoid a flying branch, rose again to see the monster now reach the putrephallus stand. It hesitated there, drew back and began to skirt it, but still it came on.

Erlin laboured up the slope to the highest point on the island. Many times she had come to this rocky prominence to survey the surrounding gleam of green-blue balmy seas. Even as she reached this height she realized there would be no safety here. A tentacle slammed down only metres below her – the creature, now past the putrephallus, had slowed not at all. Her only option was to just keep on running round and round the island. Even if she managed to stay ahead of the monster during the approaching night, and not make just one fatal error, her tough Hooper body would eventually give out. For the giant whelk only needed to be relentless. Erlin felt sure she was going to die, and all her thoughts on the matter of her death – the malaise that had first brought her here to this planet to find Ambel, and here to this island to 'think' – seemed so inconsequential in that moment. She had never felt so alive.

'Fuck you!' she shouted at the monster.

'Face Death, and know it as the enemy,' spoke a voice, as wings boomed above her and shadows occluded the darkening sky. Then long-fingered claws gripped her shoulders and hauled her up into the firmament.

The juvenile glister, being small and necessarily opportunist, had been waiting in the depths for just such a moment, its antennae up as it ascertained that the giant whelk had definitely gone ashore. It rose up onto its multitude of legs, flicked its tail, and just gently touching the bottom with its sharp feet, bounced along towards the brood of young whelks. It came from downcurrent, and its camouflaged carapace gave it added advantage. Every time a stalked eye swung towards it, it changed its buoyancy, dropped to the bottom and froze. When it was close enough it gave a powerful flick of its flat tail and came down on the nearest whelk. The glister closed its claws in the flesh directly below the whelk's shell before the creature had time to draw in its tentacles and the main mass of its body. The rest of the whelks immediately withdrew into their shells, but the glister had enough here – it was not greedy. It dragged its prey clear of the others, and with one claw remaining clamped into its flesh so the creature still could not escape, began tearing away lumps of it and feeding. The whelk thrashed at the glister with its tentacles, but those tentacles had not yet gained the concrete consistency of its parent's. Its eye-stalks slapped from side to side until the glister snipped them off with its free claw and fed them into its mandibles. Soon it was into the guts of the thing, discarding the long serrated beak, sucking in loops of intestine. Then abruptly its antennae flicked upright as it detected something else in the water. It dropped the shell, despite it still containing plenty of flesh, pushed itself off from the bottom and swam away just as fast as it could. The problem it had always found, with dining on the sea bottom, was the uninvited guests.

The turbul shoal, forever patrolling the depths – feeding and being fed upon – their outer flesh constantly needing to be replaced, were always hungry. The scent of ichor in the water drove them to a frenzy with half-remembered feasting on the contents of easily broken shells. However, the still-present other scent from the giant whelk itself reminded them of near escapes, the loss of outer flesh and sudden reductions in their number.

The first turbul nosed cautiously up out of the depths – a long five-hundred-kilogram creature with caiman jaws and bright blue fins grown seemingly at random from its cylindrical dark green body. It sucked the water in through its nostrils, blowing it out through the gill holes down its length, flicked its whip tail, the hatchet fin on the end of that dislodging rocks down the slope behind it, and came on. Ahead of it the infant whelks again extruded eye-stalks and tentacles to test the water, immediately became agitated and drew closer together. The turbul circled, joined by others of its shoal. Then it shot in.

The whelks immediately retracted excrescences they had been cautiously easing out again, and sucked down hard on the bottom. The turbul clamped its jaws closed on the shell of one near the brood's edge, wriggled its long heavy body and tugged the creature from the bottom. A few metres up it released the creature, arched its body, and slammed its tail fin into shell. The blow nearly cut the whelk in half and the turbul began champing down its tender flesh, the water growing cloudy about it.

The others began to attack now, then the whole shoal hit. It was as if someone had detonated an underwater mine. Silt and ichor exploded in every direction; iridescent shell drifted down through the water. Long heavy bodies rolled and thrashed. Whelks were jerked through all this, shattered and torn apart. Half an hour later the shoal began to lose interest and drift away, but now prill and leeches swarmed in to snap up what remained. In another half-hour they were gone. All that remained was a mess of glittering shell, and even that gleam disappeared as the silt settled down to shroud it.

Hovering on AG, Sniper watched the Island of Chel being slowly revealed by the morning sun. Below him geodesic domes nestling in the spreading sprawl of the Hooper town were licked by the yellow-green glare. The dingle surrounding this settlement was cut through by numerous paths, shadowy now, and many wide plascrete roads had been built. One extended from the greatly enlarged docks to branch into the town, another stretched in from the floating shuttle platforms. There were vehicles down there: wheeled cars and transports. Windcheater's rules concerning antigravity transport now prevented the use of AG taxis between the platforms and domes and anywhere else on the island and, for that matter, on the planet. The rules did not apply to him or the other drones, however. Windcheater liked them – did not mind them up in his air.

A shuttle rose from the platforms, not a flying wing but a long flattened cylinder with thruster nacelles to the rear. It rotated in mid-air, aiming for the horizon, and then its motors ignited, their glare matching the rising sun. Watching it go, the old war drone keyed into the

Warden's com frequencies, glad to see that the AI had not yet found the covert programs he had left in place. Sniper could now listen in to secret communications, but for how long that would last he did not know. It would end as soon as the AI changed its frequency codings.

As he had guessed, the shuttle was a planetary one that Windcheater allowed to transport reifications to Mortuary Island. He was just about to shut off the link when he picked up some unusual traffic between the Warden and numerous sources below. One particular exchange riveted his attention.

'He came through while you weren't yet back in charge here,' said a voice from the main dome. 'We were tracking him aboard some private ship concerns and expected him to join the *Gurnard*, where our agents could have apprehended him. Turns out that lead was a dead end. He in fact used the runcible network long before. We since traced his journey through five jumps from Earth.'

'Don't you think you should have informed Sniper?' the Warden asked.

'My instructions were to keep this from him. It's a touchy situation and apparently Sniper is not that good at diplomatic.'

'Agreed, but perhaps diplomacy is not what's required here.'

'I'm just following orders.'

'So you've lost this individual now?'

'Seems that way. He walked out of the Metrotel leaving his luggage behind him and just never came back. My agents are scouring the island but there seems no sign of him.'

'Yes, I'm receiving their reports now.'

'He could have gone into the sea. That'd be no problem for one like him.'

The Warden replied, 'I think you overestimate Polity technology and underestimate the dangers of the deeps.'

Sniper spun, in his frustration, like a silver coin. Who or what were they talking about? The answer was provided by yet another communication between one of those agents and the Warden.

'We've scanned the Trancept Arcade. No sign of that signal and no one has eyeballed the Golem. Chelar released a cloud of micro-eyes in there, so if he puts in an appearance we'll be on him in a second.'

Submind Seven, not so ebullient now his master was back in control, replied, 'Check the concourse now. You got nothing on secondary emitters?'

'No – there must be hundreds of them all over the planet, smuggled in over the last few years. The primary U-space transmitter could be anywhere in the vicinity of the planet – supposing there's only one of them – or it might be encoded through the runcible itself.'

'Bastard to track that down, man. About a hundred thousand constant aug links, and thousands more private messages.'

'You're telling *me*?'

'Yeah, I am. Keep searching.'

The communication cut off.

Golem? It had to be a renegade – they were not unheard of. But what was it doing here and, most importantly, would any explosions be involved? Sniper slowed his rotation as a com channel opened to him.

'Did you get all that, Sniper?' the Warden asked.

'Sneaky fucker,' the old drone replied.

'*I'm* sneaky?'

The Warden changed codes and the secret com channels abruptly disappeared. Sniper swore and wished he had left more hidden programs but, not expecting anything to start happening here so soon, he had not considered any of those channels very important.

'Do you need any help?' he wheedled.

'I don't know,' said the Warden. 'I like my drones to follow orders and I'm not sure I have use for one carrying enough armament to cripple a destroyer.'

'I promise not to blow up anything,' Sniper replied.

'You and I know that, should circumstances permit, you won't keep to that promise. However, I need someone to search the sea surrounding Chel, and to check all sailing ships that departed from there over the last two weeks.' The Warden spat down a list and the probable destinations of those ships. 'I've dropped SMs Six to Ten in geosurvey shells and am moving Eleven and Twelve into the area. You can coordinate with them.'

Sniper let out a long whoop as he arced out of the sky to hit the sea with a huge splash. As he sank he turned on his sonar and all his other useful detectors. A glister immediately scuttled out from a mass of floating sargassum to investigate the disturbance, took one look at the great shining drone, then scuttled back. Sniper tracked it with a launch tube, and loaded a mini-torpedo with a phosphorus warhead. Immediately a U-space link opened to him.

'And Sniper, show a little restraint with the local fauna. I don't want an ecological disaster,' the Warden added.

Sniper harrumphed, withdrew the tube, and began searching.

4

Sail:

with the necessity for three males to fertilize one female egg, and that egg then encysted and stuck, in its cocoon, on the side of just one location – the Big Flint – it is no surprise that the sail population remains small. The sail, however, being the largest flying creature on the planet, is not prone to predation, also is intelligent and benefits from viral immortality. It has been proven to the satisfaction of forensic AIs that there are even sails over a thousand years old, some of them remembering the first arrival of humans on Spatterjay. Those same AIs are more cautious about the veracity of claims made by some sails of having witnessed volcanic eruptions known to have taken place ten thousand years ago.

It is perhaps a sign of the sail's innate intelligence that it never fed on humans (the stories of people disappearing near the Big Flint are apocryphal . . . probably). It is a creature that feeds on the wing, and any native Spatterjay life form is a viable food resource, except leeches, which apparently give them violent flatulence, and those larger deep oceanic creatures which are just too inaccessible or too large. Sails dominate the skies, since there is only one other flying creature known on Spatterjay, and that is rather insignificant: the lung-bird –

Without any transition at all, Vrell was awake and alert. This made no sense to him because anoxia led to gradual physical shutdown, then death. He unfolded his legs and pushed himself up from the floor. Silt spilled from his carapace, but it was the only cloudiness in water which just a seeming moment ago had been murky. Now it was utterly clear and still. He must have been unconscious for longer than he had thought. With his one hand he plucked the mission timer from his weapons harness and studied it.

Impossible.

Vrell discarded the device, sure it must be damaged. Prador could hibernate for long periods, but hardly *that* long. Anyway, his kind could not hibernate at all unless in an oxygenating atmosphere – to do so underwater would lead to one never waking up. This was madness, surely. Vrell shook himself, spilling more silt from his carapace. He felt a huge pressure inside him, and a tension as if something internal was twisted out of position. He shook himself again, and felt something begin to shift inside his carapace. There abruptly came a crackling noise, jets of ichor squirting from under the claw patch, and a relief of internal pressure. Vrell stared in amazement at the translucent embryonic claw protruding from the now broken patch. Then, underneath him, followed one cracking sound after another. To check, he folded his eye-palp down in time to see pieces of medical porcelain sinking to the bottom. But to look was not even necessary as the incredible sensitivity of his new manipulatory hands told him all he needed to know. He was an adult; this was impossible. Yet another patch broke and a leg folded into view and, while he was studying this with his palp eye, the Prador realized he was now seeing a hazy image through turret eyes that should never have recovered sight after being burnt in an APW blast. Adolescent Prador regrew their limbs, but no Prador ever regrew its secondary eyes. Something quite odd and quite wonderful was happening to his body. But he was still trapped here.

Vrell turned towards the door; he required some new miracle to get him through that. Deciding to try something more prosaic, he drew his rail-gun from his harness, aimed at the door's edge, and fired. A stream of missiles slammed through the water, leaving white lines, and smashed into the side of the door, then zinged away. Some of the ricochets chipped Vrell's carapace, but he continued firing until the magazine was empty. He then took his plasma torch to the weakened metal, but only managed to cut a small hole before the torch gave out. Vrell could just about poke his claw through it, but it was still a victory, because now air was bubbling in and the water draining out. He definitely would not suffocate – just starve.

His new limbs were now growing at phenomenal speed, their growth spurt sucking Vrell's insides empty. His hunger became savage and he scoured his prison for something to eat. There was nothing evident, no living leeches, and no remains of those he had broiled with his water gun. There should have been some in here. It seemed, therefore, that the mission timer had been correct. He knew that leeches could go somnolent for long periods and that it took years for them to die of starvation. He picked the timer back up, studied it for a long moment, then returned it to his harness. What now? What should he do now?

Vrell did have a few options left to try. He detached the rail-gun from its magazine suspended on his harness, then also detached the welding unit. Both of these implements contained laminar batteries – the plasma torch having ceased to function only because he had depleted its gas supply. He disassembled these two devices, removed their batteries, and jammed them into the hole he had made, then scuttled back towards the other blast door. The water level had sunk to the bottom of the hole now. Vrell submerged and pointed his water gun towards the two batteries. Laminar batteries did not respond well to excessive heating. Lowering his eyepalps, Vrell fired.

It took just a minute, in which the air space above him filled with clouds of steam. As the two batteries detonated, the shock wave slammed through the Prador with such force that he reflexively adopted a defensive pose: folding up all his limbs and sinking. When he finally unfolded, the water was hot and acidic, and the air above it unbreathable. Vrell scrambled over to the door to see what damage he had done. The door itself seemed to have shifted back a little way, and after a moment Vrell detected a current – the rest of the water was draining away. He jammed his claw into the buckled corner and, with his feet scrabbling at the floor, shoved as hard as he could. Was he imagining that the door flexed? That was possible, since the door, though armoured, had been constructed in layers of composite, insulation and foamed porcelain so as to absorb rather than deflect shock. Then Vrell remembered the dent he had earlier put in the wall. That too was armoured.

Vrell moved back and watched carefully. The water would constrict his movements, so he must wait. Also, his new limbs had by now attained full growth and were beginning to darken as they hardened. He would need them.

Hours passed as the water level kept on dropping. When it had sunk below his now shrunken and concave belly plates, Vrell once again approached the door. He struck it hard with his old claw, eyed the dent made, hit it testingly with his new claw to find out if that one was strong enough. Seeing it was, he then began to rain blow after blow on the door edge, denting the metal back into the underlayer of foamed porcelain. A gap grew at the edge, wider and wider. All the water rushed out.

You won't stop me, Father.

Vrell thought of how he had been used, and how he would have been dispensed with. He knew that with the extent of his development he had been close to being considered a dangerous competing adult by his father, and consequently having his limbs stripped off and his shell broken. In presentient times, young Prador, enslaved by their father's pheromones, would bring food to him. But once one of those youngsters reached adulthood, it would shake off that binding control and kill its father, who by then would be weak and lacking in limbs. Prador technology had changed all that. Fathers stayed strong, enhanced their pheromones, and used thrall technology to enslave other life forms. They killed their young before they reached adulthood, or else sometimes neutered them to keep them loyal, also surgically altered them and linked them into war machines. Meanwhile the fathers just kept on living. Though this was just the

Prador way, Vrell was still angry, but he was deliberate in his anger, and it gave him strength.

The door retreated gradually under his blows, the lower corner coming up out of its channel in the floor, and the edge tearing out of the wall. Every time his energy flagged, he thought again about what his father would have done to him, and his strength returned. In his feverish activity, he noticed only subliminally how his shell was much darker now, almost obsidian black. After a wide gap was opened down the side of the door, he flipped sideways and pushed himself into it, to try to lever it open further, and was surprised how far he got before he became jammed. His whole body was now attenuated: the curve of his belly plates replicating the curve of his upper shell with not much bulk between. He levered himself back and forth, getting further through each time. Then something gave, either the door or his shell, he did not know, and he was finally through.

In the dank corridor beyond, Vrell revolved his eye-palps and inspected himself. His body, which had previously borne the shape of a flattened pear, was now concave underneath. His visual turret, at what would have been the apex of the pear, felt loose now, and with an effort he found he could move it. His main shell was also wider, more like the disc-shaped carapace of a prill, his limbs also longer and sharper. Vrell had not allowed himself to think about it closely before, but now what was happening to him seemed quite obvious. The earlier leech bites he had suffered on the island had done nothing, for an inhibitor was included in the broad-spectrum inoculations he had given himself before first leaving this ship. But obviously time and his transformation to adulthood had weakened the effect of those drugs, so they had not been enough to prevent him being infected by the Spatterjay virus from those leeches burrowing under his carapace. Now the virus was changing him. Vrell accepted the fact and shoved it to the back of his mind. Right then he had more important concerns. He went in search of something to eat.

Anything.

Taylor Bloc scanned around the inside of the shuttle, tested the air with an anosmic detector, and smelt that recognizable odour as of an open ancient tomb. In the passenger compartment, besides himself, there were twelve reifications – four of which wore the grey enviro-suits and protective breastplates of his Kladites. Aesop and Bones were not present, having gone on ahead to make arrangements for Bloc's arrival. Of the Hoopers, one was an Old Captain by the name of Ron, whom one of Bloc's agents here had hired, two were perhaps crewmen, but the fourth – a Hooper in outworld dress who seemed to spend a lot of time talking to a box on his shoulder – looked very familiar. Bloc tried to remember where he had seen that face before, but it kept on escaping him. Obviously he was not anyone of importance. Bloc was about to dismiss such speculation when the Kladite sitting alongside him turned to him.

'Forgive my intrusion, Taylor Bloc, but I've been watching him too. It is destiny,' said the reif.

Bloc paused for a long moment before replying, just to make sure this Kladite understood his insolence in speaking without first being addressed. 'Yes, destiny,' he said, though having no idea what the reif meant.

Obviously encouraged the Kladite continued, 'A

great friend of Keech himself, and he who assisted Erlin in her resurrection of him.'

As Bloc sat mulling that over, his mind seemed slow. Perhaps it *was* time for him to add some memory space. Perhaps the last fifty years of memories were spilling into the spaces his memcording used to run copies of his organic mental programs. He was about to run a cerebral diagnostic check from other programs, additional to his memcording, when what the Kladite had just told him impacted.

OUTPARAFUNCT: B.P. PRESSURE INCREASE NOT REQ

His fight-or-flight reflex, which in his organic body would have caused a surge of adrenalin and consequent increase in his heart rate, caused his internal balm pump to accelerate. That was not supposed to happen.

INFORM: STABILIZE, he instructed.

His heart would have been thundering, but now, motionless with its valves open and preserving balm flooding round and through it, it just endured.

Janer Cord Anders.

He should have known, since he had long ago formatted his memory so as never to forget a face that might be important to him. Here was the other one they had been searching for – and coming to them of his own free will. It *was* indeed destiny: further proof that he was the one to lead all reifications to the Little Flint and to resurrection. He felt in that instant the truth of his own status, and knew that in time all reifications would come to understand what he was, and what he was doing for them. Bloc undid his safety straps, jerked himself out of his seat and walked over. As he drew close to Anders, he saw that the box on the man's shoulder contained hornets.

Epiphany.

'You are Janer Cord Anders,' he said, catching hold of the back of the man's seat.

Anders looked up. 'I certainly am.'

'Might I enquire why you are on this flight?'

'I'm here with Ron.' Anders gestured to the Old Captain. 'I was hoping for a place on the ship. My friend here,' he tapped the hornet box, 'is not so enamoured of the idea, but my remit does allow for a little travelling.'

'Of course you will join the *Sable Keech*; it is inevitable. I did make an offer on the AI nets for your presence, some years ago. I am trying in my modest way to match many aspects of the Arisen One's original journey, so I would be glad to have you aboard.'

OUTPARAFUNCT: YABBER$@~*

MEMSPACE: 00055

Bloc tilted his head: another one. It had to be caused by his additional hardware and software, as such code corruptions were usually unheard of in reification software. He ran a high-speed diagnostic of the three open channels from his internal control unit. The results did not make a lot of sense. He tried linking through one channel, briefly saw bony hands sharpening a knife. He realized then that the problem was being caused by feedback from the most recently opened channel: a kind of madness, something waking up. After a second he refocused on the man before him.

Anders had tilted his head, listening to his hivelink. He frowned, showed a flash of irritation, and said, 'Then you have me.' He paused for a moment. 'I'm informed that you are Taylor Bloc?'

'I am,' Bloc replied, a little peeved that Janer had not instantly recognized him.

'You're part owner of the ship?' Janer asked.

Bloc stared at him, for a moment not understanding the question, then he replied, 'I am the owner.' The wash of anger and irritation he felt was immediate, almost seemed to come from outside him, but of course it did not show. He was not truly the owner yet, and that would have to soon change. He nodded to Janer jerkily, turned away, and began running inside himself an error-search program that though not correcting whatever the fault was, would at least clear some of the junk out of his mind. Slowly he returned to his seat.

'You've recruited him?' the Kladite asked.

'I . . . have.'

'He was not already with us?'

Bloc held up a hand. 'It was destined.'

'That is good.'

The Kladite faced forwards again, bearing no expression on his frozen and preserved face, but his mere actions told Bloc enough. He realized that whatever was wrong with himself was showing. This too would have to change.

The sail finally put Erlin down on top of a small atoll, while its two companions scattered a colony of frog whelks that had been clinging just above the waterline a few metres below her. She could hear the strange squealing of the whelks and the thunderous splashing as they propelled themselves away from the coral face. Glancing aside, she saw one of them smack its fleshy foot down on the water and bounce again. But one of the sails snatched it up on its next bounce. The pair of sails returned with two whelks each, broke open the shells and began to dine on their still living occupants. Erlin eyed their dinner for a moment – not feeling quite the same about whelks any more – then turned her attention to the sail who had carried her. Only then did she finally grasp what some part of her brain had been trying to tell her for some time.

'You're Golem?' she asked.

'They are insentient so, essentially, neither truly alive nor truly subject to Death,' the sail replied.

Erlin gazed at the Golem sail, then realized it was staring down at the other two sails as they dined. A Golem sail that was squeamish?

'I said you're Golem,' Erlin suggested.

'I'm Zephyr,' the sail replied, its gaze still fixed.

Erlin stood up, stretched her legs and rubbed her aching shoulders. 'So, Zephyr, I'd have thought it would be easier for you to take me to Olian's, or else drop me aboard some ship in that area. But it seems you've been taking me away from civilization.'

Zephyr turned its head towards her, then tossed a harness onto the stone beside her. 'Put that on.'

'Why?'

The sail gave a twisted shrug, as if in pain. 'I can carry you as before, but you might find the journey uncomfortable. There is no risk to your life. Distance . . . is long.'

'I don't *want* to go on a long journey.'

The Golem sail gave that same distorted shrug and began to extend its wings.

'Wait.' Erlin stooped and took up the contrivance of plasmesh straps. It was something like a parachute harness but with a grip bar or handle at the back where the parachute should be. She started to don it, but slowly to give herself time.

'Where are we going?'

'Mortuary Island.'

'Why there?' Erlin asked, not wanting to reveal that she had no idea what or where this place was.

'Because that is where the dead live and where we have been paid to take you.'

'You're kidnapping me?'

Again the shrug, this time with bowed head. 'Relocating . . . you.' The head came up again. 'I saved your life. I beat *your* Death.'

'I'm grateful for that. But now you are taking me somewhere I don't want to go. That's kidnapping.'

'There is worse.'

One of the other sails hawked and coughed up a piece of whelk shell. 'We could always take her back where we found her, if this gets too messy,' it suggested.

'Oh, I'll come,' Erlin said quickly. 'I see I haven't much choice in the matter.' She finished doing up her straps.

'Should we feed her?' asked the third sail, nudging the remains of its dinner with a clawed toe.

'Do you require food, Erlin Taser Three Indomial?'

Erlin eyed the chewed leftovers. 'Not right now.'

'Then we must go.'

The Golem sail launched itself, blasting shell fragments from the top of the atoll with the down-draught of its wings. Erlin turned, and it grabbed the handle at her back and pulled her into the sky.

'How far to Mortuary Island?' she shouted as the other two sails then launched with much noise and flurry.

'It is in the Cable Sea, beyond the Norbic Atolls.'

Erlin swore, and realized that at some point she would need to eat whatever was offered her. That, she knew, was *thousands* of kilometres away.

Ambel gazed through his binoculars at the island, inspecting the damage, looking for any sign of Erlin – or maybe bits of Erlin. Judging by the mess he could see, she was probably dead, but he was not *feeling* that yet. Actually, accepting someone's death was not a trait to which Old Captains could grow accustomed – most of their own fellows being so long-lived and indestructible.

'Lower the boat,' he instructed Peck, who as ever was hovering at the Captain's shoulder.

He glanced round at the rest of the crew, but none of them would meet his gaze. Sprout and Pillow unstrapped the rowing boat from the side of the ship and began feeding rope into pulleys to lower it to the sea. Ambel returned to the outer wall of his cabin, and unhooked from it his blunderbuss and bags of powder and stones. He loaded the weapon, tearing off the end of a paper cartridge and feeding it down the barrel, next shoving in wadding and pouring in some stones, then more wadding. He primed it and pulled back the hammer.

'Let's see what we've got here before we get all morbid,' he suggested.

He hung the 'buss across his back by a strap and scrambled down the ladder. While Peck peered over the side at them, Anne and the juniors – Sprout, Sild and Pillow – followed Ambel down. They were also armed: Anne carried a powerful laser carbine she had found on Skinner's Island – no longer needed by the Batian mercenaries who had gone there with Rebecca Frisk and run afoul of Hooper vengeance; Sprout carried a machete, and the other two lugged heavy clubs. Once they were all seated in the boat, Ambel took up the reinforced oars and began to row.

'What do you think happened?' Anne eventually asked.

Staring straight back at the *Treader*, Ambel replied, 'Any number of things spring to mind, but by the look of the wreckage I would guess something from the deeps paid a visit. We'll know soon enough.'

Soon they were into shallows and with a glimpse over the side Ambel noted a lack of whelks in the vicinity. He began to feel a heaviness in his chest; the signs were not good. Beaching the boat he gave a further two heaves on the oars to pull it up onto the sand, then climbed out.

'We'll stick together for the moment,' he said, all practicality. 'Let's see what we've got here first.'

Eyeing the wreckage of Erlin's home, the five advanced. They began to search under its deflated walls, to pick through broken equipment and furniture, and turn over anything large enough to conceal human remains.

'Ambel,' Anne called him over.

He came to stand next to her and gazed down at whelkish remains driven into the hard ground. He stooped and rubbed away some of the dirt, to reveal the shell pattern.

'Very well,' he said heavily. 'You collect what's salvageable and take it back to the ship. Me an' these lads'll take a look across the island. Tell Boris to bring the *Treader* round to the other side to pick us up.'

'Is that such a good plan?' Anne wondered. 'Perhaps we should all leave right now.'

Ambel turned to her. 'Erlin could be injured and holed up somewhere. I know the chances are remote, but I have to look.' He glanced back at the waves. Maybe what had done this still lurked there below the surface, but that was a risk he was prepared to take. He still hoped to find some sign, some message . . . something.

'Come on, lads, we'll spread out and cover as much ground as we can.' He turned and began trudging inland, bellowing, 'Erlin! Are you here, woman!'

Taylor Bloc eyed the Kladites arrayed in neat ranks before him, unarmed. They all wore cloth or domino masks, grey envirosuits with incorporated breastplates, while skirted helmets hung at their belts. As they raised their hands before them and started chanting 'Bloc! Bloc! Bloc!' he strode out onto the ramp waving one hand in greeting. This small army of eighty reifications he had gathered from the remnants of the Cult of Anubis Arisen on Klader, and they had all sworn loyalty to him for his promise to lead them to resurrection. Out of choice they wore a uniform created by one of their number. It was sad, though fortunate for him, Bloc felt, that even amongst the unliving there were those who felt the need to be led.

A few Hoopers stood to one side, watching the show with bemused expressions. Of the rest of the crowd, the largest proportion consisted of unaligned reifications – merely passengers – but there were others here too.

Bloc spotted the mercenary he knew only as Shive – an employee of Lineworld Developments. The catadapt was tall, thickly muscled, boosted and, now grinning, his leonine visage exposing curved fangs. Bloc surveyed the gathering, easily picking out the rest of the mercenaries; they wore black crabskin armour and made no pretence at concealment. He repressed his anger; though he had always expected Lineworld Developments to try to take over, it was doubly insulting that they used Batian mercenaries. These were members of an entire culture of one continent, on an Out-Polity planet, revolving around that frowned-upon profession. They had also, in the employ of the Eight, spent seven hundred years try-ing to find and destroy Sable Keech himself.

The chanting finally came to a halt and, turning up his volume, Bloc began to speak. 'Kladites, I thank you for your greeting, and your enthusiasm for our great venture. We have come here to walk in the footsteps of Sable Keech, seeking resurrection. It is—' There came a guffaw from one of the mercenaries. 'It is a great thing we do, but I will save the speeches for later. Right now there is much work to be done.'

Spying Aesop and Bones walking up through the ranks, easily recognizable by their hooded green flak jackets, Bloc walked down to join them. His internal search program now nearly clearing the clutter from his mind, he could link to them easily, but chose instead to speak.

'How did they get here?' he immediately asked.

'They came in the first shuttle, directly from orbit, disguised as reifications,' Aesop hissed in reply.

'As expected,' murmured Bloc. 'And the weapons.'

'They were under guard before we got here. We of course demanded that the chief mercenary, Shive, release them to us, but he refused. He said it was his job to ensure the safety of all, and that a bunch of amateurs running around with laser carbines was something he didn't consider safe.'

'No matter. How many mercenaries?'

'Only eighteen, but they are all heavily armed.'

'Weapons?'

'As required for their mission: projectile weapons that can destroy reifications and kill Hoopers,' Aesop replied.

Bloc nodded creakily. 'Not nearly enough, then.'

Eighteen mercenaries so armed was plenty enough against eighty unarmed Kladites. The rest in this crowd were all free citizens, pilgrims come here with one hope. Some of them might have had military or criminal or security backgrounds, but he had no idea of their loyalties, and so for the present discounted them. Unlike Aesop and Bones, they did not belong to him. However, it was all moot.

'It doesn't matter, I have prepared for this. We have the means . . .' he said, more confidently than he felt. He glanced around to find six Kladites had moved into a rank behind him, and the rest of the crowd was dispersing. 'Tell me the rest.'

'The Golem are hard at work and will complete the ship on schedule,' Aesop replied. 'All but ten reifs have paid their reservation fees, rental agreements on accommodation and initial bids on tickets for the first voyage. As expected, a lot of them did not bring supplies of an Intertox inhibitor that works in reification balm. Of course, with the journey's distance and time now extended, those who miss the first voyage will require further supplies and will also have to pay for extended rental agreements. Even before the *Sable Keech* reaches its destination, Lineworld will already be in profit.'

'Yes, as was always their intention, but all profits are

allocated as investment in future voyages, and stand separate from initial investment costs,' said Bloc. 'How are we now with that?'

'The cost of transporting materials and passengers has pushed us near to the limit,' Aesop replied.

'That the mercenaries have made no further move means Lineworld is waiting for us to go over that limit, then they can legally take over. Because they work from within the Polity, their actions here on the Line must have at least the gloss of legality.' Bloc felt the situation was perhaps the best he could have hoped for. He had expected Lineworld to find some way of pushing up costs, and there were many ways they could have done that. By relocating the enterprise they had untied his hands. There were things he could do now he would not have dared on Chel Island. 'Take me to the ship now. I want to see.'

Aesop turned and led the way through the sprawl of Polity accommodation units and a buzz of activity. Bloc noted the fences erected to keep the denizens of the dingle at bay, and some guard towers occupied by Batians. A few stalls and kiosks here were selling food and drink, but most sold various items of Polity technology that reifications might require. This too was part of the enterprise − a hugely profitable part for Lineworld. That organization was also raking in a profit from the currency exchange system he had arranged with Olian's. Contractually that made no difference to the initial investment, but then Lineworld's contracts served one purpose: they were the tip of a wedge into profitable enterprises started by others on the edge of the Polity. They invested, then took over − that was their whole ethos.

They came to a gate leading out of the temporary town warded by two more mercenaries who smilingly opened it for them. The Kladites now drew in closer around Bloc and keenly eyed the dingle either side of the path winding downslope.

'There's a good view from over here, unless you want to go down?' Aesop pointed to a narrow side path.

Bloc waved him on.

Soon they emerged on an outcrop above a drop, and gazed down at the *Sable Keech*.

Only the keel and ribs of the ship were yet in place, resting on the ramp leading down to the sea. Those working on it gleamed brightly, and were as skeletal as what they were constructing. Either side of the construction site, and reaching back to below where Bloc was standing, just about every tree had been felled. A sawmill, open to the air, was in constant operation; clouds of wood dust boiling out from it and turning its surroundings into powdery desert. He observed where the masts were being assembled from bubble-metal sections. He noted stacked crates, some of them the size of houses. These contained bubble-metal gears and trains, electric motors, laminar batteries and solar cells, bearings and all the paraphernalia that would allow three living sails to control the mass of other monofabric sails the masts would carry. The ship, when finished, would be nearly a kilometre long, carry nine huge masts, five hundred kilometres of rigging, square kilometres of sail, and seven hundred passengers and crew (one for each year Sable Keech had been dead). It would be enormous, a triumph and, most importantly for Lineworld, very expensive to travel on.

'I am happy to see this,' said Bloc flatly. 'Now, to my

quarters, where we must finalize plans.' He nodded slowly. 'I will not lose what is mine.'

Bones sniggered in his hood at this.

Bloc gazed at the reif for a moment, and in response Bones jerked upright as if a lead attached to him had been snapped taut. Bloc turned back to Aesop. 'We move tonight – ahead of plan.'

'I'll have to check that the . . . item is ready,' Aesop replied.

'No need. Can't you feel it?'

Reif or not, the way Aesop then reacted looked something like a shudder.

'It bothers you?' Bloc asked.

'A gun is so much more reliable,' Aesop replied.

'Guns are not a luxury we have at the moment, but we do have something better,' said Bloc, moving on.

Tarsic damned the fault in his cleansing unit that drove him to take on any job on offer so as to remain a viable reification. There were cleansing units available here, but renting time on them was expensive. The five times he had used them had made a severe dent in his funds, which were already depleted by paying for his reservation, ticket bid and the steep accommodation costs. Anywhere else, he might have been able to forgo having his own small dwelling, but here that meant you stayed outside the compound. Some reifs were attempting that, and he heard that one of them had been swallowed whole by a giant leech. The woman had remained in contact via her aug as the leech digested her corpse. Then the contact broke when the leech, it was surmised, went into the sea. Others were losing portions of their precious flesh to leeches all the time, while the

Spatterjay virus was rapidly eating away the rest of their preserved bodies. But now there was some hope for himself, and also his companions Beric and Sline.

After he was killed in an AGC accident on Klader, his grieving wife had cryo-stored Tarsic's body. Her conversion to what was then the Cult of Anubis Arisen occurred some years later. She then paid for a download from his frozen brain to crystal, and subsequently his reification. Her own reification, after death by suicide – her being anxious to become a full member of the Cult – had proved unsuccessful. Tarsic then immediately looked into getting himself installed in a Golem chassis, but discovered just how much of a bitch his wife had been. A deferred debt was awaiting him, and the moment he ceased to be a reification that debt became due and would result in his utter bankruptcy. So in his Golem chassis he would have ended up indentured to the Cult for years – a group which had since come to look upon him with contempt, for he was perhaps unique in remaining a reification out of financial motives. It surprised him when Aesop, assistant to Taylor Bloc himself, who had bought out the Cult when it effectively collapsed as a going concern, had approached him.

Tarsic turned, as he proceeded, to check that Beric and Sline were still with him. Just about all the reifs here regularly went down to see the ship being built, just as worshippers would have once ventured forth to observe the construction of a cathedral – the feeling was much the same. Tarsic and his companions had already been there a couple of times. However, it was not so usual for reifs to venture out during the night, as that was when the big leeches were most active. The guards would be suspicious, as they were of any unusual activity. As the three approached the gates, one of the two Batian guards stepped forwards.

'Strange to see you out after dark. Shouldn't you be in shutdown mode or' – the female guard paused to say the next word with distaste – 'cleansing?'

'Our night vision is good,' Tarsic replied. 'And we've concluded that we prefer to view the construction in a less *religious* atmosphere.'

The woman smiled. 'Not a Kladite then?'

Tarsic held his hands out from his sides, 'Do I look like one of those fanatics? Where's my Kervox breast-plate and skirted helmet, and my permanent link to the wise words of Taylor Bloc?'

'Well, you might be in disguise,' she suggested.

'You're auged.' Tarsic raised a shaky finger and pointed to the white bone-effect aug behind her right ear. 'They'll certainly have some kind of record on me. My name is Tarsic Alleas Smith . . .'

The woman tilted her head. After a moment she nodded. 'I see. Years working off a debt to the Cult, then to Taylor Bloc . . . and you're known as a troublemaker amongst reifs. You'll do.' She signalled to her companion to open the gate for them.

When the three were some distance from the compound, heading down the path leading to the ship's construction site, Beric opined, 'She'd think differently if she knew precisely where we are going.'

Tarsic agreed. It was all about the balance of power here. With the Batians being armed, Taylor Bloc could not augment his own forces without the mercenaries finding out and perhaps doing something drastic. But Bloc had prepared. Apparently the Kladites here, and the weapons Shive had put under guard, were merely a decoy. Down there, in a crate to which Tarsic now held the computerized key, were fifty armed reifs awaiting their moment.

Soon they came in sight of the sailing ship and the glinting movement of Golem working in the moonlight. There was no electric lighting – the Golem needed none. It would be nice, Tarsic thought, if Bloc could get them on his side. They were neutral however; here under contract from Cybercorp to perform their singular task. Tarsic led the way to the left, away from the ship, through the ankle-deep sawdust. Soon the crates loomed out of the dark, like an infant city with its power cut. He followed a map lit on the small screen of the key and eventually came to the crate indicated. He eyed the looming bubble-metal wall before him and tracked round, locating the seal clips.

'Let's get it open,' he said.

Beric and Sline moved forwards, taking crowbars from under their jackets. Beric began levering off the clips down one edge, while Sline used them on the other edge as a ladder to the crate's top. The pieces of sprung metal cracked and spanged out into the night. These had been pressed into place on the end of the crate to keep up the pressure on its seals while it was in transit in a lower-cost unpressurized cargo hold. Every time a clip went, Tarsic expected someone to come running. No one came.

'All done?' he asked, when his two companions stepped away from the crate.

'They're moving about in there,' said Beric.

'I thought they'd be in shutdown,' added Sline.

'They *were* shut down, so Aesop told me, but they

recently woke. That's why we are here now.' Tarsic pointed the key at the crate and sent over the unlocking code.

'Hang on a minute,' said Sline. 'Why lock them in a crate with no way of getting themselves out?'

With a hiss of equalizing pressures, the end of the crate jerked open and began to come down like a ramp. It was utterly dark inside. Tarsic had expected light. He considered Sline's question and realized he possessed no easy answers. But, being so happy over the promise of new cleansing units for the three of them and a confirmed reservation on the ship's first voyage, he had not thought to question.

The crate end settled on the ground with a dull whump, stirring up a small storm of sawdust. The darkness within it seemed packed with thick loops of something that shifted with a sound as of rocks grinding together. He realized he was seeing something segmented, maybe two metres thick, crammed into this box in coils. One loop of it began to unravel out of shadow, then something horrible exploded out then up into the night like a demonic jack-in-a-box. Tarsic gazed up into an open cowl of armour plates containing two vertical rows of hot red eyes. Glassy limbs and other sharp appendages ground and clattered together before those eyes like scythes being sharpened. Tarsic stumbled backwards, not comprehending what he was seeing. Sline made a strange keening sound as the terrible hood drenched him in its shadow, then came down like a cupped hand, slamming him to the earth and trapping him underneath. A ripping tearing sucking and disgorging ensued.

'That hooder must be very hungry,' said Beric, his

tone utterly flat. 'They normally feed a lot slower than that.'

'Hooder?' said Tarsic, still backing up.

Beric turned to him wearily. 'There's no point running – and we're lucky that we feel no pain.'

The creature reared again, dripping reif balm and scattering the now clean bones and various metallic additions that had enabled Sline to survive long after his own death. Beric bowed his head as it slid above him, the rest of the long armoured body uncoiling from its prison, then came down on him like an immense fly swat. Tarsic turned and ran, trying not to hear the horrible gobbling sounds, but he too was quickly smashed down and trapped in hot red shadow, surrounded by a thousand ever-shifting knives. As they closed on him and began cutting, error messages started to burn his night vision. He shut the messages off. Eventually, as the hooder severed his power cables, he went into shutdown knowing now that all hope of the resurrection of his human body was gone. He had just watched it disappear piece by piece into a thousand hungry little mouths.

5

Glister:
*glisters bear a striking resemblance to lobsters, though with
more fins and other adaptations to oceanic life, even though,
like many of Spatterjay's sea creatures, they do venture
ashore. They travel in pods of between three and twenty: one
dominant female and the rest of them males. Adolescent males
remain solitary, but on becoming adult and therefore sexually
active, they are recruited by a female to her pod. The theory
has yet to be proven that this mating behaviour developed due
to there being some viral infection in male glisters – the female
ejecting any infected male seed, and only allowing virus-free
matings to fertilize her eggs. Like lobsters, glister females
attach their eggs to their under-carapace until they hatch.
One hundred and forty varieties of glister have been catalogued, some no larger than a prawn and others up to three
metres long. They are obviously successful as a species – fossilized glister shell is a sought-after gem on the planet – but
individually their lives are usually short and brutal. Hoopers
relish their meat and, because a glister contains psychoactive
chemicals in its mouth and brainpan, they usually roast the
animal alive, as the only other way to effectively kill it is to
smash in its skull, which releases these same chemicals into its*

flesh. Sometimes Hoopers do deliberately kill glisters by break-
ing open the head, usually as a precursor to some orgiastic
celebration. However, the greatest predator of glisters is by far
the molly carp –

Tasting the air, Vrell sought food. All that remained of
his own kin, within the spaceship, was empty carapaces
and dried gristle, but he still ate those for the vital minerals and calcium they provided. He found things tough
and fibrous as wood creeping slowly in hidden crevices,
and chomped them, too, with the relish of starvation.
Only later did he realize they were the burnt and broken
remains of his father's human blanks, now transformed
by the Spatterjay virus. There was however one female
blank, complete but for the loss of a hand, shut down by
her thrall, yet not beyond being returned to human
shape. She had obviously been feeding like a leech,
mindlessly, until hunger felled her, but she still lived.
The Prador snipped her into pieces with his claws and
gobbled down the still-quivering flesh. Only then, with
the mind-numbing hunger inside him partially quelled,
did he begin to think straight. Immediately he regretted
the stupidity of his voracious hunger, for that last blank,
once he managed to suborn Father's control units,
would have made a useful tool. And with a little more
self-control he could have found meat elsewhere, since
the ship carried supplies of it. Now he headed straight
for them.

The chilling units in the ship's larder must have
recently failed, for the stored meat was spoiling and
crawling with ship's lice. He ate anyway, spoilt meat
being a Prador's preferred diet. Champing through a
slab of meat carved from a food animal of his home

planet – a decapod engineered with lungs and internal strengthening that enabled it to grow huge on a diet of kelp – Vrell observed other delicacies hanging along one rack. Only three of these human bodies had spoilt and, eyeing the tatters of clothing still clinging to them, Vrell realized they must have been snatched from some human settlement rather than specially bred back in the Kingdom. The other five humans, having been bred as blanks before being harvested for food because of some defect, contained the Spatterjay virus and had therefore retained some life. Because of their particular damage, changes were in fact being wrought upon them by the virus.

Four of the bodies were headless, and the fifth without limbs as well. Vrell recalled having snipped away these heads and limbs for Ebulan's delectation during their voyage here. The first four were now, since the failure of the chillers, growing leech mouths from the severed flesh of their necks. The fifth one was also growing them from where its limbs had been. All of them were constantly moving; writhing slowly on the meat hooks jammed through their ribcages. Vrell knew that, without those hooks, these five would be squirming about on the floor, probably feeding on the other comestibles available here.

He considered a possible option. The coring process entailed the removal of the animal's higher cerebrum and much of its autonomous nervous system. To then turn the animal into a useful tool required the connection of a Prador thrall unit in place of what had been removed. The Prador had found that such drastic measures were only required in Kingdom animals to prevent any wetware/hardware conflicts when making them do something that went against their instinct. The disadvantage to this was the loss of autonomous function. Only certain uncored animals – made to do simple tasks – could be controlled by spider thralls which burrowed in where required and connected to the nervous system. Adapting humans to either process had been difficult, as it was discovered that both methods of enslavement usually killed the host. That was until Jay Hoop cornered the market in humans infected by the Spatterjay virus, who proved tough and difficult to kill. Ebulan, to his cost, discovered too late that spider thralls could be rejected by the bodies of older Hoopers. For them only a full coring was safe.

Finishing his megafauna steak, Vrell continued eyeing the five human bodies busily making their transformation into the leech form. The fifth, limbless one, would be effectively useless, so he reached up and plucked it down, then cut its tough fibrous flesh into pieces and began inserting them one after the other into his mandibles. Perhaps, even though their nervous systems would be severely degraded by the leech transformation, he might be able to get some use out of the remaining four. Abruptly he spun towards the door.

As Vrell stepped out into the dripping corridor something cracked along his back. He turned an eye-palp, together with his visual turret and mouthparts, which had now separated from his main carapace and risen on a short muscular neck, and observed a long split in his shell, which was now knitting with fibres almost like hull repair mesh. It occurred to him that he had never heard of one of his own kind infected by the virus. Ingesting infected meat would not work because the virus did not long survive in the vitriol that was a Prador's digestive juices. The only way a Prador could become infected was by inoculation through the shell itself, as had happened to him. But surely some adult Prador would have therefore tried the virus on its own offspring? He must check the ship's data banks to see if any mention had been made of such. But not now: time to go to work.

Erlin smashed the frog whelk's shell with a rock, pulled off the eye-stalks because they were gazing at her accusingly, then took out her pen laser and began cooking its flesh. In the twilight, the glare from the device was intense, and she noted the two normal sails edge back from her as they dined on their molluscs. But Zephyr was unmoved, having nothing to fear from the laser. After a moment the device sputtered and gave out, the whelk flesh only partially seared. Erlin had expected this, as she had used it twice before: once on a chunk of rhinoworm and once on another whelk. She had no problem eating raw meat, but had been using the laser rather more to pasteurize than cook it. The less of the virus she took in orally, the slower would be the change it wrought upon her. Already her skin had taken on a bluish tint, and some of her inclinations were edging towards the irrational. But one uncomfortable fact seemed plain to her: she had *known* about the giant whelk.

Was her memory playing tricks? No, she and Ambel had talked about that creature jokily named *Whelkus titanicus*, and she recollected reading about it in one of the Warden's many reports on Spatterjay's ecology. How then to account for her behaviour on the island? That was easy. She was not immune to the ennui of long life – it had driven her here to find Ambel in the first place – but she had thought herself immune to the near-suicidal pursuits to which that boredom drove others. Obviously she was not, though in her the impulse to self-destruction was unconscious. Her own mind was playing her false. Erlin grimaced. Could that also be why she remained here on this dangerous planet? Was she, rather than trying to learn how to *live* from Captain Ambel, just staying in a place where it would be easy to die?

Damn it, enough of this!

'You know, Windcheater won't be best pleased with you,' she said abruptly, before stuffing her mouth with warm meat.

'The pleasure of that particular sail is not my concern,' replied Zephyr, who had his wings folded now. During previous landings in daylight he would spread them, blotting out the sun and casting a shadow across wherever they landed. This confirmed for Erlin that their fabric was photo-active and he had been feeding that way – no doubt to complement the power supplies he already contained.

Erlin nodded, wiped her wet chin. 'He hasn't established any laws as yet, so the right of might still rules here. Do you think you're strong enough to go up against him, or against Ambel, or any of the other Old Captains?'

'None of them know where she is.' Speaking to Zephyr, Puff indicated Erlin with one claw.

Erlin turned. 'Until Sniper, our present Warden, spots you, for he has many eyes. He'll be even less inclined to non-interference than the old Warden. He'll certainly let the Old Captains know, and might even do something drastic himself.'

The two normal sails looked to Zephyr for guidance.

'You feel that you are important,' the Golem sail stated.

Erlin frowned, realizing how arrogant she had sounded. It probably stemmed from her utter self-absorption.

Zephyr continued, almost dreamily, 'As of only a few days ago, Sniper ceased to be Spatterjay's Warden, and the old Warden, now back in control, has too many other concerns. No one is coming to rescue you, Erlin, so you might as well finish your meal and get some sleep. We still have a long way to travel.'

Erlin did as suggested. She knew there was no way out of this until they reached Mortuary Island, and at least during that time, her destiny was out of her own control. However, when they did arrive there she was going to damned well stir up some trouble. She lay down on hard stone and was soon sleeping fitfully, dreaming that a giant whelk was bearing down on her out of the darkness.

In deepest dark, the moon gone from the sky, she was woken by a hard scrabbling sound, and opened bleary eyes to look up at Zephyr. The sail's eyes were black hollows directed behind her and to one side.

'Sentience is life. Intelligence is anti-Death,' the Golem sail whispered.

'What? What's that?'

She flinched away as the turquoise flash of a particle cannon ignited the night. The scrabbling became a clattering as something fell down the side of the atoll. Huff launched and dropped out of sight, finally returning with a large glister, its front end a charred hollow. The glow in Zephyr's eyes slowly went out. Remembering her earlier exchange with the Golem sail, it occurred to Erlin

that Zephyr probably ranked quite high up on the scale
of the mighty . . . and the deranged.

The darkness, Ambel felt, reflected his mood. Leaning
on the ship's rail, he gazed across at the island and wondered what the hell he was going to do. For some years
Erlin had somehow defined his life, and now she was
gone he felt without purpose – disjointed from his 'long
habit of living'. He was calm – a bulwark of calm rested
at the centre of his being, steadily built, layer upon layer,
over the centuries he had lived – but there was no com-
pletion here, as there never was when someone died
such a pointless death. Vengeance was no good to him.
If they remained here, even though on the other side of
the island from Erlin's encampment, the creature that
had taken her might attack the *Treader*, and he very
much doubted they could survive such an onslaught.
And if they sailed away to obtain the equipment he
would need to kill such a monster, it would likely be
gone by the time they returned. Anyway, it had been
defending its young and, though the creature was no
doubt ancient and canny, there was unlikely to be any
real malice in it.

'Peck,' he said, without looking round. 'Get the
anchor up – time we were away from here.'

He heard Peck's sigh as the crewman headed away,
his shouted orders, the rattling of the anchor chain, then
the inevitable cursing as whoever had been given the
task clubbed away whatever had come up on the chain.

Ambel turned. 'Galegrabber, take us out!' he called.

The sail, which until then had been perched high on
the mast because it could smell the creature that had
probably gobbled up Erlin, cautiously lowered itself

back into position and gripped its various handholds. It turned to the wind, turned the other masts to present their fabric sails to the wind, and the *Treader* eased round. Ambel glanced to the bridge, where Anne controlled the helm. He ignored her querying look and headed for his cabin. He closed and locked the door behind him, unstrapped his blunderbuss and placed it on his table, then went to his sea chest to remove a silvery Polity device. It was hemispherical, inlaid with touch controls. Placing it flat side down next to his weapon, he clicked down one control and waited, still and utterly patient. It took half an hour before, with a slight whisper and a flicker of light, Captain Sprage materialized in the cabin.

'Well then,' said the other Old Captain, sparking up his pipe with a laser lighter.

Ambel felt sure he could smell the tobacco, but the holographic conferencing device was on a low power setting, so produced only sound and image.

'Erlin was taken by a titanicus. It seems she grabbed one of its young for dissection,' said Ambel woodenly.

'Taken? You mean dead.'

'Yes. I searched the island. She's gone.'

'Not clever, taking one of their young.'

Ambel felt a surge of irritation, repressed it. '*I* was the fool. I assumed she would know not to do something like that. Because of me she is dead . . . or maybe even worse.'

'Seems to me you're still a bit attracted to the idea of guilt,' said Sprage.

'Only when I'm guilty.'

'Really, then I wonder who it was that Verlan spotted

being carried off east of you by a bloody great big Golem sail called Zephyr?'

'Ah . . .' said Ambel.

It was one of Bloc's sidekicks, clad in a hooded flak jacket over a uniform grey envirosuit. Shive knocked the shrivelled hand away from his shoulder and swore.

'Sorry, friend,' said the reif, and moved on.

Shive sniffed the crabskin armour at his shoulder. Some horrible stink. He would have to disinfect it later. Had he his own way here, he would take a flame-thrower to the lot of them. It was unnatural keeping one's body going like that after death. Bloody things should load to Golem chassis or clones, or biostructs, or any of the more natural alternatives available. He continued on about his nightly patrol around the fence, to check the guard posts and make sure his people were not slacking. Few of them did so now, ever since Saolic had lost one side of his face to a leech the size of a potato sack. Shive knew, from his check of Batian records, that this was a dangerous place. It had eaten up a small group of mercenaries led by one Svan who had been a soldier like himself, very efficient and capable. He did not like the rumours he had heard about what might have happened to her.

Reaching the gates he approached the two guards. 'Anything to report?'

'Three deadbeats went through earlier, Commander, but I checked one of them out and his reasons were valid – not a Kladite and having no love for Bloc, according to his record. I think to the normal reifs the Kladites reek the same as they all do to us.'

'You mustn't judge them so harshly. Everyone has a right to their own beliefs no matter how imbecilic.'

'Why, yes, Commander.'

Shive grinned and was about to move on. Then he frowned. This was after all the first night Bloc was here and, though Shive had this area sewn up, he would not put it past the reif to try something rash. He keyed the comlink at his collar.

'Saden, three reifs down your way. I guess you've got them in your sights, but if not, find them and see what they're about.' He paused. 'Saden, if you're chewing some of that damned squeaky weed again I'll come down there personally and pull out your teeth.' Still no response. Shive turned to the guard again. 'I want one of you to—'

The entire fence shuddered, scattering sparks, the gates rattling together behind the two guards. Explosive charge – had to be. Shive switched to general com.

'Eyes up and lights on. Watchtowers report.'

One and Two immediately reported in: something had definitely hit the fence. There was a pause, nothing coming from Three, then Four and Five reported.

'It took out Tower Three. Something took out Tower Three,' babbled the watcher in Four, when given the opportunity.

Shive was already running. 'I want the response squad to Tower Three, *now*!' He swung his weapon down from his back and gripped it before him. Through his aug he initiated the link between his vision and the sight on the weapon, then set the weapon to three-round bursts. When the lights were tardy about coming on, he was about to set his vision to infrared, but then suddenly they did come on, flooding the area with light bright as day. The response squad came in from every direction and by the time Shive reached the third watchtower, all of them were with him. Only there was no Tower Three.

'Missile launcher,' someone suggested.

'Lights, out on that jungle,' Shive instructed over oom.

Beams stabbed into the close foliage, revealing the wreckage of the tower. Just then someone started screaming in the shadows beyond. Shive ignored the sound – it was an old trick probably meant to lure them out. He upped the magnification of his eyes and studied the ruined tower. If a missile had been used, it had to have been a zero-burn variety fired from inside the compound, else the wreckage would be here where he was standing. The screaming stopped.

'Someone is going to pay for that,' a trooper muttered.

'Shut it.' Shive held up his hand. There was something moving in the dingle. Big leech, that explained it. The damned thing must have stretched up and torn down the tower, whose guard deserved whatever had happened to him out there. He should have paid better attention. Then, concentrating on the presumed leech as it flowed through the thick undergrowth, Shive saw it consisted of rigid segments. Something else caught his eye and he looked up and caught a glimpse of two vertical rows of red eyes.

'Oh . . . hell,' someone said slowly.

Shive took a step back, glanced down at his weapon and almost unconsciously switched it to continuous fire, with the charge in each round unrestricted. He reasserted self-control, deliberately took that step forwards again.

'Okay, you in the towers, get down here now. It's now learnt there's fresh meat there so it might attack your towers. Everyone listen,' he raised his voice, 'we've got a hooder out there, a small one I estimate, probably about twenty metres long, and thin, so it's hungry. Pull back to cover amidst the buildings, and designated troops break out the armour piercers. When it comes, hit it with everything we've got.' He turned to the two nearest to him. 'You two, with me.' He headed away, with the two men running behind him. He was aware, though, that everything his men had got, including the missiles used for taking out armoured aircars, might still not be enough.

Leaning against an inflated wall, Aesop stripped off his transparent surgical gloves as he observed the watcher scrambling down from Tower One. The hooder had hit Tower Three, on the other side of the compound, and so hopefully it would still be over there. But Aesop waited cautiously. Only when he heard the buzzsaw racket of Batian weapons on full automatic did he head for the nearby fence.

Bloc was positive that the monster would only go after those marked with the pheromone extracted from the glands of a certain grazing animal from its home planet. Thus he had been assured by the lunatic who sold it to him. Aesop felt Bloc was losing it, and now with the thrall unit inside him not directly under Bloc's control, Aesop intended to get as far away as possible while the thing attacked. All he knew about hooders was that they went for anything moving and, pheromone or

not, everyone was in danger. And since he had spent most of the day marking Batian mercenaries with the stuff and was himself probably saturated with its aroma . . .

At the fence Aesop removed a small pen laser from his belt and began to cut. No one would notice as, with the present furore, all alarms would be attributed to the hooder attack. It was all damned madness, and it seemed very likely to him that many would not survive it. Aesop's main hope was that the creature would kill Bloc himself, and then he, Aesop, would be free for the first time in his . . . death.

The wire fell away and he ducked through, moving swiftly out into the night. Pushing into dingle he knocked away leeches that fell on him. He was dosed up on a balm-soluble Intertox-Virex cocktail so it was unlikely the virus would establish inside him, but he at least wanted to get through this retaining some of his flesh. That was not because of any Cultist belief that true resurrection could only come about through preserving intact the original flesh. He just did not want to end up like Bones.

Neither he nor Bones had ever considered the remaining dregs of the Cult anything more than a bunch of idiot fanatics the time they had gone to collect on a contract put out on Taylor Bloc, then a Klader scientist studying alien technologies. Bloc's interest in reification had been only a hobby then, until Aesop and Bones murdered him, when it became a total obsession. It was a killing they of course wished they had never carried out, especially when the reified Bloc pursued and then killed them. Awaking thereafter to reification had come as a surprise. It became a nasty surprise when they discovered Prador thralls had been connected in to their memcrystals, and that they were now Bloc's slaves.

In the shallows surrounding the island the giant whelk encompassed bitter loss and it was an organic pain, so she ignored the presence of the ship directly above her. Stirring silt she picked up pieces of cleaned-out whelk shell, and one by one stacked them on the skirt of flesh within the embrace of two tentacles. She tasted the strong aromatics of turbul in the water and the scales of those creatures still glittered in the silt, but there was no recourse: this shoal was already gone, since no turbul would voluntarily come anywhere near her, and she was not fast enough to catch even one of the creatures.

After a time she had gathered every last piece of shell, and closed her fleshy skirt around them like a large sack. Her impulse to protect was still there, and anger grew in slow waves in some lobes of the fibre-bound organ that was her brain. She turned an eye-stalk to watch an anchor being hauled up from the bottom, snaked out a tentacle, and knocked it against the familiar object, but could not summon up the inclination to find out what might happen if she pulled. She vaguely recollected another instance like this, long in the past, when the result had been . . . No, the memory was gone again. *Whelkus titanicus* began dragging herself to the shore.

As she emerged from the sea the whelk's anger took on a sharper edge. If only . . . if only . . . Abruptly the supply of oxygenated ichor flooded to one of the dormant brain lobes. If only she had not gone ashore after that other . . . thing that had killed one of her young, then when she came after it, managed to abandon its one shell and flee. It was all the fault of *that* one.

On the shore the whelk stacked the remains of her young where they would be safe from the further attentions of the sea's denizens. Then she turned an eye towards the remains of that other's shell, snaked out a tentacle and probed the wreckage. There were new scents here, connected to the object earlier floating above her. This puzzled her, as did the fact that there now seemed less . . . small objects – things had been taken from this dwelling. Another brain lobe abruptly fired up. The giant whelk turned her eyes to look back at the sea. The . . . ship . . . was gone. She remembered then when she had once hauled on an anchor chain and pulled down a large object made out of island trees. Those who tumbled from it, and on whom she had fed, they were the same – the same as that other!

She tasted and sensed the ground again, detected trails leading inland, swivelled her eyes to look out to sea again, could not decide what to do, then understood she had only the land trails to follow. Abruptly she surged forwards, knocking over trees and following those trails to the lane she had earlier cut across the island. From a high point, in darkness, she dimly discerned the ship turning into the wind beyond the far shore. She hurtled downslope, staying to her previous trail as on it she could move faster. Soon she reached the tideline and paused. Then she surged on.

Throwing a huge wave before her the giant whelk slammed back down into the sea. She remembered things so much more clearly now. The *other* had done this and . . . other . . . was in the vessel heading away from her. Licking her corkscrew tongue through the water she detected the taste of them, and the vaguest hint of the *other* from the island. Confusing memories arose: sounds with meanings disconnected from their inherent meaning within the sea, objects fashioned like shells but extraneous to the body, hints of understanding of things beyond her watery home. But the ship, yes the ship, contained others like the killer of her young, connected to that one by small objects taken from its dwelling on the island.

And she would avenge.

Janer jerked awake to the sound of explosions, glanced towards the window of the bunk house he had been directed to the previous evening. He had quickly realized that there were certain tensions here. Now it seemed they had come to a head. He rolled off his bed, pulled on his trousers and slipped on his envirosuit boots. As an afterthought he took up the skinstick box containing two hornets and pressed it against the bare skin of his shoulder.

'What the bugger is that?' said a Hooper in one of the other bunks.

'Shut yer gob, Loric.'

'Let's be taking a look at it then, lads,' said the calm voice of Captain Ron.

'*Batian weapons*,' the hive mind informed Janer. '*Perhaps you should not have come here.*'

'No shit,' said Janer, moving to the door.

He paused for a moment, glancing back at his belongings, but decided against collecting one particular item from among them. Opening the door he peered out.

The mercenary Shive ran across in front of him, two comrades dogging his footsteps. They reached a storehouse, quickly opened its door and darted inside.

'Big leech?' Janer wondered.

The hive mind just buzzed at him.

He stepped out as the Hoopers bestirred themselves behind him, and turned towards the staccato crackling of projectile weapons. A group of six Batians were firing at something between units. Something large.

'Big leech,' he confirmed, and began walking in that direction to watch the show. He did not suppose it would be a long one, since the weapons the mercenaries carried would make short work of the soft-bodied creature, no matter how large it was. He was ten metres from his unit when a group of reifications ran past him with that off-balance gait they assumed when trying to move fast. Something rose up into the night from further over in the enclosure. Large and spoon-shaped, it turned and he glimpsed two vertical rows of glowing red points. Weapons fire began to impact on it, lighting it up. He glimpsed armoured segments, saw that the weapons were having no effect. Then a missile streaked in from the side and exploded against the creature, which dropped out of sight.

'*That is not a leech,*' said the hive mind. '*I suggest you hide.*'

Janer glanced round. The missile had been fired by Shive or one of his two comrades, who were all now carrying missile launchers. After that initial shot they disappeared off between buildings to the left. The other visible group of mercenaries also headed on out of sight.

'You know I'm not the kind to hide,' muttered Janer, moving after them.

'*That creature is a hooder.*'

Janer paused, having heard of such things. They were no natives of this world, and where they came from they were implanted with locators so people could know when to run. Very tough and difficult to kill, apparently.

Janer at once wanted to take a closer look at it. As he advanced, however, something else gave him pause. Bloc's Kladites – either troops or worshippers, Janer was not sure – had appeared from behind the storehouse. Some of them now entered it and began dragging out heavy crates for others of their number to take away. More weapons, he assumed. Janer moved on.

Around the corner two Batians were firing repeatedly at the glistening side of the hooder as it hammered between the buildings, lit up with multiple concussions. Janer saw it bow under the impact of them. One of the buildings crashed over, still intact, at an angle, and that nightmare cowled head swung into clear view. The creature paused, its cowl swivelling like a searchlight. Janer took cover behind a stack of plasmel barrels. Something caught his eye and he looked down. Bones. Stripped of flesh but bloody. A head, one side of it stripped clean. Pieces of crabskin armour. Janer ignored the weapon that lay there – it had not done its owner much good.

The hooder came on over the tilted building and swerved towards the two marksmen. Someone else launched a missile, blowing its front end up off the ground, but still it came on, up over one of the mercenaries, then hard down on him even as he fired up into its hot eyes and surgical cutlery. It reared again, scattering human detritus, then swung sideways, chopping the other man in half with its cowl edge. Janer abruptly realized that no one was firing at it from this side of the enclosure. He moved further back into the shadows and glanced at the gore-bespattered weapon lying in the dust. Fortunately the hooder had turned towards the firing coming from behind it.

'*Now would be a good time to hide,*' the hive mind suggested.

Janer ran from cover, following the creature. In a narrow alley between accommodation units he noted the rips in the nearby walls caused by the passage of hard-edged carapace. Further along it had obviously caught a number of mercenaries, their number Janer could only guess by counting heads. Probably five or six? It was a gory mess, and blood-soaked dust caked his boots as he moved on.

In the clear central area of the enclosure the hooder was swinging around in an arc. Two mercenaries were crouched behind some crates nearby, tending to one of their fellows on the ground. Janer ran over and saw it was Shive. He was coughing blood while his comrades slapped drug patches on him and hooked an oxygenator into his jugular. The two glanced up at Janer and continued working. He supposed they preferred doing this than being out there in the beast's path.

'The Kladites are arming themselves,' Janer said, testingly.

Shive just exposed bloody teeth then turned his head for the device to be attached to his neck. Returning his attention to the monster, Janer saw it rear up over a small group of Hoopers.

'Oh shit . . . Ron!' Janer stood upright.

The Old Captain stood at the fore, directly facing the hooder, a huge machete held ready to deliver a blow. The hooder came down on him hesitantly, as if it thought there might be some danger here. The Captain struck it hard with his machete, unbelievably hard, for the blade dug well into shell the Batian missiles had only pocked. The monster jerked back, pulling the blade from the Captain's grasp. The Hoopers behind him began retreating. Perhaps realizing he might have been a tad overconfident, the Old Captain also retreated, but the hooder came down on him like a cat's paw.

Janer began running towards the Captain, not knowing what he intended but knowing he must do something. Then the cowl lifted up, higher and higher, Ron heaving himself upright, Herculean, but it slammed down yet again. Then fire ignited the night: a ragged beam of violet energy struck the hooder centrally. Janer went down feeling heat on his face and along one side of his body. For a moment the hooder's tough carapace resisted the energy directed at it, then it burned like straw in an acetylene flame. Whoever was directing the weapon brought his aim back across, going for the monster's head, but already the front ten-metre section of the hooder was coiling up and away. It crashed against a house, slid up over it and down the other side. Two more blasts, focusing on the still-thrashing tail of the monster, and two body segments flamed before the fire shut off.

Stillness now, but for the thrashing of what was left of the beast's tail. A fog of smoke rolled across the enclosure, and sticky black strands fell through the air. People began calling to each other. Someone was groaning. To one side a reification, missing the lower half of his body, was dragging himself out of a crushed accommodation unit. Janer stood and observed Kladites armed with laser carbines coming in to surround the severed tail, which was now jerking just occasionally.

'Ah, the reinforcements have arrived,' said Janer sarcastically.

'*But for which side?*' the hive mind wondered.

Janer broke into a trot, heading for where a figure was

lying prone. After a moment the man moved, then with a curse heaved himself upright. The skin of his arm had been stripped down, like a sleeve torn off at the shoulder, and was concertinaed around his wrist. He pulled it up again and patted it into place, then frowned at the rips in his clothing. The holes sliced into his body were now visibly closing. There was no blood on him. None at all.

'Now that was a nasty bugger,' growled Captain Ron.

6

Land Leech:
from a large encystment clinging to the bottom of a clump of
sargassum, protected in sprine-laden jelly poisonous to preda-
tors, leeches hatch out as globular diatoms with extended
plug-cutting mouths already working. They drift in the sea,
feeding and growing – forming the largest proportion of what
is referred to as Spatterjay's 'vicious plankton'. However, they
do not have it all their own way, being fed upon by anything
large enough to eat them and small enough to gain any
benefit from the meal – including their own kind. When they
reach the size of a pea, they become somnolent, and it is at
this stage the predation upon them is at its greatest. It is esti-
mated that less than one in a million are finally washed
ashore. Exposed to higher oxygen levels on the beach, they use
stored fat to transform into fingerling leeches, and crawl
inland to find a peartrunk tree in which to roost. A symbiotic
relationship exists here. When heirodonts strip tree bark from
it, the tree shakes, dropping leeches on the grazer to drive it
away. But that relationship is simple compared to the rela-
tionship between leeches and the Spatterjay virus.

In prey infected by leech bite, the virus imparts resistance
to damage and disease, and huge powers of regeneration.

*However, the regenerative process uses both the leech genome
and fragments of other animal genomes which the virus has
acquired over a billion years of evolution. Severely damaged
animals can transform entirely into leeches — and other
things.*

*The mechanism that finally drives leeches back into the
ocean is dependent on land food resources and the island leech
population. They can enter the sea at any size from that of
a human arm up to something weighing many tons. Some
never enter the sea, moving inland to deep dingle — becoming
tougher-skinned, more tubular and of a reddish colour —
where they feed upon larger varieties of land heirodont —*

Captain Orbus was peeved that no one had been in a
hurry to join his ship, that in fact three crewmen had
abandoned it. Yes, his mate had been murdered and two
of the crew executed for the crime, but new recruits
would not be in any danger, and anyway Hoopers should
not be so choosy or so cowardly. He guessed that what
put them off was the atmosphere of despondency and
bitterness aboard the *Vignette*, a mood that had better
soon disperse or he would want to know the reason why.
Even the sail, which had joined them with no knowledge
of the events back on Chel, was beginning to get uneasy.
Good thing sails now worked under contract. Without
that piece of paper, this one would have abandoned
them long before.

As he reclined in his chair on the Captain's bridge,
enjoying the hot morning sun and gazing out across pale
green ocean, Orbus knew this was not going to be a particularly enjoyable journey, nor a profitable one. He discounted at once any thoughts of going after sprine. Being
short-handed would push such a dangerous venture over

the edge into lethality. Orbus did not mind losing the odd man when he had them to spare, but now he did not. It seemed his only option was to do a bit of turbul fishing, if the opportunity arose, on the way to find the particular variety of sargassum that had been the downfall of his mate. Collecting squeaky weed would be the only way to turn a profit, again. And perhaps this time he would not have to push his crew so hard. He would take it easy on them. There would be no keel-hauling on this journey, no thrashings . . . Yes, he would take it easy. He eyed the desultory way his crew now went about their tasks. At least, no punishments unless they were called for. He heaved himself out of his chair and stood.

'Lannias, have you greased the ratchets?' he demanded loudly.

'Yes, Cap'n.'

'Drooble, isn't it time you stowed those ropes?'

'Yeah, probably,' Drooble replied, leering up at Orbus.

'Do you want to be the first strapped up against the mast, Drooble?' Orbus asked.

Still leering up at him, Drooble licked his lips. Abruptly Orbus felt a sudden disquiet. The other Old Captains, though agreeing there could be only one punishment for murder by sprine, had been scathing of his abilities. What was it Captain Drum had said?

'Your crew can leave you at any time, Orbus, and being the bastard you are, do you ever wonder why any of them stay?'

'I am a strict man and Hoopers need the discipline,' Orbus had protested.

'More like,' Drum opined, 'they like the discipline.'

Orbus was aware that in the eyes of the other

Captains he was too strict and too ready with the punishments, and his crew too ready to receive them.

'Get on with you,' he said to Drooble, and turned away.

It was then that the sail's head snapped up to peer at something casting a shadow on the deck. Orbus looked up into sun-reflected glare. For a moment the experience was religious — he felt on the brink of some revelation — then a voice said, 'Okay, Captain, I've distance scanned you, but our quarry might be using chameleonware. I'd like to search your ship.'

Orbus blinked, and his vision finally resolved the huge gleaming nautiloid drone descending beside the *Vignette*. There were other shapes higher up he could not discern, and to the right of the big drone was a small iron-coloured one bearing the shape of a scallop, and another fashioned like some mythical fish swimming through the air, its large scales glinting metallic green.

'The Polity has no jurisdiction here,' said Orbus, still angry because of his previous feelings. 'Any of you try to enter my ship and you will know the cost. Now bugger off!'

Orbus had not seen this particular drone before, but the others of the Warden's drones, he recollected, usually went away if you shouted at them loudly enough. They were all frightened of stepping outside of the complicated charter laid down for them by Earth Central, and they all tried to keep out of trouble that could result in them being subsumed back into the Warden. There had apparently been some changes a number of years back, but Orbus had not been interested enough to find out what they were.

'Are you threatening me?' asked the big drone.

The fish drone piped up, 'Bad move, Captain.'

The scallop added, 'A possibly injurious move.'

Orbus glanced aside and saw that all the remaining twelve members of his crew were out on deck. It seemed it was now a matter of keeping face. He reached over by his chair and picked up the weapon propped there. It had cost him a shipload of squeaky weed to buy this. He flicked a switch on the side of it and the gas-system pulse rifle whined up to charge. As an afterthought he then picked up the glittering coil of his flexal bullwhip. The big drone, he expected he could only drive away, but if he could get a coil of his whip around one of the little shits and pull it close, he knew, with his Old Captain strength, he would be able to tear it apart. He stood silently waiting. In a minute they would decide he was too much trouble and be on their way. And, after that happened, he would go down to the lower deck and wipe that smirk off Drooble's face.

The big drone sighed theatrically. 'You know, while I was the Warden I had access to all the files on the Old Captains and now carry copies of them inside myself. Yours makes interesting reading: a sadist in charge of a crew of masochists. Now my view has always been one of "Live and let live",' the big drone paused for a second after a snort issued from the scallop, and Orbus guessed at some quick unheard communication, 'but what about those Hoopers who joined you out of foolishness or desperation? As far back as your file goes, you've had six murders and four suicides aboard your ship, and eight others missing without explanation.' The drone shrugged in mid-air. 'What do you say to that?'

'I say bugger off,' said Orbus. He flipped his whip out behind him and levelled his pulse rifle.

'Oh sod this,' said the drone.

Orbus fired. A gleaming tentacle slid out from the drone with deceptive speed. The shots from the rifle just puffed into nacreous clouds on the drone's skin, as the tentacle wrapped around the Old Captain's neck and hauled him into the air. Other tentacles sped in, and he felt his whip and rifle snatched from his grasp, then he was upside down, a tentacle around his ankles, being jerked through the air. Next thing he knew he was hanging upside down from a spar of the foremast. He peered up at his ankles and saw them bound to the pearwood with his own whip.

'Search it,' said the big drone.

The two other drones zipped down to the deck and hovered over the forward hatch. Drooble ran over to them, stared at them for a moment, then reached down to open it.

'Leave that bloody hatch alone!' Orbus bellowed.

Drooble leered, then dragged it open. The drones shot inside.

'Let me down from here!' Orbus yelled, not liking the way his crew were now grinning up at him. He hauled himself up and tried to undo the whip, but not only had it been knotted around his ankles, the flexal coils had been welded. He dropped back down, to look into the upside-down crocodilian face of the sail.

'Dumb,' it said. 'Surprisingly dumb.'

Shortly the small drones came back out of the hatch.

'Clean as clean can be,' prattled the fish.

'Not a Golem in sight,' added the scallop.

And with a low roar all three of them ascended into the sky.

'Get me down from here!' Orbus yelled again.

'Minute, Cap'n. I got that rope to stow,' said Drooble.

'I think I missed one of the ratchets,' said Lannias.

Other crewmembers took their lead from those two, and set about their many assigned tasks. All ignored the Captain's bellowing for the best part of the day. When they finally decided to cut him down, they cut through the spar – it was the only way – and Orbus fell headfirst to the deck. He was very angry when he finally managed to free his ankles. Most of them liked that. Others were terrified.

There were traps upon traps layered into the programming, their parameters changing over seemingly random time periods. There were so many that Vrell wondered how his father had kept track of them all and not fallen foul of them himself. Like the blast doors Vrell had earlier opened, and jammed by fusing the motors that drove them. For them the input locking codes changed at periods ranging from a few minutes to entire days. But at least this control pit and its array of screens in Father's sanctum continued operating once Vrell short-circuited the gene reader with a lump of gristle he'd found attached to a piece of his father's carapace.

With increasing bewilderment Vrell worked his way through the programming systems of the ship. He was finding the traps and nullifying them, but knew that at this rate he would not clean the system until some years hence. It made his major ganglion ache and, as he worked, pressure grew inside him. Inevitably there came a dull crunch, and he turned his eye-palps, and what was now his head, to observe another crack in his carapace. Relief was immediate, and with it came sudden inspira-

THE VOYAGE OF THE SABLE KEECH 141

tion. Of course, there had to be a separate tracking and reformatting program. It was clearly not in the system itself, so Father must have accessed it through one of his control units – one that was still active. And it was even more obvious that his father used the same unit to access the whole system. How could Ebulan have done otherwise? He had no hands. It was so blatantly obvious, why had Vrell not seen this before?

Vrell spun round and clattered across the room picking up the hexagonal control units once welded to his father's carapace. Using a remote reader, a second device that mated into the socket in the face of each unit, he tested each one in turn. The first three were dead – obviously linked to the thrall units rendered defunct by the destruction of the blanks they ran – but the fourth was still transmitting. The Prador took it over to Ebulan's private storage area – now open – went inside, unplugged the reader, then plugged a cable from a diagnostic tester into the same socket. All the control unit required, apparently, was another nanofibre rooting module. He found one of these, removed the old module from the back of the unit, and plugged the new one into place. With another hand he picked up a multihead carapace drill, placed it against his underside and triggered it. A high whine and puff of powder resulted in a neat pepperpot of holes in his undercarapace. He brought the unit up to these and paused.

There was danger here from two sources: the rooting module carried the format for Prador physiology, and Vrell was not exactly a normal Prador any more; and there might be more traps. He thought the latter possibility remote. The traps were all outside this chamber, since Ebulan had not expected an enemy to get this close, which was why, in the end, he was now in pieces on the floor. Vrell pushed the control unit into place, felt the sudden heat as it shell-welded, took his hand away.

Nothing for a moment, then a nauseating sensation much like he had experienced when the leeches burrowed inside his carapace. Then slowly, inexorably, he saw with other eyes and reached out with invisible hands into the systems of the ship. Programming within the unit itself automatically corrected his course so he did not fall afoul of the traps, physical or otherwise. Slowly he began to encompass it all. He saw the blown reactors and burnt-out generators both through cameras and in the constant cycling of diagnostic programs. He knew that, with a great deal of work, some fusion reactors were salvageable. Weapons systems were no problem: most of them were functional though lacking in sufficient power or projectiles. He set a small autofactory to suck in sea water and electrolyse required chemicals. Metals in storage were also made available to the factory, and within an hour the first gleaming missiles were clicking into place in weapons carousels. He cleared other glitches, circumvented damage, brought online and gave autonomy to repair systems that Ebulan, in his paranoia, had controlled centrally. Eventually he reached a point where there was no more he could do through the ship's computer systems. It was time for grunt work. Shaking himself, Vrell pulled out from that omniscient ship vision and gazed around. From a nearby rack he took out four control units, and four thrall units, together with the required equipment for their installation. Then he headed for the ship's larder – more than one purpose in mind.

*

Some of his Kladites had fetched an autohandler up from the construction site. Peering out of the window, Bloc watched it trundle on its treads up to the abandoned tail section of the hooder, open and swivel its pincer grabs to pick the thing up. The tail was still moving and, from what he knew of hooder biology, each of its segments could grow into a new creature. He had no wish for any more of the creatures in this vicinity so had ordered it taken away and burned outside the enclosure. Others meanwhile were collecting human remains in motorized barrows, and still another group was pulling one of the accommodation units upright with a winch. Bloc turned away from the window.

'Who fired that antiphoton weapon?' he asked.

'I've no idea who fired that proton weapon,' Shive replied pedantically. 'But, then, what lunatic brought a hooder here and released it?'

Bloc studied him. Shive could stand upright, though a little unsteadily. Two of his five remaining comrades were not so lucky. Both were on AG stretchers, one with his leg terminating at the knee, and one with a chrome autodoc clinging to her side maintaining life in her badly shattered body until such time as she could receive better attention than would be provided here. It had not been difficult to disarm them in the aftermath of the attack. Eighty Kladites armed with laser carbines had been sufficient.

'Why, *you* did, Shive,' said Bloc.

The mercenary bared his teeth. He was not so impressive now without his armour or his guns.

'You think anyone is going to believe that?'

Bones took a step towards the mercenary, but Bloc reined him back. There was no need for any violence now Bloc had won. He glanced to the Kladite guards standing around the walls of the storeroom. They were completely loyal.

'The passengers will believe. Apparently Lineworld Developments had the creature shipped here in order to sufficiently damage this enterprise to push its start-up costs over a certain limit, whereupon they would be able to take full control. Just like when they relocated us. In fact, the relocation was the first part of the plan, and the hooder the next part. Everyone knows how Lineworld operates.'

'Reifications were destroyed by that creature, but many more of my men died.'

'Oh yes . . . I didn't say it was a very *good* plan.'

'So what now?' Shive asked.

'When the shuttle comes to take away the construction crew, you and your comrades will be put on it. Surprisingly few reifs will be departing, despite what happened here. Fewer still when I have had a chance to speak to them. You will go back to your masters at Lineworld and tell them that they will not be taking over this enterprise after all. They will not be able to do anything about that, because by then the ship will be built.'

'Do you think they'll just accept that?'

'What can they do? They can send more of your kind, but how will you take a ship at sea? Remember, AG transport is not allowed on this planet, nor are powered boats. And even if you should reach the ship, under sail, it will be well protected.'

'We have been well trained in taking such objectives.'

'But you will also tell your masters that I still consider our contract valid. Their initial investment will be repaid, and they will make a profit from the first voyage,

and subsequent voyages. I think they'll find that the cost of mounting an operation against me will far outweigh such profits, especially when you tell them that should any operation be mounted against me, their initial investment will end up at the bottom of the ocean.'

'Bloc,' Shive almost snarled, 'I don't care what Lineworld does. I'll be back.'

That was enough indication to Bloc of how Shive's masters would ultimately react: they were all about profit, not pride. He stared at the mercenary, his spectacle irrigator spraying a fine mist into his eye. Why should he tolerate such threats from a messenger? There were others here who could do the same job.

'Bones,' he said, and mentally let that individual off the leash.

Bones stooped, then came upright fast. Secondary orders brought the Kladite guards in, with weapons aimed. Shive grunted, staggered back, a small cylinder of wood protruding from his right eye. The Kladites now covered the other mercenaries; the stubby snouts of their laser carbines under chins, against heads. Bones leapt forward and brought their leader down and, sitting on his chest, grabbed the wooden handle, turned it with a wet crunching, then in a gush of blood pulled out the ten-centimetre ceramocarbide blade.

Bloc studied the other mercenaries. 'You'll deliver my message?'

After a pause one of them said, 'We'll deliver it.'

'Then make yourselves comfortable – you'll be here for some little while yet.' Bloc headed for the door, Bones following him, wiping his knife on his sleeve before returning it to his boot sheath.

Outside, in bright sunshine, Bloc spotted Aesop

walking towards him. He stopped and waited until Aesop was close, then asked, 'Where were you?'

Aesop seemed reluctant to reply until Bloc accessed him through his thrall unit and applied pressure.

'Outside the compound,' Aesop explained.

'And why were you out there?'

'It seemed the safest place for me to be, considering I was soaked with that pheromone.'

'Did I give you permission to go?'

'No, you didn't, nor did you deny it.'

Bloc stared at Aesop, moisture again filling his dead eyes from his spectacle irrigator. Aesop and Bones were becoming increasingly rebellious. Had that occurred only recently, Bloc would have put it down to the extra channel he had enabled through his control unit – meaning that his attention was more divided – but it had been going on for a long time now. Perhaps, though they could not physically reject their thrall units, as could Hooper humans, they were somehow mentally rejecting them? He must check their hardware and run some deep diagnostic tests on the software. He did not want to have to shut them down, as they had been such useful tools – comfortable as well-worn shoes.

'Very well,' said Bloc. 'Our Batian friends are well guarded now, but I want you and Bones to find out who fired that APW.' He gestured to Bones who stood right beside him, head tilted staring at something on the ground.

'How many Batians did it kill?' Aesop asked.

'The weapon?'

'No, the hooder.'

'Twelve of them.'

'Other casualties?'

Bloc closed the one eye he was still able to close and disconnected visual reception from the other. He then turned an inner eye to the control unit inside his skull, and to one of its three open channels. Aesop was resisting the order he had been given and pursuing a frankly irritating line of questioning. Bloc did not want to talk about the eight reification memcrystals now being packed into a box for shipment back to Klader, nor the reports he had heard of some scatterings of heavy, slightly distorted bones, which meant the creature had also killed Hoopers. He increased the signal strength from the unit down the channels connecting to both Aesop and Bones.

'Obey my orders,' he said tersely, and opened his one lidded eye.

Aesop nodded and turned, while Bones jerked his head up again and followed his partner. Closing his eye again, Bloc focused his attention through the unit on something else, something wild and red and dangerous. He tried to exert his will over that entity, tried to—

WARN: EXTREMITY PROBE LA76 REG. CELLULAR DAMAGE

What?

Bloc fully restored his own vision, and for a moment could not fathom what the message might mean. Was it another glitch? Some ghost signal coming back through the control unit?

LA76?

Leg/ankle, he realized, and looked down.

The leech was not large: merely the size and shape of a cucumber. He realized now that this was what Bones had been staring at, probably even as it slithered across the ground towards Bloc's ankle. He stepped on it with

his other foot and pulled his ankle away from it. The
creature stretched to almost twice its own length then
snapped back to normal size, a lump of grey flesh disappearing into its pink tubular mouth. Bloc put his full
weight on it and twisted his foot back and forth until it
burst like a huge blackcurrant, then finally stepped away.
He tried to remember when last he had updated his dose
of Intertox. The new formula lasted longer in reification
balms than the stuff Sable Keech had used, but it did
need to be frequently renewed.

WARN: CELLULAR REPAIR REQ. SHUTTING
BALM FLOW LA76

OUTPARAFUNCT: YABB@~*

MEMSPACE: 00048

Ignoring the corrupted messages, Bloc glanced down
by his ankle and saw balm soaking into the dusty soil.
He needed to seal that quickly, then he needed to make
sure the fence was back up, and the compound scoured
of native life forms. He hurried to his quarters. He also
needed to update his Intertox dose. He was a long way
from the Little Flint and the transformation that awaited
him there. To be infected by the Spatterjay virus now
could be catastrophic.

Only two of the four human bodies were serviceable.
The nervous systems of the others being so badly
degraded by their transformation into the leech form,
Vrell was unable to use them, so ate them instead. Now,
with two extra control units bonded to his carapace, he
constantly updated the programming of the remaining
two so that they worked as an adjunct to his mind, two
extra pairs of hands as was intended. Glimpsing them
through ship's eyes, he watched one of them clearing

wreckage and feeding it into one of the multi-furnaces Vrell had earlier ignited, while the other welded cracked bulkheads. Of course, in their earlier state with only leech mouths growing between their shoulders where their heads should have been, they had been of little use. It was only when he connected two cameras into the thrall units of each to give them binocular vision that he managed to utilize them. Now they looked like humans with strange trunklike proboscs and insectile eyes rearing up on stalks. Even so, they were not enough.

Vrell checked the reading on his mission timer. Much time had been counted away by the slowly changing glyphs. He had accomplished much, but there was still very much to do. He needed to work faster than this, else he would run out of food long before he was ready.

It had puzzled him why Ebulan, knowing the dangers, had used only a spider thrall on an Old Captain called Drum, rather than fully core the man. Now he knew. Full coring removed every last trace of the original inhabiting intelligence, but most importantly it removed that part of the intelligence best described as 'know thyself'. To control fully cored humans, like the two below, required a great deal of practice, for the controlled body did not instinctively know simple things like the length of its arms, how far a single pace would take it, or how tightly to grip an object to hold it, and so on. They also did not sense or react to pain. Consequently it had taken Vrell a long time to learn how to control these two, and still they were clumsy and constantly damaging themselves.

Once again fully connected into the ship's system, Vrell searched for other tools to employ. He found a few small quadruped robots, whose purpose was to act as landward spies, and used them to clean up loose contaminants where a ceramic pile had fragmented. There were few other machines in the ship like them, and Vrell cursed the paranoia that had for so long prevented Prador using AI and other self-governing machines. Then, remembering his entry into the ship, he turned his attention to the drone cache and found there one of his kin.

'We will kill the old drone,' came the comment from the flash-frozen and stored brain of a Prador adolescent – still cycling some previous instruction from Ebulan.

Vrell studied diagnostic returns and peered through sonar cameras in the cache. Ebulan had used the brain as a backup recorder for the mobile war drones, so new drones would benefit from the experiences of their predecessors. The brain was stored behind the armoured bulkhead and had been disconnected from its group, probably so no signals could be traced back to the ship itself. Vrell felt his curiosity stirring: what was this old drone it wanted to kill? And, most importantly, what had obliterated the rest of the drones? Could it be the same thing that had brought down the ship itself?

Vrell tried to ascertain as much as possible from the ship's memory, but there were gaping holes caused by feedback damage, and holes he himself had necessarily made to excise the alien programs remaining in the system from when the Warden had turned Ebulan's own blanks against him. All he knew for certain was that, while Father had been distracted by this takeover, something had punched through the ship. He keyed into the control drone's memory and found part of the puzzle. He observed how, one after another, Ebulan's drones had been duped and destroyed by an ancient ECS war drone.

'Father,' said the drone mind.

Vrell ignored it. The adolescent brain presently had no way of knowing, being controlled now by the ship's systems rather than Ebulan's pheromones, that it was not the old Prador currently plumbing its memories. Vrell was still curious about what had hit this ship. His survival might depend on knowing that. There was a risk involved in what he decided to do next, but not too serious. Checking system memory, he knew that there were still some of Father's secondary emitters out in the ocean, and many of them would have stored the last memory downloads from the remaining drones. He laboriously began to decode program traps so he could reinstate outside connections. When that was completed, some days later, the U-space links established in microseconds, and within further microseconds memory returned to the backup brain.

'Not Father,' said the adolescent, now knowing Ebulan was dead, before Vrell finished assessing those memories.

Vrell saw the last of the war drones, gutted by the ECS drone but still transmitting, taken high and brought down hard, along with that old ECS drone, to punch through Ebulan's ship. The blow had been as simple and effective as that. In a way that was a relief, for Vrell had feared some powerful weapons strike from the Warden itself.

'You are not Father,' said the adolescent.

'Obey me,' said Vrell, reinforcing the order through the ship's systems.

'We will kill the old drone.'

As he isolated the brain from the secondary emitters, Vrell thought not. The other drones had not managed the task, and anyway the old drone had destroyed itself in that last attack. Thinking very clearly, Vrell realized what the problem had been: not the weaponry or armour but the minds behind them. That wily old ECS drone had been utterly out-gunned yet won every skirmish. Vrell himself could see how the Prador drones had been far too direct, and blind to the diversity of the ECS drone's attacks. Knowing what he knew now, Vrell would have been more circumspect, and that was why he opened up a programming link, began to rearrange his sibling's brain, and to map memories and thought structures across. When he had completed that task, he disconnected the adolescent brain from the ship and opened the bulkhead that protected it. Then he started pumps emptying the cache of sea water, before going in search of the tools he required.

In a time unknown to him, 'Vrell' surfaced to awareness, clamped in the cache of his father's ship. He did an almost instinctive systems check, and immediately discovered his non-standard alterations: extra grav-units, double the thickness of armour and double the power supply, additional Polity tech usually treated with contempt by the Prador, and even claws. He turned an eye-pit towards the other drone shell, and saw that it had been cannibalized to supply him with some of these additions, though the claws themselves were utterly new. He was much more powerful than any other drone ever launched from this ship, but this did nothing to stem the tide of bitter anger that filled him, knowing he was a copy of the original Vrell mapped into the mind of a flash-frozen sibling. And he was unable to disobey the *real* Vrell, who had long ago returned to Ebulan's sanctum.

In the gloom of the *Treader*'s hold, Ambel studied the ship's manifest on his palm-screen. Then he eyed the crates of bottles filled with Intertox-laced fruit juice, the garlic bulbs and onions hanging in nets, the packs of desiccated proteins and vegetables, the salted pigs and various other items of dome-grown food. At a bit of a stretch there was enough here to keep himself and the crew from going native throughout the long journey he planned. Just one of those bottles of juice could keep the change at bay for the best part of a week. However, there was not enough food overall. He listened to the noise up on deck, which told him they were ready up there, then turned off the screen and headed for the ladder.

Climbing up onto the bridge of the *Treader*, Ambel turned and surveyed his crew. As instructed, all of them were now up on deck, some of them looking tired and irritable after being woken while off their shift. There were only four seniors: Peck, Anne, and now Sild on the deck below, and Boris at the helm beside Ambel. Of the junior crewmen there were eight, Sprout being the most senior. Fourteen mouths to feed, including the sail.

'Listen up, lads,' Ambel called, and, once he was sure he had their attention, continued. 'You all saw the island and think you know what happened there. You don't, and neither do I really. Erlin is still alive.' He allowed them to mutter amongst themselves and toss dubious glances at each other. 'I know this quite simply because she was spotted being carried away from the island by that big Golem sail, Zephyr, and his two companions.'

'So she's safe?' said Anne delightedly.

Standing next to Ambel, Boris was rolling the end of his moustache between his fingertips, but even he could not remain dour at such news, and began smiling. Even Peck was showing his teeth, though whether or not he was grinning was debatable. Sild also looked happy. Other crew members, knowing Erlin less well and not having shared in this ship's history, showed varying degrees of happiness or scepticism.

Ambel winced. 'I'm not so sure about her being *safe*. The sail is heading due east, and the only habitation that way is what has recently been named Mortuary Island – where reifications are building a big ship called the *Sable Keech*.'

'Why would she want to go there?' asked Anne.

'I'm not so sure she *does* want to go there,' said Ambel, 'as she would have communicated her intention, if not to me, then at least to the Warden. I've learnt that one Taylor Bloc, a reif, wants her there so she can do for him and his followers what she did for Sable Keech himself.'

'The sails kidnapped her?' said Boris.

At this one of the juniors spat, 'Bloody sails.'

Ambel eyed the man, a one-fifty Hooper called Pillow – which was a comfortable name for a man who had taken to discomfort in a big way, by the look of his various body piercings. Ambel was about to utter some sort of reprimand when he saw Galegrabber's head swing over the crowd, on the end of its long muscular neck, and dip down until it was breathing in Pillow's ear.

'You got a problem with sails, junior?' hissed the sail.

Pillow nervously revolved his nose stud between forefinger and thumb. 'Nooo, no problem.'

'Good.' Galegrabber rose up and turned back towards Ambel.

'Now,' said Ambel, 'I could ask for help from the Warden, but I've always felt we should settle our own problems. I intend now to sail to this Mortuary Island and rescue Erlin.'

'That's a bloody long way,' someone muttered incredulously.

Ambel went on relentlessly, 'We'll detour to the Sargassum first, picking up some turbul and amber-clams on the way to supplement our supplies. I'm told there's at least seven ships in that area, so any of you who don't fancy the journey can hitch a ride from there.'

As the crew began to disperse, Galegrabber stretched his neck even further and brought his head level with Ambel on the bridge.

'I got a contract,' said the sail. 'And this journey ain't written down in it.'

Ambel reached into his pocket and pulled out a wooden box.

'The aug you're wearing,' said the Old Captain, 'it's the basic cheap datalink kind. Bottom of the ladder really.'

'So?'

Ambel opened the box and displayed the shiny new aug inside. 'I thought about fitting this to myself, but never got round to it. It's an Orion 3000, top of the range. From your present aug we can record across the alignment program for sail physiology, and then it'll be ready to attach. What do you say?'

The sail licked its lips with its bifurcated tongue. 'I'll want that in writing.'

Ambel produced a new contract from his other pocket. 'Just sign here.'

The sail took the paper from him in its soft lips and took it up to the top of the mast to study. By the time it finished and signed the new document – surprisingly remembering its new name – Ambel was down on the deck organizing some fishing gear, for a shoal of turbul had just been sighted.

The Hoopers, to make their bunkhouse distinct and for their own comfort, constructed a veranda on which many of them would lounge during the day while they grumbled about the cost of living here. Janer felt they did not really have much to complain about: they were on a retainer until the *Sable Keech* launched, at which point they would go onto a full crewman's wages. Anyway, as well as a veranda, they had also put together a couple of rafts to go fishing for boxies and turbul in the nearby shallows, so all they needed to buy from the various commercial concerns here was some Earth food, which was sensibly sold to them fairly cheaply. Forlam, showing uncharacteristic enterprise, had even brought along a still, and the distinctive smell around their bunkhouse came from the numerous buckets ranged outside, all full to the brim with fermenting seacane. Captain Ron thought Forlam a good lad.

'He's speaking again,' Janer observed as he stepped out onto the veranda. He blinked in the bright light, rubbed his aching head – too much of Forlam's rum last night.

'Haranguing more like,' rumbled Ron from where he sat in a chair tilted back against the wall. 'It don't seem to be working.' He sipped from a beaker of coffee.

Bloc stood on a crate in the central clearing before a crowd of reifications. Picking up the gist of what he was saying, Janer realized the reif leader was telling them it was their duty to support him in defiance of Lineworld Developments' attempted rip-off.

'Maybe that's because the intended target of that rip-off was Bloc himself,' said Janer.

'I dare say,' Ron replied.

The hive mind then chipped in, '*I have been checking: Bloc now fully controls this operation here, yet has maintained his contract with Lineworld. That means no reduction in ticket prices, accommodation costs or reification spares.*'

Janer relayed that to Ron. They had both heard plenty of grumbling, and knew that when the shuttle finally returned over two hundred of the reifications currently here would be leaving on it. But maybe that was not all down to economics. There was still the front end of a hooder out there somewhere.

'How are you now?' Janer asked Ron.

His injury hunger – that ravenous appetite Hoopers experienced after any physical damage as their bodies rebuilt themselves – had been immense, and had required the other Hoopers to chip in funds to buy sufficient dome-grown food.

'Right as rain.' Ron patted his shoulder.

Janer took hold of a chair and sat astride it. He watched Bloc, the crowd, the armed Kladites scattered all around the area.

'Lineworld really screwed up, shipping that thing here,' he said testily.

Ron just grunted at that.

'I note that no APW has turned up yet, and no one

has admitted to owning one. We still don't know who it was that cut the hooder in half.'

'Not for lack of effort on Bloc's part,' Ron observed. 'His lieutenants ain't stopped turning this place over ever since.'

Janer nodded then emphatically wished he had not. He finally relented and took some pills from the top pocket of his shirt to swallow dry.

'*You should not have drunk so much last night. You are not here on holiday*,' the hive mind informed him primly.

Janer squinted down at his shoulder. 'I'm not sure I give a damn.'

Muttered imprecations issued from the hivelink. Janer returned his attention to Captain Ron, who was gazing at him queryingly. 'Hive minds are big on temperance, probably because they don't like what happens to their hornets when they eat rotten fruit. You were saying . . .'

Ron shrugged and went on, 'Curious how desperate Bloc is to find that weapon and its owner, considering they saved so many lives.'

'They're all a bit odd here,' said Janer.

'Yes.' Ron nodded. 'Not normal folk like us.'

A snort issued from the hivelink. Janer stood up and stepped down from the veranda, leaving Ron to nurse his coffee. Crossing the enclosure he eyed the damage the alien beast had wrought and noted that most of it had already been repaired. Most of the human remains had been collected, but it was still not uncommon to step on something nasty concealed in the dust.

'They were burning the dead last night,' he observed. The pyre had been built over the tail section of the hooder in an attempt to burn away some more of that as well. Hooder flesh did not combust very easily. 'I wonder what they'll do with the rest – the reifs are still extant, despite their bodies being ripped apart.'

'*Their memcrystals will be sent to Klader. Possibly the reifs now lacking bodies will be resurrected in Golem chassis or in cloned bodies, or destroyed, depending on the strength of their beliefs.*'

'Destroyed?'

'*Yes. Fanatical cultists believed the body was all, no matter how decayed it might be, and that without the body there can be no real return to life. Though the Cult itself is now defunct, many reifs still ascribe to its beliefs. Most here, incidentally, are Kladites.*'

Janer grunted an acknowledgement then said, 'I'm surprised.'

'*What, surprised at such primitive belief systems?*'

'No, that for three whole days you haven't tried to persuade me to return to Chel. Or, rather, I'm not so much surprised as rather certain there's something you aren't telling me.'

'*Our agreement was for me to fund your journey here and to pay a bounty when you performed certain tasks. I have other contacts on Chel who will keep me apprised of anything I need to know. Meanwhile, I am curious about this . . . situation.*'

Janer winced. There were no facial or verbal cues from a hive mind, but he knew it was lying. By now he had reached the edge of the compound, and saw that a female Kladite guard stood at the gate, which seemed to Janer rather redundant as over to her left a huge swathe of the fence was down.

'Not advisable to go out there,' said the woman.

Janer paused. He thought about arguing with her. But

he was unarmed, being reluctant to carry around the weapon he had brought, and was now remembering how lethal Spatterjay life forms could be. And out there lurked something even worse than hippo-sized leeches, prill or the occasional adventurous whelk. He was not Captain Ron's age, so the hooder could turn him into mush. He started to turn away, when a voice spoke from behind him.

'I'll keep him out of trouble.'

Janer turned around fully. It was the Golem, Isis Wade.

'Why should you manage any better out there than he would?' the guard asked.

'Bloc seems to think the hooder is some distance away now, and I'm sure, like myself, Janer wants to see the ship.' Wade shrugged. 'Anyway, surely you are here to protect Bloc's interests, not the likes of us from our own stupidity?'

'Well, it's *your* life.'

The dead woman opened the gate and the two of them strolled through.

'Now that's interesting,' said Janer, once they were some distance away from her. 'She doesn't seem to know you're Golem.'

'Yes, it is,' concurred Wade. 'The Batians, if they had still been in charge here, would have found that out soon enough. Bloc's Kladites, however, are not so well-equipped. Unfortunate that, isn't it? It's probably also why they cannot find that APW.'

Janer grimaced. 'Can you keep me out of trouble?'

'I could pick you up and run a lot faster with you than the hooder can move. Though I shouldn't worry about that creature. It'll be licking its wounds as far away from here as it can get.'

'You know about hooders then?'

'I've travelled some,' said Wade.

Janer nodded, let the conversation die for a moment, expecting the hive mind to interject some comment. It remained ominously silent.

'I never got to ask you,' said Wade. He nodded at the transparent box affixed to Janer's shoulder. 'As I understand it you're no longer indentured, and since certain events here a decade ago you haven't carried a hive mind's eyes. So why now?'

Janer did not question how Wade had obtained this information – anyone with access to the AI nets could know it. 'Money,' he explained smoothly. 'After my indenture I continued working for this hive mind. As you say, after the events here, I broke the contract, but I've since renegotiated it.'

'It was my understanding that you are now independently wealthy?' said Wade.

'You can never have too much,' Janer replied. 'The mind pays well for the small inconvenience of carrying round a pack of hornets in stasis and a couple of living ones on my shoulder, and all I have to do is be the tourist I'd pay to be anyway.'

Wade did not reply to that; instead he pointed ahead to where one of the reifs was trudging up the path towards them. 'That's Aesop – one of Taylor Bloc's lieutenants.'

They both halted and stepped aside as Aesop walked past them. Janer only knew which reif this was because of the recognizable flak jacket he wore and because Wade had identified him. This was the first time the reif's features had been visible. Aesop's face was damaged – new damage – but that was nothing in comparison to his old and all too obvious death-wound. A segment of his skull between twelve and one o'clock was completely missing above his left eye. He acknowledged them not at all, as they moved on.

'Do you know much about the history of reifs?' Wade asked.

'I learnt a fair bit from Keech. They were reanimated murder victims sent after their killers, mindless in the beginning, then becoming AI as the facility to memcord dead minds became available. The Cult came along after, its leaders twisting doctrine to fit the reality only when that reality suited them.'

'Simplistic,' said Wade.

Janer glanced at him. 'I only recently learnt about how the Cult imploded, when reifs many centuries old could no longer espouse such simplistic beliefs. I know things are more complicated than that, but do I care enough to find out exactly how? Not really.'

A turning in the path revealed considerable industry below, around the huge, nearly completed ship. Janer now saw that what he had first taken to be the stripped trunks of dead trees in the dingle ahead were in fact nine masts rearing from the ship's decks and its tiered deckhouses. Skeletal Golem glinted in the sunlight as they connected rigging, hauled up spars, cable motors, and the enormous rolls of monofabric sails that the living sails would control.

'Impressive,' he said.

'It is,' Wade agreed. 'The designs for such vessels have been around since before we left Earth, and improved upon considerably over that time. But, with abundant energy and gravmotors, there's never been the need to actually build one.'

'Until now.'

'Yes.'

They continued down to the deforested area, where Janer observed huge open crates from which equipment was being lugged across to the ship by treaded robotic handlers. This was the big stuff that needed to be placed inside the hull before the Golem bonded the last hull-planks into place. He paused to watch this work, letting Wade get ahead of him.

'What do you think?' he subvocalized.

No reply from the hive mind. Janer peered down at his shoulder box, then after a moment tapped it with his finger. One of the two hornets inside toppled over. Janer removed the box, pressed an indentation along the edge to flip up the lid. He prodded both hornets with his fingertip. They were both dead. He closed the box and transferred it to his pocket.

'Your hornets dying should not disconnect the com-link,' he said quietly. He reached up, pulled the hivelink from his earlobe, and dropped that into his pocket too. 'I think I'm exactly where you want me to be, but it would seem you and I are not the only ones to know that.'

He walked on after Wade.

On the planet Hive, the ancient hive mind sensed the probing presence of one of its brethren, but ignored it, aware that its own gradual fragmentation made it vulnerable to such inspection. The schisms inside it were becoming difficult to bridge or heal. It realized that this had happened to an earlier aspect of itself some time in a past immensely dim and distant. It had also happened to one of its ancient brethren a mere ten thousand years ago and – that event occurring during an ice age – all but one of the fragments of the mind concerned had died. The remaining fragment had then, over the intervening time, grown into the *new* mind – the youngest and most coherent of them all, and the most naïve. The one now trying to make contact.

'*What are you doing?*' was the essence of the young mind's question, though hive mind communication was not so easily amenable to human translation.

Ignoring it, the old mind considered its own future, or lack of one.

This was the way hive minds procreated: the networks of hives grew large and unwieldy, began to divide, as did the consciousness that spread across them, those portions of consciousness warring with each other as they sought self-definition, *ego*. In any other time the mind would have had to accept the death of self, but now it seemed the humans and their technologies offered alternatives. But were they real? Only just managing to still hold itself together, the mind could not decide.

'*You cut my link. (What are you doing?) Why did you cut my link? (What are you doing?)*' The younger mind was growing more insistent; linking itself closer in through the gaps growing in the old mind.

'*Stop interfering. Go away.*'

But the young mind kept asking questions – kept probing. The old mind tried to shut out the babble as it again returned to introspection.

If it loaded itself to crystal, memcorded itself, would it truly continue? Even humans, whose technology this was, were undecided. The reifications were a prime example of this indecision. They believed the body sacred, and that there could be no real life without it. They claimed their cult was not a religion, for they did not believe in souls or an afterlife, yet the foundation of their cult was just as irrational. The mind itself badly wanted to live, but was now truly divided over the issue: both accepting the inevitability of physical death and wanting to load to crystal, yet not accepting Death in any form. The latter attitude arose from the more physical aspect of it, and the most visceral and emotional. Reality did not impinge one wit. That part of the mind railed against Death, wanted to bring it down and sting it into oblivion. It viewed Death as some entity that needed to be fought, as a personification like the Grim Reaper which, if defeated, would remove any ending to life. That part was insane, but nevertheless its presence deadlocked the mind's more logical side. Internalized, the dispute would not end, would only become the source of a greater splitting of the mind's mentality.

'*I know you're going after sprine. You'll get yourself killed, then the AIs will restrict us further.*'

Despite its concerns for its own mortality, this evinced amusement in the old mind.

'*Naïve,*' it told the other.

'*No, just not senile,*' the youngster spat back.

The old mind's amusement grew.

'*Don't do this. Recall your agent,*' the young mind begged.

The old mind groped for internal perception, located some information in partially dislocated memory, and showed reams of code to the younger mind.

'*What? What?*'

'*Child, it is the genome of the Spatterjay leech.*'

The young mind retreated in confusion: '*(What are you doing?) (What are you doing?)*'

Amusement faded as the old mind perceived how very little time it had left. Isolating its less sane aspects had accelerated the process of its internal division elsewhere. And loading itself to crystal in its present state would not halt that process, for it would merely then be mirrored in crystal. It needed instead the schematic for sanity that could only be created quickly enough in the faster outside world. The two recordings – one of this self and one of the isolated self – must clearly find that schematic soon. It was unfortunate that the less sane self, which had departed first, still believed it possible to kill Death, and had created the means . . .

7

Hammer Whelks:
the hammer whelk is close kin to the frog whelk, but is also its
chief predator. Like their kin, the large adult hammer whelks
breed in the ocean trenches, releasing eggs to float up to the
surface and hatch. The baby whelks, washed inshore, settle in
island waters and congregate in packs. Physically, hammer
whelks differ from frog whelks in two main respects. Their
single foot, rather than used for leaping, terminates in a large
bony hammer used for smashing shell, and they possess a
tubular sucker for capturing prey. Their mouths are equally as
nightmarish. Every year they decimate the frog whelk pere-
grination out to the depths, but, just as the frog whelks are
vulnerable to the hammers, the hammer whelks themselves
are vulnerable to the crushing jaws of the rhinoworm –

The day was growing oppressive, cloud hanging in a jade
ceiling above them, as threatening in its aspect as was
the reality of life aboard the *Vignette*.

'They're all lash-happy,' said Silister, leaning over to
whisper into Davy-bronte's ear. 'Take that Drooble.' He
nodded towards the foremast where the man named was
tied, the wounds in his back already healing after the

thrashing Orbus had earlier given him. 'Orbus flogged him three times on that last trip, and I heard he has keel-hauled him twice before that.'

'Keep your voice down, *and* your head down,' said Davy-bronte. 'With luck we can jump ship at the Sargassum – get some other Captain to take us on.'

Silister eyed his companion. 'We should have left with the rest of them.'

'Yeah, but we were greedy and foolish.'

'We weren't greedy. We wanted what was owed us.' Silister winced as he said it. Orbus had fed them enough seacane rum to pickle a rhinoworm, then brought them aboard on the pretext of finding them their wages, where he commenced being profligate with even more rum. The next thing they knew they were waking up from a drunken coma with the *Vignette* out of sight of any port. 'You realize we're the only normal ones aboard,' he added.

Davy-bronte nodded as he continued working the caulking between the planks of the ship's lifeboat. This had been their only chance to talk openly for some time: alone here in the lifeboat hanging, horizontal, from its davits over the side of the ship. Silister had tried bringing up the subject below decks once, then quickly mumbled off into silence. It was only then he had realized all the other Hoopers aboard with them were in love with pain. They were all much older than himself and Davy-bronte, and all bore that certain glassy look in their eyes.

'Are you two done in there yet!' Orbus bellowed from his chair up on the bridge.

'Nearly finished, Cap'n!' Davy-bronte called.

'So you'll not be needing a little motivation?'

'No thank you, Captain Orbus,' said Davy-bronte, glancing at Silister with his expression unreadable.

Silister swallowed dryly, and wondered how much longer he could contain his anger. He reached out and ran his tar-smeared fingers down the blade of the panga he had brought into the lifeboat with him. 'No way, absolutely no way at all is he going to put me up against that fucking mast.' But even as he said it he knew it was a promise he could not fulfil. Orbus could break him like a twig, and for that matter so could any other member of this older crew.

Davy-bronte nodded, then reached inside his shirt to pull free and partially reveal the weapon he carried.

'Hell,' said Silister, 'where did you get that from?'

'Cost me all my savings, plus a loan from Olian's I'll be paying off for a few years yet.' Davy-bronte pushed the quantum cascade laser back out of sight.

Suddenly Silister found hope. Maybe they might be able to get out of this.

'Aw, not you again. Bugger off!' yelled Orbus, then anything further he said was drowned out by a loud roar.

The two juniors looked across into a blast of spray blowing over the ship as if a squall had just hit. A flattened ovoid, four metres across, was rising out of the sea on turbines. It was fashioned of brassy metal bloomed with the marks of heat treatment, and streaked with weedy growths and rashes of orange barnacles. It seemed a patchwork of old and new, for gleaming armour abutted old tarnished surfaces. Deep in dark hollows all about it, red lights glinted. From other hollows protruded the barrels and launch tubes of various weapons.

Davy-bronte grabbed the back of Silister's shirt and

hauled him down. Cupping a hand around his friend's ear he hissed, 'No way is that thing from the Polity!'

'Now I said bugger off!' Orbus bellowed, standing firm.

'Is he blind?' Silister asked.

The thing revolved slightly, as if scanning down the length of the ship. One square indentation in its surface widened like a camera shutter, and extruded a square tube. The huge drone rose higher and Silister saw that underneath it trailed a large net bag fashioned from cable. He glanced aside and saw Davy-bronte gripping the butt of his QC laser, but thought that a pointless gesture. He felt this confirmed when the drone folded out two large gleaming claws – evidently a new addition – from its surface, leaving claw-shaped recesses behind. It drifted to the bows, still kicking up spume, then swung in, crushing the rail and shoving the ship sideways. It reached out one claw and snipped off the foremast, then with the other claw snatched Drooble up over the stump and dropped him into the trailing bag. Shadow opened above – the sail abandoning them. Something whined and swivelled. A black line cut up from the drone. There came a flash and a dull detonation, then pieces of sail were raining down on the deck.

'Get off my fucking ship!' Orbus screamed, and began firing his pulse rifle.

The square tube extruded further and spat something trailing a line. From behind Orbus, Silister saw a harpoon punch right through the Captain's body, then open out four barbs. The huge drone reeled the bellowing Captain in, hard, smashing him through the side rail. It then tore him off the harpoon and inserted him into the same bag as Drooble. By now other crew were reacting:

one firing an old shotgun, another causing still more danger to his fellows through ricochets as he opened up with some ancient automatic weapon.

Davy-bronte began drawing his laser till Silister, panicking, grabbed his arm.

'We've only got one chance.' Davy-bronte pointed at the davit rope nearest to Silister. 'On my signal, you cut that one!'

It took a moment for Silister to grasp what his companion intended, then he understood. Releasing Davy-bronte's arm he took up his panga and turned to the rope nearest to him.

'Now!' commanded Davy-bronte, aiming and firing his laser.

With his panga, Silister chopped straight through his rope. Davy-bronte's laser cut slower, so the lifeboat fell at forty-five degrees down the side of the ship into the sea, but fortunately the bows bounced up rather than penetrated the surface. Silister was flung over the side, came up smacking his head underneath the boat, then ducked back up beside it where Davy-bronte hauled him. It had fortunately happened so fast no leeches had time to attach. The small craft was now in the lee of the ship, sheltered from the storm blast of the drone's turbines.

'Under this,' urged Davy-bronte, pulling across a tarpaulin.

'That thing'll have scanning gear.'

'Then let's hope it doesn't use it. I don't think rowing away now is going to help us.'

They hid under the tarpaulin as the courses of their boat and the *Vignette* itself slowly diverged. But the mainmast came down with a horrible crackling and splashed into the sea only metres away from them. A couple of loops of rigging hooked over their little boat, tilting it and binding it to the main ship. Over the roar of turbines, the screaming, bellowing and weapon fire continued – and now something was on fire up there. Silister listened to the metronomic regularity of the harpoon firing, then the sounds of weapons ceased. Only the turbines and the bellowing and screaming continued.

'Shit!' yelped Davy-bronte.

The huge drone was now moving around the beleaguered ship blasting a cloud of spindrift ahead of it, its cable bag packed full of the *Vignette*'s struggling and shouting crew. The drone slid above them, its turbine blast driving their small craft down and nearly swamping it, but the two crewmen lay perfectly still. It spat something that smashed through the side of the main ship and detonated. Then the drone rolled to one side and dropped down into the waves, taking its catch with it.

Silister hurled back the tarpaulin and brought his panga slicing down on the rigging that was dragging them down. Davy-bronte immediately started bailing with just his hands.

'No antigravity – so it didn't want the Warden to detect it,' remarked Silister, shakily, then turned to help his friend with the bailing.

Waves of steam fogged over them as the *Vignette* quenched its fire in the sea. By the time they were sure their own boat would not sink, the ship had gone under.

An iron-coloured seahorse with topaz eyes unwound its bifurcated tail from its roost in a peartrunk tree, turned and drifted gently away through the foliage. SM13's instinct had been to immediately contact the Warden and spill everything it had seen and all it thought might have happened here. However, Thirteen was now a free drone and no longer under orders to report such things to its master, and was currently on an Out-Polity world where there was no legal requirement to inform any authorities of possibly nefarious doings. The drone did feel some moral obligation to report, but not because of what had happened to some reifications or to the Batians. The former were no more dead than they had been before, and for the latter death was an occupational hazard. No, the little drone felt obliged to report because five Hoopers had died.

Thirteen drifted down to a level where the foliage was not so thick, then followed a path between globular scabrous peartrunks from which bark had been ripped so that now green sap oozed out like engine oil. On the other hand, reporting those deaths would not help the dead . . . Thirteen bobbed in the air – the only outward expression of the frustration the little drone was feeling. Really, the presence of a hostile alien life form on Spatterjay did come somewhere within the Warden's remit, even though it was no longer Thirteen's responsibility to report it. The little drone just feared contacting the Warden because, even though now a free drone, Thirteen still feared subsumption. Eventually it braced itself and opened a channel. The reply was immediate.

'What is it, Thirteen?' the Warden asked.

Thirteen transmitted a copy of the image file recorded last night, and waited.

'I am aware of the hooder's presence, but wonder why it should be my concern?'

'I just thought you'd better know,' said Thirteen grudgingly.

'I know. The creature was transported here in the cargo aboard the *Gurnard*. That ship is a free trader and so the Polity has no responsibility for its cargo.'

'I thought . . . alien life forms down here . . .'

'The hooder is merely a dangerous animal. If I took responsibility for every dangerous animal on the surface of Spatterjay I would probably need a couple of SMs down there covering every square kilometre of land and every cubic kilometre of sea.'

'What about the Prador when it came?'

'Do you need a lecture in precisely what comes within a Warden's remit?'

'Perhaps I do.'

'The relevant sections stipulate that I am to watch for anything representing a danger or a potential danger to the Polity, and I am empowered to intervene when any such danger generally threatens the population or the biosphere of Spatterjay, but especially when caused by anything proceeding from the Polity itself. The Prador, Ebulan, fell under both sections.'

'Ebulan came from the Prador Third Kingdom.'

'Then the danger he represented was general and not especial.'

'Seems a bit specious.'

There came a long pause from the Warden, then, 'I could stretch the terms of my remit and interfere, but I do not want to, in a situation where the danger to this small group – which they dealt with adequately enough – was brought on by themselves.'

'And the Hoopers?'

'Unfortunate, but I cannot take responsibility for the individual lives of any who are not citizens of the Polity.'

Feeling a sudden daring, Thirteen said, 'You've changed.'

Again that long pause, then, 'I may send Sniper, when he is available.'

'Sniper? What's Sniper doing?'

The communication link cut and now, as well as being free, Thirteen realized it was completely out of the circuit. Perhaps this was why drones like Sniper sought employment with AIs like the Warden. Independence did have its drawbacks.

Eventually Thirteen dropped lower, entered an area where a stand of putrephallus plants had been crushed, and viewed the discarded dead segment of hooder lying on the plant's stinking phallic bed, then it slowly turned in mid-air. This was where the drone had tracked the hooder to last night, before returning to the compound. The creature had been moving very slowly, and because of its starveling condition and the damage inflicted on it by the APW, the drone had not thought it would be going much further for a while. It was gone now, however. Thirteen rose up from the trees, turned on all its scanning gear, and began to search.

You've changed. The Warden came at that statement from every angle. It was specific enough to be worrying, yet vague enough that no clear confirmation seemed possible. The AI ran diagnostic programs through itself, ran system comparisons between its backup memories and present attitudes. There seemed a vague indication that it had returned to an earlier mindset in which it more closely adhered to its Polity remit, and was generally

more circumspect. This could have been caused by the
compression process it had undergone to escape being
subsumed by the drone, Sniper. That had certainly been
hurried, after the shock of discovering the ancient war
drone possessed a larger and more powerful mentality
than itself – built upon the foundation of a life centuries
long. Perhaps that was the problem: the whole experience had been humbling. However, a further possibility
was that Thirteen's own perception had changed:
becoming a free drone could prove both an illuminating
and frightening transformation.

'Yes, what is it, Seven?'

The submind had been trying to attract the Warden's
attention for some microseconds.

'Captain Sprage, boss. He's opened a channel up here
again through that conferencing link of his.'

'Then you can again inform the Captain that whilst
Erlin Taser Three Indomial is a valued Polity citizen, her
stepping outside the Line and putting herself in danger
is none of my concern. And, Seven, I am not your
"boss". I am the Polity Warden of Spatterjay.' As the
Warden finished speaking, it felt something akin to a
flush of embarrassment. *Would I have said something like
that before?*

'He's not calling about that. He's calling about a
missing ship.'

'That happens. Again, it is not my concern.'

'But . . . Warden, he's got some coordinates from the
point where the conferencing link to the *Vignette* went
offline. He's very concerned about it, but only wants to
know if you might have seen anything with any of your
eyes.'

The Warden did a fast scan through its Polity remit

and found that this situation fell in one of those grey
areas. Though this might concern only the loss of a few
individuals, it had been communicated to the AI via one
of the sort-of rulers of the human population here, and
so might pertain to something important.

'Very well.'

Seven transmitted the coordinates and the precise
time when the link went off. The Warden scanned the
memory of the satellite eye concerned – it was memory
they held for a few days before deleting. The coordinates
centred on a cloud mass, which immediately aroused the
AI's suspicions – if anyone wanted to hide their actions
from it, they would perform them underneath such a
mass. Searching through the range of the eye's scan, the
AI found very little until moving into infrared. There –
the vague blob of the ship, an explosion then a fire, then
the heat flickering out, along with that blob itself, as
the ship no doubt sank. An accident? Hoopers were not
particularly prone to them, though they did carry gun-
powder, explosives and sometimes Polity weapons
aboard. Moreover, the *Vignette*'s record was not a good
one. The Warden ruminated over the response it would
give, before reluctantly packaging the relevant information and transmitting it.

'Sniper, check this out will you,' the AI also sent –
then fretted that it might be sending napalm to put out
a fire.

The industry of the Golem and other Cybercorp
machines was fast and frightening. Ron had earlier
expressed an interest in being involved in the construction, but Bloc had told him no humans were allowed on
site – it was just too dangerous for them. As he saw a

skeletal Golem rush past with a ten-metre beam on its shoulder, halt abruptly, spin the beam round then throw it up through a gap in the hull planking, Janer now understood why. A moment's inattention might result in a human ending up smeared into the woodwork.

'You note, they are not only using wood,' said Wade, pointing through the perimeter fence.

Janer scanned the site, noting composite beams resting on a row of trestles nearby. A spiderlike robot was hauling a sheet of some sort of metal up the side of the ship. The huge rudder, which even now was being swung into place and hung from a crane located on the deck above, bore the logo of a company Janer knew specialized in the production of bubble-metals – alloys foamed with inert gas and cast in zero-G so the bubbles remained evenly dispersed. The air around him was also redolent with the smell of fast-bonding epoxies.

'Not a nail in sight,' he commented.

'Even Hoopers don't use nails in the construction of their ships,' said Wade, turning to walk along the perimeter. 'They use pegs and dovetails and mortise joints, and that has not changed even since abundant metals have become available to them.'

'You know about shipbuilding?' Janer asked.

'That's just plain woodworking I'm talking about. However,' Wade tapped his own forehead, 'I have recently loaded much about the craft.'

Janer paused to consider that. Humans could load information directly into their minds, but to do it they required some kind of hardware in their heads. The process was very much easier for Golem. Just in this short walk down from the compound, Janer had almost forgotten what Wade actually was.

'Why are you here?' he asked.

'Why are *you*?' Wade countered, studying him. He then went on, 'I'm a free Golem, I go where the interest takes me . . . Now, that looks like a weak point.' Wade pointed, and it took Janer a second to realize the Golem was indicating at a join in the fence beside one of the pearwood posts.

'Yes . . . ?' said Janer cautiously.

Wade gave him an unreadable look, reached out and shoved his fingers through the fence mesh. Janer smelt hot ozone, then Wade pulled, and, sparking and crackling, the fence parted.

'See, shoddy workmanship,' said Wade. 'Shall we?' He gestured through.

It was certainly dangerous in there, but Janer had always found that avoiding danger usually resulted in danger blindsiding him. Anyway, he was already bored with the prospect of sitting around with the rest of the Hoopers, seeing if it was possible to drink the rum as fast as Forlam could distil it, for they seemed intent on doing little else. That was, he realized, a sign of them having accepted immortality: they were able to be still for long periods. He was not.

'Okay,' he said, ducking in ahead of Wade.

The Golem soon overtook him and led the way into the site. Janer hung back for a moment.

'*You still gone?*'

No response from the hivelink. He quickly caught up with Wade.

Now, drawing closer to the big ship, Janer began to get a better impression of its sheer scale. The side of it was like a cliff ahead of him; its bows rested on the beach and its stern abutted the first slopes ascending to the peak at the centre of Mortuary Island.

'How are they going to launch it?' he asked.

Wade pointed to the bottom of the hull, which was largely concealed by construction materials and machinery. 'There's a ramp under there, and a few hundred motorized pallets on which they laid the keel.'

As they passed a stack of timber, Janer peered through a gap to see the gleam of a metal caterpillar track in the undershadows. They moved on past an open container half-filled with pipe fittings and prosaically domestic plumbing items. Another container just behind it contained electrical equipment and next to this rested a half-used reel of insulated and combined five-core S-con and fibre-optic cable. Seeing such standard items here was a bit of a disappointment to Janer – until Wade gestured to something on the hull itself.

'I knew it would be here,' said the Golem.

In the side of the ship was a large open portal containing the kind of iris door more commonly found on space stations. It would be submerged, Janer realized, below the waterline. As they drew closer he saw that inside, resting on a ramp leading to this door, was the flattened-torpedo shape of a large submersible. Around the door itself were the familiar arc-shaped sections of black metal that were the business end of a shimmer-shield generator. Of course a shimmer-shield was perfect for this, since it could let the craft out without letting the water in.

'Not quite what I would have expected,' he said.

'To the letter of Windcheater's laws, though not exactly in the spirit of them,' explained Wade. 'That sail wants only sailing ships on the surface of the ocean, and no AG vehicles at all in the sky, but no other technologies have been proscribed.'

'Why do they need this, anyway?' Janer wondered.

'That'll be Lineworld Developments. No doubt they originally had some profitable enterprise in mind.' Wade shrugged. 'Of course they'll not be pursuing it now.'

Just then a paint-bespattered skeletal Golem stepped in front of them.

'You should not be here,' it said. 'It is unsafe.'

Wade ignored it, just walking on past.

'Yeah, you're telling me,' said Janer, following his new friend.

Someone hammered him hard on the back, and Orbus responded by spewing the sea water from his lungs and taking his first shuddering breath of frigid stinking air. He opened his eyes and immediately wished he had stayed drowned, but that was unfortunately an impossibility for any Hooper over a century in age.

'This is not a nice place,' said Drooble, going on to smack his fist against the chest of another crewman to bring him ungently back to consciousness.

There were ten of them confined in the dank space. The cable bag was now hanging from one weed-covered wall which seemed to be scaled with rough slabs of metal. Orbus guessed that one of the crew had broken the frayed strand he could see, to spill them all out on the floor. Certainly their captor or captors would not have thought to free them, for Orbus recognized, from old memory, what this place was.

He had been only fifty years old when the Prador had seized Imbretus Station and herded human captives aboard their ship, before targeting the station's reactors

with particle beams to leave it a spreading cloud of
debris and incandescent gas. The brutality and horror
of the ensuing journey was not so clear in his memory,
though he did know that he had done terrible things in
order to be one of the few survivors to reach Spatterjay.
But once on the planet he now called home, he clearly
remembered being made to walk through tanks of
leeches to ensure infection by their virus, just as he still
felt the shame of how he avoided coring by being ready
to play an active part in the sinister games of the
Eight . . .

Orbus stood up, a little shakily, and probed the rip
across the front of his plasmesh shirt. The harpoon
wound was sealed now – just a star-shaped indentation
in his solar plexus. He felt around his back and ran his
fingers over lumpy nuggets of scar tissue. He was starv-
ing – injury hunger. The others, similarly injured, would
feel the same. Drooble had probably been one of the
first to rouse, because the drone had captured him without harpooning, his only injuries being those Orbus
inflicted earlier with a lash because of the man's disobe-
dience – and the drowning, of course. The Old Captain
looked around. Most of his crew did not look so good.
They had bled, and some of their wounds were still raw
and red. One of them remained unconscious despite
Drooble's pummelling, and all of them appeared thinner. Their skin was now blue, but not with cold.

'Well, Cap'n, what do you reckon?' Drooble asked.

Orbus reckoned that his own brain had not been
working right for a large portion of a thousand years.
The other Captains were right: there was something
wrong with him. He must have been mad not to have
recognized a Prador war drone the instant he set eyes on

it. But then, even if he had, what more could he have done?

'I reckon we're fucked,' said Captain Orbus.

Drooble turned and gazed at him. 'No shit?'

It was a typically provocative response from a crewman who enjoyed being punished, but Orbus felt too weary to respond to it.

'If Prador take prisoners, it's for one of two purposes,' he said. 'That means we're either to be the main course, or we're going to be cored and thralled.'

'Prador?' someone murmured incredulously.

'You want pain, Drooble?' Orbus asked. 'Well you're going to find more of it here than you'd ever think possible.'

As if to emphasize his words there came a crack from behind him. Orbus stared at Drooble, saw the horrible avidity in his expression, and wished he felt the same inclinations, but for a sadist pain only holds any attraction when it is someone else's. He turned and eyed the wide door constructed for a shape that certainly was not human. It had split diagonally and now the two halves of it were revolving in opposite directions into the uneven wall. He stepped back amongst his men, noting they possessed the same avidity as Drooble, yet with some hint of doubt. Perhaps their wiring was not quite so twisted as his.

Then it came through the door and Orbus could not help but gape. This was no Prador he knew. It was fully limbed, like an adolescent, but no adolescent grew to this size. This one was black rather than the lurid purples and yellows of that kind. Its main body was no thicker than its vicious claws; its visual turret, palp eyes and underslung mouthparts had detached and risen higher on a corded neck, which seemed to be in the process of growing ringed plates of armour. Orbus slid a hand down to his belt, found the handle of his skinning knife and gripped it. He would go for the neck; that seemed the most vulnerable part.

'If we all go for it at once, we might be able to bring it down,' he hissed.

No reaction for a moment, then Drooble stepped forwards. The distorted Prador reached out almost gently, and closed its claw around the man's waist. Drooble gasped as the pressure came on. It merely picked him up and backed to the door.

'We should attack it, all of us together,' repeated Orbus, stepping forward.

But not one of them moved with him.

He turned to them. 'We'll die here!' he said urgently.

They just stared at him glassy-eyed, then turned away as behind him the door swiftly ground shut.

Perhaps they had found something more alluring than him.

Ambel was quite puzzled, and beginning to feel a little annoyed. They had sighted three turbul shoals over the last few days, then moved the *Treader* to intercept them, and on every occasion the shoals had veered aside.

'That's bloody odd,' said Peck. He was standing with his bait plug cutter in one hand and his new boat line in the other. The line and related equipment was of Polity manufacture: braided monofilament with a breaking strain of tonnes, ceramo-carbide hooks, an electric reel powered by a laminar battery which in turn could be recharged by sunlight, attached to a stubby fishing rod with a big solid rubber-grip handle. Peck had been wanting to try out his new toy for a long time, but it seemed rather excessive to use it just for catching apple-sized boxies.

Ambel slapped him on the shoulder. 'Never mind, we'll hit some of the lads soon.'

Even so, Ambel could not understand why the three turbul shoals had turned away like that, Were they learning to avoid Hooper ships? He had heard nothing of it. Or was there something leaking down in the hold, causing some scent to emanate through the hull and put them off.

'Just keep an eye out. I'm going to check below.'

Ambel headed for the ladder leading into the hold itself, climbed down inside and looked around. When he thought about it, there was not much on board that would put off turbul. Most of the stores here would do just the opposite. Maybe leech bile, but he had none of that, as he had refined it during the journey so as to take only a yield of pure sprine to Olian's. And, anyway, having just come from there . . . Perhaps there was something else he had missed? Just then, while he was puzzling, there came a loud thump against the hull.

'Turbul! Turbul! They're coming under!' came Peck's excited cry.

Ambel rushed back on deck as his crew began casting their lines. Anne was the first to hook one, and pulled up a two-metre-long specimen with a shiny tubular body, randomly spaced blue fins, caiman head and whiplike tail ending in a hatchet fin. She snatched her hook from its jaws, and it landed thumping on the deck. With an apologetic look she kicked it sliding and struggling across to Ambel, as he was the one who always dealt with anything this large. He stamped his foot on its lashing tail, clamped its jaws shut in his right hand, then placed his left hand behind its head. Releasing the tail he pulled with his right and pushed with his left. With a sucking crunch the head came out half a metre, the fins disappearing into its body. He heaved again, and the quivering tube of flesh slid off across the deck, so he was left holding the head, the long spine and attached bag of internal organs. From the spine, fins sticking out all round at the end of jointed bones flicked and quivered, and at the opposite end the tail still thrashed. He cast this remnant over the side and watched it swim away, while the rest of the crew continued pulling in more of these piscine creatures, but smaller ones. The shoal, he saw, was heading under the ship then turning abruptly away to port. Something was definitely spooking them. Perhaps there was a big deep-sea heirodont somewhere nearby, which accounted for the behaviour of the previous shoals? But he dismissed this thought as he baited his hook with a plug of rhinoworm steak, cast his line, and immediately hooked another turbul.

Soon the deck was littered with their tubular bodies and glistening with slime. Anne brought over a turbul, leech-scarred and painfully thin, which told them they were reaching the tail end of the shoal.

'Barrels and spiced vinegar,' he told her when she unhooked this sorry creature and cast it back over the side.

'Bugger me,' said Peck. 'This'n's a big bugger.'

Ambel glanced across at the crewman, who was leaning back against the pull of his line, which, now humming like a power cable, angled down at forty degrees into the sea. Peck, Ambel knew, was not exactly a weakling, so it would take a seriously large turbul to give him any trouble. He coiled his own line and moved over behind the man, while other crew members, discarding leech-hit rejects, coiled up their lines and turned to watch.

'Bugger,' said Peck again – it was his favourite word.

Ambel eyed the short composite rod, which now actually had a bend in it Peck's knuckles were white around the handle. For anyone else, Ambel would have suggested they had snagged the seabed, but Peck knew when he had a live one on, and the way the line was moving in the sea also confirmed this.

'You might have hooked a heirodont,' Ambel suggested.

Peck was now beginning to slide against his will towards the rail. Ambel stepped forwards and hooked an arm around his waist.

'Not . . . getting me bloody . . . tackle.'

Peck's torso was as rigid as stone, and even Ambel had to strain to prevent him going over the side. A turbul body slid down against his feet, then another one. The deck was tilting.

'Any suggestions?' Ambel asked generally.

'Switch . . . on the side . . .'

Ambel peered round at the reel. There were three switches there. Suddenly the line cut round to the stern of the *Treader*. As it chopped into the rail, Sild threw himself sideways to avoid being decapitated. Then the line began to drag down, till it was cutting into the deck. Ambel had visions of it going through the ship like a cheese wire. He reached round and clicked a switch.

'No . . . that one!'

The reel started droning, pulling them towards the edge, their boots tearing up splinters from the deck.

Boris grabbed the back of Ambel's belt and held on, but found he was being dragged along as well. Ambel reached out and clicked another switch. The sound was a kind of slither; that of a very sharp knife cut hard through air. The three men collapsed in a heap as the tension abruptly came off.

Peck was the first to his feet. 'Breaks the line where it's weakest,' he explained.

Ambel stood and eyed the man's new fishing gear, wondering if he would be wise to throw it over the side right then.

'Fuck me,' said Boris.

They turned to look at him and he held up the stump of his hand. His fingers were lying scattered on the deck at his feet.

'Peck, fetch your needle, lad,' said Ambel mildly. 'Then I think we're going to have a little chat.'

With the tip of one finger Erlin probed the end of her tongue, and was sure she could feel a hollow developing there. She had been well supplied with dome-grown food upon her arrival at the island, but in the last few months had needed to eke that out. Now that she had none to eat, the Spatterjay viral mutation seemed to be trying to make up lost ground. Perhaps, she speculated, it was this that also seemed to be altering her perception? No, she decided, things only looked different because she was far from any regions she had previously explored with Ambel aboard the *Treader*.

This island was recently volcanic, in geological terms: basalt guts running in a highway down from the classically shaped volcano behind her and spearing out to sea to form a natural jetty. The end of this promontory was occupied by a cluster of frog whelks, like a flock of sheep driven to the sea's edge. From what she could see at this distance, they were of a different variety from any she had encountered before: their shells were squatter in shape and the two yellows of old butter. The rise and fall of the waves along the stone perimeter also occasionally revealed the three larger hammer whelks creeping up on them. These were also different: more streamlined, their shells tilted backwards and wide and flat on top, like Nefertiti's headdress. But then Erlin had been rudely awakened to the fact that she had not yet seen, in the flesh, all the whelks that Spatterjay offered.

'It's very different here,' she commented, as she drew out her meal of rhinoworm meat. Perhaps she did not need to do this, as Huff, Puff and Zephyr seemed equally as interested in the drama unfolding on the promontory.

'It is catalogued,' Zephyr replied.

'Really?' she replied.

'The Warden now back in charge has spent many years using its subminds to study this planet thoroughly. Probably a necessary diversion.'

'From what?'

The Golem sail looped its neck round and down so its head came level with hers. 'From its very limited duties here. It is a runcible AI, with the capacity for governing a high-tech, civilized planet, yet it here only possesses limited power to intercede in matters beyond the Line. That is something Polity citizens arriving here tend to forget.'

Erlin merely grunted, and continued chewing on her meat. She then turned her gaze inland to where the dingle was swamping the old volcanic outflow. The peartrunk trees there were lower than usual, their trunks standing like the open cageworks of mangroves. Further inland grew yanwoods, and scattered amid them were trees resembling pines. On the beach, which seemed comprised of obsidian fragments, a couple of small armadillo-like heirodonts were snuffling about. Erlin finally returned her attention to the whelks.

The hammer whelks had nearly reached their prey, and were now poised on the ledge below them. The attack was fast. All three whelks flicked upright, at the perimeter of the frog whelk cluster, everting their tubular suckers. Immediately the frog whelks exploded from the stone, each propelled high in the air by its single powerful foot and splashing into the sea all around. All but three of them. The hammer whelks flowed over their victims, extruded their bone-tipped hammer feet and began working on them like a team of blacksmiths. Scattering fragments of shell around like broken crockery, they soon exposed the meat they sought. But then one of the de-shelled frog whelks escaped, bouncing along the promontory, a glob of pink flesh shaped like an inverted carrot with two eye-stalks above and one cantilevered foot below. Puff launched and, with a couple of flaps, was soon directly above the fugitive. Noticing the sail, the denuded whelk tried to leap into the sea, but Puff snatched it in mid-air and quickly chomped it down. That was perhaps merciful, since it would never have survived without its shell, and its death would have been slower in the sea. Erlin returned her attention to the others. Two of the hammer whelks were now fighting over a single frog whelk, whilst the third hammer whelk dragged its own catch out of range. The two contestants tore their victim apart between them, then seemed content with their separate spoils.

'It is all the time. Everywhere . . .' said Zephyr, gazing with what Erlin thought was a peculiar intensity towards the whelks.

'What is?' she asked.

'They are not alive,' said Zephyr, turning to her.

'Of course they are.' Erlin shrugged. 'Well in some cases not any more.'

'Dead?' Zephyr asked, something leaden and weird in his voice.

'Well that's the way it goes.'

'Time we moved on,' said Zephyr.

Erlin did not bother to argue. She stood and turned her back to Huff, who had been carrying her for some time now, but it was Zephyr who grabbed the handle protruding from the harness she wore and hauled her into the sky. Perhaps Huff had grown tired of her chattering. As she was carried back over the island, Erlin stared with fascination down into the caldera. This contained a steaming lake around which a herd of half-seen somethings were moving. Then, in the ocean extending beyond the other side of the island she saw huge floating plants much like water lilies. Large pale blue blossoms floated on the surface.

'Look, flowers,' said Erlin, continuing to munch on the steak she had retained. When she finally finished it, and licked her fingers clean, she saw that her digits had become much the same blue as the blossoms below, and acknowledged that maybe Zephyr was carrying her because he was the only one safe in doing so now.

'Lilies,' said Zephyr. 'Of course.'

The giant whelk closely focused one of her dinner-plate eyes on the ceramo-carbide hook embedded in the tip of her tentacle. The thing had actually ripped through her flesh; nothing else had caused her such damage in a very long time. This only made her angrier, as certainly this hook, and its ten metres of line attached, had come from the ship above her. She had seen turbul being hauled up there and in all the excitement had tried grabbing one. Big mistake. She then recalled other injuries she had suffered: memories reawakened in the newly functioning lobes of her brain.

The brood comprising herself and her siblings had been large, but over the years had been whittled down. Initially, nearly all the other denizens of the ocean had presented a problem to them. Leeches, given the opportunity, would snatch plugs of flesh; prill often planed through to scythe off the occasional tentacle of the unwary. She herself had lost a tentacle that way, but soon regrew it. Turbul took half their number, avoiding only those whose shells had hardened sufficiently, like her own. Glister ambushes took her kin, but only when the parent went off to feed its gargantuan appetite. One once attacked her, too, but had been unable to dislodge her. Then, beginning their long migration into the depths, they began to mature and grow stronger. In time her own skin became too tough for leeches to penetrate, and her shell too hard for turbul to crack. Only larger prill and glisters managed to snatch away the odd tentacle, but that soon became a dangerous option for them, as even they eventually became prey for herself and her kin. But deeper down the brood soon learnt that there were other, larger predators.

A monstrous heirodont had assailed and crunched

down many of them before the parent attacked it. The
giant whelk remembered that battle, remembered hiding
in a crevice with her shell broken and ichor leaking out
around her, attracting prill. She remembered the death
screams, then a long silence before finally her parent's
shell tumbled down the slope past her, utterly cleaned
out. She stayed in the crevice until her own shell healed,
feeding on anything that got close enough. Then she
emerged and dragged herself down to rejoin her own
kind below.

The giant whelk again studied the hook and saw that
quickly forming scar tissue had sealed it in place.
Whipping her tentacle back she observed the line loop-
ing above her. Different movements of her tentacle
caused changing patterns in the line: there a sine wave
travelling its length, and there an endlessly revolving
coil. These patterns pleased her, and rather than tear the
hook out, she drew the line back and wrapped it around
her tentacle.

8

Packetworms:
these segmented worms obtain most of their nutrition by bor-
ing through compacted mud layers and sedimentary rock. It
is theorized that the evolutionary pressures driving them into
this lifestyle were in force before the rise of the leeches. A bil-
lion years ago, after five billion years of competitive evolution
and no mass extinctions, Spatterjay was seemingly over-
burdened with life, resulting in every possible niche being
competed for and exploited. Few people have actually seen
living specimens of this creature, its home environment being
far below the seabed, but they do make their presence known.
The casts they throw up – of ground rock, calcined limestone
and clay – are of a similar composition to cement, and set as
hard. And since some packetworms grow to two metres wide
and fifty long, those worm casts can be large enough to
protrude from the ocean surface. Their almost cubic con-
figuration has in the past caused them to be mistaken for the
ruined buildings of some alien race, and they form the foun-
dations of many atolls and even some islands on Spatterjay.
The packet-worm's physical biology, working five degrees
hotter than that of most other native forms, and being highly
acidic, is inimical to the Spatterjay virus –

The SMs numbered six to ten, in their standard format geosurvey shells, were not built for speed as that was not necessary for them to catch or escape rocks. Each of them measured two metres from top to base, and about a metre wide. If they bore a resemblance to anything, it was, with numerous blocky additions, to ancient paraffin tilley lamps sprayed sky green. They were also now devoid of the 'attitude' program they had run while occupying enforcer shells and attacking the Prador ship ten years ago. They were also unarmed.

'Okay, you lot,' Sniper addressed them. 'Keep searching for that Golem. I'll get back to you.'

'Yes, Sniper,' they all replied at once.

'Eleven, Twelve, you're with me,' Sniper then sent.

SM12 had been the Warden's lieutenant during that crucial battle a decade earlier, and though being physically destroyed, had yet managed to upload from its cockleshell drone body. When Sniper displaced the Warden he did not subsume the surviving SMs, but allowed them to choose their own course. Twelve opted for a new body much like its previous one, but a scallop shell this time, two metres across. Eleven, having missed all the action while acting as a signal-relay station, decided on a drone shell made in the mythical dolphin shape more commonly seen as a door knocker than in any ocean, but one two metres long. Both of them were armed with needle rail-guns and lasers, both of them possessed fusion boosters, and both of them had loaded a slightly adjusted version of 'attitude'.

Sniper turned in mid-air, watching the drones approach. Twelve had opened his shell to fold out two boosters, and was hammering towards him rearwards. Eleven's booster was positioned with anatomical humour.

Sniper transmitted coordinates to them, then accelerated, and the drones adjusted their course to match his.

'Problem, boss?' asked Eleven.

'Seems the *Vignette* might have burned and sunk,' said Sniper.

'Could we be the cause?' asked Twelve. 'That Captain did seem to resent us, and his crew weren't in any hurry to cut him down.'

'Maybe we were the catalyst,' Sniper allowed. 'That's what we'll find out.'

As they hurtled across the sky, Sniper transmitted to them all that the Warden had sent him.

'Underneath thick cloud,' Twelve mused. 'It would be interesting to find out how many other ships have been in a similar position recently.'

'I did check,' said Sniper.

'How many?' asked Eleven.

'None,' Sniper replied.

Within an hour they were hovering over the sea twenty kilometres east of the last known coordinates of the *Vignette*. The cloud was dispersed now, and the sun a watery green eye above them.

'Why here?' asked Eleven.

'The bottom's two kilometres down and the current easterly,' Sniper said. 'The ship ain't going to be directly below where it sank. Can you both pressure seal?'

'Can do,' said Eleven.

'It was how I was designed before, and how I am designed now,' said Twelve.

The three of them dropped towards the waves.

'We'll use U-space com. Stay alert, and keep all your detectors at maximum range,' Sniper ordered, just as all three of them splashed down.

They stabbed into the sea, punching white-water trails like icicles, then allowed themselves to drift and sink with the current. Sniper scanned the other two, to witness Twelve retracting its boosters, and Eleven becoming stone rigid. Both of them would be filling their interstices with crash foam and adjusting other internal structures to withstand the pressure. The old war drone himself briefly tested his underwater tractor drive, and left his ports open to the water. He was itching for an excuse to use his supercavitation field, but supposed reluctantly that travelling at mach three underwater would not help him find the *Vignette* any quicker. He also opened his various weapons ports, to prevent sudden pressure inclusions should he need to shoot anything. Opening a port, with normal air pressure inside, to sea water under high pressure, was not a good idea, especially if you were in the process of trying to rapidly launch a mini torpedo. Also, the tractor drive needed its internal pressures equalized to its environment in order to function quickly and efficiently. But this was all the preparation he needed. Most of his new body was as dense as iron with very few air spaces, and his shell could take a great deal more than the water pressure he would find two kilometres down.

As the three drones descended through clear water, leeches, streaming towards them like shoals of flat eels, grated mouthparts against their armour then dropped away. When a leech the size of a small ship started to show an interest, Sniper brought to bear a device he had been anxious to try out. Loosely based on the Prador water gun, this weapon ionized and field-accelerated a jet of superheated sea water. Sniper called it his dissuader.

'Remember what the Warden said,' Twelve warned him.

'Like a few leeches less might be a problem?'

The leech came on. Underwater, its body was leaf-shaped and moved with slow undulations that swept it forward rapidly. It went for Sniper – the larger prey – its stem an extending metre-wide mouth, starting to bell out to encompass him whole. Sniper fired, and it was as if a bar of hot metal stabbed out between himself and the leech, super-heated steam exploding in enormous bubbles away from it. Where it struck, the creature's flesh just melted away in dark clouds, retreating like butter before a blow torch.

'An effective weapon,' commented Twelve.

'Now that's gotta smart!' exclaimed Eleven.

The leech coiled in on itself, globular, and began to ascend in a mass of bubbles. The three continued down.

Deeper, and leeches were now somnolent strands drifting in the water. Glisters swam here, but never too close. A shoal of boxies turned away with geometric precision, and a small heirodont flicked its vertical sharkish tail and swept past with its mandibles clattering. Distantly came the moan of one of its larger cousins. The water was murky now, but Sniper soon discerned a mountain range below them. They swept the bottom with refined sonar beams, looking for sign of the ship. Sniper identified slopes of shell scree, and some intact empty shells so large he could have motored inside them.

'I'll do a wide scan over *this* grid. You two search one of the squares starting *here*,' he sent. The drones' method of underwater locomotion consisted of squid jets, so

they would not be able to keep up even with just his tractor drive.

'No need,' said Eleven, broadcasting coordinates to
his two companions.

They scanned down where he indicated, found the
broken mast lying on one peak, then tracked a half-
kilometre slide mark down the mountainside to where
lay the ship in two halves.

'Try to find its crew – they might still be alive,' sent
Sniper.

Hoopers, he knew, might survive even this.

The two little drones circled the two separate halves
of the vessel, then entered one half each. Sniper held
back, mapping the wreckage and building three-D models in his cortex. There, he brought the two halves
together, correcting for damage obviously caused by it
striking the underwater mountain and its long slide
down here. It took him only moments to discern that
something had exploded inside it.

'No one here,' said Twelve.

'Not a single one,' added Eleven.

Sniper closed in on one half, centring himself over
where the explosion had occurred. He reached out with
a tentacle and picked up one charred pearwood beam,
then ran another tentacle over its burnt surface. The
dense sea water all around prevented him using his laser
spectrometer, so he drew in a small sample through a
microtube, up through his tentacle and inside himself to
analyse in his internal spectrometer. He removed from
the results the signature for carbonized pearwood, then
for burnt sea-gourd resin, leech and turbul ichor, and
anything else commonly found on Hooper ships. Soon
he had fined down the results to certain elements in

certain proportions. Some kind of explosive, but this told him nothing he had not already guessed. He tried another sample at a different location, while Eleven and Twelve searched the surrounding area for any stripped fish. His fifth try revealed a definite spike for an uncommon element. It was one of the exotic metals; one of those discovered by humans only after they had left the solar system, but which another race had discovered long before. Sniper recognized it instantly – enough of it having been shot at him over the years.

'Let's go,' he said. 'There'll be no survivors here.'

Having lost one claw, a few hands, a large proportion of shell and very nearly his life to an Old Captain called Drum, Vrell was bemused by the behaviour of his captives. But then perhaps this was the way all Hooper crews behaved: as meek as Prador children controlled by their father's pheromones? No, that wasn't right. Prador children were only meek towards their own father, not to some outside threat. The prisoner Captain himself was not so obliging, and had twice escaped Vrell's grasp. But why did he not order his crew to attack? It was all very strange.

Vrell had chosen to use spider thralls. He knew the danger, but the benefits of using blanks with some autonomy outweighed it. Anyway, before any of these humans rejected their thralls he would fully core them. But, right now, the first three he had enslaved he needed to immediately put to work. Thralling the others would have to wait.

The first blank he programmed to be a pilot, the second a navigator, and the third an engineer controlling below him the two blanks recently resident in the larder.

The first two now stood at the rebuilt consoles in the control section. The third waited, with patches and welders, near the ship's weak point – where it had been penetrated. Vrell himself monitored the overall systems of the ship. It was a relief to relinquish some control, yet running three more slave units shell-welded under his carapace presented different difficulties. It required a light touch and eternal vigilance. When the navigator finished mapping the hundreds of kilometres of sea-bottom between the ship's present location, just off the Seagre Islands, out to the deep Lamarck Trench, it was all Vrell could do to not interfere with that blank's plotting of an optimum course towards the trench. The navigator had already been programmed to find a route that continued as deep as possible, but high enough above major accumulations of silt so as not to disturb them unnecessarily. And when the pilot started the four big underwater turbines, Vrell let out a bubbling yelp before remembering this was all according to plan.

Via a probe floating outside, the Prador watched the ship, seen on one of the hexagonal screens before him, rise off the bottom in an explosion of silt and glittering shell. As it began sliding out towards the deeps, he observed huge funnel-headed worms exposed from underneath the hull, now retreating into their burrows. Stress readings located for him weaknesses he had earlier missed, but none of them were critical. The damage inside, mainly caused by power surges and blown generators, was not structural. In a perfect world he would have preferred to use the five gravmotors he had repaired, even though they did not function quite so well with such a mass of water above them. But that level of AG usage would immediately attract the Warden's attention.

Bringing the probe on after the ship, Vrell felt some relief when he saw the massive vessel plane out over an underwater cliff and begin to descend. Most of the detritus on the hull had been washed away now, so the trail was not so obvious. Vrell just hoped the disturbance already caused would go unnoticed, as the currents swiftly dispersed it.

Like a great marine city fashioned vaguely about the shape of a Prador's carapace (though not Vrell's own, now), the ship descended. Vrell returned the probe to its port and settled back to eye the other screens giving him outside views. There were not many seagoing leviathans nearby, they having quickly sensed something larger moving in the water. The seabed was now a wide flat plain scattered with broken shell, black bones and the occasional forest of kelp trees rising hundreds of metres tall.

Vrell spotted a large herd of whelks trundling along the bottom like an armoured division, then the open yellow vaginal splits which, when Vrell sonar-scanned them, were revealed as the mouths of massive clams. He saw prill with saucer carapaces five metres across tilting back to observe the ship, eyes running round their rims like ruby searchlights, sickle feet coiled underneath. These sprang from the bottom in a cloud of silt, and planed up like attack craft. In his sanctum Vrell heard distant clangs and scrabblings, then on a screen watched the frustrated creatures dropping away. He badly wanted to employ some of the ship's weapons against them, but again that would be too revealing.

Then, after hours of such progress, the ship reached a tributary trench leading down into the Lamarck.

It was in the vast oceanic trench lying ahead that Ebulan had originally concealed the ship, so there was the possibility that any new search for it might be directed here. However, the trench was thousands of kilometres long, and in places many kilometres deep. If he concealed the ship well, and used no traceable energy signatures, Vrell felt his chances of going undetected were good. He settled down, trying to feel some pleasure from his achievements, but that was strangely lacking. He felt a hollowness inside him, like hunger or the deprivation from some addictive substance. This feeling was certainly a result of changes the virus was making to his body – changes he needed to learn more about. Now, in this breathing space, he called up a file he had discovered earlier in his father's diverse collection. It dated back to near the end of the war when the Prador had been employing their drones and adolescents, but most importantly armies of blanks, in ground assaults against Polity worlds. Vrell had been very interested to learn that there had been other Prador infected with the virus before him. He began now to scan through the story of their catastrophic return to the Second Kingdom.

As he stood with Captain Ron and the other Hoopers, Janer surveyed the surrounding crowd, trying to ignore the occasional waft of decay that reached his nostrils. It was a convention of the living dead, and even though he had now been here for many days, he still could not get used to them.

At the forefront of the crowd, arrayed in neat ranks, were Bloc's Kladites, all in grey, their helmets and masks tucked under their arms, laser carbines slung across their backs.

Here, around him, were the other reifs. Some were clad in a mixture of fashions, as if their deaths had also frozen time for them at that point. The rest wore utile garments similar to those worn by Keech when Janer first met him, but not necessarily in boring shades of grey. Few of them displayed death wounds, as did Taylor Bloc up there on the platform, or Aesop, though some bore signs of tissue repair, or covering patches which were often ornamented. Many more were just the usual shrivelled individuals, and Janer supposed that what had killed them was either invisibly repaired or now concealed by their baroque clothing, if concealed at all. There were many routes to death that caused no visible damage to the body.

Janer returned his attention to the platform. Bloc had been going on for twenty minutes now and, after the preamble about this 'age of the Arisen' and the 'flame carried down the years', Janer had tuned him out. Aesop and Bones lurked in the background, hooded like sinister priests, and yet more Kladites stood to either side, surveying the crowd suspiciously.

'This reif is a world-class bore,' said Ron ruminatively. 'What's all that business with the bottle?'

'To launch the ship, they smash it against the hull,' Janer explained.

'Seems a criminal waste to me,' Ron opined.

Janer swung his attention to Forlam, who stood at Ron's side. The man looked not so much bored as quiescent, as if waiting for an opportunity to exercise his rather unhealthy inclinations. Wade stood with his arms folded and a look of tired patience, so again Janer had to remind himself that this was emulation, not some unconscious attitude on the Golem's part, and certainly no indication of what was going on in his mind. He turned back to Ron.

'She is certainly impressive. I suppose it would be stupid of me to ask if you'll be able to handle her?'

'Ship that big,' said Ron, 'you've just got to know how quickly you can stop it or turn it. And never forget how little it is, compared to the ocean, and how fragile compared to some rocks in that ocean.'

Janer nodded. Yes, the ship was huge and wonderfully complete, with its long blue and black hull, hundreds of square chainglass windows, its tiered decks and many other structures up there, and the forest of masts and spars above them. Things seemed quite complicated in the rigging, and he wondered how the sails would cope. Having asked, he now knew that they would not be hanging upside down, batlike, as was their custom. Nor would they be using plain muscle power to change the angle of the other fabric sails, for even they were not that strong. They would turn themselves to the wind as instructed by the helmsman, Forlam apparently, but this movement would be transferred via sensors to the relevant mast and spar motors, and cable winders. Much of their other work up there – reefing fabric sails and rigging changes – they would control through consoles mounted on the masts. There was still much for them to learn. Perhaps foremost was working with their fellows, as never before had there been more than one living sail to a ship.

'Ah, at last,' muttered Isis Wade, 'the outflow of verbal effluent comes to an end.'

'. . . so now, without any more ado, I name this ship,' Bloc announced, 'the *Sable Keech*!'

He pulled down a lever on the framework. An arm, which until then had been concealed, arced up with the bottle attached to the end, and smashed it against the hull. Immediately the grumbling of motors set up a vibration in the air, and the *Sable Keech* began to move down to the water. Peering through the crowd, Janer observed the treaded pallets running smoothly under its huge weight. As its bows touched the sea, the Hoopers all cheered, then the reifications followed suit, but that seemed to be just noise with no feeling in it. The cheers died away as the ship continued its slow progress into the waves. Soon it revealed behind it the alloy ramp, dented with the marks of pallet treads. It trailed cables being wound out from motorized reels on the deck to shore anchors. Each of the reels was manned by a skeletal Golem. Once it was fully in the water, one of these reels began winding in, pulling taut the cable to Janer's left, drawing the bows round to a predetermined position, whereupon another Golem aboard dropped an anchor. The ship turned, the stern swinging out until the vessel drew parallel to the coast. More anchors slid down. Now, the motorized pallets returned from the sea, and to Janer's surprise the ramp began to rise. It drew level, creating a jetty protruding a hundred metres out over the waves, supported underneath by rams. The end of this was only a few tens of metres from the ship itself.

'Neat,' he said.

'Golem know how to build,' said Wade.

'They had good teachers,' Janer shot back.

'You mean the AIs?'

Janer grimaced at that and made no further comment.

The Golem were now manipulating both anchor chains and shore cables to draw the ship closer to the jetty. An upper section of hull hinged out, and down, drawing a wide collapsible stair out from under the main deck and down to the jetty. It moved with the roll of the sea for a moment, until clamps folded up from underneath the jetty and crunched it into place. What struck Janer here was the strange combination of the anachronistic and new: a sailing ship but all this technology as well. He wondered what other Polity technologies, besides that submersible, might be aboard, then he watched as the army of Golem began to disembark.

'Here's the new toy we've built for you,' he said.

'Quite,' said Wade.

Janer turned to Ron, as Bloc began speaking again. 'I guess we should go get our stuff.'

'Why not,' said Captain Ron, looking at Wade thoughtfully.

Wormish tangles of packetworm coral rose in the sea like three Hindu temples, beaches of grey sand accumulated around them. Ambel scanned their destination through his binoculars, and grimaced as he noted the mounded shape of a leech washed up on the shore. It was unmoving so was probably dead. Leeches, which sat at the top of the food chain here, were surprisingly more mortal than everything below them in that chain. The sprine they used in their digestive system tended to percolate through their bodies, negating the growth of the viral fibres.

'Must be fairly recent.' Boris nodded towards the

huge corpse. He was holding the helm with one hand and contemplatively flexing the fingers of his other hand. Ambel lowered his binoculars and eyed the man. Stitching the fingers back on had not been such a problem, but reattaching the tendons that had snapped back up into his arm had been messy and painful.

'We're not going to have any problems are we?' Ambel asked.

Boris shrugged. 'It was an accident.'

'Then take us in.'

Boris turned the helm to bring the *Treader* round, then he shouted, 'You awake up there?'

Galegrabber hurriedly turned himself, and the sails he controlled, to catch the best of the wind to bring the ship in towards the grey beach. Ambel glanced down to the deck to make sure someone was ready to drop the anchor, then returned the binoculars to his eyes.

It was a recent death. The leech's rider prill were milling about just beyond it, not yet aware that their ride was dead and so might now have made the transformation into dinner, and no other creatures had yet arrived to join in the potential feast.

'Might be a bit risky,' said Boris.

'But there's something to gain.' Ambel lowered his binoculars. 'You get that deck cannon loaded.'

They changed position and Boris kicked open the ammunition box situated below the swivel-mounted cannon. He took out a paper-wrapped charge and shoved it down the barrel, ram-rodded it down, followed by wadding then a pack of stones. Then he pierced through the ignition hole and primed the flash pan.

'Anne, up here!' Ambel called. In a moment she came up from the deck, where she had been readying the rakes and riddles used to harvest amberclams. 'Take the helm,' Ambel told her, 'I need to ready my 'buss.' As she took the helm he scrambled down the ladder to the deck, unhooked his enormous blunderbuss from the forecabin wall, and prepared it in much the same way Boris had prepared the deck cannon. Both weapons were equally effective, but only Ambel was strong enough to hold the blunderbuss and aim it properly.

'Juniors below!' he ordered as at the last moment the *Treader* came about, the sail reefing both fabric sails and itself, and climbing high up the mast, out of reach. The ship drew up sideways against a bank of sand, next to which the water was still deep. Sild dropped anchor then hurried off to find his musket. Peck swiftly freed his shotgun from its wrapping of oily cloth, fed some shells into it, then pumped one into the chamber. Already the prill had spotted the ship and were running across the sand in their curious revolving manner, leaving spiral trails behind them.

'I said juniors below,' said Ambel.

Sprout hung his head and, trailing his machete behind him, slowly followed the other junior crew. Ambel hoped Sprout would soon understand juniors do not heal as quickly as older Hoopers, and this was the only reason Ambel sent him below on such occasions.

'And leave your machete – I'll be needing it.'

Anne tied off the helm, then half scrambled and leapt down to the deck. In a moment she had reached the rail, taken a case from one of the lockers, and out of it her laser carbine.

'Save your shots,' Ambel warned. 'You've only got one more energy canister for that.'

Anne nodded just as Boris fired the deck cannon.

The leading prill fragmented in a great gout of sand, broken carapace and detached sickle legs. Ambel fired too and blew more of them to pieces, then hurriedly reloaded. Sild fired once, splitting one prill into two halves, which flipped over backwards with legs wriggling in the air. Anne picked off the ones closest to the ship with brief pulsed shots that caused them to leap in the air, trailing steam from the holes burnt through them. Then the remaining creatures hit the side of the ship with a sound like hail on a wooden board. Ambel and Boris fired yet again, simultaneously, fragmenting more of the creatures below. In a second one of them was up on the rail, red eyes shooting around its rim like some nightmare music centre. Sild smashed it away with his musket butt, but more of them swarmed over. Anne calmly replaced her carbine in its box, picked up Sprout's machete, then began laying about herself, chopping the creatures to pieces. Peck continued blasting them as they came over the rail then, having emptied his shotgun, he reversed it to use as a club. As always, using his fists and boots, Ambel turned the sur-rounding deck into a shellfish bouillabaisse minus the vegetables. Boris was soon down with him and joining in. The last prill over the rail he caught under his hobnail boot, then pressed his full weight down, crush-ing its shell.

'Juniors up!' Ambel bellowed. He walked over to Anne and held out his hand for the machete. With a quizzical look she passed it to him. 'You take Sild and the rest of the lads and get all the amberclams you can.'

'And you?' she asked.

'Peck can guard my back,' he slapped the gory blade

against his gory hand. 'I'm gonna get me the best part of a leech.'

Erlin gazed down at the island, and it seemed a perfect agate in the pale green ocean, but for one flaw near its edge. This flaw had obviously been scraped out and repositioned just offshore. As Zephyr began to spiral down through cold dispersed cloud, her view became clearer, and she realized she was seeing an enormous ship. Ah, so a piece of the island had been scraped out and beaten into a ship mould to produce this. You'd think it would sink being made of all that stone and mud . . .

On some level Erlin knew she was not thinking in any logical manner. The craft rising from the island she recognized as a planetary shuttle, but also thought it a huge fly rising from the island's wound. She wondered if the ground had bled, or if the island had squealed when that big leech, now resting offshore, had bitten from it such a huge bloody lump of its flesh.

'There the Golem leave to serve out the rest of their indenture to Cybercorp elsewhere. Perhaps some of them, in time, will wear bodies like mine. I envy them such choices,' said Zephyr.

Bodies . . . lump of flesh . . . blood . . .

Before she knew what she was doing, Erlin was trying to claw at the creature above her. She was suddenly so very hungry. Then abruptly she saw her extruded tongue waving before her face and some sanity returned. She gaped at her broken fingernails and vaguely recollected that she had attacked the sail before. Then she stared at her dark blue fingers, mesmerized.

'What we going to do when we get down there?' asked

one of the other two sails. 'We can't let her loose like this. Things might get a bit . . . hectic.'

'Arrangements have been made,' Zephyr replied.

Gazing down at the planet through satellite eyes, the Warden observed Erlin's arrival at Mortuary Island, and though the AI had not interfered, it felt some shedding of responsibility. Then, gazing through many other eyes at ground level, it felt frustration. The Golem agent of the ancient hive mind was practically untraceable now. In the time frame posited, thousands of Golem had arrived and departed, including the indentured ones who had built the *Sable Keech*. This was worrying, for no one could be sure what the hive mind's motives or intentions might be.

That hive mind, being old and nigh incomprehensible, did not have much official contact with humans and AIs, though through its own kind it did have some converse with those skirting the edge of the Polity and its laws – humans, aliens and AIs. Through them it must have gained access to the technology enabling it to accelerate its thought processes beyond pheromonal transfer, and to send out its eyes and agents beyond Earth. It was supposed that, like the younger mind before it, it was here after the formula for sprine, but that was dubious. Some claimed that a breed of hornets carrying sprine in their stings would counterbalance the strength and nigh indestructibility of Hoopers, and that Polity AIs were not averse to this. It was a myth, which, foolishly unchecked, led one young hive mind (a mere ten thousand years of age) to attempt colonization here with adapted hornets. Had it succeeded, the Warden's drones would then have been busy with canisters of insecticide until every last hornet here was dead.

The Polity contained many other individuals potentially as dangerous as Hoopers: free Golem, augmented humans, dracomen and the ineffable Dragon that was their source, and various other aliens. Moreover, just the existence of sprine acted as a counterbalance. Of course Polity AIs had long ago analysed that substance and could easily manufacture it. The Warden knew that one runcible jump away lay a stock of weapons that employed it. A rail-gun firing sprine-tipped darts would certainly be more effective than any hornet, and that was just the least of the weapons available. The young mind's claim to be seeking personal armament for defence, just like any other Polity citizen was allowed, was rather weak when individual hornets comprised only a minuscule fraction of it. Hornets with killing stings could not be allowed, especially since they could inadvertently wipe out the limited population of an alien race, the sails, who owed their incredibly long life spans to the virus inside them. Surely the ancient mind knew this, which again begged the question, why was it here?

The Warden turned its attention to files that one of its subminds had hunted down from all quarters of the Polity, and began to examine them. The hive mind, though incommunicative to Polity AIs, was very active and constantly monitored. Its eyes – carried by some indentured to that same mind but mostly by those it employed, now the indenture periods were so reduced (perpetually increasing hornet populations of each hive mind resulted in a reduction of the sentence for killing one hornet) – had been to many locations. It travelled to Hive, to most of the planets and stations in the Sol system and, seemingly at random, to other planets across the Polity. But then other hive minds operated in the same fashion: they were looking around, ever curious. Also, like other minds, it searched regularly for information on the nets. And by studying what the mind searched for, the Warden began to see a pattern emerge.

In the beginning the mind had studied the various religions of Earth, paying particular attention to the concept of afterlife those primitive ideologies espoused. It then moved on to a brief spell of investigating the mind-wiping or execution of murderers, swiftly followed by a detour into memcording. At precisely that time, the Warden noted, it had sent its agents to Klader and, both through them and the nets, studied the changing organization of the reifications. It also looked into the history of human medical technologies, paying particular attention to the time when it first became possible for people to live forever. Noting the direction of the mind's interest, the Warden realized the mind's physical explorations were anything but random. Its agents visited war graves, the pyramids, the sites of ancient concentration camps, the Solar System battlefields of corporate wars, the planet Samarkand, and planets denuded of life during the Prador War. Its agents purchased for it numerous items with one constant theme: a crystal Aztec skull, reproductions of medieval art, antique weapons, gravestones, funeral urns . . . the list even included a dinosaur skeleton. So, given its ghoulish interests, Spatterjay should most certainly be high on its list of places to visit. But this was not exactly what worried some Polity AIs.

The mind had studied Spatterjay, and around about the same time there had been a successful raid on an ECS information repository. This unlinked storage system contained, amongst much else, the deciphered genetic codes for numerous Spatterjay life forms. This occurred while the hive mind relocated to Hive and purchased equipment from human genetic engineers there. The AIs were immediately suspicious, but could not prove the mind responsible for the information raid. But they watched very closely thereafter, and began really to worry when warned, by the younger hive mind, that the old hive mind was sending a Golem agent to Spatterjay.

The Warden returned its attention to the base on the Island of Chel. Still no trace of the Golem, and only one hivelink had been operating through the runcible, though one not connected to the old hive mind. But the Golem was here, and its guiding hive mind was very very interested in death.

Janer dumped his backpack on the floor and surveyed his cabin. He had expected it to be cramped, but on reflection a ship a kilometre long should have room to spare. It contained a desk against one wall with a screen above it and a swivel chair before it. At the foot of the fold-down bed running along the opposite wall a partitioned area held a washbasin and toilet. The tap he found only ran when he put his hands directly underneath it, and he soon discovered it would not operate if he placed some other item in the way of its sensor. There were cupboards, light panels in the ceiling, a small area supplied with a microwave cooker which also supplied boiling water for hot drinks. But most importantly, this cabin was on the side of the corridor adjoining the hull, so he had the benefit of one of the metre-square chain-glass windows, before which rested two form chairs on either side of a coffee table.

He was quite happy with all this, but what aroused in him some suspicions was the bottle of hornet syrup in the cupboard, and the fact that his name was already carved into the door.

This set of crew quarters lay to the stern of the ship on A Deck, whilst there was another one in the bows. Separate quarters were necessary simply because of the sheer length of the *Sable Keech*. Hoopers working at the bows would not take kindly to having to walk the best part of a kilometre to work each shift. There was a galley and a mess at the end of the corridor outside, and a food store beyond that. The reification staterooms were located on Deck B, a level below. While exploring with Ron and Forlam, Janer had seen how different these were: without toilets and with flat unpadded bunks – no doubt for them to take the weight off their servomotors but certainly not for sleep. There was also no refectory down there, no storage for food, no need for either. He had later learnt that such spartan conditions were misleading, as each reification stateroom could be swiftly converted to house living humans, which their current occupants hoped one day to become. Restaurants, shops and bars – at present mostly closed – in the third tier of the central deckhouse, and on all three tiers of the stern deckhouse, were there to cater to their needs on the return journey.

Sitting on his bunk, Janer dragged his backpack up beside him, pulled out all his spare clothing, then the short hexagonal stasis case. He pressed his fingertip into an indentation, whereupon the case split in half longitudinally and silently hinged open. He eyed the ten small cylinders arranged inside, with their tubes connecting to the transparent reservoir. Each time a hornet died, he would open this and release another one – just revived. There were none presently in the reservoir. He now took the diamond stud of his hivelink out of his pocket and fixed it in his earlobe. This device was only a relay to the implant in the bone behind his ear. By removing this earring he broke the connection between that implant and the transceiver inside the case. The hornets were also linked to the case, which in turn was U-space-linked through the runcible on Coram back to the mind on Hive. He heard nothing, not even a buzzing to signify that the link was operating.

Janer ruminated. Something could have gone wrong, but in all his years communicating through the hivelink, Janer had never known that to happen. It was odd, just as it was odd that the two hornets had died simultaneously. They were always of different ages so as to prevent this, so the hive mind could have an unbroken view through at least one of them. Perhaps something else had occurred: some attack on the hive mind's communication system, and on its hornets? Janer grimaced, loath to jump to conclusions, but definitely suspicious of one individual in particular. He closed the case then removed another item from his pack and studied it warily, wondering how he would know when to use it now.

The gun looked little different from a regular gas-system pulse gun. In fact it did fire pulses of ionized gas, but it was also something more. Its appearance was a facade, but would never have fooled a runcible AI, which was why Janer had come here aboard the *Gurnard*. The older hive mind's agent was a Golem, so would be very difficult to stop. An APW would do the job, but only one above a certain energy level, but such weapons were usually bulky carbines or larger, and therefore difficult to conceal. This one he could conceal, however, and with it he could prevent that agent from acquiring sprine. It was a weapon for the assassination of a Golem. Unfortunately that Golem seemed likely to be Isis Wade – and Janer rather liked him.

The trench was deep here, its bottom four kilometres below the ocean's surface, and hundreds of kilometres from where Ebulan had originally hidden this spaceship. Scanning outside with sonar and an infrasound sampler, Vrell ascertained that the cliff rearing beside the vessel was loaded with weed and drifts of silt caught on ledges, but that there seemed no dangerous faults in the underlying stone. Selecting one of the underwater turbines he revolved it until it was pointing up at the cliff, then turned it on. This only succeeded in pushing the ship harder against the bottom for a while, then the stream of water hit the cliff, and clouds of silt, weed, shell and other detritus began to boil out and avalanche down. He listened carefully to the sound of rocks, larger shells and other odd unidentifiable objects impacting against the upper hull, and was reminded of the time he had to bury himself in the ground to escape the rampaging Captain Drum. He felt a sudden anger and nearly shut off the thruster. Why should he hide? Why should he be afraid? He could tear them apart. But he got himself back under control, and only shut off the stream of water when the silt was metres deep and beginning to impinge on the function of outside scanners and cameras. When he was ready he would fight, but not until then.

Heaving himself back up onto his legs, Vrell flexed his new pair of back limbs, which had unaccountably replaced those that had, on the island, dropped away to expose his sexual organs. These new legs were still soft, and not yet long enough to reach the ground. Did this mean he was an adolescent again? He wasn't quite sure what it meant. No matter. He would set his blanks to work, then return to studying the account concerning the virus-infected Prador.

The pilot he programmed to repair gravmotors, and the navigator he set to dealing with the various generators and transformers. He set them to replacing coils and components with those kept in storage, or manufacturing new components in the ship's machine shop. Setting them these tasks was not too onerous, as Ebulan had stored many thrall subprograms for this very purpose. Vrell also designated the two headless blanks to assist where they could; usually just to fetch and carry and help lift heavy items. The other blank he decided he would make dispensable, and with the quadruped robots set it to work on the ship's fusion plants. One of those was operating so needed no attention, two required realigning and restarting, others were severely damaged and radioactive. Vrell doubted this last blank would survive this to repair them all. Then, setting alarms to alert him should the blanks encounter anything their programs did not encompass, Vrell returned to the story.

The ship, a huge exotic metal destroyer, had returned to the home system, but was ordered to take up orbit around one of the furthest cold planets and there await inspection. The council of Prador leaders, who governed the Second Kingdom, had communicated with the adult Prador aboard, but remained wary.

The report they received from the ship did not tie in with what Prador spies gleaned of the action in which it had been recently involved. Two ships had been sent to drop from U-space outside a Polity system and run in at fast sublight speeds firing antimatter missiles to intersect the course of a defence planetoid. This had all gone according to plan, and the planetoid blown to glowing dust that spread in a ring around the sun. The moon's defences had been weak, the reason for this becoming evident when the orbital sun lasers of the system's real defensive weapons began firing. Both ships escaped. However, this returned ship's report claimed that the lasers had managed to destroy the other ship. Either the spies or the Captain of this surviving ship had been lying.

The order to stand off and wait was disobeyed and the ship in question dropped into U-space, managing an incredibly accurate jump into the orbit of the home world. Immediately, heavy destroyers were ordered to intercept, but not managing so accurate a U-space jump, arrived thousands of kilometres away from the planet. They also could not fire on the ship for fear of causing damage to the groundside population.

Planetary defences opened up and the ship took a terrible battering as it descended into the sea fifty kilometres off the King's island. The then King, an ancient Prador who had ruled the Second Kingdom unassailably by keeping his council members squabbling with each other, ordered in every available force to defend him. The sea was depth-charged continuously for a month, then a hundred of the early-style Prador drones called in, too. The battle that followed Vrell was able to observe from recordings recovered from those drones lucky to survive. He saw some weirdly shaped Prador, black as night, ascending from the deeps where few should have survived the depth-charging. He recognized many similarities in these to himself now. Many were badly shattered by drone weapons, but they did not die easily and fought back hard, destroying the King's drones one after the other. They carried the regular Prador weapons, but also ones they had modified, advanced, made more powerful.

Eventually fifty of them gained the shore, clustering about a huge one of their own kind – the size of an adult but hollow of carapace and retaining its full complement of legs as in childhood. Its head jutting forward moved independently of its body on a corded neck. Ashore they faced a force of five thousand adolescents, including armoured drones, some on the ground and some in the air. The battle should have been brief, but it dragged on as these strange new Prador rebels employed energy defence fields and even managed to survive tactical atomic blasts. As they advanced, the King retreated with a personal guard of his own adolescents, giving also the order for the withdrawal to his other forces. But their retreat only allowed the new Prador to more quickly advance. The King finally ordered a massive CTD strike, thereby sacrificing thousands of his own fighters.

What happened next became increasingly unclear to Vrell, as it was difficult to separate truth from propaganda. The island was scoured to the bedrock – nothing remaining of the attacking Prador. The King, out at sea, was deposed by an aggressive faction of his council. All his adolescents were slaughtered, and he himself was apparently injected with a slow-working diatomic acid and floated out above the sea on his own AG so other Prador could watch him die screeching and bubbling. A new King grabbed power, called Oboron, a name unfamiliar amid the previous factional infighting of the council. And so the time of the Third Kingdom began.

This stuff was all utterly new to Vrell. He had known how the present King had scrabbled to power over the burnt-out carapaces of his predecessor and that King's supporters, but nothing about any attack by virally mutated Prador. Delving deeper, he discovered that the returned ship had been the first to carry human blanks imported from Spatterjay, and read Ebulan's speculations about experiments, using the Spatterjay virus, being conducted aboard. He scanned a brief report of some discovered wreckage being identified as that of the missing ship used in the attack on the Polity, and supposed the chief Prador aboard it had discovered what was happening aboard its companion vessel, leading to a dispute in which the mutated Prador decided to act pre-emptively. Nowhere could he find the name of the Prador Captain of the returned ship. And Vrell reflected on how the Third Kingdom had survived for so long, guarded by Oboron's ruthless army of adolescents constantly encased in layers of concealing armour, and how the same king had remained in power for some seven hundred years, unseen.

After scanning all the records, Vrell ruminated over everything he now knew. Aggression warred with intellect inside him. He wanted away from this planet so he could establish himself back in the Third Kingdom, but he would have to be very careful and very clever in doing so. Though he knew his mind was now functioning differently from that of most Prador – more intelligent and, if it was possible, more ruthless – he was one against many, and should he make the slightest error in his plans for his return, he would not survive the wrath of his own kind . . . all of his own kind.

9

Amberclams:
these molluscs are one of the best-known of the many genera
of burrowing bivalves that live in the ocean floor, or in 'cast'
sands. Their name stems from the amber colour of their flesh,
which is much relished by Hoopers. Pickled amberclams are
a staple of the Hooper diet, and the product 'amber sauce' –
made by allowing de-shelled clams to dissolve in seacane rum
– is greatly valued by them. It would be well to remember that
this sauce is poisonous to non-Hoopers, causing intoxication,
hallucinations, convulsions and sometimes even death. But
perhaps the worst side-effect of this product on Polity citizens
is that, while hallucinating, they experience the overpowering urge to take a swim – which is never a good idea on
Spatterjay.

Perpetually growing larger, old clams slowly migrate down
into the deep ocean muds, where have been found specimens
weighing many hundreds of tons. But for viral infection, the
amberclam life-cycle would be brief, and confined to the sands
washed from the worm casts of packetworms –

Janer walked down the corridor to the communal wash-
room, glanced inside and saw it noticeably devoid of

Hoopers or any sign that they had ever been there. He had been surprised, when first coming to Spatterjay, that such an apparently unwashed people smelt only of things they caught and handled, and remembered a conversation with Erlin on that subject:

'You'd think they would stink,' he said, pulling his own shirt out of his sticky armpits and wishing he himself could wash. But they were returning from the Skinner's Island, fresh water supplies were limited, and even sea water clear of visible life could contain a plankton that started eating one's skin.

'That's not through any conscious effort on their part,' she informed him dryly.

'No?'

'No, the Spatterjay virus immunizes them from the bacteria that cause body odour. It also kills many other parasites to which humans are prone, and even some bacteria normal humans need.'

'Like?'

'Intestinal flora. They may look like us, but how they function inside has changed a great deal,' she explained.

'But you're a Hooper in that respect, and I'm on the way to becoming one.'

'Mmm . . . quite.' Erlin seemed annoyed by the observation. 'Perhaps I'm just thinking more of the Old Captains.' She peered back down the deck, towards where Ambel and Captain Ron were deep in conversation.

She went on to tell him at length how Old Captains did not sweat, probably not containing sufficient moisture, how their kidneys shrank and their livers changed, how they digested food; and how, by the colour of their urine, they seemed to have over-indulged in beetroot.

Now Janer was seeing signs of these changes in himself, but he still liked to wash. Habit probably.

He showered, used the built-in hot air blast to dry himself, then donned clean clothes: tough monofabric combat trousers, a blue silk shirt, and boots from an envirosuit. His jacket was of vat-grown leather, with an inner layer of ceramal mesh and a temperature-controlled lining run from a power pack the size of a coin which in turn was kept recharged by a gridwork of solar cells across his upper back and shoulders. After putting this on he slid his gun into an inside pocket. He now felt ready, and was anxious for this strange voyage to begin.

Janer stepped out to the sound of Hooper voices echoing down the corridor and numerous other sounds probably from the mechanisms of the ship itself. Turning to head for the nearest stair, which spiralled up around the lower internal section of Mizzenmast Two outside the forward bulkhead of the crew quarters, he passed the cabin door next to his own, then halted and backed up. There was a name carved into this other door too – one he had missed. He was just contemplating this when Aesop found him.

'Bloc requires you ashore.' The reif passed him a plasmel box. 'Here.'

'What does he want me for?' Janer eyed the sidearm the reif wore.

Aesop gestured to the box. Janer opened it and studied the contents: some bottles of the supplements Hoopers now often used to stave off the transformation the virus could cause, a hollow-core laser injector – the only kind that could penetrate Hooper skin – and cartridges of Intertox inhibitors to load into it. He looked at Aesop questioningly.

'Come,' said the reif, not elaborating.

Aesop led him through the bulkhead to the stair he had been heading for anyway, then up and out of the stairwell below the mizzen, and onto the main deck. Janer looked around.

Each one of the nine masts penetrated right down into the ship's bilge, and each of them was wound around with a spiral stair, though these ended at the maintenance deck, three decks below. This particular mast stair lay between the rear two deckhouses: a large one positioned amidships and a smaller one stretching back from here. In the latter deckhouse he had earlier seen automated restaurants, bars and shops, and others that would eventually be run by many of the Hoopers now aboard. Only glimpsing into the midship deckhouse, he had seen rows of chainglass tanks, like aquaria, and racks of medical equipment. Apparently the first two tiers were totally taken up by these, the third tier containing more catering facilities.

From the forward deckhouse jutted a raised bridge. The cabins and staterooms underneath were to be occupied by Bloc and his lieutenants, and also by Captain Ron and his command crew. Up in the bridge, behind enclosing chainglass, he could just see some people moving about, though from where he stood they must be about seven hundred metres away. He supposed Ron, Forlam and other Hoopers must be checking out their command, and trying out the controls, for he could hear movement from the laser turrets positioned on the hull below the rails. Positioning lasers there was only a sensible precaution. There were some nasty creatures here quite capable of scaling the side of a ship.

Just ahead of him, by Mizzen One, extending up the

side of it from the midship deckhouse, rose a crane, positioned over the movable section of main deck between that deckhouse and the stern one. Above him was a forest of rigging in which some Hoopers were either working or just climbing for the hell of it; reefed monofabric sails, control cables and electric winders to drive them; solar panels, mast-mounted consoles and the places ready to be occupied by the living sails.

Aesop led him through a milling crowd of reifications, past Hoopers wandering around bemusedly, and groups of watchful Kladites. They traversed the wide area of deck beside the Tank Rooms, passed midchain anchor points, where Janer peered down the length of the three ceramal chains reaching down into the sea, and finally reached the embarkation stair. Two Kladites stood below, armed with laser carbines, watching out for hostile life forms, since already some frog whelks had tried to board the ship.

Janer's admiration for the Golem builders was tempered by the fact that they had neglected to put up some kind of fence along the jetty's edges. Just then, shadows drew across him, and he glanced up to see two living sails gliding in to land up in the rigging. Then transferring his attention ashore, he saw, on the beach, Bloc, a group of his Kladites and Bones, all standing beside some large metallic object. Halfway down the ramp and he saw the metallic object move, and realized it was a sail holding something flat to the beach with one talon. That something was struggling, and after a moment he realized it was human; and that what he could see of its skin was very blue.

Returning his attention to the one holding it, he said, 'That is a very odd-looking sail.'

'Golem,' Aesop replied briefly.

Janer noted that the reif's head was moving back and forth, scanning the island as if worried about something there, though it was difficult to be sure, what with Aesop's lack of expression and a distracting lump missing from his head.

The beach consisted of polished quartz pebbles lying in drifts on pale grey sand, seeming like something tipped out of a giant lapidary drum. As he approached the group gathered around the Golem sail and its captive, Janer pulled out the hollow-laser injector and clicked a cartridge of Intertox into it. Obviously here was someone undergoing the viral transformation which, if left unchecked, might result in something nasty.

'We have one more passenger,' said Bloc, turning towards him. 'One even more important than yourself.'

Janer did not like this obsequious and oblique compliment. His distrust of Bloc was growing on every contact with him. Bloc walked beside him as he stepped over to the sail. The great Golem turned and fixed him in its emerald regard, then simply bowed its head to indicate its prize with its snout. The sail was holding a woman face down with some sort of handle jutting up from a harness she wore. From this Janer surmised the creature had been carrying her. She was struggling and grunting with effort to escape. Only when he stooped down to pull back her collar did recognition dawn. He set the dosage at its highest, and placed the injector against her neck. It burned a pinhole deep into her flesh and squirted a stream of Intertox into her as she continued struggling. His mind running scenarios and discarding them one after another, Janer stood and turned to face Bloc. He knew Erlin would never have risked any journey so unprepared as to end up in this state. But would it be a good idea to voice his suspicions right now?

'I'll give her another shot in about an hour or so,' he said, 'but we need to get some supplements inside her.'

'You can do that aboard the ship. We have restraints there for anyone undergoing cybermotor nerve conflict as they Arise.' Bloc's spectacle irrigator sprayed his eyes.

'I see.' Janer remembered how he and Erlin had ministered to Sable Keech when, as a reification, he had arrived stinking, half-decayed and half-alive on the deck of Ron's sailing ship, the *Ahab*. Keech's convulsions, shortly after he had returned to life, had been the result of cybermotor nerve conflict. It was because of this that Bloc wanted himself and Erlin along. This was the reason for all the chainglass tanks aboard. This was the entire purpose of the voyage. He was not here for a celebrity's free ride; he was here to work. He wondered, judging by her condition, how willing a volunteer was Erlin.

Bloc gestured in turn to a couple of Kladites. 'You two take her to the ship.' He turned back to the Golem sail. 'Zephyr, release her now.'

Not thinking this a good idea at all, Janer stepped back. The sail released the handle with which it had clamped Erlin to the ground, and shuffled out of the way. Erlin paused before heaving herself to her feet.

'Jaannersss!' she hissed, her leech tongue waving about obscenely. 'Lovelllies!' She launched towards him, her hands open in blue claws. The two Kladites tried to grab her, but she shrugged them off as if they were not there. Bones stepped forward aiming a flat-nosed weapon. Janer flinched at the first stun blast – and the one after it. Erlin dropped face down at his feet, sighing into unconsciousness.

'It is well to remember Hooper strength,' said Bloc, irrigators again working furiously.

Damned right, thought Janer.

Huff's memory of the time prior to his receiving severe injuries aboard Captain Drum's *Cohorn* was not so good. But the horrible occasion when he actually received those injuries he remembered in lurid detail. Admittedly, his memory would never have been so clear now without the assistance his Polity aug gave his fibre-locked brain, but certainly he would never have forgotten that time even without it. The memory of that mad woman Rebecca Frisk boiling his head with a laser still made his eye sockets ache sometimes, but going to see her confined in her tube at Olian's was always a pleasant remedy. A taste forever on his tongue was of the two human blanks whose heads he had bitten off at the time he escaped and carried Captain Drum ashore to hunt that Prador adolescent. The memory of Shib, the Batian mercenary, stapling his neck to the mast elicited a psychosomatic choking. This last memory was why Huff, surprisingly, felt happy now. Via his aug, he had learnt of the recent events here on this island. And discovering that a number of Batian mercenaries had been torn to pieces was cheering news indeed.

Growling contentedly to himself, Huff spread his wings and gripped the control spars with his spur claws. Being this way up felt very strange, but was not entirely unpleasant. He shifted his position and felt the assister motors cutting in to move the spars above and below him, and on foremasts behind and in front of him. Turning his head he checked the mast console and, onlining the program in his aug, understood it perfectly: these controls to adjust trim, reefing controls on a percentage scale so that he could put just as much sail to the wind as he wanted, cable motors he could set to change the angle of the other fabric sails in relation to himself – but all these controls within parameters set by Zephyr, who would occupy the middle one of the three mainmasts, controlling those ahead and behind him. Puff was towards the stern of the ship, controlling the two mizzenmasts and the jigger mast.

However, still studying the console, Huff came across many terms unfamiliar to him. He knew about course, gallant and top sails, but only through his aug did he learn about skysails, moonrakers and staysails, and numerous terms for the different kinds of rigging. He realized that this job would not be quite so easy as he had supposed, and understood then something Windcheater had once told him: 'Technology means you work harder with your brain than you did with your muscles, but the rewards can be greater.'

Huff agreed with the first part, but wondered when the second part might materialize. However, his speculations were cut short when Zephyr arrived on the central mainmast, his voice issuing from Huff's mast console.

'Now, we begin to learn,' said the Golem sail.

The quarter deck was crowded with reifications gazing back towards the island as it retreated from view. Above them the hundreds of square metres of doubled staysails cut up into the sky like blades and, forward, more sails were opening to the wind all the time, as if the ship were a closed flower brought out into the sunshine. Many other reifs, John Styx knew, were, out of long habit, shy of company and so would be watching through their cabin windows – those with hull-side cabins that is, which on the whole had been occupied by Bloc's people. Others, he knew, had no interest at all in the voyage itself, and had immediately interred themselves in their quarters, shutting themselves down until it ended. It occurred to him that those on deck were evidently the ones still with some appreciation of life, even though they were dead. He surveyed the crowd, studied their varied dress, varied styles of reification, various visible death wounds. It did not matter to him how accustomed he was getting to the sight of dead people walking; this was still a macabre scene.

'Aren't we a grisly crew,' said a female reif standing beside him. 'And here comes our grisly leader.'

Styx turned to her as she gestured with one tatty hand – flesh worn through to the bone and replaced at the fingertips with rubbery pads. He inspected his own wrinkled hand as if unsure of its provenance, then gazed at where she indicated. Instantly recognizable in his long black coat, Taylor Bloc was walking down beside the stern deckhouse towards them, Aesop and Bones trailing along behind him as usual, but now with four armed Kladites behind them. As soon as Bloc reached the edge of the crowd, some of its members approached him. Out of this group stepped one individual who by the look of him had died before attaining full growth. This dead youth, with stringy blond hair still clinging to his scalp, wore clothing Styx recognized as being the fashion of Klader a few hundred years in the past.

'Bloc,' began this reif, 'we have some complaints.'

At this the others began to speak up too: '. . . damned inner cabin . . .' '. . . expect a reduction for . . .' 'I don't see why it's necessary for . . .' They all spoke in dead flat voices and kept on interrupting each other.

The ringleader held up his hand until the others fell silent. 'As you can hear, we are somewhat troubled by your treatment of us. We may be dead, but you should know this does not give you the right to steal from us, or treat us like your personal property.'

'You'd think that death would be an adequate cure for whingeing, wouldn't you?' the female reif murmured to Styx.

Styx tilted his head, and would have grinned if he could. 'Perhaps it's all those years of having no one to complain to, and all those years of independent existence.' He pointed to the one who was now going into more detail about the complaints of those hovering behind him. 'Who is that?'

'Ellanc Strone – recently reformed Kladites are always the angriest. And who might you be?'

Styx held out his hand. 'John Styx.'

After a hesitation she took his hand. 'Santen Marcollian.' She turned his hand in hers and inspected it. 'You recent?'

'Relatively.' He approximated a shrug. 'And I use reconstructive cosmetics.'

She released his hand then stared at her own. 'I considered that, but never saw the point. I'm a corpse, why bother being a neat corpse?'

Now the crowd around Bloc and his crew continued with their litany of complaints while Ellanc stood with his head bowed and his arms crossed. Had the reif possessed the facility for expression, Styx supposed he would be smiling now.

'Enough!' Bloc turned up his volume. He was now holding up his hands, which he continued doing until the bitching around him dropped to an acceptable level.

'Cabins were allocated at random. If any of you wish to move, then I suggest you work out some arrangement with your fellows.'

'Yeah, but I would have paid—' began one of the complainers.

'Please!'

Bloc's eye irrigators seemed to have some sort of fault, Styx surmised. His eyes surely did not need that much moisture.

Bloc continued, 'I have given you this opportunity of resurrection, and you complain?' Despite the even tone issuing from his voice synthesizer, his incredulity was evident. 'We are reifications—'

'Well screw you and your platitudes,' Ellanc interrupted. 'We're not Kladites following you on the promise of resurrection; we're paying customers.'

Someone else interjected, 'He's right. We paid good money and we've been conned and robbed ever since arriving here.'

Another said, 'Yeah – five hundred shillings for a replacement joint motor.'

Yet another: 'Last I heard, it'd be a short voyage from the Island of Chel.'

And the whole furore started up again.

'Some definite hits,' said Santen, 'and some rather unfair criticism.'

'They need to be rather careful,' said Styx. 'They

seem to be forgetting that they are no longer protected by Polity law.'

'That could be a problem?' she asked, looking at him.

'Remember the hooder? Did you see any ECS monitors afterwards, any of the Warden's drones? Bloc's Kladites are armed now, and they will enforce Bloc's law only.'

'I guess that's true.'

Styx continued relentlessly, 'When you live in a society governed by uncompromising law, it is a mistake often made to think you somehow carry it with you when you step outside the safe confines of that society.'

Bloc turned up his volume again and bellowed for silence. When he finally got it, he eyed the various rifts developing in the crowd.

'Obviously there are some issues that need addressing,' he continued, ignoring a muttered 'Fucking right' from Ellanc.

He went on, 'I will arrange some meetings so that you may present your complaints in an orderly manner. You will be notified about them through your cabin screens. Now, this is a ship upon which a crew needs to work, so your presence on the decks does not help them. If you would all please return to your cabins, you will duly be notified.'

But the crowd did not clear. The complaining started up again. Bloc retreated, but they followed him across the quarter deck and down beside the stern deckhouse. There, Aesop and Bones suddenly turned on them, while the four Kladites shepherded Bloc away. Some pushing and shoving ensued, only to result in Bloc's two companions hurling Ellanc Strone and a couple of others to the deck.

'You should be careful,' Aesop said evenly to the prostrate figures. 'You might accidentally have gone over
the side, and then the weight of your internal hardware
would have taken you right down.'

None of the crowd subsequently tried to follow Bloc.

'Thus it begins,' said Styx.

Sturmbul was certainly impressed with the enormous
ship, but as a Hooper nearing his three hundredth year
he had not survived by trusting other people's workmanship, and as a shipwright himself, employed by
Bloc, he had wanted for many days to make a closer
inspection of the vessel. On the day of its launch he had
watched the stair fold up into the side of the ship, and
that section of hull close after they brought that woman
aboard. He then wandered over to a Hooper who was
standing idly by, watching the massive midship anchor
chains being hauled up

'That chain ain't greased,' he observed.

The other Hooper turned to him. 'The top few links
are automatically sprayed with Nilfrict as the anchor
goes down and hits the bottom. All morning I've been
watching frog whelks scrabbling for a grip and falling
off.'

'They could come up with the rest of the chain,' suggested Sturmbul.

The other Hooper just pointed, and Sturmbul went
over for a closer inspection. The chain was crashing up
through a funnel-ended hole in the upper section of hull,
up through the deck over ceramal reels, around a motorized capstan, then down into a chain locker. He watched
a hammer whelk ascend gripping the chain and go into
that funnel. A wet squeaking squelch ensued, and as the

chain emerged up over the reels it was thick with ichor and broken shell.

'Ah,' said Sturmbul, turning to the other man. 'What's your job?'

'Anchorman. Buggered if I know why. All they do is flick a touch panel up there.' He stabbed a thumb towards the bridge.

Sturmbul shrugged.

Over the ensuing day he encountered a lot of the same: Hoopers standing around gazing with bemusement at all the machines doing their jobs for them. However, the same did not apply to him. He spent time studying the plans on his cabin screen, making occasional forays to check this or that. Half a day he spent replacing some pulleys the Golem sail had ripped out of their fittings. Then he took a further half-day reorganizing the machinery and spares on the maintenance deck. But now he was finally free to look around.

Standing on the main deck, he looked up when shadows slid across the midship deckhouse and he observed some fabric sails reefing with automated precision, and the Golem sail on Mainmast Two turning its rig to the wind. For such a huge vessel, this ship moved very smoothly. Sturmbul found it almost too smooth, but understood the *Sable Keech* would not be tossed about much in seas like these. He headed for the stairwell of Mizzen One.

The stair took him down ahead of the crew quarters, through a section that was open with gantries either side. The decks below were similarly open down to the bilge, to give access for the crane above. He departed the stair on B Deck, strolling along a corridor between the reifications' staterooms, and could not help slowing his pace to peer in through an open door. Inside he observed a dead woman swabbing her shrivelled breasts with a sponge soaked in blue balm, felt slightly sickened by the sight and quickly moved on before she spotted him. Then, encountering a squad of four armed Kladites marching down the corridor, he stood aside and eyed them suspiciously.

Reaching the third mainmast, Sturmbul took the spiral stair down to the maintenance deck. Here, he had been told, was stored every conceivable component that might be required, barring an entire new ship, of course. He sniffed the familiar smell of newly cut wood and glanced back through a wide sliding bulkhead door, beyond which were stored stocks of planking, beams, sheet bubble-metal, and some of the ship's larger components, on either side of a wide gangway supplied with rails and pallets for shifting those heavier materials. Further beyond lay the open section through which larger items could be craned up above. Ahead of him were machine shops where they could make new items: cutting and shaping wood and metal into the most minuscule item if necessary. He waved at Lumor and Joss, who were joyously shoving a lump of wood into a robotic router and tapping things into the machine's console. The misshapen object coming out of the other end appeared utterly useless, and it was obvious the two were playing around, but he thought it better not to berate them just yet. He glimpsed, in partitioned booths, the planers, lathes, mills and other machines less familiar to him as he moved on.

The next bulkheads, sectioning off the stair of Mainmast Two, led through to a storeroom containing smaller items. Cages were filled with a shipwright's cornucopia; one was packed full of monofabric. Boxes contained metal and wooden fixings; other items rested on long racks, all clearly labelled: *cablemotor mizzen staysail 1B, pulley – standard, cable clamp* . . . the list went on and on. Yet more racks contained components for the cabins: taps, sinks, light panels and other electrical fittings. He moved past these, and spotted Rymund standing before a cage containing a miscellany of bottles and cans.

'All right, Rymund?'

'Just seeing what we got here, Sturm.'

Sturmbul glanced at the notescreen in Rymund's hand. 'And *what* we got?'

'Seagourd resin, paints, greases and oils – all the usual – but we've got glues that could stick a giant leech to the Big Flint, also solvents and acids and a shitload of other stuff I'm still trying to figure. Here, wood metalizer – you got a rotten beam all you do is soak it in this stuff and a few minutes later it's full of a steel fibre grid.'

'You got a rotten beam,' said Sturmbul huffily, 'and you ain't been doing your job right.'

'Just what it says here.'

Sturmbul snorted and moved on, entered the stair at Mainmast One, then at the next bulkhead pressed his hand against the panel beside the heavy door, which admitted him to a more secure area. He was allowed in here for inspection purposes, but was immediately aware of the swivel-mounted camera with its underslung laser. He eyed a locked cage containing QC hand lasers, some laser carbines and energy canisters. Just what was left – the rest of the armoury the Kladites carried constantly.

Other open cages about him contained reification spares and medical equipment, and Sturmbul guessed they were stored here simply because there was space to spare. He moved further on through, the camera tracking him. It was a standard security camera: large enough to be seen and by its obvious presence prevent wrongdoing.

The next door admitted him to an area containing two immense water tanks and a desalination plant – the latter an upright cylinder made of brushed aluminium. From this pipes punched down through the deck, some of them eventually opening into the sea below. Other pipes connected to the water tanks, and a wider one exited sideways through the hull. He had already seen this last pipe spewing salt sludge waste as the plant filled the tanks with fresh water refined from the sea. He listened hard for the sound of pumps, but heard none. This was Polity technology: if it made any noise, that meant something was going wrong.

Rather than now go on to the less interesting chain lockers, Sturmbul climbed down a ladder into the misnamed bilge. This area rose three decks in height, with partial decks and enclosed areas scattered all around it. There were many items and mechanisms here that he could only guess about. Fat cylindrical bubble-metal shrouds he felt sure concealed Polity technology. Similar, though larger, shrouds covered something far back in the stern, where in any other ship the engines might be positioned. He guessed what lay hidden there was not something Bloc or Lineworld Developments would want Windcheater to know about. On a railed deck directly opposite him, he observed racks of laminar storage batteries which connected to solar panels up in the rigging, and thereby fed all the electrical systems of the ship. Along with them, also connected into the system, were a couple of squat, sealed chrome cylinders.

No one had told him what these were for, but the fact that they required a pure water feed from the desalination plant above led him to suspect they were fusion plants. A section of the bilge, at midships, was utterly sealed off. He guessed that was where they kept the submersible no one was supposed to know about. But there were many other things here of which he knew nothing: many concealed machines, hidden corridors, strange nooks and sealed compartments.

He stepped off the ladder and walked across the gratings, eyeing the lower hull and the massive keel, confirming for himself that this place was misnamed, for the bilge contained not a single drop of sea water. He moved forward along aisles, checking corridors, finding his way to the hull wherever he could and rapping it with his knuckles. Nearer the bows, below the chain lockers, he almost got lost in the twists and turns, odd corridors, ladders and different levels rising amid concealed machines. When he heard a sound of chains, he wondered what had gone wrong. Why were they dropping the anchor again? But the sound was not from the locker above, but nearby.

He turned towards it and died.

Eventually.

The leech was coiled up like a giant slug poisoned by a huge slug pellet. Captain Ambel inspected it while behind him Peck pumped a cartridge into his shotgun's breech and eyed the surrounding sea. Deep wounds had been burnt into the creature's front end – not injuries it might naturally have received in the depths. The Captain walked down alongside the length of this hill of slimy flesh, slapping the flat of the machete blade against his leg. When he reached what he considered the correct position on its body, he stabbed the machete in and drew it across for three metres, like opening a zip. The purple and yellow lips of the cut everted under pressure from inside, but the spill of ichor was thick and sluggish. He reached out and touched the raw flesh. It was cool. The leech had been dead for at least a day. Nodding to himself, he chopped downwards at one end of the long slash, and more inner flesh bulged out. When he then sliced down from the other end, a great meaty flap peeled down and the edge of the leech's translucent intestinal sac bulged out, packed with unidentifiable lumps. He sliced across this, and quickly stepped back as dissolving chunks of heirodont flesh avalanched out, before being blocked by something larger. The half-digested head of a small molly carp oozed into view, tatters of translucent flesh clinging to its skull, its eyes gone and the jagged teeth in its mouth revealed dripping and gleaming. Another hack, and the carp slid out over the stinking mass and flopped over on the grey sand.

'Greedy bugger,' Peck observed.

Ambel stepped around the mess and peered into the rapidly collapsing cavity.

'Further back,' he muttered, then cut open another three-metre flap. This time the stuff that emerged was less easily identifiable. Certainly it included undigested sections of glister shell and what looked like a load of rotten apples, which it took him a moment to identify as probably a whole shoal of boxies. The rest was just meat fibres, bones and dilute green bile.

'Here we go!'

Ambel cut his way in, scooping aside the garbage with his machete, careful not to get any of the bile on himself.

Eventually he revealed a large baggy organ the size and shape of a potato sack, fringed with wet combs of white flesh. Pulling some string from his pocket he tied off the intestinal tube leading from it to the main gut, cut that, then cut around the organ until he could pull it free. It dropped and slid out, and he dragged it down to the sea to wash it off. There were boxies nosing about in the shallows, but the moment spilled bile washed off the bile duct and clouded the water, they shot away. Ambel could feel a slight tingling in his hands and a hollowness in his stomach, of either hunger or nausea. This had happened to him before: the slightest contact with leech bile – from which sprine could be refined – poisoning some of the viral fibres in his body. It would not kill him, since only swallowing the stuff could do that, though it could make him feel unwell.

'A good un,' he said, hauling the duct up out of the sea by its tied-off tube. Then he noticed Peck peering into the slimy cavity, his expression puzzled. Still carrying the duct, he walked up to stand beside the other man. 'What's up?'

Peck gestured with his shotgun. 'What's *that* bugger?'

Lying in the base of the cavity was a segmented silver sphere the size of a cricket ball. As they watched it opened out, like a pill-bug without legs, began emitting a low hum and rose up into the air, turning so it pointed towards Ambel and Peck. The two stepped back.

Peck aimed his shotgun, but Ambel reached out and pushed the barrel down.

'It'll be gone in a sec,' said the Old Captain.

The object floated out into the open air, turned towards the sea, then abruptly shot away. In moments it was out of sight.

In response to Peck's querying look, Ambel said, 'Warden stuff. Likes to know where all the adult leeches are, and who's getting hold of the sprine.'

'Ah,' said Peck. 'Like mebbe hornets.'

'Yes, certainly them,' Ambel agreed.

As they headed back towards the *Treader*, Ambel glanced across to where the others were raking amber-clams out of the sand. Really it was meat like that they most needed, but he had been unable to resist the lure of a bile duct obtainable without having to harpoon a living leech and cut it open out at sea.

'Gettin' some local activity now,' announced Peck.

Ambel glanced back to see a rhinoworm rearing out of the sea, ten metres behind the beached leech – and other disturbances in the water to either side of it. He had observed this sort of thing before. It was as if the local fauna sensed the most poisonous part of the leech had been removed and that now it was time to feed. Often, seeing activity of this kind – the curious behaviour of molly carp, the awareness of danger in some whelks – Ambel wondered about the intelligence of some of the creatures here. The sails were obviously intelligent, but other Spatterjay animals definitely reacted in ways that were noticeably . . . *odd*.

Back at the ship, Boris threw him a rope, which he then tied to the bile duct.

'Stow it carefully,' said Ambel, as Boris hauled the organ aboard.

Ambel and Peck then returned to join Anne and the others. There was a stink in the air of the dried fish flakes scattered over the wet sand to lure up the molluscs. The juniors were now raking up the big amber-lipped white clams, while Anne and Sild collected them in riddles, washing them off in a nearby pool, and filled sacks with them.

'Wonder if there'll be any pearls?' Peck was watching Ambel.

Almost unconsciously Ambel patted his pocket where he kept the only pearl he had ever extracted from a clam. Peck was wise to his trick of seemingly discovering this same pearl just prior to some dangerous venture – a sign of good luck. Ambel glanced back at the leech. Two rhinoworms were now arced up over the rear of it, like pink question marks, turning their rhinoceros heads from side to side as if trying to figure out what might have happened to it. Their behaviour was similar to vultures approaching the corpse of a lion: aware that here was available meat, but cautious of the possibility that it might still have some life in it. Then one of them plunged down, bit deep, thrashed from side to side, and tore off a chunk of brown and purple flesh. Ambel decided there was little time for play-acting when, over to one side, a single prill splashed up on the beach, and behind it sharp cones rose like teeth emerging from the waves as a flock of frog whelks came marching in.

'That'll be enough, Anne,' he decided. 'We'll have more company soon.'

The juniors stopped raking to help collect the clams already raked to the surface, and soon they were all trudging back to the ship, laden with their booty. With two heavy sacks gripped in each hand, Ambel kept an eye on the host gathering around the huge leech corpse. Something there focused his attention. One of the rhinoworms appeared to have gone, which surprised him as, with such bounty available, the creature should not have left until utterly bloated. He kept glancing back, then saw the second worm being wrenched back down under the waves, disappearing like a lead bar dropped end-on into the water.

'Looks like a molly carp just arrived,' remarked Anne, also having witnessed this.

Ambel wondered. It would have to be a very big and powerful carp to drag a rhinoworm down that hard, so surely they should see some disturbance in the sea there. There was none.

'Pick your feet up, lads,' he said calmly.

Prill and frog whelks were now swarming over the massive corpse, like flies on a turd. Suddenly the body jerked. The prill still clung on with their sickle legs embedded in slimy flesh, but frog whelks were bounding away in every direction. A large flat tentacle rose up out of the sea, hovered like a cobra, then slammed down on the leech to get a better grip.

'Boris! Up anchor!' Ambel bellowed. Then to his fellows he said, 'I think we should . . . *run*.' He really had no need to say that last word, as by then they were all sprinting off ahead of him. Shortly they reached the ship, and while the juniors scrambled up on deck, Anne and Sild threw up to them the sacks of clams. Ambel dropped his own sacks for them to deal with, braced himself against the side of the *Treader*, and pushed, hard. The woodwork before him creaked and groaned, and he sank down into the sand up to his thighs. Heaving himself out again, he found another spot and pushed again. The last sack now up on deck, Sild and Anne climbed aboard as the ship slowly drifted out from the sand bank. It was already a few metres clear, Galegrabber unfurling and turning into the wind, when Ambel leaped the gap, caught a ladder, and scrambled aboard.

'Not too close to the wind,' he said casually, striding over to take up his blunderbuss from its hooks. Boris was now loading the deck cannon while Anne turned the helm.

'Quickest way,' Anne replied.

Ambel shook his head. 'We need deep water. This breeze'll take us straight over there.' He gestured towards where the remains of the leech were disappearing into the sea. Anne nodded and swung the helm back a little. Galegrabber turned both himself and the fabric sails to the optimum angle.

A tense few minutes passed as the *Treader* eased out into deeper water.

''Bout now,' said Ambel.

Anne swung the helm over, and the ship turned full into the wind to take it past the grey beaches. As they drew athwart the groove left in the grey sand where the leech had lain, something groped stonily along the hull for a moment and slapped the rudder so that the helm spun from Anne's grip. She quickly grabbed hold again and straightened up. A tentacle, more rounded in section this time, and with a pallet-knife tip, speared into the air behind them and slammed down on the sea, spraying them with spume.

'Easy now,' said Ambel.

Further long minutes passed and then, as the packet-worm corals dropped behind them, they began to breathe easier.

'Same one?' asked Peck, hugging his shotgun.

'I reckon,' said Ambel. The Captain then eyed the deck, which was scattered with sacks spilling amberclams. 'Best we get them shelled quick and into vinegar,' he said. Later, when Sild opened a particularly large amberclam, yelled delightedly and held up a pearl to show everyone, Ambel grunted noncommittally.

So bloated with leech flesh she was ballooning from her shell, the giant whelk slapped her tentacles in frustration against the edge of the underwater cliff. Behind her the seabed sloped up steeply to the beaches and packet-worm corals. She could feel the constant vibration of the long tubular worms boring their burrows into the rock as they sought the minerals they required, and felt a sudden surge of anger. She wanted to slide back to dig them out and rip them to pieces, as if it were their fault. But still she clung to the edge, watching the ship's hull moving away above her. When it at last became difficult to discern, she directed her dinner-plate eyes downwards.

The cliff dropped hundreds of metres into a rocky terrain scattered with forests of kelp trees, tangled with vine wracks, and prowled by pods of glisters. Though the glisters would be unable to actually hurt her, their constant probing attacks could prove very irritating, and this would slow her down just as much as the terrain itself. She might easily lose the scent; lose the ship.

The giant whelk knew that her own intelligence had increased due to her previous efforts and requirements. She could feel the increasing heaviness of the organ inside her that was the source of that increase. Now also available to her were memories she had never before needed, and one of them was of gliding through the depths like a heirodont. This further frustrated her: the knowledge that at one time she had swum, rather then dragged herself along the bottom. She strained away from the cliff edge, yearned for that ability again.

Her guts rumbled, their load of leech flesh churning

acidically, and she began to pump them. After a moment she lifted on a massive fart. Huge bubbles of gas boiled out around her, and she felt the rush of nutrients pumping around her ichor-stream. Then something inside her wrenched open painfully, up and back into her shell, some occlusion. Her shell crackled and, turning one eye, she observed flakes of deep encrustation peeling away from her living shell and falling off. Pressure grew and again she lifted up trying to expel it, but this did not pass through its usual route. The pressure dropped and the occlusion wrenched further open. Still watching her shell, she saw noxious clouds squirting from hundreds of raw little orifices that had opened up in it. Her guts continued rumbling and sloshing, until eventually gas began bubbling from her shell itself, and the orifices then closed. Realizing she was now much lighter, she rose up on her tentacles, lifting her fleshy skirt off the ground. She spread her skirt, engulfing cubic metres of sea water, then slammed it closed again, driving herself up and out, over the cliff edge. She began to fall, but shrugged her shell again and tonnes of encrustation slewed off it into the depths. Her shell now possessed the colouration, pattern and shape of a juvenile. Engulfing more sea water she tilted towards the distant ship's hull, and jetted on.

10

Land Heirodont:
there are many thousands of species of this creature cata-
logued, and probably more yet to find. They range in size from
creatures as small as a pinhead to the wood pig, which can
grow as large as an elephant. All of them are herbivores.
Fossil evidence proves that there were once carnivorous vari-
eties, and that heirodonts dominated the biosphere before the
rise of the leeches. Their overall appearance is vaguely mam-
malian, with heirodonts being comparable to many Terran
animals, though possessing the mandipular mouthparts of
insects. There are two sexes, and the females give birth to fully
developed young carrying a thick layer of back meat. No
other kind of offspring would survive to adulthood, for the
land heirodont spends a life of pain feeding upon foliage and
bark, while perpetually being fed upon by falling leeches. This
lifetime of pain is little different for the ocean heirodont –

Since the spaceship had stopped moving and shut down
what sounded like large turbines, the weird Prador had
been coming to fetch its captives regularly. In the last
five hours it had taken four more of them. Now just
Lannias, his wife Shalen, and himself were left and, by

sitting as far from the door as he could, Orbus hoped it would be the other two that the Prador would come for next. They seemed ready – almost anxious to join their fellows in whatever hell the monster provided. Even so, that would only delay matters for Orbus. There would be no escape from this. By the way the drone had come at them from the sea, the pressure changes he had felt, the sounds and the movements of this spaceship, he surmised they were deep in Spatterjay's ocean.

Captain Orbus sighed and leant back against the rough wall, transferring his gaze to a big leaf-shaped louse creeping towards his leg. A couple of these had already nipped him, and he supposed they had developed a taste for human flesh – their main purpose being to clean up food scraps the Prador dropped. He waited until the louse's front end began to rear, antennae waving and tri-hooked mandibles opening, then snatched the thing up. Its back curled around his hand as it tried to stab him with its ovipositor. Counting the large outer legs and the short spiky inner legs, he wondered for a moment how close a kin it might be to the monsters after which it kept house, then he drew his knife and began hacking away those multiple legs. Shortly he was left with just its flat armoured body, still bearing mandibles and antennae. Now being quite proficient at this, he thrust in behind the mouthparts and levered. With a crunch the mandibles popped out, and he tore them away from gristly flesh and tossed them aside. He then worked his knife in along the carapace edge, stuck his thumbs in, and folded the body open like a book. The green sac at the back was edible, as one of the now removed crewmen had discovered, though it smelt of shit and naphtha. Orbus cut it out and discarded it before using the tip of his knife to winkle out the soft bits from the creature's many internal compartments. They tasted something like raw hammer whelk, and there was just enough to stave off his hunger.

Lannias and Shalen, Orbus noted, had not eaten in some time, and showed no inclination to dine on the lice coming near them, rather waiting until the creatures first bit, then crushing them with their fists. The two were apparently competing to see which could end up with the most sets of louse mandibles embedded in their legs. This, Orbus felt, was adequate demonstration of how twisted his own crew had become, and how twisted he himself had become to encourage it. It almost seemed that what would soon happen to him was a deserved punishment.

He tossed away the empty shell and heaved himself upright, noticing how deeply blue the other two looked, and how their ridiculous giggles kept growing louder. He himself was not so blue yet; his diet of ship lice must be staving off the change in just the same way as did dome-grown food. Stretching his aching limbs he realized the other two were now staring at him.

'Ca'in,' said Lannias, smiling brightly, unable to articulate the 'pt' because of what was now growing in his mouth.

Orbus just looked away and tried to ignore him, not liking the immediate urge he felt to go over and kick the man insensible. Shalen started giggling uncontrollably. She thrust her hand down the front of her trousers and began playing with herself. She seemed unable to keep her eyes still and her chin was wet with drool.

'Captsss!' she hissed.

Lannias stood up. Orbus recognized the man's expression as one possessed to a lesser extent by all his old crew. But now it turned the man's features grotesque. Lannias drew his own skinning knife and began stabbing its tip into his own chest as if to test it. Surely he didn't think himself capable of taking on an Old Captain? Apparently he did for, when mutilating himself abruptly became too much of a bore, he suddenly rushed towards Orbus.

Orbus crouched, and slashed his own knife in an arc before him as a warning. But Lannias did not even slow. Orbus straight-armed him in the face with a flat hand, snapping the man's head back and flinging him to the floor, then circled round.

'Want a little tussle do you?' he asked nastily.

The hell with it, he thought; this might not improve their situation, but it would make him feel better.

Lannias rose quickly, his tongue wagging as he spat out a couple of teeth. Grinning, he jumped forward, slashing at his Captain's face. Orbus swayed back and cut up, opening the man's forearm. Then there came a sound that sent a shudder through him. The door was opening again.

'Ca-a ca-a ca-a!'

Lannias tried to bury his knife in Orbus's guts.

'Fucking idiot!'

Orbus slapped down Lannias's knife hand and cut hard across his face, bursting one of the man's eyes and feeling his knife crunch through the gristle of Lannias's nose.

'Urg,' said Lannias, staggering back.

Suddenly a weight came down on Orbus's back, arms and legs wrapping around him, and something wet licked round his ear.

'Nicesss Captainsss,' said Shalen.

He reached back, grabbed clothing, ducked, and slammed her down on the floor.

'Damned bitch! You . . .'

A huge claw closed hard around his waist. He felt several ribs breaking and he vomited a stream of louse meat.

'Fuck you! Fuck you!' he kept repeating as the Prador retreated with him to the door. He snapped his knife trying to puncture the adamantine claw, struggled to no avail, and wished with all his heart that he had some sprine.

The third day's Intertox injection immediately stopped her struggling against the braided monofilament restraints. Janer was glad about that – her bonds had been stretching alarmingly. Her breathing became stentorian, rattling that horrible flaccid tongue in her mouth. For a second she looked at him with tired sanity, before her eyes started rolling again. He uncapped a bottle of supplement and watched her speculatively, not liking what he must do next and wondering if the clamp gripping her head would hold. He stepped forwards, thrust the bottle neck deep into her mouth, and pinched her nose closed. She struggled at first, thrashing like a beached turbul, then abruptly started swallowing. Once she had drained half the bottle, her eyes opened wide and she stared at him directly. He withdrew the bottle, recapped it, and wiped her chin. Enough for now. As she closed her eyes and slept, Janer moved away.

Having now had time to look around, Janer fully realized what tasks awaited himself and Erlin – if she did not decide to throw Bloc off the side of the ship when she recovered. Four rows of chainglass tanks extended for hundreds of metres in both directions, two rows on either side of a wide aisle interspersed with three wide pillars which enclosed mast stairwells, and the same arrangement on the deck above. With each tank came a set of equipment similar to that they had used on Sable Keech himself: a chrome autodoc, diagnosticer, sets of body probes with optic connections, and a voice generator with an assortment of connections for the varying kinds of reification hardware. Pipes ran along the floor beside the tanks, and connected into each. Others ran along the ceiling, also with spurs leading down to each tank. These were obviously for filling and draining them, but he wondered what with? They had used sea water as an amniot for Keech. It contained microbes as hardy as any other Spatterjay life form, and had been a nightmare to sterilize. There were also stretchers and trolleys here – no doubt intended to bring in the half-dead half-alive reifs after their religious experience on the Little Flint – and there were restraint tables like the one Erlin currently occupied, for holding reifs should they go into conflict with their own cybermotors, as had Keech.

Janer turned back to Erlin, wondering how long he should leave it before administering yet another injection. He watched her for a while, then went out to take a turn around the outside of the deckhouse as the sun set. He next took the stairwell down to the crew quarters in the stern, obtained food in the galley, and chatted for a while with some bored Hoopers sitting around in the mess, before returning to the Tank Rooms to sleep the night away on the table next to Erlin. The following morning he administered more Intertox. The day after that she tried to talk, but her tongue still got in the way.

It did, however, seem to be shrinking, and her colour was less blue. Another night and the best part of the next day passed before he dared consider freeing her.

'What the hell is this?' Erlin asked, as she shakily stepped out across the main deck towards the port rail. The sea stretched endlessly before them, the dark green of laurel with not an island in sight, but the vista divided by ratlines and stay cables. She eyed some reifications standing a short distance away, scanned around the ship, then turned and peered up at the forest of masts, spars, cables and fabric sails in which lurked the three sentient sails, two living and one debatably so. 'Bastards,' she added.

'This is the *Sable Keech*,' said Janer. 'I was willingly recruited. I gather you did not come of your own free will?'

'Damned right I didn't, though the alternative at the time didn't seem so good.' Erlin suddenly looked uncomfortable and added, 'At least that's what any sane person would think.'

Janer glanced at her questioningly, then wondered if he had released the restraints too soon when she went on to describe her nearly terminal encounter with a giant whelk.

'Why weren't you with Ambel?'

'I needed a break,' was all she allowed, then went on, 'What's this all about here?'

'You're on a ship full of reifications sailing towards the Little Flint – sort of following in the footsteps of Keech. A pilgrimage.' Janer stabbed a thumb over his shoulder at the Tank Room. 'I think you can guess what happens when we reach that destination.'

'Whose bright idea is this?' Erlin asked.

'A reif called Taylor Bloc. He was financed by Lineworld—'

Erlin snorted at that.

Janer continued, 'Yes, I know. But with a little help from a hooder he now has *them* off his back.'

'Hooder?'

Janer explained what happened back at the island, then went on with, 'He and his followers are fanatical – as far as you can tell with reifs. I gather that having us aboard, being one-time companions of Sable Keech himself, is something of a coup for Bloc – something akin to having some Apostles at a Christian church service. Though I rather suspect we are expected to feel honoured and humble.'

'So objecting to being kidnapped, and demanding I be released, might not be too bright. Anything else I need to know?'

Janer shrugged. 'Some things going on here I haven't quite fathomed yet, but that's about it.' He grimaced. One of those things concerned Isis Wade, but he was not about to complicate matters by telling Erlin about that. He gazed back along the deck, observing a group making its way down an outer stair from the bridge. Soon the group was close enough for him to recognize some of its members. He pointed. 'Here comes Bloc and a few others.'

'Damn me,' said Erlin, as they drew closer.

'Erlin!' bellowed Captain Ron. He was the first to reach them and he swept Erlin up in a hug.

'Put me down, oaf.' After he did so she continued, 'Janer here neglected to mention you. Last I heard you were off-planet. So what are you doing here?'

Ron waved a hand about. 'I'm the Captain.'

Erlin glanced at Janer and raised an eyebrow, before turning to the others. 'And Forlam's here, too,' she said, her tone neutral. 'How are you doing, Forlam?'

'I do well enough.' Forlam looked slightly guilty, for some reason.

Erlin turned to the reifs. 'And one of you three is Taylor Bloc.'

Bloc stepped forwards, from between Aesop and Bones. 'That would be me.'

Janer could tell nothing from his tone, but doubtless he was wondering what Erlin's immediate reaction would be to being kidnapped and hauled all the way out here. He wanted to warn her to be very careful, but need not have worried.

Erlin held out her hand. 'Then I want to thank you for saving my life, though that was not strictly your intention.' She paused. 'It is precious to me.'

After a hesitation Bloc gripped her hand, his eye irrigators working over-actively, which was, Janer now realized, the only indication of this reif experiencing some strong emotion.

'I am glad to have helped. Zephyr has told me of the circumstances in which he found you. I also must apologize for bringing you here like this, but our need is great . . .'

Erlin released his hand and smiled around. 'No need to apologize,' she said smoothly. 'I'm sure I can allow you months or even years from a lifetime that could possibly last thousands of years for me. Whether intentionally or not, directly or indirectly, you *did* save my life. Anyway, as you are perhaps aware, one of the greatest dangers to a person of my many years is boredom, and this,' she waved a hand to encompass the ship, 'looks interesting.'

'So, when required, you will apply your considerable knowledge and abilities to helping my people . . . Arise?' Bloc asked.

'Certainly. The possibility of my refusing you is doubly remote now that I see that my friends are here willingly.' She indicated Janer, Ron and Forlam.

Bloc nodded woodenly. 'Perhaps you can prepare yourself as soon as possible. It has come to my attention that some reifications are already infected with the Spatterjay virus, and that the Intertox inhibitors merely slow its progress in them.'

'Not surprising really,' Erlin said offhandedly. 'Any form of Intertox, whether in balm or blood, possesses a short active life. It won't therefore access those places the balm reaches by slow percolation, like your bones, where the virus also grows.'

Bloc turned slowly to gaze at one of his companions, before turning back. 'This sort of knowledge is precisely why we need you, Erlin Taser Three Indomial.' He paused, eye irrigators working so hard that moisture was now running down his wrinkled face. 'Please consider yourself welcome aboard the *Sable Keech*, and if there is anything you require, anything at all, please contact me at once. Now, I have some matters to which I must attend. Perhaps later I can give you a tour of our ship?'

'That would be wonderful,' said Erlin.

Even Janer could not fathom whether or not her delighted smile was genuine. Bloc turned and departed, with his two companions in close step behind him. Once he was out of sight, Erlin scanned her surroundings before turning to Ron.

'Okay, Ron, what the fuck are you really doing here?'

'Someone's got to keep an eye on things,' muttered the Old Captain.

'Why you?'

'It's my job.'

'Job?'

'Yeah. Pays well too.'

'And who's paying you?'

Ron shrugged resignedly. 'Windcheater.'

Oh hell, thought Janer.

The cave had been excavated over the millennia by a stream wearing gradually through flinty chalk then limestone running down alongside a basalt column that had been created some time in the island's volcanic past. Packetworm burrows also intruded, to confuse matters, and the drone spent many hours scanning tunnels that led out promisingly sometimes thousands of metres, but always ended at some ancient collapse. On the third day, Thirteen thought it had found the hooder, on coming upon the petrified corpse of a massive packetworm a metre in diameter, its grinding head resting against the basalt that had finally defeated it. The creature must have been dying when it hit this obdurate rock, and just did not have the energy left to turn around. Passing it, the drone explored deeper.

Other living creatures also attracted Thirteen's notice. There were no leeches in the cave, so a species of land heirodont had escaped their attention. These creatures were no bigger than the drone itself – pallid armadillo forms with stunted mandibles. In pools swam their prey: globular white fish that appeared to share ancestry with boxies, diamond-shaped jellyfish, and strange animals mistakable as bonsai baobabs until they scuttled along the stream bed on their rootish feet. But of the hooder there was still no sign.

Eventually, the cave system now completely mapped in its mind, the drone returned via a winding route to the surface. It had scanned every square metre of the island. It had run geoscans into soft ground and, though finding some strange items it might like to investigate later, had found no sign of the alien monster buried there. There were other cave systems, but none large enough to conceal the creature. Thirteen was certain it had missed nothing. Now it reviewed what it had downloaded via the planetary server regarding hooder biology.

They were incredibly tough, and incredibly difficult to kill with most weapons available to the Polity. Like flatworms, if they were broken into segments, each of those segments could eventually grow into another hooder. Their home environment was swamp, on a planet with very little oxygen in its atmosphere. However they did still need oxygen to survive, a small amount of which they obtained from the atmosphere itself, some by eating the oxygen storage cells in their prey, and the rest by cracking CO_2 in photochemical and electrochemical reactions. Such creatures could survive underwater for a considerable time, but they could not swim – were too heavy for it. On their home planet the only specimens found in the sea had been those that had drowned. Had it ventured into the sea? Thirteen thought this unlikely. So where was it then? Thirteen rose high out of the dingle on Mortuary Island, revolved in the air and gazed out across the ocean, tilted itself towards the horizon, and set out.

Leaning against the stern rail, Santen Marcollian gazed out across the sea. She had been a cultist for her first fifty years of existence as a reif – after her unfortunate accident with a grenade – but even being dead did not prevent one growing up. That half a century taught her a lot, and in the end, feeling she had outgrown the Cult of Anubis Arisen, she rejected it and went her own way. Consequently, it peeved her that this voyage was controlled by the likes of Bloc, who though not a cultist of the old style, still espoused some of its ideals. And, after that scene on her first day aboard, she was beginning to wonder if she had made a big mistake.

Bloc's armed Kladites were everywhere, and that worried her. Yes, this was a ferocious world, but they were aboard a large ship protected by automated laser turrets dotting the hull. Nothing nasty was going to get aboard, so perhaps it was the case that the nasty thing was already here. She looked around, noting a few other reifs strolling about out on deck, experiencing what they could of their surroundings in their own limited way. The prospect of actually returning to life, like Sable Keech, had brought her here – to actually be able to *feel* again: wind against skin, movement through the inner ear, the roughness of this metal rail against her palm . . .

'How are you enjoying the ocean life?'

Santen turned and saw that the reif John Styx had stepped up beside her. Studying him, Santen wondered what had killed him, since there was no visible damage to his body, and for a reif he moved with a surprising smoothness. Prior to their earlier encounter aboard this ship, she had witnessed him, when the hooder had attacked, taking up a Batian weapon and firing on the creature while other reifs, herself included, merely took cover.

'It is becoming somewhat boring,' she replied.

'After just eight days?'

'Yes, after just eight days.'

'Never mind, I'm sure that will soon change.'

'What do you mean?'

Styx shrugged – which was not an easy thing for a reif to do. 'Have you received Bloc's summons?'

'Yes.' Santen checked her internal clock. The meeting was due in only half an hour in a hall down in the bilge, immediately above the rudder. Santen wondered where the intervening time had gone. 'He's probably going to lay down the law for us. And I somewhat doubt he's going to be making any concessions, perhaps rightly so.'

'Will he have us standing in ranks practising our salutes?' Styx asked.

'Let's hope not. I already left the Cult of Anubis Arisen, and have no intention of joining its bastard off-spring.'

Styx nodded. 'Apparently he's been delivering some lecture to us all a hundred at a time. At least this is what I've been told, though those already called in are rather close-mouthed about what went on. His own people, of course, don't need any instructions.'

'It's Cult shit, I guarantee. Even if he and his follow-ers are technically not supposed to be cultists.'

Styx remained silent.

'You know,' Santen went on, 'I find it difficult now to understand how I swallowed all that garbage for as long as I did: *The Cult is to give us identity; the Cult empowers each individual with the strength of all* . . . and the rest. It took me far too long to realize the Cult is just a way of making its leaders wealthy and powerful.'

'Like a religion,' suggested Styx.

'Like a religion,' Santen agreed. 'And this is no different. Shall we go down and see what our tour guide has to say? It might at least be amusing.'

'Let's hope so,' murmured Styx.

They began making their way along the deck.

'At least the Hoopers don't have to put up with this crap,' remarked Santen, eyeing one man who was cleaning some organic mess from the visible section of one of the massive bow anchor chains.

They reached the jigger mast stairwell and Styx went down ahead of Santen. She noted again how easily he moved, not checking his handholds on the banister, nor watching where he put his feet. Probably he was a later reification than herself, therefore running on more advanced hardware and software. Soon they exited on the maintenance deck and walked along to another short stair leading down to the meeting hall itself, joining others heading for the same destination. They entered a room in which were crowded the reifs summoned this time around, talking in low voices to each other. Santen observed Bloc standing at one end facing them, Aesop and Bones on either side of him, and a squad of Kladites arrayed behind. Studying the room itself she noted the floor was polished wood, and that there was a line of cupboards along one entire wall. The door to one of them stood open, revealing stacks of folding chairs. Doubtless this hall was intended for conferences, but Bloc had not thought to put out the seating.

'Please close the door,' he said to the last reifs entering. When this was done Bloc continued, 'Welcome, fellow searchers.'

Ellanc Strone, who had positioned himself near the front, interrupted. 'Ah, it now seems I'm not supposed to be here.' He turned to go.

'Please wait. What I have to say is important, and concerns you all.'

'It better be good,' said Strone, turning back.

'Oh it is,' said Bloc, his spectacle irrigators misting moisture all around his face. 'It concerns discipline aboard this ship, and the establishment of an efficient regime. This is not a pleasure cruise; it is *my* ship and I do expect obedience.'

'That's interesting,' replied Strone.

'Yes,' Bloc nodded, 'it is. Now you all received notification of the ship regulations, through your cabin screens, when we set out, but it seems some of you require a reminder. You have all been allotted specific times when you can come up on deck, you have all been clearly informed of those areas where you cannot trespass, but many of you persist in ignoring such simple instructions. May I remind you that this is not a Polity world, and so Polity law does not protect you.'

'You see,' muttered Styx.

'What's it to be then? A flogging? Walking the plank?' someone said.

Bloc eyed the reif who had spoken. 'The former will obviously have no effect though the latter is a possibility.'

At this many of the crowd protested, perhaps remembering Aesop's implied threat earlier.

Ignoring the hubbub, Bloc continued loudly, 'I am personally affronted by the attitude shown by many of you.' Bloc eyed Strone in particular. 'Without me and without this ship, you would not be here at all and would not have this chance of Arising.'

'The bite of a leech is not so hard to find on this planet,' retorted Strone.

'Yes,' said Bloc. 'But what about the expertise of Erlin Taser Three Indomial here onboard, what about the tanks I have provided, the presence of Janer Cord Anders, the opportunity to more precisely follow the path Sable Keech himself walked?'

'I don't recollect anything about him coming right out here,' sneered Strone.

'I will bring you to the Little Flint,' continued Bloc, ignoring him. 'And what do I get – nothing but complaints about matters that are almost ephemeral?'

'You're cashing in on us. You and that fucking Lineworld,' said Strone.

'I am not,' Bloc protested. 'If it was not for me, Batian mercenaries would now be running this ship, and then . . .'

In the pause John Styx muttered, 'Now that's very interesting.'

The protests and interruptions started up again. Every time Bloc tried to say something, he was shouted down.

'What is?' asked Santen.

'Well, the bulk of those mercenaries were killed by a creature supposedly shipped to this world by Lineworld Developments, so you would think it hardly due to Bloc that they are not currently running this ship.'

Santen felt a horrible disquiet as she returned her attention to Ellanc Strone, speaking again on behalf of all the complainers.

'So this is better, is it?' Strone pointed to the Kladites gathered behind Bloc. 'You cheat us, expect our obedience, and now you're prepared to enforce it.'

Bloc bowed his head as the verbal assault continued, then he held up his hands. 'Quiet! Please, quiet!' When the noise had dropped to a mutter, he continued, 'Obviously we are getting nowhere here today. I shall have to look into the matter of compensation, for which I will need to contact Lineworld. When I have done that, I will meet with you again, and we will sort all this out.'

He stepped forwards, the crowd parting before him. The Kladites fell in behind him as he left the room.

'So the complainers are getting somewhere,' observed Santen.

'Precisely where, I wonder,' replied Styx.

Visually checking his hand- and footholds as he climbed, Wade experienced a momentary amusement. Who would have thought *he* would ever fear heights? It was the human facade, for to be an anthropoid Golem required a high level of human emulation. He did not really fear heights, just ran a program to adjust his behaviour to that of a human aware that to fall now would mean death. In defiance of that same emulation, he paused for a moment, turned and gazed around him. A cool breeze was blowing off the sea. On the horizon the sun bloated as it set: a dull lime orb poised at the far end of the ocean, cloud boiling up around it like steam it created as it seemingly submerged, this spreading in a static explosion, shredded across the sky, its inner faces green and yellow, the outer faces gold and red. A trail, as of green-tinted mercury, cut across the dark sea to the ship. The occasional frothy wake appeared as mid-sized leeches surfaced and probed the air with their trumpet mouths. Wade nodded, as if the view confirmed something for him, then peered up the length of this massive mainmast he clung to, which at this point tapered to a mere half a metre thick. Only a little way still to go.

Eventually reaching his destination, he stretched up and grabbed a spar. A hook claw released its hold right next to his hand, and the expanse of monofabric wing above folded in on its many-jointed spines. Wade hauled himself astride the spar, then looked upwards.

'I was hoping you wouldn't come up here,' said Zephyr.

'I gave you a few days to learn the ropes, so to speak, and there has been much here to divert me. But our business is only just beginning. You must still be undecided to have come all the way out here.'

'Time is not an issue,' said the sail.

'I disagree. It very much is an issue.'

'It might be for you, but I am a complete entity. I owe nothing to how I was made.'

'Then death is an issue,' said Wade.

The Golem sail hissed and swung its head away, then abruptly swung it back, stopping only half a metre from where Wade sat. He was uncomfortably aware that not only was he the focus of a pair of emerald eyes, but also the focus of a particle cannon. It was utterly illogical that an entity so hating death would carry such potent means of delivering it. Wade turned his head away and peered down towards the activity on the deck.

'And it is certainly very much the issue aboard this ship, hence our interest. Are reifications dead, and once dead can they live again? Why do Hoopers value the potential of death, then bank it?'

'They know Death, and they fight to defeat it.'

'Then we are in agreement. You understand, and it is time to tell your other self.'

'We are not in agreement. Reifications are truly dead. Hoopers are alive.'

'So you believe, as humans once did, in a soul?'

'Life is the totality: body and mind, and their sum, their synergy. Death is the antithesis that must be destroyed. I will begin that destruction and . . . live.'

Zephyr's eyes were flickering like faulty lamps, and Wade sensed some of the turmoil the Golem sail was suffering. He knew that turmoil: the war fought between emotion and intellect inside all conscious beings . . . even sane ones.

'You are not alive,' he said.

'I *am* alive,' Zephyr growled.

'No. You claim reifications are dead, yet how are they different to you? They are minds loaded to crystal, just like you are, and just like our progenitor could be, if you could persuade *yourself* of that fact.'

'Am alive!'

Zephyr swung his head away, then cracked it back hard. Wade went backwards off the spar, then was hurtling down towards the midship deckhouse. Human emulation made him grab air as if trying to slow his descent, then he overcame this reflex and relaxed. Hitting the bubble-metal roof of the deckhouse with a crash, he cratered it. Lying there, reflecting on the changes the real world had already wrought in Zephyr, he heard the sound of approaching footsteps. As they halted, one of the Hooper crew leaned over to peer down at him.

'That were a hard landing. What happened?'

Heaving himself out of the man-shaped dent, Wade looked around as if dazed. He noticed the rails all around the roof; the tables bolted to it ready to take umbrellas and be surrounded by chairs. After a moment he realized he was not fooling this Hooper. For some reason they had known what he was almost immediately. He guessed that the sizeable dent was also a bit of a giveaway.

'Just a little disagreement.' He winced.

'Your evidence is not entirely satisfactory,' said the Warden.

Hovering a hundred metres above the sea, with the two smaller drones on either side of him, Sniper repressed his frustration. Returning to the search after locating the *Vignette*, he tried repeatedly to convince the Warden that its sinking should be investigated further, but the Warden had a hornet in its bonnet about this hive-mind agent, and considered finding that intruder a lot more important. Sniper disagreed; Prador, as far as he was concerned, were a lot more dangerous than stinging insects.

He protested, 'I ain't trying to convince a legal submind. I just think this is something I should investigate. And we've looked under every rock in this area, and checked every ship – but no agent.'

'Then it is time to widen the search.'

Sniper hissed and spun about like a coin.

The Warden continued, 'If you believe Prador are down there, did you neglect to record their ship's arrival while you acted as Warden, or did they come by rucible?'

'No need to be sarky. There's another possibility.'

'Yes, the newly adult Prador that left the Seagre island ten years ago. It would perhaps have been better if you had ensured its demise at the time.'

'Well, I set a molly carp after the bastard, and he was at least fifteen kilometres from its dad's ship,' Sniper replied grumpily. 'Anyhow, I was busy, and most of the SM shells were scrap by then.'

'Busy?'

'Well . . . it took me a while to take on your role. It's complicated up there.'

'Complicated,' the Warden repeated flatly. Then after a long pause: 'Actually you were right. The chances of the Prador surviving the molly carp were slim, but the chances of it surviving aboard its father's ship were utterly remote.'

'There, y'see?'

'So where did the Prador come from that supposedly sank the *Vignette*?'

'Bollocks,' Sniper muttered.

'Precisely, as you say, "Bollocks." Now let us look at the facts. The Golem agent of an ancient hive mind is loose down there for as yet unknown purposes. Has it not occurred to you there may be a connection?'

'Why would a hive mind want to sink a ship and take its crew?' Sniper asked. 'That's the Prador way of operating – taking the human crew to use as blanks.'

'I don't know, but some connection does seem likely.'

'Nope,' said Sniper stubbornly. 'I still think it's Prador.'

'Then what do you propose?'

'Check out Ebulan's ship. I can get there in a few hours.'

Again a long pause. Sniper sensed something like

confusion through the link. It occurred to him that the Warden's long confinement might have sapped the AI's confidence.

'Very well, do so. But I want the geological drones to continue the search, and you to return to it the moment you've ascertained the position.'

The Warden then cut the connection.

Sniper did not try to analyse why the Warden had now changed its mind. He dropped out of the sky, then engaged his fusion engines. As he shot away he sent back to Eleven and Twelve, 'Come on slowpokes, get those burners on.'

As Ambel peered through his binoculars, what he saw evinced in him some surprise, and for the Old Captain that was no common occurrence.

'Definitely a ship's boat, and there's someone waving from it,' he announced.

'Can't have been out at sea here for long – wouldn't have survived the first rhinoworm to come along,' observed Boris.

'Well let's pick 'em up before one does happen by,' Ambel replied.

Boris eased the helm over, and Galegrabber eased himself and his fabric brethren to the optimum angle. The *Treader* curved in towards the smaller craft, foaming out a white wake in the stiff breeze. The men in the boat began rowing hard to intercept the ship's course.

Climbing up to the bridge, Anne observed, 'We'll have to reef to pick them up – it'll slow us.' Down below, Peck had already unwrapped his shotgun.

'That's as maybe,' said Ambel, 'but we can't leave the lads to die. Anyway, we're out over deep water now, so

there shouldn't be any problem with big angry molluscs.'

'That's good.' Anne turned to stare behind them.

As they finally drew in beside the small boat, Boris
shouted at Galegrabber, 'Reef 'em!' after the sail seemed
a little reluctant. Muttering to itself, it pulled the reefing
cables that wadded the fabric sails up against their spars,
then climbed high up the mast, peering nervously all
about. Ambel frowned at it, then climbed down to the
main deck.

'You all right there, lads?' he asked, leaning over the
side. He vaguely recognized the two men in the boat,
which probably meant they were juniors, as he clearly
recognized every senior crewman. How could he not,
having known them for centuries?

'Captain Ambel!' said one of them delightedly. He
was a thin-set lad with blond hair tied in a pony tail. The
other one was of squatter build, his ginger hair patchy on
the dome of his head. Another few years and it would
likely all be gone – just like Ron's.

'Do I know you?' the Captain asked.

'I'm Silister, and my friend is Davy-bronte . . . from
the *Vignette*.'

'Ah . . .' said Ambel. 'Well get aboard sharpish and
you can tell me all about it.'

The two men scrambled up the rope ladder Peck had
cast down to them. Ambel observed chunks taken out of
the side of their craft, some burns, and the remains of a
rhinoworm on which the two had obviously been dining.
The boat was also partially awash. He nodded to himself
– they had been adrift for a while and survived, doubtless with some Polity assistance. As soon as the two men
were on deck and standing before Ambel, he shouted up

to Galegrabber, 'Let's be moving along then!' The sail
seemed intent on something out at sea, so he yelled.
'Galegrabber!' Eventually it obeyed and, under the
boom of fabric sail, the *Treader* journeyed on.

'What about the boat?' Peck was peering over the
side.

'Tie her off at the stern,' Ambel replied.

Muttering imprecations Peck took up a coil of rope
and climbed over the rail.

'All right, lads, which of you has the laser?'

The two of them looked uncomfortable. Eventually
the squat one, Davy-bronte, opened his shirt and pulled
out a QC laser handgun. He hesitated for a moment,
then turned it round so as to present the butt to Ambel.
The Captain took the weapon, inspected it for a
moment, then handed it back to him. The look of surprise on Davy-bronte's face both amused and saddened
him.

'This isn't the *Vignette*. It's your weapon, so you keep
it. I just want to know who has it so I know who to call
on should it be necessary.' He pointed up to the bridge.
'Anne up there's got a laser carbine. And that over there
is mine.' He pointed to where his blunderbuss hung.
'Now, speaking of the *Vignette*, where exactly is that ship
now?'

After a long hesitation, the one called Davy-bronte
replied, 'A couple of kilometres down, I reckon.'

Ambel winced. He might not have much time for
Orbus, but no Captain liked to hear about a ship going
down. The best that could be hoped for crew from a
stricken ship who ended up in the water was that something big might grab and kill them quickly, since only
very young Hoopers would have the luxury of drowning.

Ambel knew, only too well, what happened to older Hoopers left helpless in the sea.

'Why's that then, lad?'

'A big Prador war drone shot a hole through the side.'

Coming over the rail with the end of the rope, the other end of which he had just attached to the boat, Peck said, 'Chewin' bloody squeaky weed bugger.' He then headed for the stern, flipping the slack along the rail as he went, while the rowing boat drifted out behind the ship.

Ambel ignored his muttering. 'Prador war drone?'

Silister now replied, 'It come out of the sea. The Cap'n thought it was that other big Polity drone at first an' it harpooned him, then it rained sail meat an' it got Drooble first . . .' He trailed off, looking confused, then brightly added, 'We were caulking the boat. We hid.'

Ambel patted him on the shoulder. 'Perhaps you'd better start—'

'Aaargh!'

Ambel stepped past them and hurried to the stern, in time to see Peck leaning back hard, his feet slipping along the deck, the rope now a taut line to the stern rail, then out to the boat beyond. Ambel stepped to the rail and saw the boat, half sunk, waggling from side to side.

'Let it go, Peck.'

'Umph.'

The line slackened. The boat turned a circle, lifted up out of the water and fell back upside down. A familiar flat white tentacle rose behind it, then came down hard, smashing it to matchwood.

'We got all the sail on?' Ambel asked loudly but casually.

'Yes, Captain!' shouted Boris. He was also turning the *Treader* quickly, so it would run with the wind.

'What?' asked Silister, who had followed with his companion.

'One thing at a time,' said Ambel. 'Now tell me again what happened to the *Vignette*.'

The giant whelk chewed on the fragments of wood, sucking every nuance of flavour from them. She located and gobbled up the slightly rancid chunk of rhinoworm. She was very hungry, having discovered that swimming used up more energy than crawling along the bottom, but all this unaccustomed activity also made her feel more alive than ever before. Also, such were the changes she had undergone, mentally and physically, she was beginning to question her earlier motivations of revenge.

The bulk of her young had been eaten by a shoal of turbul, but should she ever encounter any of that species again she would treat them no differently than before. She would kill and eat them just the same. The human . . . yes the word was now clear in her mind . . . had only killed one of her young, and she was not exactly pursuing that particular human, but any with some connection to it. No matter. She gave an underwater shrug. She would kill and eat them just the same. That was what she did. Anyway, she was enjoying this chase. It was with a growth of something new inside her – humour – that she recognized that she killed and ate any living thing she could lay her tentacles on. And so she laboured on after the *Treader*.

The heirodont, closing in from five hundred metres behind her, possessed no sense of humour at all, probably because it spent most of its life being fed upon by parasitic leeches. However, it did enjoy a chase, and it definitely ascribed to the same creed as the whelk: it killed and ate anything it could get its mandibles around.

11

Sea Leech:
upon entering the ocean, the leech's body-shape becomes leaf-like to more suit it to the pelagic life. It grows huge on a diet of flesh taken from boxies, turbul, oceanic heirodonts – anything soft enough for it to bore into with its plug-extracting mouth. By the time a sea leech becomes whale-sized, such prey is too small to provide sufficient nutrient by plug feeding. However, it would be dangerous for the leech to take prey down whole as, with the incredible durability and voracity of all Spatterjay's fauna, that prey would eat the leech from the inside. Hunger drives the next transformation. The leech grows a sprine-producing bile duct and feeds upon whole prey – poisoning them with sprine inside its intestines. Again genetically programmed to respond to their environment, they mate only when the surrounding population of their own kind drops below a certain level (this measured by the quantity of particular pheromones in the water). Leeches are hermaphrodite: they will close against another of their kind and exchange genetic material. After this the leech dies during the process of attaching its own body-segments to the bottom of masses of floating sargassum. The segments then collapse into hard encystments, and the cells inside them turn into eggs

encased in sprine jelly. Each of these hatches a diatom, which then begins its long journey to shore to become a land leech –

In his stateroom, Bloc sat on the edge of his wide, soft and unneeded bed and stared at the polished, oak-panelled wall – an occupation that seemed more and more frequent to him lately. Internally, he gazed into the red tunnel comprising the third channel from his control unit. He felt that what he barely controlled there was his only option now. Ellanc Strone and those aligned with him had not needed to come on this voyage, but they had, and now their earlier complaining was turning into open defiance. Bloc realized that Strone understood Bloc's position here; that he was isolated and could possibly be usurped. Could it be that the other reif was secretly working for Lineworld? No matter, Bloc must quickly assert full control aboard this ship, and remove all dangers to himself and this enterprise. As if to illustrate, the reason for this now appeared on his internal visual display:

OUTPARAFUNCT: B.P. LOAD INC. 15%

He had increased the amount of Intertox in his balm to a fifth, but still he was getting those warning messages. How long he could hold on before having to go into a tank he did not know, but it seemed unlikely he would reach the Little Flint before his transformation. He realized how he resented those reifs who would. He resented their knowingness, their lack of respect for him. *He* had done all this. This ship was *his*. And he refused to allow them to be so casual, dismissive and contemptuous in his presence. He stood up abruptly.

VIRAL INFECT

Again that message.

IDENTIFY he instructed almost automatically.

SPATTERJAY VIRAL FORM A1

He cleared that one, then another immediately appeared.

MEMSPACE: 00037

Annoyed, he quickly cleared that too, while considering all the potential dangers.

Strone and his followers numbered thirty-six – he had identified them all. Now, Bloc could simply order his Kladites to dispense with them, but that would not go down well with the other six hundred reifications aboard. Also the Hoopers, though primitive, were necessary at the moment and, despite the automation aboard the *Sable Keech*, it might be foolish to annoy them. The sails, even Zephyr, worked to their contracts for money and that was all. If they became a problem, though, this ship had the facility to sail on without them. It had the facility to keep going without any sails, either living or plain fabric. That left Janer Cord Anders and Erlin Taser Three Indomial, who he certainly wanted to keep on his side. So, no overt action on his part, but there was another way.

Bloc closed his eyes and turned his attention inward to the partitioned control unit he used to control Aesop and Bones. Those two channels were familiar and easy for him. The third channel was something else, however: a red tunnel of madness. He ignored it for the moment and turned his attention to his servants.

Bones he put on hold: utterly motionless in the corridor outside. Aesop he summoned inside. Bloc opened his eyes as the door opened and closed.

'Summon Ellanc Strone and his friends to the stern meeting hall,' he said.

'You'll not settle anything with them,' said Aesop.

Bloc eyed him. 'Did I ask your opinion?'

Aesop remained silent.

Bloc continued, 'Seven o'clock this evening. When that is arranged, I'll have another task for you, which you must complete before that meeting begins. I think you know what it is.' He turned away, but Aesop was not leaving, so he turned back.

'Leave now,' said Bloc with finality, and *pushed*.

As he stepped off the ladder Isis Wade paused to study his hands. The human form, he felt, was interesting: perpetually on the point of toppling from its mere two limbs but never doing so. The limitation of possessing only two legs, however, was more than made up for by the complicated dexterity of the hands. No doubt, had the body he occupied actually been human rather than a mechanical construct, he would be surprised by many of its other . . . functions. But he was Golem and, behind all this emulation of humanity, something utterly else. He turned from the ladder and scanned the bilge.

There was a great deal down here, most of it at Lineworld's insistence, some at Bloc's, and he suspected there was something else that nobody wanted here . . . perhaps. Making his way along walkways and through hidden corridors he approached the ship's bows. Being Golem, his hearing was superb; he could hear the beating of a human heart, hear it stop.

Wade shook his head – another human gesture, as if the thoughts in a mind could be physically shaken free. It did not work, for the fact remained that he was allowing these distractions to divert him from his prime purpose here aboard this ship. But the human dramas were so much easier . . .

In the twisted conglomeration of rooms, corridors and walkways below the chain lockers, Wade began scanning about himself as he proceeded. Eventually, on a grated walkway affixed directly to the lower ribs of the hull, he found what he was searching for. He stooped and picked up a pair of bloody trousers, slashed to ribbons. He shook them, and caught something that fell out: a piece of bone. It was white, with bluish striations through it, and looked as if someone had roughed out its shape from the main bone with a small drill, then snapped it out. Wade flipped it aside then peered over the edge of the grating. After a moment he moved over to one side, clicked across the catches securing one section, then hinged it up. This gave him access to what had been deposited below the walkway. Down there were many more pieces of bone, fragments of cloth, strings of fibrous flesh, a skinning knife and a screwdriver. He picked up the knife and inspected the name etched into the blade: Sturmbul. Wade accessed the list of passengers and crew he had loaded, and after a moment nodded. Gazing into the darkness, towards the chain lockers, he carefully reached out to pull the section of grating down, stood back, and headed quietly in the other direction.

Halfway along the length of the hull, Wade came to his second objective down here. The enclosed section had one metal bulkhead door with a manual wheel and a code-input palm reader. He stared at the reader for a long moment, then took out the skinning knife and inserted its blade under the small keypad. One twist and this flipped away, exposing optical circuitry. He smiled –

something else he had been practising – traced the circuitry with the knife point, then selected a plug-in chip, levered it out and pocketed it. He next moved over to the manual wheel, braced himself and began to put on pressure. After a moment something snapped inside the door and the wheel spun freely. As he pushed the door open, pieces of shattered locking mechanism clattered to the floor. Stepping inside, he stooped to pick them up and toss them out of sight, before closing the door behind him.

Wade first eyed the row of glass-fronted lockers containing breather gear and ceramal chainmesh diving suits, then turned his attention to the flattened-torpedo submersible. He approached the ladder, climbed up to the squat conning tower, where he opened the hatch and lowered himself inside. Then, dropping into the pilot's seat, he studied a large screen and numerous controls. After a little while he went back outside and more closely inspected the craft's hull. Very quickly he found the harpoon ports and slidable sections covering folded manipulators and chainglass vibroblades.

'Naughty,' he said, and shook his head.

Lineworld Developments had certainly been out to cash in wherever possible. Wade wondered what the Hoopers aboard would have thought about them using a submersible to harvest sea leech bile ducts. No matter, since this option was now closed to them. Nevertheless, here, should anyone require it, was a perfect way of obtaining the prized poison, sprine.

He again smiled to himself.

As Aesop made his way down into the hull he felt his terror growing, but Bloc's control of him was as rigid as a cage. Stepping off the ladder onto the maintenance deck, he observed a couple of Hoopers gazing through the protective cover over a ceramal powder forge, and wondered if the ship would soon be urgently in need of their skill if what was to happen inside it did not sink it. He knew that the hull was double-skinned, sandwiching a layer of crash foam, but would that be enough?

Eventually he made his way down into the bilge. Moving stealthily via stairs, platforms and hidden corridors, he came eventually to the area Bloc had designated: the room above the rudder hydraulics and motors where he had earlier lectured groups of the passengers. It was dark until he touched a pad beside the door, then star lights lit up all across a low ceiling, revealing the room space stretching hundreds of metres from port to starboard. Aesop had no idea what its intended purpose might be, but there were many places like this aboard. Perhaps it was for some celebration after they reached the Little Flint – though the bars and restaurants some way above him would be better for that. Aesop reached into his pocket and took out an aerosol can, and as if spraying invisible graffiti, began working his way around the wall.

'*Get a move on*,' Bloc instructed, and pushed.

Within twenty minutes Aesop was back at the door. Now, as he headed towards the ship's bows, he began to spray also along the corridor wall. He resisted all the way, but to no avail – Bloc was not relaxing his control in the slightest. He wondered if Bloc would ever allow Aesop's memcrystal to be recovered. Probably not, since Aesop's mind contained far too much damning evidence. He wondered if being destroyed would feel anything like dying. At least there would be no pain this time, just physical destruction then . . . nothing. Up ahead somewhere: *movement*. The sound was like someone sorting through a huge wooden tool chest, though slightly more rhythmic than that. Suddenly there came a crash, and the sound was moving towards him.

'*I've done it now*,' he pleaded with Bloc.

There was no response from the reif. Through his enslaving link, Aesop could feel Bloc directly controlling Bones. Through Bones's vision he glimpsed armed Kladites creeping along a corridor on one of the upper decks. The clear-up party, almost certainly. With Bloc's attention elsewhere, Aesop could fight the control. This he did, trying to pull his finger away from the aerosol can's spray button. With all his effort he broke through to Bloc, fed back, and managed to ease the pressure of the programmed order. His finger came off the button. But this was not enough to enable him to survive. He strained harder, trying to break the link, but it was like trying to cut through cable with a butter knife. Then suddenly he realized he was no longer walking – just standing in the corridor, straining forwards.

'*Please let me . . .*'

He jerked his hand forward, releasing the can to send it bouncing down the corridor, just as a darkness slid, clattering, round a further corner. Aesop desperately wanted to run: he picked one foot up and tried to turn. He would have to fight for every step, yet knew he could not. There was a recess in the wall beside him – the moulding for a doorway that had never been cut through. He took one swinging, jerky step and fell into it. As he turned his head, something passed him thunderously. Aesop might well have sighed with relief, but

considered it perhaps lucky he did not possess that ability, for *it* would have heard.

Janer, sitting in the crew mess, eyed two Hoopers
gobbling down pickled hammer whelks at a nearby
table. The equipment checks in the Tank Rooms now
finished, Janer felt the pressure had come off him, so it
was time to turn his attention towards his primary purpose for being here.

The hive mind had paid him to hunt down the Golem
agent of another hive mind, who was supposedly here
after sprine. He was to 'stop' this Golem, though being
armed by the mind with a perfect Golem assassination
weapon made the method of prevention somewhat
implicit. Janer had his reservations about this, but he
was never one to turn down money, and the venture
promised to be one that might keep his perennial boredom at bay. As he saw it, he would make a serious effort
to stop this Golem without recourse to the weapon.
Golem were not stupid after all. Upon his arrival here he
had realized the hopelessness of the task. His joining
Ron's venture was a reaction to that, as had been his
attempt to return the hive mind's payment. The mind
refused it, probably hoping to persuade him back to
the task. But now his hivelink had shut down and the
hornets were dead. This had happened while he was with
Isis Wade, a rather inscrutable Golem, and Janer was
convinced Wade was the one he had been sent here to
find. But what now?

Janer stood up and took his empty dish into the galley to wash it. Now, he felt, it was time for him to start
trolling for information. As far as he had been able to
gather, Isis Wade's job was to monitor and keep running

some of the ship's more high-tech systems – a make-work task at best. It seemed more likely that the Golem was ensconced in his cabin, so Janer headed there.

Wade's cabin was in the forward section, along with the quarters of those employed to oversee the more technical systems of the ship. Finally reaching it, Janer undid his jacket, then knocked on the door.

'Something on your mind?'

Janer froze, then slowly turned. Wade was standing directly behind him.

'We need to talk.'

'Is that so?' Wade stepped past him, opened the door and ducked inside. Following him, Janer wondered where to start.

'Where have you been?' he asked.

Wade sat down on the bed while Janer closed the door and rested his back against it. Some species of almost painful amusement flitted across the Golem's expression. But it was solely emulation – Janer felt he must never forget that.

'I went to have another look at that submersible. It was most interesting.'

'In what way?'

Wade shrugged. Damn, but it was *good* emulation. 'It would seem Lineworld was prepared for every opportunity to make some profit, though of course it will now profit them nothing.'

Janer repressed his irritation. 'Profit?'

Wade stared at him directly. 'The submersible is especially equipped to catch leeches and remove from them their bile ducts. No doubt somewhere else on board this ship there are facilities for refining sprine.'

Janer felt himself tensing up. Was that it, then – had

this hive-mind agent come here to take advantage of this opportunity? Certainly, obtaining sprine from Olian's was out of the question, yet surely one of Wade's capabilities could obtain that substance from any incoming ship – could have grabbed some before it ever reached Olian's?

'Is that why you are here, Wade?' he asked.

'Certainly not. I'm here to learn some things, and to apprise an individual of certain truths, and possibly – though I hope this will not be necessary – to prevent a cataclysm.'

'Can you be more specific?'

'I can, but I won't,' Wade replied.

'All right then. Can you at least answer me this: are you the agent of an ancient hive mind?'

Wade abruptly stood up, and Janer slid his hand nearer to his concealed weapon. He didn't much rate his chances against Wade in this situation – in any situation really. The Golem turned his back, opened a cupboard, and from it removed a long box. This he placed on the bed and flipped open. Janer eyed the weapon revealed, and felt his mouth go dry. Sable Keech had once carried something like this. It was an APW carbine. Fire burned inside its glass body.

'It was you . . . You fired on that hooder?'

Wade waved a hand dismissively. 'Yes, of course. But let's keep to the subject of our discussion. In a sense, I *am* the agent you describe.'

Janer closed his hand on the butt of his own weapon, expecting the Golem to turn on him at any moment. But even as Janer quickly drew his gun, the Golem made no move.

'What the hell is that weapon for?' Janer asked.

'I might well ask you the same.' Wade indicated with a nod the gun now pointing at him.

'Self-defence,' said Janer.

'Equally,' said Wade, 'I have not as yet told you what else I discovered down in the bilge.'

'I'm listening.'

Wade told him.

Ellanc Strone admiringly checked the working of the Batian weapon before placing it on his sleeping pallet next to a collection of grenades. Quite remiss of Bloc to have not collected all this. He turned and looked at himself in the mirror. Now it was time to move on. He had believed in the Cult for some years, but grown out of that, then come to hate it. He had in fact come to hate the whole idea of reification and would have gladly dispensed with the corpse he now saw before him. Only one thing stood in his way: money. Though the Polity did provide Golem, clones and sometimes the bodies of mind-wiped criminals for human beings recorded to crystal, the waiting list was fifty years long. To actually step over that list and buy a replacement cost a great deal and Ellanc's funds did not stretch so far. His dislike of the Cult and its bastard offspring, also his need for money, were what had made him accept Lineworld's initial offer to spy on Bloc. They were also the reason he had accepted the offer he recently received over secure com.

He would turn Bloc into a heap of scrap metal.

Ellanc donned his long coat, concealing the Batian weapon which hung from his belt underneath it. Quite probably he himself would be destroyed by the Kladites. However, Lineworld had made promises, guaranteed by independent arbiter, to load him to a Golem chassis, and pay him a disgustingly large quantity of money. Ellanc himself had made provision for one of his fellows to retrieve his memcrystal. Thereafter, Bloc's people would be leaderless and easy prey for other Lineworld operatives, who were already on their way to Mortuary Island to await this ship's return, and seize control of it before the next voyage.

It was 6.30 now, and time to get going. Ellanc stepped out of his cabin and strode along the deck that housed the reification's staterooms, picking up his followers as he went. As Oranol joined him he said, 'Remember, you do nothing. Don't make any hostile moves – just ensure you get hold of my memcrystal.'

'I understand,' confirmed Oranol.

So he should – Ellanc would be paying him a lot of money for that understanding.

Twenty-five minutes later they reached the jigger stairwell and filed down to the meeting hall. They entered, looking around, but the hall was empty.

'I don't like this,' said Oranol.

'What's to dislike?' Ellanc asked. 'Bloc is probably still trying to figure how he's going to get out of this.' Ellanc knew that Bloc was near bankrupt, and that definitely no further funds would be forthcoming from Lineworld.

'Someone's coming,' said one of the reifs.

Ellanc listened – and heard a rumbling sound. Probably a troop of Kladites coming to back up some more of Bloc's threats. Maybe some of those threats would even be carried out. Ellanc did not care really, just so long as Bloc came along with them. Precisely at the moment he turned, the door and half its surrounding woodwork exploded inward, and the hooder careened into the room like an out-of-control train.

The hard, segmented edge of the creature's carapace cut across one reified woman like a saw, flinging her back with her clothing torn away and chest ripped open to expose shrivelled lungs. It slammed down on another reif, then instantly reared up again, tossing aside something ragged and spraying blue balm. Ellanc swung up his weapon, knowing it was useless. He fired continuously, explosions flashing along the creature's surface, blowing small cavities and flinging off pieces of tough carapace. Another victim was smashed into the back wall, yet another cupped under the monster's hood, while its new spiky tail lashed sideways and someone's head bounced across the floor. It loomed up, with pieces of reification hardware and bones falling away from underneath its hood, whipped its head from side to side sending reifs sprawling in every direction.

Ellanc fired at it repeatedly, aiming for the same spot on the body segment just behind its head, trying to excavate his way in. Five reifs down in as many seconds, possibly more. This was worse than what he had witnessed back at the enclosure. The thing seemed maddened. He pulled a grenade and rolled it underneath the monster. It lifted slightly on the blast, a hole blown through the floor below it. Then it came down again and again, like a draughts player profiting by an opponent's fatal error. One two three four: four others shredded to bones and tatters of milky flesh, torn clothing, spreading pools of balm.

'Get out!' Ellanc shouted needlessly. 'All of you, get out while you can!'

Just seconds of distraction, and the tail, like a swinging

steel girder, struck him in the chest and hammered him back against the wall. He glimpsed one of his fellows being smeared across the floor like a bug under a fingertip. Then darkness loomed over and above him as he struggled upright and brought his weapon again to bear. Perhaps striking it underneath the armoured hood would do it? Ellanc remembered seeing a Batian try the same, and fail, so instead he fired down at the floor by his feet as the hood slammed down on him. And had not the floor given way at that moment, the hooder would have collapsed him into a grotesque dwarf.

In a shower of burning wood Ellanc landed on the cowling of a big hydraulic motor. Fluid was squirting from a damaged ram, and the back end of the huge ship's rudder was sliding towards him. On the other side of it, he glimpsed, in the tangle of pipes, rams and motors, a fire burning below the grenade hole, further over. He looked up and saw the vertical rows of burning red eyes, and glistening scalpel mandibles groping after him through the gap. But by the time he brought his weapon up, it had swept out of sight. He backed away from the rudder and sat down on a pipe. He gave a hacking sound, realized it was a laugh. For a dead man he had not felt so alive in a long time. Then, as doors behind him opened, he stood up and turned. Fire slammed into him, hurling him backwards. Hitting pipework, he tumbled to the floor. Error messages slid up into view, one after another. The smoke cleared enough for him to see Kladites standing beyond it.

'A few others got away,' announced one of them.

Another replied, 'I don't care – we get out of here now. You saw what it did to the others?'

Ellanc stared at the two of them. One turned and

aimed his carbine at Ellanc's upper torso, where his memcrystal and main control hardware was located.

'No . . .'

Fire and smoke blasted up before his face, and Ellanc slid into blackness.

Janer gazed down at the weapon he was holding. It seemed he would be getting just about all the excitement he could stand. As he holstered it, he noted that Wade had now tilted his head as if listening.

Emulation.

'Do you hear it?' Wade asked.

Janer listened intently. He could hear nothing but the usual sounds of the ship and the sea, but then he did not have a Golem's hearing.

'What?' he asked.

'A distinctive sound, something like a tank rolling across wooden boards, then a Batian weapon . . . and now laser carbines,' Wade told him. 'Down in the stern.'

In a fraction of a second, with a kind of snapping sound, Wade was on his feet, holding his carbine across his stomach. *Could he have got me before I pulled the trigger?* Janer wondered, and answered himself: *Probably.* He reached round and opened the door, stepped out into the corridor and turned to head for the nearest foremast stair. Reaching it, he made to go down towards the bilge.

Wade caught his shoulder. 'Not that way. We'd have to go through most of the bilge itself to get there. We go along the main deck and down.'

They climbed the stair and stepped out onto the nighted deck. There Janer witnessed something that almost physically jerked him to a halt. He felt a further rush of adrenalin, immediately followed by confusion, as memories surfaced in his mind's sea. Before him, a few metres above the deck and regarding him with topaz eyes, hovered an iron-coloured seahorse drone. Thirteen – the Warden's drone that had been present during those events on the Skinner's Island ten years ago.

'You're armed. Good. We need people armed. Can't find any of Bloc's merry crew. I reckon they're down there after it.'

It took Janer a moment to realize Captain Ron was speaking to him from a few paces beyond the drone, and that behind him stood a crowd of Hoopers and two reifications.

'What?' Janer asked stupidly.

Ron stepped forward, the drone shifting aside for him. 'Thirteen here tells me that nasty bugger is aboard.'

Janer nodded. 'Yes, I know.' He gestured to his companion. 'Wade just told me.'

Ron eyed the Golem. 'How might you know that?'

Wade stepped forwards, pulled a knife out of his belt and handed it across to the Old Captain.

Peering over Ron's shoulder, Forlam said, 'Sturmbul. I wondered where he got to.'

Wade said, 'What's left of him is lying under a walkway down in the bilge. The hooder is down in the stern of this ship, and I heard weapons firing down there.'

'Heard?' Janer asked.

'It has ceased,' said Wade, glancing at him.

Ron peered at the APW that Wade held. 'Mmm, well, best we go see what's happened.'

Ron was armed with a heavy machete and a QC laser pistol. The others carried weapons which, in their variety, seemed to cover human history. They ranged from clubs and blades to muzzle-loaders, cartridge-fed weapons to various designs of pulse gun and laser. One of them even carried a machine gun. It was a pathetic collection of arms with which to go up against a hooder.

'Have you been able to contact Bloc?' Wade asked.

'Can't find the bugger,' said Ron. 'Didn't try too hard.'

'Maybe he's down in the stern with his Kladites?' Janer suggested.

Ron snorted. 'Maybe leeches will fly. Best we get down there and lend a hand before anyone else gets 'emselves killed.'

'People die,' said Wade, a strange expression on his face.

'Not if I can help it,' said Ron.

Wade looked up into the rigging, smiled, then said, 'But surely you are risking your own life and the lives of others by becoming involved in this?'

Janer understood that the Golem was playing to an audience of one, for Zephyr's hearing was just as good as Wade's.

'Nobody wants to die,' growled Ron. 'But life without risk ain't living.'

'Could it be,' said Wade, 'that life without the possibility of death is not life at all?'

Ron stared at him hard. 'I don't know what your agenda is, Golem, but we ain't got time for it right now.'

Wade shrugged. 'Well, we do have weapons . . .'

'Come on!' Ron turned and led the way back towards the stern.

12

Ocean Heirodont:
like the whales, these creatures long ago abandoned the land
to return to the sea. Only forty-seven species have been cata-
logued, for they have obviously not well survived competition
with the vast oceanic leech population. They are cast in the
same mould as Terran fishes and cetaceans: on the whole,
those with horizontally presented cetacean tails are herbivo-
rous, whilst those with sharkish tail fins are predators. They
grip their food in mandibles, be that kelp stalks or a strug-
gling turbul, and feed it into the grinding bony plates in their
throats. The largest kind can grow half again the size of a
blue whale and is a carnivore. Its favoured prey is giant
whelks, if it can drag them from the bottom. But even some-
thing so large is subject to the predation of giant leeches,
sometimes losing a ton or more of flesh to one in a single
strike. The only relief these creatures can find from leech
attack is to drop below the depth leeches are able to reach, but
they must perforce return regularly to the surface for they are
air breathers. But even when they go deep enough to avoid
leeches, they might still be attacked by giant prill –

From high up, Sniper observed the Skinner's Island,

being implicated in the same ancient crimes, those would certainly not be the same as its father's. Even under Polity law, the crimes it committed while under the control of its father's pheromones were ones of which only its father was accounted guilty. However, there was the *Vignette* to consider. Its crew was missing and the ship itself at the bottom of the sea. Admittedly no Polity citizens had been hurt and the crime, if such it was, had been committed outside the Line. But this did not bode well for what else the Prador might do – possibly things that could easily fall within the Warden's remit. There were also political ramifications. Perhaps it was time to pass the buck? Before the Warden could decide, Submind Seven started shouting for its attention.

'Seven?'

'Captain Sprage again, Bo— Warden. Says there's someone you need to talk to.'

This time the Warden fully engaged with the conferencing link, relayed through Seven, and gazed into the Old Captain's cabin. The man stood lighting his pipe with a laser lighter, his expression sombre.

'What is it this time, Sprage?' the Warden asked.

'Not me this time. Ambel wants a word.' Sprage reached out and adjusted something out of view. The link jumped and the Warden found itself looking into a similar cabin in which stood Captain Ambel and two junior crewmen.

'Captain Ambel.'

'Hello, Warden.' Ambel looked equally sombre. 'Good to have you back. That other fella was a bit irascible.'

'Yes, quite. How can I help you, Captain?'

'Not so much how you can help me . . .' Ambel gestured at the two juniors. 'Let me introduce crewmen Silister and Davy-bronte, lately of the *Vignette*.'

The Warden abruptly focused more of its attention through the link. 'You are from the *Vignette*. What happened to your ship and the rest of the crew?'

Both the juniors stepped back, looking somewhat startled. The Warden realized it was projecting one of its many avatar images through the link, and that the two men were now looking at a two-metre-long grouper floating before them. It changed the image to something more human and acceptable.

'Well the Cap'n was right pissed-off with Drooble, an' the harpoon went through him, not Drooble you understand . . .' Silister babbled, until Ambel put a hand on his shoulder.

'I think, lad, you should let Davy-bronte tell it, just like he did earlier.'

The explanation from Davy-bronte was much more concise, and the description unmistakable.

A Prador war drone, evidently upgraded, thought the Warden. *Sniper will be pleased.*

'Thank you for informing me,' said the Warden.

'One other thing,' added Ambel. 'You will be telling Windcheater about this?'

'Certainly. He is, after all, your ruler.'

Ambel gave an ambivalent shrug and the comlink cut.

So, confirmation, if any more was needed. An upgraded war drone had been used, which inferred that systems aboard Ebulan's ship were in a good state of repair. The same could be inferred from the fact it had been moved undetected. Also, the fact that the adolescent Prador – the Warden checked its records – Vrell, had survived Ebulan's traps meant it was a very capable Prador indeed. Deciding it needed further advice, the Warden opened a communication channel through its own runcible, and through five other runcibles, right to the heart of things.

'Yes?'

The Warden transmitted all it had recently learnt, in detail, the information zipped into a package even some AIs would have had trouble deciphering. A microsecond later the reply came back.

'Work to your remit as best you can, Warden. Thrall codes within the ship will have been changed, and without signals for you to intercept you will not be able to break them, so there will be no repeat of Sniper's . . . lucky shot, and you do not have the armament to deal with a functional Prador light destroyer,' the Earth Central AI advised the Warden. 'I am now informing all interested parties.'

'Interested parties?'

After a delay of nearly half an hour, EC replied, 'The nearest Polity warship is two hundred light years from you. However, there is another warship much closer.' Earth Central then transmitted all relevant information, and a recording of a recent conversation in which it had participated.

'Is that a good idea?' the Warden asked.

'It is in the nature of a test of agreements.'

As the communication channel closed, the Warden could not decide if things had got better or infinitely worse. Certainly the stakes had just gone up: Earth Central was gambling with a planet and its population. The AI scanned round inside the moon base at the crowds of Polity citizens. No need to start a panic just yet, so it put a message up on the bulletin boards in the main concourse and arrivals lounges:

BUFFER TECHNICAL FAULT DETECTED

The submind at the planetary base immediately queried this, and the Warden told it what the real problem was.

'Oh fuck,' said the submind.

The Warden added, 'It would be convenient if those travellers on the surface were encouraged to leave.' Shortly after, the Warden observed that the departure bookings began to rise when the news-net services began speculating about a rumoured mutation of the Spatterjay virus into a lethal form – a rumour neither confirmed nor denied by the planetary base submind.

Then an hour later:

FAULT CONFIRMED. INCOMING TRAVELLERS ON BLOCK OR DIVERT. WE APOLOGIZE FOR THE INCONVENIENCE. FURTHER MESSAGES TO FOLLOW . . .

Now no more Polity citizens would be coming to the moon, and increasing numbers of them were already leaving. This meant that if things went pear-shaped, at least the body count would be lower.

'Okay, lads,' said Ambel, leading the two crewmen out of his cabin onto the deck. 'Peck will show you to your bunks. Tomorrow we should be reaching the Sargassum.'

'You gonna put us on another ship to go back?' asked Silister.

Ambel paused.

'Be a bugger to stop,' said Peck, who was standing underneath a lamp, peering out into the darkness.

The man, Ambel noted, had been very reluctant to be more than a pace from his shotgun, and cradled it now.

Perhaps understandable with what was evidently following them. And he was right about stopping, too. The moment they did, the giant whelk now somehow swimming after them would be all over the *Treader* in minutes.

'Peck's got that right, I'm afraid. We'd end up in the sea if not in our friend's guts.' He stabbed a thumb behind the ship. 'So you'll have to stay with us for a while.'

'Good,' said Davy-bronte.

Ambel peered at him curiously.

Davy-bronte continued, 'We been on the *Vignette*, Cap'n, so we know a good ship when we're on one.'

'Okay, lads. You get some rest now.'

Ambel turned away as Peck took the two juniors below. He glanced up to Boris at the helm, nodded to him, then strolled to the stern. Ambel – always calm and not prone to panic – realized Silister and Davy-bronte's service aboard the *Treader* might be limited indeed unless he could think of a way to deal with the giant whelk. Perhaps after the Sargassum, find an island, break out the harpoons and every other available weapon, beach the ship and . . . get things sorted. Ambel winced at the thought. Jabbing harpoons into giant leeches was all very well, but he knew a bit about the thing following them.

Sticking a harpoon into it would not be easy. Only himself and elder crew would be able to accomplish that, as it would be equivalent to ramming a knitting needle into a tree, and about as effective. So what to do? As far as he knew, only large heirodonts were capable of killing a giant whelk, and they were massive creatures with mandibles capable of crushing rocks. Be nice to have one of them on his side, but they spent as much

time as possible down deep where the leeches were not
so thick, only ever coming up for air. And when one did
that, and any Captain spotted it, he would quickly take
his ship out of the vicinity. There were no stories of
heirodonts sinking ships, but maybe that was only
because no one had survived to tell such a story. No,
that was a fancy, and he still had to find a way.

The function of the ship's harpoons, of course, was
not to kill but to harpoon. Ambel stared into the darkness and reflected on an old old story about another
kind of giant.

A kilometre behind the *Treader*, the giant whelk experienced a bowel-loosening moment which clouded the
water sufficiently for her to jet out of the attacking
heirodont's path. The great creature cruised on with
leisurely insouciance, utterly aware that the whelk had no
convenient rocks to which it could cling. In panic the
whelk released gas from her shell and began to sink, but
the bottom was a long way down and there was no guarantee there would be stone there to which she could
cling. She spread her harder tentacles out towards the
heirodont and tried to draw as much of the rest of herself
as possible into her shell. It was hopeless. By extending
her tentacles she was only offering the predator a starter
to munch on. Then she saw a wisp of something cutting
starlit lines across her vision. The line from the ship, its
hook still jammed into one of her tentacles. It was strong
in a way that nothing else in the sea was, she realized,
since it had managed to cut into her flesh. Perhaps it
could equally cut into the flesh of a heirodont? She
caught the end of the line and wrapped it about another

tentacle, stretching ten metres of the stuff horizontally before her.

The heirodont circled twice, lazily flicking its tail to change course. It sighed contentedly as, deeper now, leeches began to detach from its body. Rolling its head from side to side, as if to ease a crick in its short and powerful neck, it began grating its mandibles together – a sound sure to strike terror into the heart of any sea creature large enough to be lunch. Then it turned and headed directly towards the whelk.

The whelk kept the line on target, just below the predator's eyes. The heirodont opened its mandibles wide, the black bony plates in its mouth clashing together like a row of sliding doors. It hit the line and suddenly the whelk was hurtling backwards through the sea, mandibles clashing only twenty metres away from her. Then she was rising.

The heirodont shook its massive head, a trail of juices oozing from where the line cut in. The whelk rode up over its head and then bounced down the length of its back, getting cracked once by the huge tail on its way past. She spun, spread her skirt to stabilize herself. The heirodont turned hard and circled round again. The whelk eyed her tentacle where the line had bitten in but not cut through, unwrapped that length of line and shifted it to undamaged flesh, and held the rest of the line out again. The heirodont drew close once more, then abruptly turned away. The whelk felt new terror; it had spotted the line. Now began a long and horrible duel: feint upon feint, attacks defeated, the heirodont increasingly maddened by the deep cuts to its head. But the whelk was learning, and soon began to see a way.

The fifth attack, from above, went much the same as

before. The line cut in below the heirodont's mandibles. As it shook its head, the whelk swung round to fall past the side of the head, only this time she reached out with her other tentacles to grasp the heirodont's hard armoured breast. This was something utterly new to the predator: whelks normally wanted to get away as fast as possible, not cling on. It accelerated, flicking its tail hard from side to side, and rolling to try to shake off the unwanted passenger. Using all the strength in her tentacles the whelk began hauling herself up and round. Behind the heirodont's head, she gripped hard and sucked down. Now the heirodont was panicking. The whelk uncoiled one end of the line, flung it around her attacker's neck, finally managed to snag it on the other side. Again coiling the line around her tentacle, she drew it taut around the beast's throat, then began to pull.

The heirodont suddenly stopped shaking itself and headed for the surface. Hundreds of tonnes of heirodont, plus many tonnes of whelk, rose high into the night. The enormous tail thrashed the waves for a second, then the two crashed down again. But the whelk did not lose her grip.

Aboard the ship, only a few hundred metres away, Captain Ambel gripped the *Treader*'s rail as the wave hit. He was the oldest of Old Captains, and thought he'd seen all this ocean had to offer.

'Fuck me sideways,' he muttered.

A low boom reverberated through the ship and Janer stumbled aside as the floor tilted, and caught himself against a rack of dowelling rods. Other items here in the maintenance section, where Ron had brought them in search of further weapons, crashed to the floor.

precisely in position, for they contained tens of thousands of microscopic individual filaments. While this was running, he headed off to the ship's larder and fed himself, noting as he did so that supplies of food were getting low. By the time he returned, the program had run its course and he was now getting diagnostic returns. He inspected the screen readouts for a long time, then abruptly turned and knocked the tool chest across the room, to smash into another bank of screens. Then he settled down onto the ashy floor, with a hiss like something deflating.

Forlam flushed with embarrassment. Styx, himself and just five other Hoopers up against Bloc, Aesop, Bones and a small army of Kladites – what had he been thinking? He could easily have got them all killed. The obvious reason for such rashness was those unhealthy impulses to which Styx had referred earlier.

'Sorry about that,' he muttered.

'No matter,' said Styx. 'Just try to control yourself.'

'Yeah, right.'

They reached the door to the nearest Mainmast stairwell, and clattered down to the reifications' deck. Once there, Forlam turned to head for the stern. Captain Ron, in his own calm and lugubrious manner, would have to deal directly with Bloc. Maybe they could open the embarkation stair and lure the hooder there and somehow force it out into the ocean. Maybe Erlin could sort something out, since she was clever . . .

Styx abruptly caught hold of his shoulder. 'Not that way,' said the reif.

Forlam stared at him, puzzled.

'Don't you want to fetch those weapons for your Captain?' Styx asked him.

'Well . . . yes.'

'Then follow me.'

Styx broke into a lope that was surprisingly smooth for a reif, leading the way towards the bows. Some other reifications were crowding the corridor, and from them one female reif approached him.

'What's happening?' she asked.

'I haven't the time to explain right now, Santen,' Styx replied. 'Suffice to say that I think Bloc has dealt with a particular problem of his in a way that endangers us all.'

What is he on about? Forlam wondered, as he followed Styx on through the crowd. The female reif hesitated for a moment, then abruptly followed. Shortly they reached the stairwell by the third foremast, which led up eventually to the bridge.

'We have to be quick,' said Styx. 'Bloc and the others may be coming back here.'

Soon they reached the doorway leading through to the staterooms on this level. Styx peered through the porthole in the door. 'Two Kladites, armed. Deal with them, Forlam.'

'Right.' Forlam glanced around at his five companions. 'Come on, lads.'

Forlam crashed through the door, saw the two guards turning towards him. He launched himself at the nearest one, grabbing the reif's carbine and driving his head into the guard's face. Hands slipping from his weapon the guard staggered back against the wall, while Forlam brought its butt up hard into his face. The other guard managed to fire just one blast, then disappeared under three Hoopers. The one Forlam had hit was struggling to get upright again.

'Tie them up,' said Styx. 'You won't be able to knock dead men unconscious.'

Sufficient belts and straps were found, and shortly the two Kladites were writhing about on the floor, leaking blue balm from their injuries.

'You,' Styx pointed to one of the Hoopers, 'go watch the stair.' He then strode down the corridor, checking each door before halting at one. 'Forlam, here.'

Forlam kicked hard, his foot going right through the woodwork. 'Bugger.'

Styx relieved him of the carbine, as he struggled to free his leg, and fired into the lock. After Forlam pulled himself free, he slammed his palm against the door above the smoking lock. It swung slowly inwards.

'I'll be damned,' said Forlam. 'How did you know?'

On the big wide bed rested a neat row of Batian projectile weapons, stacks of ammunition, energy canisters and grenades. It was the missile launcher that caught Forlam's eye, however.

'I knew because I watch and I listen.' Styx turned to the female reif. 'It always surprises me how much most people miss.'

'Oh I missed it at first, but not now,' said Santen Marcollian.

Styx just stared at her. Forlam knew he was missing something about this exchange between the two, but ignored them to take up the launcher and eye it greedily.

'You be careful with that,' said Styx.

The Hoopers collected the weapons, making a bag for them out of bed sheets, and were soon piling out of the room. Forlam shouldered the launcher and watched as

Styx walked around the double bed and picked up something that had fallen on the floor. It was a plasmel box, and he opened it. Inside were four divisions, one of them empty. From one of the others he removed an aerosol can of some kind, no label, slightly dented. He sniffed it in a very unreif-like manner.

'This was the stateroom assigned to Aesop,' he said, 'though he never uses it. Such luxury is wasted on the dead.'

'Someone coming up!' came a shout from the Hooper watching the stairwell.

Styx nodded briefly, led the way out of the room and along to the other stairwell, then down.

Travelling under the ocean at what would be Mach 1 if airborne, Sniper followed the silt trail for a hundred kilometres before it faded into the normal background micro-debris of the ocean. Shutting off his S-cav drive, he coasted for a time while assessing collected data. Obviously the ocean currents would have shifted the trail, but how far? The war drone overlaid the present silt trail on his internal map of the sea bottom. Then, taking into account the ocean currents and tides, he tracked this trail's position back day by day. The twisting line deformed, grew wider to account for possible error, but still – at a point in time a few days after the disappearance of the *Vignette* – it seemed to match some seabed features. Sniper turned, opened up with his drive, and returned with all speed to the spot where the spaceship had originally rested.

'What you doing?' asked Twelve from above.

'The silt trail is just about gone, but I've plotted its

original location. I'll follow it and see if I can get into our friend's thinking.'

'Oh, right,' said Twelve, with more than a hint of boredom.

Propelled by his tractor drive, without the S-cav field engaged, Sniper followed the winding trail he had configured along the ocean's bottom. After fifty kilometres of this and two dead leeches, he still could not plumb the Prador's thinking. Apparently it was heading towards the Lamarck Trench, but then it would have needed to circle back round the Skinner's Island to go anywhere else. Then Sniper picked up a sudden surge from his magnetometer as he detected something far off to one side. He turned to trace the source, travelling two kilometres away from his current course. Finding only a piece of Ebulan's ship which, judging by its encrustations, must have fallen away prior to it crashing ten years ago, he cursed repeatedly as he returned. It was only as he motored back through his own silt trail that he realized the Prador had made a compromise between depth and silt disturbance along the most direct route leading to the trench. It had clearly never expected any of this trail to last long enough to be followed.

'He's definitely gone to ground in the trench,' Sniper sent.

'That's good,' sighed Twelve.

'What are your intentions?' the Warden interrupted.

'Well, this trail will only show me where he entered the trench, not where he is positioned now. Reaching it, he could have turned either left or right, or even into one of the tributaries. My chances of finding him are the same from wherever I begin my search. What can you give me?'

'The geosurvey drones would not be able to sustain the pressure, and Thirteen is presently otherwise occupied. You will have to make do with Eleven and Twelve.'

'You don't seem that anxious to find this bastard – and its bastard drone.'

'This bastard probably just wants to leave the planet, and though the loss of the *Vignette* crew is lamentable, it does not warrant major intervention on my part. Anyway, this may soon no longer be our concern.'

'What?' Sniper asked, then grunted almost physically as he began to decode the information package the Warden sent. 'I see,' the drone muttered. 'We just got shat on all the way from Earth.'

Janer studied the still-shifting remains of the hooder and wondered who was now in charge of the *Sable Keech*. About ten Kladites were now little more than piles of bones and reification hardware. The Hoopers waiting all around him were now well armed.

'Steady, boys,' said Ron, standing up at the sound of marching across the deck above.

The thirty or so Hoopers down here looked steady enough to Janer.

The Kladites started descending the two nearby ladders. A group of about twenty gradually gathered at the base of each, then milled around confusedly when they saw what awaited them.

'Shall we do 'em?' asked Forlam eagerly. It seemed he was anxious to try out his new toy.

'No,' said Ron, 'we'll just make sure our position is clear, then get on with the work we're being paid for.'

Taylor Bloc, carefully checking his hand- and footholds, finally worked his way down the ladder.

'Looks a little shaky,' opined Wade.

The Kladites parted to allow their leader through, then fell into ranks behind him. A few metres from Ron, the reif halted. He turned to stare at the remains of the hooder.

'How was it killed?' Bloc asked.

'Well,' said Ron, 'I reckon whoever originally hit it with the APW came and finished the job this time. Never saw what happened myself. I was waiting for Forlam to bring us these weapons.'

'I see,' said Bloc, eyeing the gathered Hoopers, only a few of whom did not carry some of the hardware Forlam and Styx had obtained from Aesop's stateroom. 'Does anyone know who owns this APW?'

A general shaking and scratching of heads was all the reply he received.

'So it would seem the present crisis is over.' Bloc glanced back at his own men, then around at the Hoopers. To Janer it seemed the reif was weighing the odds. Laser carbines against Hoopers armed with Batian weapons: it seemed that Bloc did not rate his chances very high. 'I don't want any further trouble. We have already had . . . sufficient.'

'That's fine by me,' said Ron pleasantly. 'We've got work to do now if this ship is not to founder,' Ron looked beyond Bloc to his gathered Kladites, 'and more trouble would just mean more mess for us to clean up.'

Bloc did not turn or say anything out loud, but his people began heading back towards the ladders. After a moment he followed them. Forlam and many of the other Hoopers appeared slightly disappointed by this retreat.

'I would dearly love to pull his head off,' muttered Ron.

Stepping out of the shadows behind, John Styx said, 'I understand your feelings, Captain Ron, but his attempt to prevent you obtaining weapons that would have proved ineffective against this creature hardly seems sufficient justification.'

'Yes, I guess so.'

Styx held up a battered spray can and inspected it. 'Patience – I think we will know soon enough,' he said.

Ron sighed. 'Okay, let's go to work then.'

Just two ships were in sight: one moored to a clump of sargassum, the other heeled over and heading away. Ambel recognized the moored ship as the *Moby* (which it was generally called rather than by its recorded name of *Moby's Dick*) at just the same time as he recognized the figure on her bridge staring back at him through binoculars. After the loss of his ship *Ahab* the other Captains had pooled their resources to buy Captain Drum another vessel, for in sinking his own ship, which contained a Prador CTD, Drum had saved all their lives. Many said that Drum, who had been implanted with a spider thrall that he ejected from his body before sinking his vessel, was now slightly mad and dangerous to know. Ambel, who had lived through experiences more nightmarish even than that, thought this criticism unfair, for in reality it was a description that applied to all Hoopers.

'Take her in. We'll anchor just off the *Moby* and pay a visit,' he told Boris.

Boris eyed him. 'What about our friend?'

The helmsman still did not quite believe Ambel's story about a *Whelkus titanicus* attacking a heirodont.

But then a whelk managing to pursue a ship as far as it had was an unlikely story in itself.

'We've seen no sign of it, and the turbul and boxies have been behaving normally. I reckon if it survived the heirodont, it probably lost our trail.'

'You'd bet on that, Captain?' Boris asked.

Ambel patted him on the shoulder. 'We can't live our lives expecting that thing to turn up all the time, lad.'

Boris nodded and spun the helm. The *Treader* heeled over and after a while Galegrabber furled himself along with fabric sails. Just ahead of them a mass of sargassum floated on the ocean: rotting woody stalks and wadded ribbons of weed. A couple of hammer whelks occupied it, but nothing else. Any prill there had no doubt been disposed of by Drum's crew, for the *Moby* was moored to this mass. Ambel climbed down to the deck and walked over to the bows. There he took up a heavy iron grapnel attached to a long coil of thick greased rope. The ocean was too deep here for bottom anchors, and this was the only way. He spun the grapnel over his head and released it. It arced out, trailing rope, to thud into the weed just by the hammer whelks, sending those creatures lolloping into the sea. Then, drawing in the slack as the *Treader* nosed into the weed itself, he checked the grapnel's hold and tied off the rope.

'Hey up, Drum!' Ambel bellowed. 'Got anything cooking?'

'Prill!' Drum bellowed back. 'I got prill on the menu today!'

Ambel turned to his gathering crew. 'We won't be staying here too long. You two,' he pointed at Davybronte and Silister standing uncertainly in the background, 'this may be your opportunity to catch a ride back to Chel. Drum may have some more sailing to do, but he'll certainly be going back that way before we do.' He turned to the others. 'Anne and Boris will also come across with me. Anne, find us a cask of seacane rum. The rest of you, get the ship's boat lowered.'

'Aye, Captain,' replied Anne, moving away. Silister and Davy-bronte, with the help of Pillow and another junior, set about lowering the ship's boat, while Ambel turned his attention to Peck.

'You're in charge, Peck. I know you're feeling a tad nervous,' Ambel eyed the shotgun Peck was clutching, 'so it's best you stay here and keep an eye on things.'

Peck did just that, watching with unnerving intensity as the five scrambled down into the boat and rowed across to the *Moby*.

Like most Old Captains, Drum was built like a tank, but unlike many he had retained his hair, which he tied back into a pony tail. He was a wide-faced individual who always had a welcoming grin for his friends. He wore it now, but there was something unnerving about it.

'How you doing, man?' Ambel said, shaking Drum's hand and looking round.

Drum's crew was a relatively new one, as his previous crew had all been murdered by Batian mercenaries and the adolescent Prador, Vrell. Some of them, Ambel noticed, were from Ron's old ship. There stood the appropriately named Roach, a raggedy weasel of a man who was honest because no one gave him any other choice, because he looked more untrustworthy than he actually was. Others were gathered around a couple of braziers on which prill roasted. Some of them were already eating: holding prill upside down on their laps with belly plates hinged open, scooping out the fragrant contents with spoons. Many of them, Ambel also noted, bore healing prill wounds.

'They can be a bugger to catch intact,' Ambel observed.

'All you need is a little perseverance,' said Drum, rubbing his hands together. 'What's that there, then?' He nodded to the cask Anne was carrying on her shoulder.

'A little gift,' said Ron.

'Then best we get it open! I'd guess you don't want to hang around too long.'

Ambel raised an eyebrow. 'Captain Sprage?'

'Oh yes, we all know about your rescue mission.'

'Do you know these two lads?' Ambel gestured to the two *Vignette* crewmen.

Drum eyed the two men while scratching contemplatively at the back of his neck – a habit he seemed unable to break ever since digging a spider thrall out of there. 'I know their faces . . .' Then his attention wandered to where Anne and one of his own crewmen were driving a tap into the rum barrel. Suddenly realizing what he was doing with his hand, he snatched it away to rest on a nearby rail.

'These are all that's left of the *Vignette* crew.' Ambel kept a close eye on the other Captain as he explained the next bit. 'Seems the rest of the crew was grabbed by a Prador war drone before it sank their ship.'

'Really?' Drum turned back to look at Ambel. His apparently calm demeanour was belied by a loud crack as his hand splintered the rail. Most Old Captains' horror of what Prador had done to their human captives, and their resulting hatred of the aliens, was a pale reflection of Drum's views on them.

'Seems,' said Ambel, 'that Prador you were hunting on the Skinner's Island might have survived. The Warden didn't say so, but no others have come here.'

Drum released the rail, now reduced to half its original thickness. 'I think I'll be needing a drink.'

So they drank, and Ambel related recent events. Whether Drum believed what he was told about the whelk and the heirodont (a name for a fable if ever there was one), Ambel couldn't tell. Drum obviously had other things on his mind, murder probably being one of them. Later, Silister and Davy-bronte together approached Ambel.

'We'd like to stay with the *Treader*, if we may,' said Silister.

'Why's that, lad?' asked Ambel.

Davy-bronte answered. 'He's not there yet, nowhere near, but he could turn too, like Orbus. We don't want to be here for that.'

'You think so?' Ambel asked, and they both nodded vigorously. 'All right, let's get ourselves back, then.'

As Ambel and his fellows made their farewells, Drum said, 'Looks like a storm's about due,' and Ambel knew he was not referring to the weather.

Drum was so very right, in more ways than he knew.

The movable deck section hinged up on hydraulic rams, and the crane ran on high-powered electric step motors, but it took Hooper muscle to heave the still-squirming remains of the hooder into the cargo net. Hovering ten metres above the deck beside the central mainmast, Thirteen watched as the crane hoisted into the sunshine what was left of the creature – writhing like some great black maggot – and swung out over the sea to drop it.

The drone watched a sudden activity in the water, spotting leeches and the long writhe of a rhinoworm closing in, and wondered if the life forms of Spatterjay would be able to digest this tough alien flesh. Then, turning its attention to Taylor Bloc and the watching Kladites, Thirteen assessed the situation there.

The Hoopers could probably wipe out these Kladites very quickly, and many of them were eager to do so. However, Ron kept them on a tight rein, reminding them that they had yet to be paid, which seemed to do the trick. The Captain was biding his time, and had quietly opined to Thirteen that something stank about recent events. The particular group of reifications the hooder had attacked had been those who had been giving Bloc a hard time – also some of them had been incinerated by laser carbine. Bloc's explanation that this had happened accidentally while the Kladites fired on the hooder was weak at best. The present situation seemed precarious to the drone, who felt sure it would not last. Thirteen moved out from the mast and headed for the open deck as Bloc and his followers returned to their bridge staterooms. From down below came the sounds of industry.

With the hooder now out of the way, the Hoopers could all continue with the task of repairing the rudder. The drone descended a couple of levels, then hovered to observe the maintenance section. Several reifications were shifting movable floor panels from where they had been stacked to one side, and slotting them back in place. Two Hoopers had disassembled a large ram, earlier disconnected from the rudder and carried up here by Captain Ron. Hydraulic fluid ran out of the ram's incinerated seals, trickling off the bench on which it rested. Another Hooper was returning from the stores carrying a box of new seals, and yet more Hoopers were coming up from the bilge with various other components of the rudder control system which were in need of repair or replacement.

Thirteen now dropped down further, into the bilge, and headed back towards the rudder. On the way the drone halted where a reif and a Hooper were busy scooping up the rest of the hooder's remains.

'Why would Janer Cord Anders be carrying such a weapon?' the drone sent his inquiry to a far-away listener.

'I would guess that the hive mind he consorts with supplied it to him,' the Warden replied. 'This is a situation that bears close watching, and it seems evident that the Golem, Isis Wade, may be the hive-mind agent I am seeking.'

'And if that proves to be the case,' said Thirteen, 'what action should be taken?'

'None at the moment. Our actions are dependent on what the Golem actually does. If he ever attempts to take any sprine off-planet, he must be stopped, which I suspect were Janer's instructions, too. It is, however, doubtful that this is truly Wade's aim.'

'And what might be his aim, then?'

After a long pause the Warden replied, 'I have no idea.'

Thirteen moved on, finally entering the meeting hall at the stern. Here again floor panels had been pulled up, but to expose the tangled and incinerated wreckage around the rudder's rear tang. The Golem, Isis Wade, was unbolting the electrical control of a hydraulic pump, while Janer detached various servo-switches and their charred loom of optics. Others were replacing melted pipes and heat-seized valves. The work was nearly done, but the rudder remained jammed over at the full extent of one ram, the ram on the other side having been removed.

This was where Captain Ron came in. While Thirteen watched, the Old Captain heaved against the rear tang of the rudder, as if against the bar of a lock gate. Slowly the rudder began to move round, fluid jetting from melted pipes and valve holes as the remaining ram closed up. Dragging behind two large iron wedges, and with a sledgehammer resting over his shoulder, Forlam followed the Captain.

'Now,' said Ron, once the rudder lay straight relative to the ship.

Forlam dragged the wedges into position underneath the tang and hammered them into place while the Captain continued to prevent the rudder from swinging back.

'That'll do it,' Ron opined.

Thirteen just filed this further example of how physically strong Old Captains were. It observed the dents made in the bubble-metal floor by the Captain's feet, then swung away to scan, by ultrasound imaging, Janer Cord Anders. Within a second the drone ascertained that the man still carried his singularity gun – the drone receiving strange feedback from its vicinity. Abruptly Isis Wade looked up and located Thirteen.

By radio, Thirteen sent, 'Are you a hive-mind agent?'

'Yes,' replied Wade, without opening his mouth.

'Why are you here?'

'To repair this rudder control system.'

'No, I mean why are you *here*.'

'I was never much good at metaphysics.'

Wade returned his attention to his work, no longer responding to Thirteen's questions. The drone swung away, floated out into the bilge, and once again ascended up to the deck. It observed Erlin contemplatively studying formulae on a screen while, nearby, five reifs floated in tanks of sea water and tried to live. It saw a Hooper inspecting the hull where it had impacted against an atoll, only to find no discernible damage. Other Hoopers tossed sacks of human bones and wrecked reification hardware over the side, and one of the living sails departed its mast to snatch up a rhinoworm this commotion attracted. The drone transmitted a signal to Zephyr, and as ever received no response.

Then, once the rudder was repaired, over the ensuing days and nights Thirteen watched the continuing voyage of the *Sable Keech* settle into an uneasy rhythm.

The trench was a vast canyon under the sea, up to seven kilometres deep in some places, and sometimes twice as wide. As Sniper cruised down the long slope leading into it, he observed a wide trail in the sand and mud, then eventually encountered its source, perambulating along the bottom like a mobile mountain. From below the slope of gnarled pyramidal shell cut through with glimmers of iridescence, dinner-plate eyes turned to track his course, and thick white and grey tentacles groped out of the murk after him. He accelerated beyond their grasp.

'Eleven, Twelve, how are you doing?'

Twelve replied, 'We'll be with you in two hours.'

'That the best you can do?'

'Without imploding, yes,' Twelve replied dryly.

Sniper grumped to himself and moved on.

Soon he was travelling alongside a vast cliff occupied

by diamond jellyfish like glinting blue glass eyes, roving glisters black as midnight, and populations of smaller molluscs roaming like flocks of vertical sheep. All his detectors were operating at maximum efficiency: his magnetometer checking for anything metallic around him for a distance of a kilometre, he probed the ground below with ultrasound and to a wider radius with infrasound, constantly sampled the sea water for unusual compounds, and just watched, listened . . . As the canyon grew wider, he moved to its centre to maximize the efficiency of his scans. Detecting metal he immediately put his weapons systems online, until discovering a vein of silver in the rock. Another return had him digging down into mud, using his tentacles and the blast of his tractor drive. But he only revealed a very old piece of ceramal hull, quite possibly from the same craft Jay Hoop crashed onto what later became the Skinner's Island. Then Sniper reached the first side canyon.

He was undecided about entering this tributary, as it seemed too narrow here, but checking his map of the trench he saw that further along it became wide enough to hold Ebulan's ship – or rather Vrell's ship, now. He motored between the narrow walls, paused to listen to the sound of packetworms grinding through obdurate stone, ascertained that the rumbling disguised nothing else, and moved on. Passing through a blizzard of diamond jellyfish that had detached from the walls, he found glistening tubular structures sticking to his armour, so combed them away from his surface with his tentacles and jetted on beyond the clouds of microscopic eggs thus released. Another of the giant whelks was wedged in a crevice ahead of him, its cracked shell gaping open, one eye missing, the remaining eye directed above him to a circling heirodont the size of an ocean liner. The heirodont ignored Sniper, intent on larger prey. Beyond them, where the canyon widened, no spaceship was revealed, though huge pieces of iridescent shell were scattered on the ocean floor. Turning to head back, Sniper realized his was a walk-on role in a drama played out down here many times before.

Moving beyond the tributary, Sniper zigged and zagged as the canyon grew wider, picking up two metallic sources that came to nothing. Another three tributaries branched off just ahead. Two of them, by his internal map, were over fifty kilometres long. Assessing how far he had come and what area he had covered in what time, Sniper made a rough calculation of how long this search would take him, presupposing he would have to search the entire trench on his own. The resulting figure depressed him. However, he was no longer alone. Up above him now he detected two metallic objects descending, and scanning them by sonar he recognized the shapes of a fish and a scallop.

'Each of you take one of the longer side canyons,' he instructed, 'and maintain constant link to me.'

'So you'll know when we're obliterated?' enquired Eleven.

'I see,' said Sniper. 'I thought your descent overly protracted.'

Neither of the other drones replied as they descended to the separate canyons and sped off into their individual darkness. Sniper turned into the remaining canyon, there exploring a killing ground used by a large prill – the creature surrounded on all sides by the dismembered remains of a pod of black glisters. It leapt up from the bottom at him, turning at the last moment to present its array of sickle legs revolving like the blades of a food processor. He caught hold of it with his two larger tentacles, held it for a minute as its bladed limbs grated harmlessly over his armour, then shoved it away.

'I haven't the time,' he muttered.

'What was that?' asked Twelve distantly.

'Lively down here,' Sniper sent.

'Yeah, we've seen,' replied the other drone.

Sniper returned to the main trench, ruminated for a little while as he searched it, then came to a decision. Abruptly he programmed some missiles in his carousel, and fired them off along the trench. After a few minutes a detonation broke the night a few kilometres ahead of him, and his sound sensors nearly overloaded internal programs with data.

'What are you doing?' Twelve asked.

'Call it extended sonar,' Sniper replied.

Seeing with sound, he had just shone a very bright torch into the darkness.

'Better,' he opined, but he still knew this search could take him weeks.

Close to utter exhaustion, the giant whelk pulled herself ashore, discovering that her buoyancy detracted from her ability to grip the bottom. But still she refused to release her prize even though it soon became utterly covered with leeches from the shallows. Reaching the tide line, she stretched tentacles up the beach and grasped a rocky outcrop to help pull herself and the heirodont's severed head finally out of the sea.

The massive head was now just one great writhing mass of leeches. Irritably she stripped them away, feeding one after another, like sweets, into her beak and champing them down. A strange whistling sound distracted her, and she kept searching around for its source, finally locating it as the gas issuing from the now open orifices in her shell. But she returned her attention to the leeches, soon revealing the head itself, badly pocked but still recognizable. She prodded the beast's mandibles and they snapped at her. Its remaining angry eye blinked and glared. Groping along the beach till she found a small boulder, she heaved it up, then smashed it down on each mandible in turn, but this was still not enough. The whelk hauled herself and the head further up the beach and, using the rock outcrop as an anvil, again smashed the mandibles until there was nothing left of them. Next she turned over the head to inspect the severed neck, then began to chew on the tough flesh. It took her hours to eat away all the skull's exterior flesh, but she left the monster eye still blinking and glaring at her.

Only after another few hours did she discover that no amount of chewing would get her through the thick skull itself. She glanced towards the sea and observed huge movement out there. The heirodont's body still seemed fairly lively, and somehow had stayed with her despite its lack of a head. Memory again nudged her. She then finally pecked out the eye and shoved the skull further inland. It seemed the safest thing to do in the circumstances. Now replete, she moved on across the island to the beach on its other side. She settled down contemplatively, gurgling eructations regassing her shell.

Now what? she wondered.

Depression slowed Vrell's return to his sanctum. Some of the U-space engine's super-conducting power cables must have had their insulation damaged, for they had

transmitted a massive temperature surge inside it, cracking and blowing minor components all the way through.
The main components remained undamaged, as they
were built to withstand forces far beyond mere heat. The
casing of the line-singularity generator was intact, as
were all its internal parts. The Calabi-Yau shape expan-
sion matrices (a technology stolen from the humans)
could not be damaged by heat, though they could have
been collapsed into one of the smaller dimensions of the
quantum foam. And the phase emitters had gone into
safety mode, folding a few degrees out of phase with
reality, though those systems that could bring them back
were trashed. Overall, the damage was beyond anything
one Prador adult, even with slaves, could repair. In normal circumstances the functional parts would have been
salvaged and all the rest scrapped. Yet, as Vrell entered
his sanctum, he began to think the unthinkable.

Bringing back the phase emitters would be the most
taxing task, but then the repairs to their support systems could be countenanced. Perhaps if he used an
expanded Calabi-Yau shape as a tool . . . Such shapes
were, after all, six-dimensional. All he needed to do was
work out the formulae controlling energy input into a
matrix, so as to distort the shape into the spatial analogue holding the phase emitters. At a rate of one base-
format calculation per second, using all the ship's
computing, this would take Vrell approximately four
thousand years. Too slow, therefore. But aboard there
was further computing capacity he could use, in the
form of human minds. He turned his attention to his
control units and the spider thralls they controlled. It
should be possible to use those minds to increase the
computing power by an order of magnitude . . . It was

then that Vrell noticed some interference to the thrall channels, and immediately put a trace and decode program onto it.

More Prador? Here?

The program did its work with surprising speed, and Vrell studied the results. In the ocean, not very far from him in planetary terms, he had detected the code spillover from nine interlinked spider thralls. That was very strange. The readings he was getting told him they linked through only one channel back to a control unit up on the sea's surface. This did not seem like the work of Prador, for there was no encryption in the coding, yet their technology was definitely being employed.

Nine thralls . . .

This meant a mind, or minds, he could use. He must take the risk.

'Brother, retrieve this.' He sent coordinates and the signal to trace to the drone cache. 'If you are seen, do not return here until you have destroyed the watcher.'

'Yes, brother mine,' the earlier version of Vrell replied, as it motored its war drone body out into the depths.

It had been another slow day aboard the *Sable Keech*, but it would not be long before things started to get more interesting. Forlam, who of course was fascinated by the ship's grisly passengers, had informed Erlin of the recent events below decks, and of the discovery of some reifs incinerated by laser carbine. So it seemed Bloc might be beginning to exercise his power. Did she feel good about the possibility of danger? She was not sure. However, whatever he might do did not negate what she felt were her responsibilities here. She looked across the lower Tank Room to where Janer was working. She had spent most of the day running diagnostic checks of the control equipment and, at her behest, he was visually checking filters and scanning for contamination in the small autodocs each tank employed. She would let him go once he seemed about ready to start shouting at her, which would bring them full circle to the end of their last relationship. But the equipment needed to be ready. *And here*, she thought, turning to the reif who had just stepped from the stairwell, *is the reason why*.

'Just lie down on the table,' she said, when he finally approached.

The reif, a man without visible signs of a death wound, twisted his face in what looked very like a grin. 'I'm not here for a medical.'

Erlin felt there was something not quite right about him – but then that could just be her. She had been sane for only a little while now, and even so knew that the virus had wrought changes in her mind. Some day she must make a study of the psychological damage the *change* caused.

'Then why *are* you here, John Styx?' asked Janer, who had rapidly found this an excuse not to continue with his mind-numbing task.

'Janer,' said the reif, then looked at each of them in turn before tilting his head to stare up at the ceiling, focusing on one of the camphones attached there. Erlin did not need any further hint. She beckoned him to follow her into an area separated by partitions erected by one of the Hoopers. Here, on wide work surfaces, sophisticated equipment lay at her disposal. It was also her base and her refuge.

'Unfortunately, when crewman Lumor put up these partitions, he accidentally smashed the camphones. Very clumsy. He's also sadly been unable to locate replacements for them.'

The reif grinned. It was definitely a grin this time. Erlin shot a look at Janer, taking in his slightly bemused expression, before returning her attention to the reif. He reached into his pocket and withdrew a dented spray can. She took it and held it up.

'And what am I supposed to do with this?'

'I would like you to analyse the contents.'

'It may have escaped your notice, but I am rather busy.'

'This will only take a moment of your time, Erlin.'

Something familiar . . .

Erlin shook the can and turned with it to her nanoscope, which included a viewing screen mounted above the glittering mechanisms of the scope itself. Using the side console she designated an empty sample cylinder from the carousel of six. The carousel turned, and in a moment the small chainglass cylinder folded out from the scope's mouth.

'Could this be dangerous?' she asked.

'Not now,' Styx replied.

She grunted and just held the spray can over the top open end of the cylinder, and sprayed inside. 'Right,' she said, working the console, 'could this be nanotech?'

'I think not,' said Styx. 'I rather suspect some animal product.'

The cylinder folded back into the scope. 'In that case I'll just use straightforward molecular analysis.' The screen blinked on displaying a shifting cladogram. Chemical formulae began to scroll up below it. 'You're right; looks like some kind of hormone.'

'Would you be able to find out what kind?'

Erlin began running a program to compare the substance in the scope with the billions listed in the scope's database, then she turned and gazed at him. 'Who are you and what do you want?'

'I want some answers,' the reif replied.

'You didn't answer *both* of Erlin's questions,' said Janer.

'For all present purposes, I am the reification John Styx. However . . .'

Styx rolled up his sleeve to expose an antique watch. He did something with the controls and pressed his thumb against the face. After what ensued, both Erlin and Janer laughed out loud – which was obviously not the reaction Styx had been expecting.

14

Sea Lily:

these plants are a close relation to the seacane, but the fact that they sprout flowers has provided the source of much contention between xenobotanists. Flowers mean pollinators and there is only one pollinator on the planet – the lung bird – which usually stays inland and needs to be attracted out by a very strong (and fetid) perfume. So how did this variety of seacane evolve flowers? The issue is further complicated: seacane was, far in the past, a land plant but, like the ocean heirodonts, it moved back into the sea. The lung bird is a crustacean that came out of the sea and took to wing. So in evolutionary terms the two life forms were travelling in opposite directions. Many theories have been posited to account for this, including alien interference. Probably the truth has much to do with six billion years of uninterrupted evolution. The same truth accounts for the lily's symbiotic relationship with rhinoworms, and the relationship between leeches and pear-trunk trees –

The spaceship surfaced from U-space like a volcanic island heaving up out of the ocean: something hot and titanic, vaporizing anything that touched it. Immediately alerted, the Warden observed it through some of his deep-space eyes, and in that interval the rent through from U-space had yet to close. The thing was three kilometres long, nearly as wide, and a kilometre deep. Inevitably its shape was similar to a Prador's carapace, but one distorted by encrustations that the Warden was uncomfortably aware were powerful weapons systems.

That was quick, was the AI's immediate thought.

This Prador ship must only have been days away from the system.

Immediately upon that thought, the Warden's suspicions were aroused: *Why so close?*

'Prador vessel, this is the Warden of Spatterjay opening communication,' the AI sent.

The huge ship continued into the system on a dirty fusion drive that caused a lot of interference with the Warden's link to its scattered eyes. The AI knew that Prador fusion drives were as efficient as Polity ones, producing less than $15^{-12}\%$ total fuel burn as isotope pollution. The interference was deliberate, which probably meant this spaceship contained technology the Prador did not want the Polity to know about. Such an action could be simply a sensible precaution of creatures keeping their offensive and defensive capabilities secret, but there could also be a more sinister purpose behind that.

'Prador vessel, this is the Warden of Spatterjay. Please respond.'

Nothing. The Warden became uncomfortably aware of how Coram lay, at present, directly in the vessel's path. The AI now considered initiating the moon base's defence systems, but that might be taken as undue provocation. Instead it sent signals to move its eyes in closer – a different kind of provocation. Side thrusters now fired, turning the behemoth round. The rear drives dropped to a spluttering low-power burn, then went up to full power when the vessel lay rear-end towards Coram and the planet. This burn lasted only a few minutes before shutting off. It was perfectly timed so that the ship now drifted in surrounded by a screen of radioactive gas. Then a powerful signal came through and the Warden was looking into a Prador captain's sanctum.

'Communication acknowledged,' came the reply in human tongue, but there was no sign of any Prador in that sanctum.

'How do you wish to proceed in retrieving your citizen?' the Warden immediately sent.

Now a shape finally moved into view, and the AI wondered about the paranoia evident aboard the Prador ship, for the respondent wore heavy exotic metal armour. Then he realized that this individual must be one of the King's Guard, for they all wore armour like this.

'Transmit details,' said the Prador.

By transmitting most of those details verbally, the Warden gave itself long seconds to think. 'I was informed of the disappearance of a sailing vessel on Spatterjay and sent my drones to investigate. Traces of Prador exotic metal were found in the sunken wreck of that ship – *map location inserted* – and the crew is missing. I sent my drones then to the location of Ebulan's spaceship – *map location*. It has been moved, most likely to the Lamarck Trench. It seems likely that the Prador Vrell, who was Ebulan's first-child, now has control of Ebulan's ship.'

'Why is this first-child alive? I was informed at the time that Ebulan and all his kin were terminated.'

Interesting. The Warden could not help but speculate how long this ship had been waiting outside the Spatterjay system. Ten years perhaps? Had Ebulan succeeded here, would he have been allowed to return to the Prador Third Kingdom?

'How should I address you?' the Warden asked.

'I am . . . Vrost.'

'Vrost, please send me all you know concerning the events here,' said the Warden.

After a long delay an information package came through. The Warden opened it in programming space designated for potential viral/worm attacks. There was no danger in it, however, and the AI soon ascertained that though the Prador knew most of the story, there were certain critical gaps in that knowledge.

'As you know,' said the Warden, 'Vrell was sent to the island on a suicide mission to kill those Old Captains who could bear witness to Ebulan's involvement in Jay Hoop's human-coring trade. But, transforming into an adult there, Vrell was able to disobey his father's orders. After Ebulan's ship went down, he made the attempt to return to it. No further action was taken against him because, first, it was unlikely he could survive the underwater journey to the ship and, second, it seemed an impossibility that he could survive the remaining booby traps his father would have installed in it.'

'How did you bring down Ebulan's ship?' the Prador asked.

'How long have you been waiting outside this system?' the Warden countered.

There came no reply, nor for another six hours. After

that time the Prador ship again activated side thrusters, this time to divert its course behind Coram and down towards Spatterjay. The Warden's patience then ran out.

'Vrost, since you have seen fit to cease communicating, I can do no less in response than activate my lowest level defensive/offensive capability.'

The Warden activated the moon base's defensive system, and observed weapons turrets breaking up through Coram's icy sulphurous crust all around. They rose like giant tube-worms into vacuum, folding armoured plates away from the business ends of near-C rail-guns, anti-photon cannons and particle-beam projectors. Racks of smart missiles folded up into view like collections of pan pipes. This was not the AI's 'lowest level defensive/offensive capability', but all it possessed. It was also something the citizens in the base could not avoid witnessing through the chainglass panoramic windows. Queries started coming in through personal comps and augs. The Warden put up a bulletin:

BUFFER TECHNICAL FAULT DUE TO MICRO-METEORITE PUNCTURES. FURTHER METEORITE ACTIVITY IMMINENT. RUNCIBLE IS NOW OPEN PORT TO ALL SYSTEMS.

Of course, the Warden had been here before.

FOR YOUR CONVENIENCE AND SAFETY, ALL CITIZENS PLEASE PROCEED TO THE RUNCIBLE GATE.

The runcible was soon throwing people away from the moon just as fast as possible, to be caught by whichever runcibles were available to catch them. Some of those travellers might find themselves hundreds of light years away. There was no real panic, but then many Polity citizens had never faced a physical threat at *any* time in their lives. For most of them this seemed an enjoyable bit of excitement. Fielding a growing number of queries, the Warden noticed a small percentage of people who were clearly dubious about the board messages.

'You lying fuck, Warden,' said a three-hundred-year-old woman as she hurried towards the runcible. Checking her ident package and cross-referencing it to traveller lists stored from ten years ago, the AI ascertained that, like the rest of the doubters, she had been here the last time this happened, too.

'Lock down and full defences,' the Warden told the submind running the planetary base.

'Ah, it's getting nasty, then.'

'Not yet, but it would be best to be prudent.'

Just then the Prador captain communicated.

'None of your present weapons are capable of bringing down a Prador light destroyer, such as Ebulan's, let alone my ship,' it observed.

'I am glad you have decided to continue our communication. I would not want to proceed to defence level seven, nor six.'

'I have scanned the moon on which you are situated. You possess no further armament.'

'Ever heard of chameleonware?'

An encoded message came through from a different source. 'Ooh, what porky pies you've been telling.'

'Shut up, Seven,' said the Warden, observing that the turbot drone was now moonlighting by carrying passengers' luggage to the runcible.

This time the reply from the Prador captain took an hour to arrive, while its ship went into orbit around Spatterjay. The radioactive cloud surrounding the vessel was dispersing now, but still isotopes coating its exotic metal surface concealed much. Some areas were also very well shielded. However, the Warden now had a clear and detailed exterior view, and could see huge blockish shapes shifting position on the warship's hull. This time the communication began with a map, *sans* ocean, of Spatterjay's surface, the Lamarck Trench being indicated by Prador positional glyphs.

The warship captain asked, 'Is this sub-oceanic feature the Lamarck Trench?'

The Warden considered denial, but only momentarily. 'It is.'

Shapes began launching from the warship and spreading out through space. Some of them were war drones, others were Prador in that heavy armour, hundreds of them. Then out of the ship's hull folded one of those titanic blockish structures, and the Warden picked up energy signatures it knew indicated the charging of a massive coil-gun.

'Your actions would indicate,' suggested the Warden, 'that Vrell is not to be welcomed back into the Prador Third Kingdom?'

Detecting a slight rise in background residual radiation, Sniper suppressed a surge of excitement. There were deposits of pitchblende on the bottom of the ocean, and the briefly radioactive current could have picked up some of that anywhere. Scanning into ultraviolet, he watched a scarf of blue water dissipating behind him. There were similar blue areas in a chaotic boulder-field where part of the cliff had collapsed. He rose higher to get a wider view over the field, then descended at an angle towards the largest area of blue. It seemed to be seeping from some kind of cavern. Sniper hesitated at the entrance. Certainly no Prador vessel was concealed in there, but perhaps here was some clue.

As he made the decision to enter, a black glister surged out with its claws spread threateningly. Upon observing him, it began frantically sculling itself to one side. It held something in its mandibles – something that glowed into the ultraviolet. Snipper stabbed out a tentacle and slapped hard behind the creature's head, and in a cloud of blue the glister released its prize, but clamped a claw on the offending tentacle. Sniper flicked the glister, tumbling, away and turned his attention to picking up what it had dropped. At first it was only identifiable as a lump of flesh and gristle clinging to a bone, but Sniper needed no new programs to quickly recognize the bone as a human tibia. He dropped the remnant just as the glister attacked again, this time closing both its claws together on one of his tentacles. He reached out with two more and tore the creature in half, before finally entering the cave.

Ultraviolet revealed killing levels of radiation as a luminescent blue fog that obscured all view in that part of the spectrum. Infrared revealed seven glisters fighting over something. Two of them turned towards him, and he hit them both with his dissuader. Broiled bright red, they sank to the bottom. Only then taking some notice of the Warden's instructions concerning the local fauna, he slid around behind the feeding creatures and tried to drive them out of the cave. They would not be driven, he being of a size that perhaps this pod of glisters thought they could handle. He tried ultrasound, infrasound, just simply pushing them with his tentacles, then, his patience at an end, he hit them all in turn with high-power ultrasound pulses. When, internally shattered, they all sank to the bottom, he closed in and pulled their twitching hard-shelled bodies away from the prey.

There was little left: just disjointed bones, torn flesh and skin, and some rags of clothing. The skull of this crewman, who must have come from the *Vignette*, had been crushed, and the brains sucked out. A spider thrall lay nearby. Sniper scanned it, but it was offline, emitting no carrier signal, so there was nothing for him to track. He backed out of the cave and sent a description of his finds to Eleven and Twelve.

'So we're close, then,' replied Twelve.

'Certainly hot,' Eleven quipped.

'Possibly,' said Sniper. 'We don't know how far this corpse was carried by the current or by those fighting for a mouthful of it, and it might also have been dumped from Vrell's ship while it was in transit. Make sure you scan for radioactivity.'

'I have been,' said Twelve. 'I'm coming up out of the end of my particular tributary, and I've detected something about a kilometre out from me.'

'Send it,' said Sniper, then viewed the distant blob, blued by ultraviolet and rendered unrecognizable by distance. Now Twelve was sending a narrow-beam sonar image, slowly building. Sniper guessed what he was seeing, just by the size and general spherical shape. His guess was confirmed when things began detaching from the distant object and heading towards Twelve.

'Fuck, not again,' said the drone. 'Warden!'

The view tilted, levelled again. The distant object must have moved very quickly because now it was gone from view, though the underwater missiles it had sent were closing fast. Sniper then received a close-up image of a nose-cone, just before the transmissions from Twelve blinked out.

'Warden, Prador war drone detected,' sent Sniper, winding up his tractor drive as he turned towards the surface, then engaging his S-cav field and taking off like a rocket.

'I can't say I'm surprised,' the Warden sent. 'Twelve just joined me. Now, you and Eleven get out of that trench right now, and get as far from it as you can, as quickly as you can.'

'What—' Sniper began, but upon receipt of another image, this time from one of the Warden's spatial eyes, he fell silent for a moment before saying, 'We'll lose track of that drone.'

The coil-gun fired, the projectile only becoming visible on reaching atmosphere – an orange line stabbing down towards Spatterjay's ocean. Spectral analysis of the trail told the Warden that it was left by a large slug of exotic metal. The Prador captain had not actually resorted to planet busters, but this was bad enough. The missile hit with no visible effect for a fraction of a second, then the ocean rose and opened around a white-hot cylinder, a disc of cloud rapidly growing above it. The cylinder collapsed as it spread out into a tsunami travelling at over a thousand kilometres per hour. The ocean-level winds would move just as fast, and blast-furnace hot. Luckily the only sentient life forms in the vicinity were Sniper and Eleven, and some tomb robbers the Warden had been keeping an eye on over the other side of the Skinner's Island. Most of the explosion's energy would be spent by the time it reached civilization, though some ocean-going vessels were about to be in for a rough ride.

However, the worst damage would be precisely where intended, in the oceanic trench many kilometres below the surface.

'Prador vessel, cease firing on the planet forthwith!' the Warden sent.

The coil-gun was charging again. The Prador clearly intended to work along the entire length of the trench to drive Vrell out from hiding. If it did that, the effects would certainly be felt all the way around the planet. Tens of thousands would die, environmental damage would be vast, but that would only be the beginning. The resultant volcanic activity in the trench would drive whole trench-dwelling species into extinction and cause climatic changes around the planet. The Warden could not allow this, and preventing such a catastrophe was totally within its remit.

Immediately, the Warden completely shut down the runcible, even though there were still many travellers ready to leave. The AI briefly observed someone stepping into the Skaidon meniscus extending between the device's bull horns, then stepping out the other side and looking utterly bewildered to find himself still on Coram as the meniscus dissolved. The Coram runcible buffers were galactic upside, which meant that for travel more energy came into the runcible here than went out. The Warden had to periodically arrange pure energy transmissions to a runcible out on one of the many cold worlds that were still being terraformed, where it could be usefully employed. But it had not done that in some time, and now found a use for the surplus.

'Cease firing on the planet, or I will be forced to take action,' the Warden sent.

'And what action might that be?' the Prador captain sent back.

The AI's bluff was being called. It realized that in this situation neither rail-guns nor other missile launchers would act fast enough, as the coil-gun was launching near-C kinetic missiles. Only light itself would do. The Warden selected one heavy laser that stood furthest away from the moon base. The weapon, even though it was the biggest, was woefully underpowered for the demand about to be made on it, but would have to do.

The super-conducting ground cables would be able to take the load, and the device itself would smoothly turn that energy into a beam until it vaporized about two seconds later. The advantage here was that it would continue to lase even as it fell apart, even up to the point of the cylinders – containing the lasing gas – melting. The Warden chose a target area and prepared one buffer to dump its energy load in a cable he was now isolating to the laser. It was ready, but how would the Prador react? It would think the AI had used the only suitable weapon available to it, overloading and destroying that weapon in the process. The art, the Warden well knew, came in what was said rather than done.

'I have no wish to cause an incident,' said the Warden, 'nor have I any wish for you to cause the same.'

'This is not a Polity world,' the Prador replied, 'and your ground base is in no danger.'

'Spatterjay is a protectorate—'

The coil-gun fired again and, an instant after, so did the laser. The paths of the beam and the slug of exotic metal intercepted in the upper atmosphere. A spectacular explosion ensued, violet-shifted fire licking down into the stratosphere while a disc of rainbow incandescence spread in the ionosphere. The Warden observed the laser turret vaporizing down the S-con cable, and a plume of glowing gas extending out from the moon. Now the Warden fed the remaining energy contained in the buffers into the runcible, transmitting it to one of those distant cold worlds. It knew the Prador captain would read that a large amount of energy was being transferred somewhere, but no more than that.

'You destroyed one of your weapons,' the Prador said.

'Obviously I was bluffing,' said the Warden. 'I possess only one level of conventional weaponry here, as you have seen. Please do not force me to resort to U-space or gravtech devices, or anything runcible-based. The result would be . . . regrettable.'

Of course the newer Polity battleships did carry such weapons: USERs and DUSERs being respectively general underspace interference emitters, and the directed kind which could cause a U-space drive to detonate; the various DIGRAWs – directed gravity weapons – which if they did not instantly shred their target, would occlude any antimatter vessels that same target contained with the same result, besides other devices bearing numerous other acronyms. AIs were reluctant to employ them in battle, as the difference between what the Warden labelled conventional weapons and those devices was the difference between a machine gun and an ICBM. However, the Prador must have some knowledge of them, since bad news like that is not easily concealed.

After a long delay the Prador captain asked, 'What do you suggest?'

Still accelerating away, Sniper saw first the underwater flash, then what looked like a fast-moving and immense aquarium glass hurrying to catch him up. He withdrew his tentacles and head, and closed and sealed his composite clypeus. The pressure wave hit him, travelling at Mach 3. His cavitating field went out, and the drive sputtered to a stop shortly after. Those senses of his relying on sound were soon providing no useful information at all, and his other senses could probe no distance into the grey chaos. But in a U-space transmission he picked up Eleven's brief 'Oh shit' as that submind – at the moment of its fish-shell destruction – transmitted itself to the Warden. Sniper was unsurprised: Eleven's shell had not been as rugged as his own, and he himself was getting a battering.

Sniper's structure distorted and components broken inside him. He noted high-pressure water forcing its way inside him through a breach in the tractor drive and tried closing its ports, but it was like trying to shut them on stone. Then the pressure wave passed on. He flipped down his clypeus, extruded his head and tentacles, and saw he was tumbling through hot clear water above a stratum of silty chaos. Activating his tractor drive and stabilizing himself with his tentacles, he watched the silt boil to a halt in its direction of flow, and all sorts of strange objects begin to float up out of it. There the carapace of a large prill, devoid of legs and bubbling hot internal gases, and there the separate carapace segments of glisters, red as cooked lobsters, and the strandy glutinous masses that were all that remained of leeches. Then something dropped past him from above and it took him a moment to identify the completely intact skeleton of a heirodont, boiled clean of flesh.

'Well, if it's fucking war they want,' he sent.

'It is not war,' the Warden replied. 'But it seems they very much don't want Vrell leaving here alive.'

'Seems a bit drastic just for one post-adolescent Prador,' Sniper opined.

'Yes, it does – and that's interesting.'

Sniper began motoring towards the surface. 'Did they hit him?'

'Not as far as I can gather.'

Sniper broke through the surface into a hurricane raging below the weirdest sky he had seen in a long time. A low ceiling of grey cloud stretched from horizon to horizon, but wherever it broke he observed the rainbow aurora of high-atmosphere ionization.

The Warden continued, 'That was in the nature of a little nudge to drive him from cover. At present no further such nudges will be forthcoming, so I suggest you find Ebulan's ship before our friend up here gets impatient again.'

Sniper located himself on his internal map by signals from one of the Warden's satellites, and realized the pressure wave had carried him eighty kilometres.

'Okay, send me a copy of Twelve's last ten minutes. That drone he detected was probably heading straight back to Vrell.'

The package arrived within a second, but it took a minute for Sniper to delete everything irrelevant: including the drone's boredom with the task in hand, a program it was running concerning the historical significance of seashells, and how it really didn't want to get splattered when so close to buying emancipation. The residue fined down to Twelve's exact position when it had detected the Prador drone, that drone's then position, and its general course before it spotted Twelve.

Sniper aligned that same course on his internal map, and saw that continuing it in a straight line brought it to a point on the Lamarck Trench five hundred kilometres from where he was. He tried to start his supercavitating field, but it was then that a swarm of error messages called attention to themselves.

'Fuckit, fuckit, fuckit!' Sniper repeated as, on tractor drive only, he headed slowly to that identified location, while shifting internal micro-welding heads to repair the breaches in the S-cav field generator.

As fast as possible, Vrell put his blanks on hold, clinging to the nearest supports and holding onto any breakable items. He shut down all internal systems that could be disrupted by a shock, isolated fusion reactors, and closed all the workable internal doors. The drone made it back inside just in time, and Vrell rapidly closed the cache door behind it. Then he himself clattered over to one side and clung to the uneven wall of the sanctum. The underwater blast wave slammed into the ship, lifting it up off the bottom so the concealing layer covering its upper hull slid away, and grinding it down nose first a few hundred metres along the bottom of the trench. Then the ship settled in a roiling cloud of silt. Debris falling through the water – boiled and broken creatures, boulders torn free from above and the silt itself – would soon conceal him again. But perhaps the time for concealment of that kind had ended.

Vrell absorbed the download from his drone. It had been spotted by one of the Warden's drones, but had destroyed that observer just before the blast. But the Warden would now know this ship was close, and so might detect it at any moment. Vrell listened again to the transmissions he had decoded between the Warden and the Prador warship. If Vrell's ship was detected down here, how long before the Prador captain fired a kinetic missile directly on target? Admittedly the captain had not yet recognized the Warden's double bluff, for it was fabricated upon the way this very ship had first been brought down. Vrell knew this had been effected by subversion of thrall codes, distracting Ebulan sufficiently for that old war drone to slam both itself and a dead Prador drone down on top of the ship from high atmosphere, with an impact not dissimilar to that of the recently fired kinetic missile. No U-space or gravtech weapons had been deployed – the Warden possessed none. However, Vrell thought it likely that the Prador captain had actually ceased firing because he did not want to cause an incident, and the fifty or so kinetic missiles he might need to work along the entire length of the trench would certainly do that. Just one missile though . . .

Vrell then considered why the captain had fired at all. Obviously the Prador King knew what the Spatterjay virus could turn other Prador into, and suspected that Vrell, having survived so long on this planet, might also be infected. The King certainly did not want that kind of competition, nor for anyone but himself and his immediate offspring to enjoy the same advantage.

'What do I do with this?' asked the drone from down in its cache.

Vrell came sharply out of his reverie, to look through his brother's eyes, and through those others' eyes down below. The drone was holding part of a segmented life form in its claws. Though one end of it was ragged, as if part of it had been torn away, it was still writhing furiously. Vrell picked up the uncoded thrall carrier signals issuing from it and, as he magnetometer-scanned it, realized there was a spider thrall lodged in each of its segments. It was then easy for him to read the carrier signal and program it into the control unit previously employed to run the radioactive blank ejected earlier. This certainly could be no setup instituted by Prador, for they were utterly aware of the interchangeability of control unit and thrall. For if you did not sufficiently encrypt signals to and from a thrall, an enemy might use it to control you instead. This had happened regularly in the Third Kingdom and, adult Prador being even less friendly to each other than to different species, the result was usually extremely painful, messy, and then terminal.

Vrell linked through with ease, quickly decoded the programs employed, and usurped the partitioned control unit at the other end. He then gazed, through human eyes, out across the ocean, discovering that Taylor Bloc's mind was a morass of contradictory conviction and frustration. The three partitions were designed for three control channels: one each for two human minds and one for what remained of the creature his drone had retrieved. But the whole system had become scrambled by the feedback caused by the creature's massive injury. The two human minds were currently offline, somnolent. Perfect, for here then was more processing space for the U-space formulae. Keeping Taylor Bloc unaware, Vrell routed through programming links to those two minds he had controlled, and immediately began using them to run formulae, then he returned his attention to the reif himself.

Only touching Bloc's mind lightly, Vrell replayed fragments of his recent memory. In these he observed the launching of the *Sable Keech* and the subsequent

embarkation of Polity citizens. Replaying more recent
events he was amused by the thoroughly human drama
unfolding. By the signal strength from the control unit
he had just usurped, he realized the huge sailing ship
itself was close.

Interesting, thought Vrell.

Standing on the top of the midship deckhouse, Janer
raised his image intensifier to his eyes and studied the
distant volcanic island. It was nameless, that place, so on
the map called up on his cabin screen bore only a number. Commenting on this island to Erlin, who at that
moment was hoisting yet another reif into yet another
tank – over twenty of them had gone into the tanks now
– she had replied, 'Flowers in the sea there – a kind of
sea lily you find out this way – that's about all I remember, because I was losing it by then.'

'Sorry?'

'I saw it as Zephyr carried me over.'

'I see.'

Janer moved on then, recognizing impatience in her
voice. *Zephyr*, he thought. There was some connection
between that one and Isis Wade, for Wade had been
spending a lot of time conversing with the Golem sail up
in the rigging. Perhaps it would all come out when Wade
made his promised explanation.

Ah, flowers . . .

The island was definitely volcanic – it could not have
borne a more classically volcanic shape. And now, in the
shallow seas surrounding it, Janer observed masses of
lily pads bearing blowsy blue flowers. There were also
things swimming amid those masses of vegetation, but

he could not discern whether they were rhinoworms or medium-sized sea leeches.

'Zephyr has a curious fascination with lilies,' came a voice from behind, 'but then he has a curious fascination with anything related to death.'

'You walk very soft, Wade,' said Janer, removing the intensifier from his eyes.

'I'm no clunking robot, if that's what you mean.' Isis Wade stepped up beside him.

'There's a lot of things you are not. What I'd like to know is precisely what you *are*.'

'Isn't that something we'd *all* like to know?'

'Don't start waxing philosophical on me. You know what I mean.'

'Explanations?' asked Wade.

'It's about time, while this calm lasts.' Janer gestured to a squad of Kladites marching along the deck below.

'Yes . . .' said Wade. 'Very well, I do represent an ancient hive mind. I in fact do more than that. Have you ever wondered why there are separate distinct hive minds rather than just one mind encompassing the entire hornet species?'

'I can't say it's been very high on my mental agenda.'

'I suppose not, and really I cannot clearly answer that question. Perhaps, just like individuality in any species, and the reasons for sex, it is a survival strategy. Perhaps, back before even dinosaurs walked the Earth, there was just *one* mind. Who knows? What I do know is that now there are many minds, and the way more are created is by the division, the breaking apart, of larger, older minds as the masses of hives that carry them become . . . unwieldy.'

'The mind I represented was young,' Janer observed.

'It was: just one fragment that survived of a mind that broke apart during an ice age. Hornets do not cope well with the cold, which is why none of the other fragments survived.'

'No, really?' said Janer.

Wade smiled and continued, 'On Hive it is warm, and on Earth hives are better equipped against the cold, but ancient minds still face that threat of division – death to them individually, or maybe just death to their individuality. The mind I represent is so dividing and would have had to accept its lot, had it not been for human technology. But now there is the possibility of memcording. The mind has managed to hold itself together, in so much as it has so far only divided into two. One half is rational and prepared to memcord itself and accept that as life. The other half is . . . unbalanced. It will not accept death, believes death an entity to be fought. Nor can it accept memcording as life.'

'Rather like our friends here, who don't truly consider reification life, merely a kind of purgatory.' Janer shrugged. 'Well, something like that.'

'I don't just represent the mind,' said Wade.

'What do you represent?'

'One half of the argument.'

'What?'

'The other half is Zephyr.'

Janer just stood there staring as he realized what he was being told. After a moment he asked, 'Which half are you?'

'The rational half, of course.'

'So let me get this straight.' Janer pointed above. 'We've got the nuts half of an ancient hive mind up there in a Golem sail. It doesn't accept memcording as life, yet it is a memcording itself. You are the sane half, if that's possible.'

'Yes, that's about right.'

'What do you hope to achieve here?'

'I hope to persuade Zephyr to accept memcording as life – to accept rationality over the visceral or emotional. If it accepts that, a template of its understanding can be transmitted via hivelink back to Hive. This will enable the two halves of my other self to come together for memcording.'

'And if you fail?'

'Then this,' Wade pressed his hand against his own chest, 'is the best my other self might achieve, and it must therefore accept dissolution.'

'So no sprine thefts, no attempts at planetary domination involved here, just a bit of literal psychoanalytical projection?'

'There is a further complication, and it does concern sprine.'

'Isn't there always? Tell me about it.'

Wade then explained to him why Zephyr was here, and Janer felt himself grow cold. He looked off past the Golem, across the ship to the further horizon.

'That's bad,' he said.

'Yes, it is.'

After a moment Janer realized he could not actually see the horizon, and he also realized that the *Sable Keech* was heeling over and turning hard. He again raised his intensifier to his eyes.

'And talking of *bad*.'

The cloud, laced with lightning, looked like a roller of solid bruised flesh. The wave, hammering towards them below it, was higher than their ship, and looked more solid still.

'Keep us turning. I want us bows-on towards that mess. Zephyr, start reefing all sail right now,' said Captain Ron. 'Then get yourself and your friends to cover or in the air – whichever you prefer.'

'Is that a good idea?' asked John Styx who, without protest from Ron, had taken up position at the coms console. 'It'll slow our turn.'

The *Sable Keech* was turning slowly while that wave, and the storm riding it, was coming bloody fast. Sideways on, the ship would capsize, and it would probably then stay that way, despite the heavy machinery acting as ballast down in the bilge.

'We'll be able to make the turn under present momentum,' Ron replied. 'If we leave sail on, that might tear out the masts, holing the deck and possibly the hull. We really don't want holes in this ship right now.'

Bows on, the *Sable Keech* might be able to stay on the surface, though Ron thought it likely the wave still would break its back. That way, however, at least the passengers and crew might survive the coming experience.

'Everybody been warned?' Ron asked generally.

'I've been repeating the warning over the ship's intercom, and putting it up on every cabin screen,' said John Styx. 'Others are spreading the word, where they can.'

'Ah, good.' Ron eyed the others on the bridge. Then, entertaining a suspicion, he turned his attention to Forlam. 'You got that rudder hard over, Forlam?'

'Certainly have.' Forlam gazed at the approaching wave with his eyes glittering.

Ron reached out to grab the helm and tug at it a little,

to make sure Forlam was not making any small but possibly fatal mistake, as was his tendency. He found the helm was hard over, however. Forlam gave him a hurt look, then returned his attention to the wave.

'Nearly there. We're gonna make it, boys,' said Ron.

Others on the bridge, looking doubtful, kept clinging to the nearest handholds. Ron himself reached out and closed his hand around a nearby stanchion. Something big had hit: this looked like the wave thrown up by a seaborne atomic explosion, of which Ron had seen his fair share during the Prador war. It might have been seven or more centuries ago, but you tended not to forget stuff like that.

'What do you reckon caused it?' Ron asked, generally.

'Dunno, Captain,' came the general reply from the Hoopers.

It struck the Old Captain that his bridge crew was not overly gifted with imagination anyway, so he turned to Styx. 'Any ideas?'

Styx studied the displays. 'It was an orbital kinetic strike over the Lamarck Trench in Nort Sea.'

'Right. And the source?'

'Prador battleship. A big one.'

'Well, that's a bugger,' said Ron, just as the massive wave hit.

The *Sable Keech* did not lie completely bows-on to the wave. Nevertheless it rose up and up on a sudden mountain of water only just visible through horizontal rain. Ron looked up at the boiling cliff of sea as it broke round and over the bows, and clung on tight as the floor turned up to forty-five degrees, then beyond that. He looked back, and wished he hadn't when he saw the seven-hundred-metre drop down the length of the ship

into the trough. The stern was now under, cleaving
through the sea and throwing up a huge cowl of water
that kept crashing against the deck. Ron tried to ignore
the groanings and crackings he was hearing, then
suddenly the bows were in clear air, and the angle of the
ship returning to normal. But the vessel now turned on
the wave's peak . . . Then it was over, and sliding sideways down the lee of the wave. Ron found himself clinging to the stanchion with both hands, one foot braced on
a console. Forlam was gripping the wheel, his feet wide
spread. A screen popped out and a waterfall roared into
the bridge as the ship bottomed in a trough.

'Rudder – other way!' Ron bellowed.

Forlam started spinning the helm – no strength being
required since the rudder operated by hydraulics. The
ship started to present its stern to the next, smaller wave,
and went up over that one at an angle. Another wave,
then another. Now came a shuddering crash as the *Sable
Keech* dropped down in the next trough. It rose again on
a wide swell, crashed down again. Staring straight ahead,
Ron observed just how much closer the island now
appeared. Steam was billowing from its volcanic cone,
and where once there had been trees there was now just
the wreckage of trees and mud. Eyeing the sea, he
observed lily pads bobbing back to the surface and then
reopening their blowsy flowers.

'We're grounded,' someone announced.

'Yup, I figured that,' replied Ron.

'How we going to get this ship off?' the same man
asked.

'Ain't figured that one yet,' admitted the Old
Captain.

*

The giant whelk dipped herself back in the sea, but could no longer detect the scent trail of the ship she had been pursuing. Heaving herself back up onto the beach, she gazed towards the horizon with her huge eyes, and experienced a feeling of panicky bewilderment. This sudden loss of purpose caused almost a feeling a deflation in the growing lobes of her brain, and she felt the loss of that, rather than of the scent, as of greater importance to her. But the ship was not gone – itself or one very much like it would be out there. All she needed to do was search, keep on searching, and never stop. It then occurred to her that if she found the same ship, dragged it down and crushed it, chewed on the crew . . . if she finally achieved her aim, that meant no more aim to achieve. She blinked, caught on the rusty nail of paradox, not knowing it was much the same as faced by all thinking beings. Then she swivelled her eye-stalks to one side, wondering why the horizon there had suddenly risen.

Uncomprehending, the giant whelk watched as a glassy hill of sea rolled towards her, then some buried instinct had her sucking back in her eyes, and bunching together her tentacles. The wave, carrying less momentum now than when it had struck the *Sable Keech*, picked her up like flotsam and tumbled her away from the island. Brief chaos ensued, then, drifting below the surface, the whelk unknotted her tentacles, extruded her eyes again, sucked in some of the offending water. Strange flavours tantalized her taste buds, and she decided immediately to track back this phenomenon to its source. Anything rather than return to her previous plodding and thoughtless existence.

15

Rhinoworm:

symbiosis, parasitism and mutualism being a feature of Spatterjay's fauna, it is unsurprising that the rhinoworm's life cycle begins this way. Its eggs are laid upon the stalks of the sea lily, where they inject tubules to feed upon the lily sap and thus grow. This stimulates the lily to bloom, attracting the lung birds that pollinate them. On lily sap the egg grows to the size of a football, and out of this hatches the four-limbed juvenile rhinoworm. Hatching takes place at the precise time when the lily is producing its seed pods, which, being high in protein, are much relished by many varieties of herbivorous heirodonts. Now the lily benefits from the presence of tens of thousands of voracious rhinoworms attacking any other creature in the island shallows in which it flourishes. The worms utterly denude the surrounding area and, as they begin to lose their limbs and change into the adult form, turn cannibalistic. Only 10 per cent of their original population will leave the area as adults. Rhinoworms have four sexes – three separate 'males' contributing three quarters of the genome to the one quarter in the female egg. Only one other life form on this world uses the same reproductive method, but no kindred spirit results, since rhinoworms are the main diet of that other form: Spatterjay's famous sails –

Erlin dragged herself to her feet and glanced around with some relief. The tanks had been well anchored, and – though having spilled much of their liquid contents across the floor, to mix with everything that had come in when the sea smashed through the side doors – only two of her reifs had been tossed out of them. Wading through ankle-deep water, which was swiftly draining into scuppers all around the edge of the room, she approached the first of the ejections and, not bothering to bring across the ceiling lift, untangled the various connections to his body, then picked him up and lowered him back into his tank, which was still a third full of amniot. She did the same with the second one, noting how real blood was seeping from splits caused by his recent violent departure from his tank. Then, seeing that the tank amniot levels were automatically being topped up, she began checking readouts.

To say they would survive was not entirely accurate since they were dead. But their trauma had in no way halted or even slowed the work of their nanofactories. There was something else, though: she felt a tingling soreness where the sea water from outside had soaked her. It was caused by the vicious plankton of Spatterjay, and any of the tanks that had taken in some of the incursion of sea water would now be contaminated with it. She definitely needed to do something about that, or the work of the nanofactories would be undone as the reifs themselves served as a food source for the plankton. Quickly she returned to the wreckage of her work area, found a pack of soluble tablets of a sterilizing enzyme,

NEAL ASHER

and dropped one in each of the twenty-two tanks currently in use. This stuff might damage the reifs, but that damage would be limited and swiftly repaired by the nanites already working in their bodies, and it would certainly kill the plankton. She then checked the readouts on the remaining twenty tanks, plugging back in a few loose sensors, but that was all she needed to do until she came to Aesop and Bones, who were safely strapped to restraint tables.

Inspecting the screens that kept her informed of the condition of the two, she realized that whatever the problem was here, it had nothing to do with the sudden storm. Both screens were scrolling what seemed the kind of formulae in which runcible technicians and AIs dabbled. She shut down Aesop's screen, plugged in her own laptop, and sent in a diagnostic check to be sure the optic plug in the reif's hardware had not pulled loose. It was seated firm. Turning the screen back on, she glimpsed the usual diagnostics a reif would access, before it clicked back to scrolling formulae. Erlin left it alone. She felt no great responsibility to these two, and she needed to find out what was going on outside.

'Wow, now that's what I call a ride!' said Janer, who had obviously been heading for the Tank Room just as she stepped out of it. The Golem, Isis Wade, accompanied him.

'What was that?' Erlin asked.

'A tsunami,' explained Wade.

Erlin stared at him for a moment, then enquired acerbically, 'Could you elaborate on that?'

'According to one of the Warden's subminds, the tsunami was caused by a kinetic missile fired down into Nort Sea from a Prador warship in orbit above us. I'm getting no more detail than that. It seems they're quite busy up there.'

Erlin turned to Janer. 'Why am I not surprised about that?'

Janer merely shrugged.

'You all right, lad?' Ambel asked.

Pillow was looking particularly peeved, and it took the Captain a moment to realize the reason for this: the junior had lost some of his facial jewellery when he bounced down the length of the deck and slammed into the stern rail. But for a Hooper the rips in his face were minor injuries, and closing up already. Peck's arm was broken, however, and Ambel saw the mechanic straighten it out with a crunch, then hold it taut while Anne splinted it. Peck, being an old Hooper, would only require use of the splint for a few hours.

There were other minor injuries amidst the human crew, but they had been lucky – Ambel counted heads – that none of them had gone over the side. Now he looked up and wondered if Galegrabber had survived while grabbing this particular gale, for the sail was now nowhere in sight.

'Any sign?' he called up to Boris, who was surveying the surrounding ocean through binoculars.

'Not of the sails,' Boris replied. 'But the *Moby* is still afloat. They must have got their cables off the sargassum in time.'

Ambel nodded, turning to the rest of the crew, who were now mostly wandering around the deck in a daze. Their reaction was understandable – none having ever experienced weather quite *that* heavy, nor needed to cling onto a deck that was pitched near vertical. But this disorientation of theirs had gone on long enough.

'All right, lads!' he bellowed. 'You three – Pillow, Davy-bronte and Sprout – I want the pumps up on deck and working *right now*. The rest of you, get down below and sort out the mess. Get everything that needs drying out up here hung on lines. Peck, I want you down below checking the racks and cogs. If Galegrabber comes back any time soon, I want everything ready and working. Take some hands with you, if you need them. Anne, I want a hull check, stem to stern – don't miss a plank.' They all stared at him, still a little bewildered. He clapped his hands together with sounds like gun shots, and began striding along the deck. 'Come on, this isn't a bloody holiday cruise! Move your arses!' Crew members scrambled in every direction, but some still hadn't realized he meant what he said. 'Pillow, what are you gaping at! I see no pumps up here!'

'But, Captain—'

Ambel picked him up by the scruff of the neck and threw him towards the nearest open hatch. Pillow hit the edge, then tumbled down inside, letting out a yell as he hit the deck below.

'Any more questions?' Ambel demanded.

There were none.

Over the ensuing hours, his crew pumped hundreds of gallons of sea water out of the bowels of the ship. Lines tied between the masts were loaded with soaked clothing and bedding. All this occurred to the sound of Anne's tap-tapping as she checked the hull's planking, and the constant clanging and occasional 'Buggering buggered up bugger' as Peck set about replacing one of the mast cogs which had sheared off all its teeth. Most tasks were completed by the time evening began to descend, and Boris set about lighting the recently replaced lanterns all around the deck. Ambel, who had just applied his Captain's strength to the task of removing a stubborn cog from its shaft, came out on deck to see the *Moby* heading towards them, towed by its ship's boat, which was rowed by Drum alone.

When the other Captain came within hailing distance, he called out, 'I'll be coming along with you!'

'Why's that?' Ambel asked.

'Out that way, the way you're heading.' He pointed. 'Sprage tells me that's where the spaceship is. Probably in the Lamarck Trench.'

'Spaceship?'

'Vrell's – that bastard Prador.'

'I see,' said Ambel. 'It caused this?'

'Nope, seems the other spaceship did that,' Drum replied.

'Uh?' was Ambel's response.

Drum explained what he had learnt from Sprage about Vrell, and about the new spaceship above them, and what it had already done and might yet do. Even more so now, Ambel wanted to get to Erlin. He was grateful when, in the morning, a bedraggled Gale-grabber and the *Moby*'s sail returned, with muttered curses, to occupy their masts.

It took Janer a moment to recognize the vicious drumming sound. Clutching a glass of a more refined version of seacane rum than he was accustomed to, he stepped out of the bar area recently opened on the first level of the stern deckhouse. Glancing to one side, he noted some of Bloc's Kladites – probably set to watch those frequenting the bar – now peering over the side. He moved to the rail to take a look himself, then halted. There was something sitting on the rail.

It looked like a partially plucked crow that someone had nailed in place because it had been dead for a week or more. Then it turned its head and regarded him with pink, blind-looking eyes, before honking loudly and winging raggedly away. It left behind it the stink of decay.

'Lung bird,' explained Ron, stepping up beside him.

'I know what it was,' Janer muttered.

'We'll have to get off here soon, before things get too hectic,' Ron added.

'Hectic?' Janer queried. 'Because of lung birds?'

Ron led the way to the rail and pointed a thumb downwards. 'No . . . them.'

Janer peered over the side to see one of the hull laser turrets swinging back into its hold position. Pieces of some pink anguine form thrashed, still steaming, in the sea, then a shoal of leeches dragged them down. Janer squinted, puzzled, sure that he had seen a limb amongst those remains, yet the swarming creatures were rhino-worms, which were limbless. Further along, he saw another laser turret fire, then distantly he heard one from the other side of the ship.

Ron pointed out towards the lily-like plants all around the ship. 'Breeding area, that. There'll be thousands of the leggy buggers.' He took his comlink from his pocket and spoke into it. 'How we doin' there, John?'

From the link a tired voice replied, 'I will get it, but I can't give you any estimate on the time. The programming is rather convoluted.'

'Okay, keep at it.'

Ron put the link away, then seeing Janer's querying expression said, 'Bloc is behaving very strangely and being stupidly uncooperative. He's refused to give us access to the ship's computer systems, even though that'll get us out of this mess. Maybe he's frightened to hand over any further control.'

'And why would access to the ship's computer systems help?' asked Isis Wade, who had just joined them.

It had been Wade who had kicked in the door and suggested rather loudly that here were facilities it seemed a shame not to use. He also served the first drinks, before starting up a metalskin barman that had been stored under the bar. The place had become a regular watering hole for Hoopers just coming off-shift from clearing up the mess below – there had been little damage to the hull itself, much to Captain Ron's surprise.

Ron glanced at the Golem. 'As you know, there's more to this ship than Windcheater would be happy about. Now, that John Styx is a clever one, knows more coms coding and programming than probably even you, Wade. He used to do that stuff on Klader before the Polity AIs got there, and before he fell off a mountain . . . So he tells me.'

'And the relevance?' Wade asked.

Ron gestured down the entire length of the *Sable Keech*. 'Only the front half is grounded on the bottom. Once Styx cracks Bloc's codes, we should be able to start the engines in reverse, and maybe that'll pull us back into deep water.'

'Engines,' said Janer, nodding. Other Hoopers had already speculated that might be what was concealed under the enormous sealed housing forward of the rudder hydraulics. 'What sort of engines?'

'The usual kind – does it matter?' Ron then downed a large slug of rum before heading back into the bar.

Isis Wade followed the Captain, but Janer stayed observing the two organic sails, Huff and Puff, winging out over the sea. He watched them for a moment, then gazed up ahead into the rigging. All the fabric sails were reefed and everything above appeared skeletal. The Golem sail, Zephyr, stood motionless like some folded piece of iron equipment affixed on a spar. Janer patted his hand against the gun concealed under his jacket, and considered the dangerous game Isis Wade was playing. Should he allow it to continue? He lowered his hand; any intervention might be provocative in the present uneasy circumstances. Better instead to wait and watch. He returned his attention to the sea, and watched Puff scoop up a great spaghetti tangle of writhing pink shapes. Then he glanced down again and saw a man-length rhinoworm, with thin newt-like limbs, attempt to climb the hull, before being lasered into smoking segments. He supposed he should not be surprised that this world had yet to reveal to him all its teeth.

Returning inside, Janer observed the small group of Kladites now sitting around a table – probably postioned there to note down the identities of those who were breaking the curfew Bloc had tried to impose. No one had been punished as yet, so perhaps Bloc was wary of upsetting the uneasy truce for the moment. Like the other reifs scattered around the room, the Kladites sipped through straws pure ethanol drinks to complement the balm inside them. He had seen Sable Keech do the same, ten years ago, and wondered if they too possessed the facility to feel or emulate inebriation. He walked past that table and went over to stand with Erlin, Ron and Wade.

'I just saw a rhinoworm with legs,' he commented.

Erlin turned to him. 'The juvenile form. They grow up in island nurseries, like this one surrounding us, and lose their legs as they go fully pelagic.'

'They're going to give us trouble,' Janer stated.

'They don't mind snacking on each other,' said Ron. 'Our problem is that every time those autolasers hit one, its remains attract even more.'

'Will there be many of them here?' Janer asked.

Erlin replied, 'The adults gather in places like this en masse, and each one lays tens of thousands of eggs under the leaves or on the stalks of those plants you see out there. There's probably *millions* of juvenile rhino-worms around this island.'

'There's always the thought to consider that we might be better off somewhere ashore,' Janer said, passing his glass back to the barman – the metalskin android was fashioned in blued metal with a flattened ovoid head and scanning red eyes. It looked like a prill mounted on the neck of a humanoid body.

'You did notice that they've got legs?' said Erlin dryly.

'Yeah, but I wasn't thinking about that. What if that Prador captain above us decides to ignore the Warden and continue its bombardment?' The Warden had lately updated them on recent events. 'How many more of those waves can this ship endure?'

'And where would we go, once we're ashore?' asked Ron.

Janer thought about that for a moment: the devasta-tion visible over the island, the steam rising from the caldera somewhere behind the highest point on the island.

'Okay, dumb idea, I guess,' he allowed.

Janer now considered revealing to Erlin and Ron what he had learnt from Wade – he trusted these two absolutely and felt the Golem should do the same – but just then there came disturbing sounds from outside, as of all the lasers firing at once.

'Ah, that's it.' Ron took out his comlink and strode to the door. Janer, Erlin and Wade followed the Captain, and this caused a general exodus from the bar. The racket originated from the sea below, so everyone moved to the rail to look over. Janer was expecting to witness some massed attack from leggy rhinoworms, but what he saw was the sea boiling towards the stern, just forward of the rudder. Large chips of wood kept bobbing to the surface amidst a spreading slick of sawdust.

'Is that supposed to happen?' asked Erlin. 'I wouldn't have thought it such a good idea to make holes in the hull.'

Wade explained for her. 'The propellers are made of case-hardened ceramal. They're mounted on telescopic shafts housed in watertight compartments inside the hull. When activated, they just bore their own way out through the hull. A concealed engine Windcheater could make no objection to, but evident propellers would be a little too much.'

'How did you know all this?' Erlin gazed at Ron, Wade and Janer in turn.

Janer shrugged. 'I didn't.'

'Styx broke into the ship's concealed plan a while ago,' said Ron. 'It's just the control codes we've been after, since.'

'And this will pull us free?' Erlin glanced back at the boiling sea.

'If we don't run out of power first,' replied Ron, watching the lasers turn more of the walking rhino-worms into macaroni.

The trench was now right below Sniper and slowly the error messages from his S-cav drive were blinking out. He descended a cliff that sprouted seaweed trees in the branches of which shoals of boxies swam like mobile silver apples. Passing a deep cave, he observed two large eyes watching him, and an ultrasound scan rendered him the strange image of something like a giant whelk, *sans* shell, protecting its softer body in stone like some kind of hermit crab. Finally reaching the bottom, he scanned at full power with each of his senses, then again picked up something in ultraviolet.

Prador were riddled with tactical blind spots – it was this that had once enabled Sniper to defeat a number of Ebulan's drones, even though they carried superior firepower and armour – and he suspected this was how he would now find the hidden spaceship. Doubtless Vrell had concealed it in a deeper part of the trench, but what the Prador had failed to conceal were the leaking radioactives, which were thick in the water here. Choosing the direction from which the current seemed to be sweeping the isotopes, he headed off. Then, ahead of him, against the base of a rocky underwater cliff, he spotted the painfully bright glare of some large pill-shaped metallic object.

Sniper scanned his find briefly, quickly realizing it was a dumped fusion reactor – its casing cracked and the isotope ash of its last faulty burn poisoning both itself and now its surroundings. Around this object the bottom was littered with dead and dying creatures: some small varieties of whelk and bleached-white heirodonts no bigger than a human arm. Checking his records the drone realized these were creatures whose vision extended into the ultraviolet. They had been attracted by the light – and it had killed them.

'Fuckit,' Sniper muttered, moving on.

The reactor could have been dumped during the journey along the trench, so the ship itself could be many kilometres from here. Almost with a sigh, Sniper transmitted his findings to the Warden, then continued trundling along just above the bottom.

The AI on Spatterjay's moon responded immediately. 'You must find that ship soon. The Prador captain is becoming impatient. His drones and his armoured Prador have dropped to the stratosphere, and I don't think they will hold there for long.'

'This could be a good sign,' said Sniper. 'If Vrell had considered the possibility of this reactor being found, he'd have concealed it better. It could be that it was only carried a minimal distance from the ship itself, and then dumped.'

He now reached the base of a rubble slope in the trench. The remaining error messages in his S-cav drive now merely concerned his jammed ports. This meant weaknesses in his armour, but did not mean the drive itself would not work.

'That is a possibility arising from optimism rather than logic,' opined the Warden huffily.

Sniper sent back a U-space raspberry and continued searching.

Halfway up the slope the drone spotted a small shoal

of those heirodonts encountered earlier near the reactor. The water was disturbed and murky around them as they fed upon something. Admitting the possibility of finding another human corpse, though by the readings in ultraviolet not a radioactive one, Sniper motored over.

The heirodonts dispersed, then circled round again – loath to leave their meal. Revealed was an adult frog whelk, much the size of Sniper himself, its shell crushed under the edge of a large slab of rock. What remained of its extended foot still moved weakly, but its eyes were gone and what he could see of its main body, inside the broken shell, was in tatters. Even while he watched, more of those same heirodonts fled from cracks in the whelk's shell. The creatures would not have been able to feed on the whelk in any other circumstance. He suspected that having most of its main body eaten had weakened it sufficiently for them to go to work on its tough appendage.

But there was nothing else important for him here.

Sniper noted another shoal now coming down towards him. That whelk would not last much longer – would never get the chance to regenerate as did so many of the animals here. Then it hit him: why was the whelk trapped underneath this slab? This slope of rubble must be a recent fall – but what had caused it? Yes, probably the shock wave, but maybe something else. Suddenly back on alert, Sniper opened his scan all around him. The moment it touched the descending shoal, that shoal accelerated. These fish were not flesh – they were black and too evenly shaped – and no creature down here propelled itself by a constant water jet.

Sniper spun upright, put his S-cav drive online, and accelerated upwards in an explosion of silt which disappeared amidst more silt rising, as the very ocean began to shake. Explosions nearby knocked out the cone-field of his drive, and set him tumbling for a moment. He saw further explosions below turning the whelk into mincemeat and slivers of shell. The remainder of the swarm of mini-torpedoes now swerved towards him.

'Found it!' he sent over U-space.

Below him an avalanche revealed a rising curved edge of metal, and the constant blast along the trench from some massive turbine.

'Get out of there, Sniper,' the Warden replied. 'I've so far dissuaded our friend from using his coil-gun, but as soon as he knows about this, I suspect he'll change his mind.'

'That's my—'

An explosion right next to him again knocked out Sniper's cone-field, even as he began to generate it. He scanned for other missiles, could see nothing, then whipped a tentacle through the dispersing cloud of the explosion and drew in, through microtubes, a sample for his internal spectrometer.

Ceramic missiles?

Suddenly every moving object around him could prove a threat – missiles fired at him did not have to be metallic. He blew out a cloud of antimunitions beads and motored sideways, scanning behind and below for the precise source of the attack, which had to have originated from somewhere on the rising titanic spaceship now filling the trench from side to side. However, the focused ultrasound pulses hit him from above. They struck the end of one of his large tentacles and tracked in, paralysing that limb then scrambling some of his internal systems when they reached his main body. He loaded and fired hunting torps upwards directly towards the triangulated source, which was behind a spreading cloud of mercury chaff. The source then speared into view, launching another ultrasound pulse. It was another torpedo.

Sniper veered, angling his course upwards at forty-five degrees away from some rising monolithic extension of the Prador ship. Rerouting internal systems knocked out by ultrasound attack, he made for the edge of the chaff cloud, as his attacker was almost certainly behind it. After firing a couple of torps towards the further edge of the cloud, these missiles being programmed to go around it and intercept whatever they found there, he loaded antimunitions. Rounding the cloud, he opened up with his own ultrasound weapon. He hit one of his own seeking torps and it blew in a flat explosion. The other one kept circling, sniffing for prey that was not here. Just then, rather than communicate, the Warden relayed a recent exchange, compressed to be read at high speed directly into Sniper's mind:

'If you fire now, you will be destroying a seven-hundred-year-old Polity citizen and ECS employee. You will also kill the crews of two Hooper ships, the Polity passengers and Hooper crew of another larger vessel – and cause untold environmental damage.'

'There is only a drone down there. A few of these Hoopers are not your responsibility. And these so-called Polity citizens, from what I have recently learnt, are nothing more than animated corpses.'

'Nevertheless, I will be forced to employ a U-space weapon, should you fire. It will certainly destroy the projectile as it leaves the coil-gun, but I estimate it will also

revolve half of your ship's bulk into underspace then
back out again, inverted.'

Almost to the microsecond of Sniper finishing the
package, a torp streaked up out of the chaff cloud and
exploded against his underside.

Where the fuck are you?

Sniper reserved his shots until he saw a clear target.
He began motoring rapidly to the surface, with the pretence of drawing his attacker away from the chaff cloud.
In reality he knew the cloud was a decoy to make him
think the attacker was there. And after the Warden's
message he had no wish to hang around playing cat and
mouse, especially as he seemed to have now taken on the
mouse role. Some five hundred metres above the rising
Prador ship he fired two missiles towards the cliff-side
nearest to him, then focused his scanners below the
tumbling rock fall that ensued.

Nothing.

He came up out of the trench, again trying to restart
his S-cav drive. It came close to engaging, then the cone-
field collapsed in a cascade of errors. He put this, and
some of the weird readings he was getting on sonar,
down to ultrasound damage. He began motoring to one
side to get out of the way of the Prador ship. It was now
elevated above the trench and sliding sideways, tonnes of
rubble and silt pouring from it. Sniper decided he
should head for the surface as fast as he could; at least
in the air he would be able to use his fusion engine. Then
something stopped him dead, as if he'd run into an invisible brick wall.

Invisible.

Sniper remembered the recording from SM12, just
before that drone was destroyed. It had seemed the

Prador war drone had moved off very quickly – because one moment it was there and the next moment gone.

'Fuck,' said Sniper, as a huge exotic metal claw folded out of nowhere and clamped on the forward edge of his shell. 'Chameleonware.'

The Prador war drone appeared in one rippling wave, and Sniper immediately fired a contact torp directly towards it. The explosion blasted the two drones aside in a spinning course. The Prador drone's exotic armour developed a glowing dent, but the shock wave, turning him against the gripping claw, bent Sniper's armour where it was clamped. A square port opened in the bigger drone and now a torp slammed into Sniper, causing a similar dent. The big drone tried to bring its other claw to bear. Sniper wrapped two tentacles around it, and underwater arm wrestling ensued. Through another tentacle touching the base of that claw Sniper directed the discharge from one of his inner laminar batteries, but the instant he did that, a similar shock slammed into him through the other claw. They were hurtling towards the surface now, both their drives applied to the same task: the Prador drone to get a potential attacker away from its ship, Sniper because he did not want to be in the vicinity of an orbital strike. Despite the shock, however, Sniper still had another option.

'Let's see you hang on now,' he sent.

He initiated his S-cav field, part of it intersecting the other drone, then opened his tractor drive to full power. Within seconds their speed doubled, and they continued accelerating. Some tightly focused ultrasound weapon began gnawing at Sniper's armour just behind his head. Sniper injected aluminium-film chaff between, to soak up some of the energy. Then they exploded from the ocean's surface. The field stuttered, went out, and Sniper engaged his fusion drive. That wrench was enough and, peeling away a piece of Sniper's armour, the big drone tumbled away, snapped taut Sniper's gripping tentacles, then fell again when the Polity drone released his hold. But, with a flash of white fire, the Prador engaged its own fusion engines and came on, now firing missiles and lasers.

Employing a hard-field, Sniper smacked the missiles out of the air, and replied with his APW. Violet fire splashed on his opponent's hard-field, then it replied with its own APW blast. Sniper fired a missile which, exploding, caused a massive directional electromagnetic pulse. He was about to follow up with another APW blast, hopefully cutting through his opponent's defences, which should have been knocked out by the pulse, when the two missiles he had knocked away earlier tried to hit him from the ocean below, where they had been waiting for this. One he shot down with a laser, but the other exploded just underneath him, delivering a similarly disabling EM pulse.

Not such a pushover, thought Sniper.

Reaching then exceeding the speed of sound, the two opponents hurtled over the ocean, leaving a trail of ionized gas, smoke and falling flakes of white-hot armour.

The coil-gun on the Prador ship was charged and ready to fire, and the Warden had no way of stopping it other than by firing on Vrost's ship with conventional weapons – thus revealing a lack of anything else effective – or by further bluffing.

'The seven-hundred-year-old drone is now no longer in the way,' Vrost informed him.

Sniper's departure from the scene had been all too evident, and the Warden supposed that the old drone was probably about as happy as he could ever be.

'That still does not negate my original assertion. Vrell's ship is now much closer to the *Sable Keech* and the two Hooper ships, and should you fire, the deaths of those aboard the three vessels would be certain,' said the Warden calmly.

With another part of itself, the AI observed one of the armoured Prador as it drifted close to one of many orbital eyes, for it was not often that one of this kind got so close to Polity scanning equipment, and such an opportunity should not be missed.

Certainly, if the King's household was organized along the same lines as others of his kind, all his guards would be first-, second- and third-children. There were no fourth-children, as any that survived the ruthless selection process in a Prador brood cave was automatically designated a third-child. The casualty rate being approximately 90 per cent for each generation, out of a thousand Prador nymphs in a brood only a hundred would survive the savage selection process so as to become *third*-children, while ten would survive to become *second*-children, and one would get to be a *first*-child. What this ensured was self-evident, for in the life-time of an adult Prador, which could be as long as eight hundred solstan years, three to four hundred broods would be engendered. However, first-children rarely made it to adulthood since they were generally killed by their father around their fiftieth year of life, before they could make that final step. This meant that, at any one time, a single adult Prador should have a maximum of twenty-five first-children attending on it. Speculation in the Polity had always been rife about King Oboron and his guard, since the King was older than any other known Prador, with his first-children numbered in the thousands, and all of them wearing that concealing armour.

'Again,' Vrost replied, 'Hoopers are not your concern, and the passengers of that ship are already dead.'

'I must warn you I cannot allow you to use that coil-gun,' said the Warden, groping around for something more to add. 'And I must also ask whether this behaviour is what passes for diplomatic relations amongst your kind. Would your King be pleased with your actions here – and the way you are threatening the new alliance between the Polity and the Third Kingdom?'

Vrost was a long time in replying, and during this delay the Warden attempted some gentle probing of the armoured Prador.

The most probable explanation for the current King and his extended family was that he had discovered some form of longevity but denied it to all but his immediate kin, and that this same serum, process or surgical technique had also stalled his kin's maturation. This had occurred with some of the earlier anti-geriatric medications used by humans. Specifically there had been a nanotech process – similar to the nanofactories used by reifications – which had read the DNA of its host, then perpetually worked to repair any subsequent damage to that DNA. The disadvantage here was that if the DNA was already damaged before this reading process, the nanomachines would maintain that damage. This meant that someone suffering from cancer would then *always* have cancer, for any attempt at correction at a genetic level would be defeated by the nanobots. It also meant that if someone took such treatment while a child, he or she would then remain forever a child.

The armour was near impenetrable: a thick layer of exotic metal sandwiching alternate layers of a superconductor and some other reflective exotic metal. The Warden tried low-level radar and microwave scans, but once the AI upped the intensity of those, the Prador clearly sensed them, because it turned to face the nearby satellite eye and projected microwave and radio white noise. But there remained another possibility.

The Warden slowly began altering the position of the nearest satellite eye, to bring it away from the armoured Prador but down into the same level of the ionosphere. Further around the planet, it dropped another eye to the same level.

'Prador do not participate in diplomacy,' Vrost replied. 'This must be settled quickly.'

Shit, thought the Warden.

'Now,' Vrost continued, 'that I have obliged you, I would prefer it if you made no further attempt to scan Father's second-children.'

One strange piece of information there: the Warden had assumed, by the size of this armoured Prador, that it must be a first-child. The AI then initiated the X-ray scan from his further eye, while using the closer eye as a receiver. The fusion detonation came a microsecond after, converting the armoured second-child into a glowing ball of gas. The flash knocked out the reception on most nearby satellite eyes.

'I repeat,' said Vrost, 'attempt no scans.'

Either suicide or remote detonation initiated by Vrost, the Warden realized. 'My apologies, that scan was initiated before your warning.'

The AI was betting on the Prador not comprehending exactly how fast an AI could react. For a moment Vrost gave no reply, and the Warden studied the X-ray picture he had obtained. It was not very clear, but certainly showed that the armour had not conformed to the shape of the being it contained. *That* looked nothing like any Prador second-child.

'The ocean ship survived the wave caused by my first strike,' said Vrost. 'Another strike would only be four hundred kilometres closer and, impacting on a spaceship near the surface, I have just calculated that its detonation would not cause so large a wave.'

The Warden found himself all out of bluffs. Either Vrost believed the AI could use U-space weapons or he did not. There was nothing more the AI could do, and Vrost, it seemed, did not believe him. The coil-gun fired again.

Tracking the missile down through the atmosphere, the AI made its own calculations and realized that the Prador captain might just be right, so long as no weapons or fusion reactors detonated aboard Vrell's ship. Then something unexpected happened, and the AI observed the projectile become a streak of incandescent gas.

'It would seem that Vrell's shipboard weapons are perfectly functional,' the Warden remarked.

After a long delay, Vrost replied, 'Yes, so it would appear.'

Something cataclysmic had certainly occurred here in the sea. The giant whelk recognized the signs by something buried deep in her memory. She recollected, long in the past, grey sulphurous fountains spewing from seafloor vents around which gathered strange green prill and enormous pale clams. Near her, magma had wormed up from the deep ocean floor with a sound like something huge tearing apart. Hints of its inner glow showed through the immediate crust it acquired on contact with the sea water, and it hardened into stone pillars that then toppled one after another. All this had been a curiosity to nearby whelks, until one of them had ventured close enough to grab one of the clams. That rash individual was caught in a stray current of water which, but for the pressure, would have been steam. It died with one long-drawn-out squeal, before floating upwards inflated by its own cooking gases. The rest of the whelks fled.

Here, around her now, drifted the remnants of parboiled leeches, cooked-red segments of glister and hinged-open prill carapaces. Down below she observed the skeleton of a heirodont and felt a surge of gladness – as she well knew, such monsters did not die easily, so what had caused this ablation of its flesh must have been strong indeed. Now all that was left of that drastic event was unusual warm-water currents cutting through the devastation. But the ocean was gradually returning to normal and, like herself, its denizens were venturing into this area to feed on the organic detritus.

First came the turbul, crunching open both shell and carapace to get at the broiled meat inside. Then came shoals of boxies, swarming like silver bees as they picked through this cornucopia in the water and juggled clean any pieces of shell the turbul dropped. Glisters remained distant, keeping well clear of the whelk herself, but prill she had to perpetually slap away. A heirodont, half the size of the one she had beheaded, cruised into view then turned towards her. She prepared her garrotte and waited, as the thing circled twice, clacking its mandibles. Holding the line out towards it, drawn taut between two tentacles, she sculled round to stay facing it. Then it attacked.

Her line cut into the slope of its head as it drove her rapidly back up through the water, then along the surface, kicking up spray from the heaving ocean. Its mandibles kept groping only a small distance from her body. When it eventually slowed, she relaxed the line's tension, sculled neatly round beside the creature's head and looped the line around its neck. It was easier with this smaller attacker than the previous occasion, and the line did not snag on any vertebrae this time. A second heirodont arrived just in time to see the whelk pushing off from the thrashing body of her attacker while its head spiralled down towards the bottom, trailing ichor as grey as any spume from a volcanic vent. As the second heirodont quickly turned away, she felt joy not so much because of this victory but because the attacker had propelled her to this particular area of ocean. For, sticking out her corkscrew tongue, she savoured a familiar taste in the water.

The ship.

16

Molly Carp:
no one really knows how this creature obtained the first half of
its name, though the second part is quite obvious, since the
creature's body resembles that of a Terran fish called a carp.
However, there the resemblance ends. It propels itself through
the sea by gripping the bottom with three rows of flat tentacles
growing from its belly. Fossil evidence indicates that these are
a further evolution of barbels. Molly carp are solitary and ter-
ritorial creatures, usually making the shallows around a single
atoll their domain. They can grow up to five metres long in the
body, with tentacles extending down fifteen metres. Hoopers
claim that once every three hundred years they all simultane-
ously leave their individual territories so as to mate in Nort
Sea. This has yet to be witnessed by any Polity observer, but if
it is the case, then they seem to have adapted well to viral
longevity. Rumour and legend abound regarding these crea-
tures: they rescue drowning Hoopers, sometimes follow ships for
hundreds of kilometres, and like magpies will steal anything
shiny they can lay their tentacles on. It is claimed that one
Captain Alber even trained a molly carp to tow his ship. This
Captain has never been found, so no confirmation can be
made. All Polity observers have witnessed are molly carp

haunting island waters, where they are voracious predators of glisters and prill, occasionally venturing down deeper to unearth amberclams –

Janer peered through the sight of the laser carbine and observed the adolescent rhinoworms tearing at each other in the island shallows. After targeting one of them he was about to fire when another surge from the ship's engines forced him to step quickly to one side to maintain his balance. Some of the Kladites on deck, who were making themselves useful by lasering worms out at sea, were experiencing the same problem. Hooper crew up in the rigging, as well as having to maintain balance, were also plagued by lung birds which, apparently sated on nectar from the sea lilies, found the rigging a convenient place to roost. And they stank. But still lots of rhinoworms had been hit at some distance from the ship, diverting the attention of many of their cannibalistic kin away from those the ship's autolasers were currently massacring.

Janer stepped back to the rail and peered over.

It was a mess down there. The sea was a soup of chopped up bodies, and of thousands more come to feed in a struggling mass three-deep up the side of the ship. Smoke was billowing all along the waterline, the stink of charred flesh infected the air and, much as he had no love for the voracious denizens of this planet, Janer was saddened to see their destruction in such numbers. He turned round and glanced up beyond the Hoopers joyously popping away at distant rhinoworms. Up there Zephyr hung upside down, his head jerking back and forth as if tracking every shot. Janer glanced down again, considering switching to auto-sight – as the Hoopers doubtless had – which allowed some correction for the movement of the deck beneath him. Then he shouldered his weapon and wandered over to the ladder up the side of the midship deckhouse.

'There has to be a better way than this,' he said to Wade, who was observing the mayhem from the roof and occasionally turning to check Zephyr's reaction to it.

The Golem looked down at him. 'There is, and it's being dealt with now. Everyone but a small crew is being ordered to remain in their cabins, and all stairwells and hatches are to be closed. We'll keep the decks clear meanwhile.'

Janer climbed up to join him. 'So even Ron is getting a little tired of this slaughter?'

'It's not that.' Wade glanced at him. 'These creatures are only being attracted to the bodies of their own kind, and that's why there are so many around the ship. Left to their own devices, only a few would manage to crawl up the side and get aboard.'

'You got that in writing?'

'We have to try it.' Wade grinned. 'According to Ron, if we can lose the bulk of those now clinging at the waterline, the ship would lift as much as half a metre.'

'Have to try what, precisely?'

'Shutting off the autolasers.'

'Ah, that's—' Janer did not finish, for at that moment Wade grabbed him, hurling the both of them to one side and down onto the deck. As he sprawled, Janer heard yelling, saw a shape hurtling down, then felt the deck jounce underneath him as a Hooper slammed down on it a couple of metres away. Immediately after, what was left of a Batian weapon hit the nearby rail. The two struggled to their feet and moved over to the fallen man, who was lying on his side with his hands wrapped around his head.

'Are you all right?' Wade asked.

Janer at first thought that a silly question, until he remembered: *Of course, a Hooper.*

With a crunching sound the man unwrapped his arms from his head. His landing had been a hard one, for the Hooper found it necessary to push one of his eye-balls back into its socket.

Another crunching sound as he straightened out his leg. 'Think . . . I'll be needing a little help,' he managed.

Wade removed a comlink from his pocket and spoke into it. This was just a courtesy to Janer and the crew-man, as he was quite capable of transmitting the same words by his internal radio. 'Erlin, we've got an injured Hooper on the midships deckhouse, just above you.'

Erlin replied from the link, 'And?'

'He fell about a hundred metres from the rigging. He might need a bit of work to straighten him out, before he heals up flat.'

'Hoopers don't fall off masts,' Erlin replied suc-cinctly.

The Golem peered down at the fallen man, who was now slapping the side of his head with his one good hand to straighten up his eyeballs. 'He didn't fall. He was pushed.'

Janer looked up to where the Golem sail was crawling down the mast like a huge iron vampire bat. It was swinging its head from side to side, and a turquoise glow kept advancing and retreating in its eyes.

'Shit,' muttered Janer. 'What the hell is the matter with *him*?'

'Ah,' said Wade, 'my other half seems to be experiencing a little internal dispute.'

'Might be an idea to move away from here,' suggested Janer, aware that the turquoise glow was the emission from a particle cannon being taken on- and off-line. At that moment the sail let out a long shriek which seemed to penetrate all the way down the length of Janer's spine. It then launched itself from the mast, spreading monofabric wings with a snapping sound, and gliding away from the ship. It turned in mid-air and turquoise fire flashed down. There came an explosion from below and the sounds of hot metal skittering across the deck. Janer and Wade ran to the deckhouse rail, to again see that fire flash from Zephyr's eyes, this time striking further along the ship.

'He seems to have come to a decision,' Wade observed.

More shots blasted from the sail as it winged around the ship. Janer tilted his head to listen to the sounds of destruction from the other side. 'I don't think you'll need to shut down the autolasers – that's what he's doing for you.'

'He's probably decided they represent Death,' said Wade, then spoke into the comlink: 'Erlin, we'll be bringing the injured party down to you. Ron, are you seeing this?'

'What's that bugger doing to my ship?' came the Captain's reply.

'Destroying the autolasers.'

'I bloody well know that. *Why* is it doing that?'

'I don't know, but you better get the hatches locked down and the stairwells closed, as per plan. Erlin, stay in the Tank Rooms and keep the doors closed. Are you armed?'

'I am now.'

Wade indicated the Hooper. 'I'll carry him. You watch my back.'

They reached the nearest mainmast stairwell just as Janer saw, down on the main deck below, the first pink rhino head, *sans* horns, peering over the rail. He shot it through the mouth before it got a chance to progress any further, then himself followed the Golem into the stairwell, engaging the door lock behind them.

With the Hooper slung over his shoulder, Wade addressed his comlink again. 'Can't see what's going on at the moment, Ron. What's happening?'

'We've got a few strays coming aboard, but the main mass at the waterline is dropping away. Gonna fire up the engines in about ten minutes. Ah . . . Huff and Puff just joined in. Nothing they like better than a bit of fresh rhinoworm – barring the odd Batian head, in Huff's case.'

'Okay, you lot up on the masts, concentrate your fire around any open hatches or stairwells. We can't afford to let these bastards inside the ship.'

Janer wondered just when Wade had been appointed military commander of this ship, and whether that was such a good idea.

Meeting them in the upper Tank Room, Erlin led the way to one of the restraint tables, this one with its restraints removed and an autodoc folded down underneath on the end of a jointed arm. As soon as the Hooper was down on his back, she pulled the chrome autodoc out and up so it was poised just to one side of the man's waist. 'What age Hooper are you?'

'Hundred twenty,' he replied. He was staring at the autodoc as if wanting to get as far away from it as possible. Obviously he was a Hooper who had yet to stray into the territory occupied by the likes of Forlam or the crew of the *Vignette*. Janer understood his feelings, for despite having been operated upon by such autodocs himself, he was still wary of the things. Perhaps it was some primordial instinct impinging – the atavistic fear of insects. This particular doc looked something like a shiny metal horseshoe crab, only with longer legs which were possessed of more joints and terminated in a variety of surgical instruments.

'I've got to straighten this leg and that arm.' Erlin flipped up a lid in the doc's back, revealing a small console with a port for a memory tab. 'If they heal like that, you'll be crippled for the next couple of years until they straighten out naturally.' Out of her top pocket she took a cylindrical container and pulled from it thumbnail-sized crystal tabs. Selecting one, she placed it in the port, then tapped instructions into the console. The tab contained enough memory storage to encompass a human life – similar tabs formed the basis of memplants.

'Is it gonna hurt?' The man tried to pull himself further away as the doc wiggled its multitude of legs.

'I can't inject you with anything. Even if I could get the injection in, the analgesic wouldn't spread quickly enough anyway. But I've been well-supplied here.' She held up a simple grey cube between her forefinger and thumb. Before the man could say anything more, she pressed it against the side of his neck.

The Hooper lay there blinking for a moment, then said, 'I can't feel me body – it's like when I broke me back.'

'Do you really want to feel it right now?'

'Guess not.'

Turning to Janer and Wade, Erlin said, 'I had to make a few alterations to the nerve-blocker. It needs stronger nanofilaments to be able to penetrate Hooper flesh through to the spine.'

'And the doc?' Janer asked.

'Programmed for removing reification hardware initially, but I reprogrammed it to Hooper physiology.' She closed the lid over the console in which she had inserted the crystal tab. 'I've been studying Hoopers for quite a while now, and have operated on many of them. What I just put in here contains everything at variance to standard human biology from Hooper babies right up to Old Captains. He' – she stabbed a thumb at the prostrate Hooper – 'won't need anything to seal severed blood vessels, only arteries, and the doc won't touch any of them. But it will need to clamp open its incisions, and work fast to ensure the job is done before those incisions start healing while still open.'

'That's fascinating,' said Janer, turning to watch the autodoc swing down the length of the Hooper's body, abruptly slice open the man's trousers, and then the calf muscle of his mangled leg, right down to the bone. 'You won't be needing any help?'

Erlin shook her head.

The doc was now cutting between fragments of shattered greyish bone that were already knitting together.

'Then perhaps we should go back outside and help the others.' He looked questioningly at Wade.

The Golem bore a curiously twisted expression Janer could not fathom. Internal communication? After a moment, Wade nodded and turned away.

'Best lock the door behind us,' he suggested.

Vrell eased his ship higher in the ocean until its weapons turrets were completely clear of the surface, meanwhile recharging the massive capacitors feeding the two particle cannons. He kept his weapons aligned with the location of Vrost's ship, ready to again vaporize anything fired by the coil-gun. Other weapons he laser-ranged on numerous objects dropping through the atmosphere.

Things were turning nasty here.

Through the senses of his alternate self, Vrell observed its battle with the Polity drone. Overhearing the latest communication between the Warden and Vrost, Vrell guessed who that other drone must be, even though it now inhabited a different shell. Its subsequent familiar tactics confirmed this suspicion, but the danger it represented was minimal. He was aware of how its previous attack on this ship had only succeeded by a narrow margin and, should it try again, Vrell would burn it from the sky. Its previous success had only been due to Father's thrall codes being subverted, so that Ebulan, being attacked by his own blanks, was distracted at the critical moment. Vrell, however, would not be distracted, and his only vulnerable code transmissions, to those aboard the ocean-going vessel now only a few hundred kilometres from him, he could break instantly. Ebulan's mistake had been in thinking those codes unbreakable. But Vrell, having ventured into the realm of higher mathematics, knew no code was unbreakable. No, the greatest danger to him was still Vrost. He sent a summons to his own drone, and levelled one weapons array to cover it. He would need all of his resources if he was to survive this.

The calculations necessary to enable him to make repairs to the U-space engine were halfway completed. Vrell considered abandoning that pursuit, because to use the engine he must first get off this planet and well clear of its gravity well. It did not strike him as probable that Vrost would allow that. However, Vrell lost nothing by allowing those calculations to continue running, and some future opportunity might present itself. For the present he would take measures to protect himself, and those were predicated on the threat to Vrost of non-existent grav-tech weapons controlled by the Warden and Vrost's resultant reluctance to destroy a ship-load of mobile corpses.

Vrell was not optimistic.

Stalemate. Sniper pulled away from the Prador war drone, and it pulled away from him. Assessing the damage done to him, Sniper was quite impressed. His internal systems were down to 70 per cent, his internal power sources were half depleted and only a few missiles remained in his carousels. Externally, his once bright armour was now battered and black, and he was even missing two tentacles. However, the Prador drone was not in the best of condition either: it was missing one of its claws, radioactive gas was leaking from a crack in its armour, and its shape was no longer entirely spherical.

'You know, shithead,' Sniper sent, 'I'm saving a small imploder missile for that crack in your hide.' With any luck this would make the Prador drone more protective of that area, perhaps thus leaving it vulnerable elsewhere.

'My name is not shithead, old drone,' it replied. 'And such cheap ploys will not work with me.'

'Right, gotcha. What's your name, then?'

'I am Vrell.'

Interesting.

'Now that's an odd coincidence.'

'There is no coincidence – I am a copy.'

'I see . . . I'm Sniper, by the way.'

'Then know, Sniper, that we are evenly matched, except in one respect: my armour is thicker. Should we have finally depleted our respective armouries, I would have knocked you down onto one of these islands and pounded you into the ground.'

It sure was a lot more talkative than others of its kind that Sniper had met, and destroyed. 'Would have?'

The Prador drone abruptly turned and opened up with its fusion engines, immediately accelerating away from Sniper.

What now?

Sniper set off in pursuit but, as he did so, he immediately picked up objects hurtling down from the sky above. Suddenly their fight was no longer an even match, for Vrost's forces were coming to intercede. Sniper suddenly felt a kinship with the fleeing drone.

'Looks like your relatives have come to finish what we started,' he sent after his erstwhile opponent.

'They make clear targets against the sky. I suspect they will not survive beyond another twelve point three kilometres,' the Vrell drone replied.

Sniper abruptly cut his acceleration. *Twelve point three kilometres* was a precise figure, and certainly a strange product of bravado. At this elevation, he calculated, as drones and armoured Prador sped past him, that figure would bring them over the horizon and in direct line to the present location, within a permissible error, of Vrell's spaceship. Using attitude jets, Sniper spun round, and re-engaged his engines to send him in the opposite direction. At three kilometres he observed one of the armoured Prador turning in mid-air as it sped past. It looked something like a gigantic dust mite cast in gold.

'We will attend to the matter you have left undone,' it sent contemptuously.

Sniper considered giving these new Prador the courtesy his opponent had just given him, but rejected the idea. Obviously the Vrell drone had felt the same kinship as he had felt for it, though given the opportunity it would still have pounded him into the ground just as he would have gladly given it a missile suppository. But he felt no such kinship with these others. As far as he was concerned, Prador killing Prador could only be a good thing, despite any treaties. Low over the ocean, he turned to observe, right on cue, the flash of particle-cannon impacts, and molten pieces of drone and golden armour raining on the sea.

Ambel gazed astern through his binoculars, and frowned. The sea was choppy so it was difficult to tell, but he was sure he had just spotted something in the waves. Not that this was unusual: since all the life forms on Spatterjay were long-lived and difficult to kill, it was inevitable that they swarmed everywhere. And, tacking like this, the *Treader* was sure to pick up the odd inquisitive monster – perhaps a rhinoworm then, or a big leech.

'Something up, Captain?' asked Boris from the helm.

'I think we might have an unwelcome guest,' Ambel replied.

'Not that bloody whelk?'

Ambel shook his head. 'Unlikely – I reckon that one's long gone.' He headed for the ladder, clambered down it to enter his cabin, snatched up the holographic conferencing device, and walked back out on deck. After spending a moment resetting it to voice only, and then connecting to one other such device, he asked, 'Drum. Drum, are you there, man?'

Drum's reply was immediate. 'I wondered when you'd be getting in contact. I've been shouting into this thing on and off for a couple of hours.'

'You've seen it then?'

'Yup, something in our wake. Might be an idea to run with the wind for a while to lose it,' Drum replied. 'This blow is starting to shift the way we want to go, anyway.'

'How long ago did you spot it?'

'Roach spotted something this morning. No one believed him until our sail confirmed it a few hours ago.'

'Any idea what it might be?'

'I dunno – something dangerous by the way Cloud-skimmer's behaving.'

Ambel looked up. 'Galegrabber! What's following us?'

The sail lowered its head until it was level with Ambel's. The creature now wore its new aug, and since donning it had been very silent and introspective. 'A big swimming whelk. Its tentacle nearly snagged the rudder on that last tack.'

'Why didn't you buggering well tell us?'

The sail blinked. 'The search program I ran revealed that no one has yet been attacked by a swimming whelk.'

'Erm, and how about your memory?'

The sail looked astern, licking its black tongue around its teeth. 'My memory is clear. Yes, I do recollect this individual attacking us.'

Ambel sighed. 'Galegrabber, this is the real world, right here.' He stabbed a finger at the deck. 'I know what you see in the AI nets can be astounding, and that the programs you run can reveal all sorts of fascinating facts, but none of that stuff will help you if something tries to eat you here and now.'

'Aug trance?' asked Drum over the link.

'In a big way,' Ambel replied. 'I reckon we should do what you said. Boris, turn us into the wind!' He addressed the sail again. '*And* you.'

Galegrabber stared for a long moment, then abruptly jerked up his head and began to turn both himself and the fabric sails. Boris spun the helm and the *Treader* heeled over. Across the link, Ambel heard Drum bellowing similar orders, and saw that the *Moby* was coming about as well.

'Everyone up on deck, and armed!' Ambel now called out, then returned to his cabin to inspect a chart spread on the table. If Drum was right, and the wind did shift to take them back on their original course, then in a few days they would be reaching an island which was only a number on this chart. He again considered his earlier thoughts on how to deal with this persistent pursuer. They required a landfall for that, as they stood no chance against such a monster on the open ocean. He just hoped the wind did not die, meanwhile.

Back out on deck he observed such crew as were not moving about assigned tasks all standing armed at the rail, looking astern. He joined them in time to see a huge iridescent shell break the surface, tentacles whipping the waves ahead of it, and two huge eyes extruded on stalks to observe them.

'How ever did it survive that heirodont?' Anne asked. 'And how the hell did it find us again?'

Ambel shrugged. 'Luck, coincidence, fate?'

As she raised her laser carbine to take a shot at the creature, Ambel stepped over to push the barrel aside with his hand.

'You'll only annoy it further,' he said.

'Well, it doesn't seem that likely to calm down and leave us alone.'

'Save your shots then for when they'll really count. In the meantime I want you and Peck sharpening all our harpoons and checking their ropes.'

'You want to catch the damned thing?'

Ambel ignored this and held up his conferencing link. 'Are you listening, Drum?'

'I'm riveted,' the other Captain replied.

Ambel then outlined his plan, and observed the looks of dismay from the crewmen surrounding him.

'Has anyone got any better ideas?' he asked them.

None was forthcoming.

The Golem sail had destroyed all of the autolasers, and was now back up on Mainmast Two, scrambling about as if searching for something while occasionally letting out more of those piercing shrieks. Janer watched it for a moment, then focused on what had just slid over the rail and onto the deck ahead of him. The young rhino-worm resembled a two-metre-long pink newt with a hornless rhinoceros head. It opened its beaklike mouth and hissed, before charging him eagerly. Rather than use his Batian weapon, which would also have smashed the surrounding woodwork, Janer drew his handgun and, with it set only to standard pulse, opened fire. Drawing white lines through the air between himself and the creature, two of his shots burned holes through its head, jerking it up and back. His third shot hit it underneath its head, bursting some organ there. The creature reared up as if electrocuted, then crashed down, thrashing about as it sprayed a sticky yellow mess over the deck and a nearby cabin wall. Before it had even finished its death throes, a shadow loomed as Huff leaned down over the deckhouse side, clamped the rhinoworm in his jaws, then flung the creature out over the rail with a snap of his long neck.

'Got enough now?' Janer enquired.

Earlier, he had noticed Huff making a mound of still slowly moving bodies up on the deckhouse roof – those he did not eat, at least. Janer guessed the sail was laying in food stores for himself, but even in that there had to be a limit.

The sail eyed him. 'I grow sick of the taste.'

'Understandable.' Huff's body was now bloated from his gorging, and Janer suspected he would not be taking wing for some time. Puff, over on the stern deckhouse, had not been quite so greedy for, after feeding only a little while, she had concentrated on picking up the encroaching worms in her jaws and flipping them over the side of the ship.

'Doesn't it worry you how Zephyr might react?' Janer asked.

Huff turned and looked up at the aforementioned sail. 'Zephyr . . . is not right. Death is an absence, not a presence.'

So the living sails understood something of their Golem companion's motivations.

'He still might take a shot at you, to stop you killing those rhinoworms,' Janer suggested.

'He does not kill. He cannot kill.'

Janer did not even bother to dispute that. Instead, he turned and shot a rhinoworm that was sneaking over the rail behind him. By destroying the defensive lasers Zephyr had endangered them all for, had these creatures been less intent on devouring their kin, they could have swamped the ship. He moved up to the rail and peered over, noticing how now there were fewer of the creatures clinging at the waterline. Clumps of them were even drifting away, fighting with each other over the remains of those hit earlier by the now disabled autolasers.

'Do you know where Isis Wade is?' he asked over his shoulder. 'I lost track of him a couple of hours ago.'

'He is on deck over on the starboard side of the bridge,' Huff replied, before heaving himself up and back out of sight.

Janer began walking in that direction, his carbine slung from his left shoulder and his handgun in his right hand. Just then the ship lurched as Ron once again started the engines. A grinding vibration shivered up through Janer's feet, and he felt the ship move this time, if only a little way. Walking on, Janer observed red flashes of carbine fire from a group of Kladites gathered around the bridge on the roof of the staterooms just below it, and smelt wafts of acrid smoke drifting across the ship. They were probably huddling there to protect Bloc. All the hatches were locked down now, all the stairwells bolted shut. Crossing, behind the bridge, over to the starboard side, he spotted a rhinoworm scuttling down the further gangway, and was about to take a shot at it when a pursuing Hooper dived onto the creature and brought it down. It tried to turn on the man, but he grabbed it by the neck and smacked its head against the planking until it desisted, then tossed it over the side.

'Wade?' Janer asked him.

The man gestured behind himself with a thumb, then went to retrieve a machete embedded in a nearby wall.

Wade, leaning against the rail, was gazing down. Janer joined him there and also peered over. A number of the worms were still working their way up the hull, but none were yet within easy reach of the rail.

'Do you note their toes?' the Golem asked.

Janer saw only that the mentioned items were as flat and round as always. 'What about them?'

Wade pointed. 'The hull paint has a very low coefficient of friction – enough to prevent any whelks or leeches climbing it – yet these things still manage to get aboard. Look.' He reached down and picked up something to show Janer. It was a rhinoworm leg, ripped off at the shoulder. 'See,' Wade poked at one of the toes, 'the structure of these is very like that of an Earth lizard called a gecko.'

'Your point being?' Janer asked. Even though he himself had recently been shooting these unwelcome boarders, he could not quite accept the callousness of ripping a leg off one so as to study the toes. That seemed inhuman, which of course it was.

'Why would sea-going animals develop toes like that? What use do they have for them?'

'You might well ask the same question about the legs themselves. But don't you think we've got more important concerns?' Janer gestured up towards Zephyr. 'Your other half is still rather agitated, and to my mind looks ready to go.'

'His agitation is a good sign,' Wade replied. 'His time as a distinct being is now conflicting with his madness.'

'So he won't fly?'

'I did not say that.'

Janer wondered how he should best assess this Golem before him. Underneath that human exterior and emulation, he was not even a normal AI (if there was such a thing).

'Are you afraid to make that final decision?' he asked. 'I reckon Zephyr is a danger to the entire ecosphere of this planet, not to forget its financial system.'

Another rhinoworm poked its head over the rail, and Wade casually smacked it from view with the leg he still held. Almost as if that one worm had been holding down the entire weight of the *Sable Keech*, the roar of its engines changed, the grinding sound recommenced and continued, as the ship's propellers began dragging it back out to sea. They both turned to watch as clumps of battling worms slid past them towards the bows, bobbing up and down in the first waves generated by the shifting hull.

Parting his feet to maintain his balance, Janer said, 'Perhaps I should make the decision for you?'

'That will not be necessary.'

'How can you be so sure? You're too close to the problem.'

Wade glanced at him. 'Zephyr will not use the virus . . . not yet.'

A cheer arose, and Ron beamed round at his crew gathered on the bridge.

He slapped Forlam on the shoulder. 'Keep us on this heading until we're well clear – a couple of kilometres at least – then take us round and back on course. On the other side of the island we'll put on sail and shut down the engines.'

'What do you reckon Windcheater'll do about this? We have broken his law.'

Ron tapped a finger against the comlink in his belt. 'I asked him before we started those engines. He won't do anything drastic – just work out how big a fine the owners of this ship will have to pay. I must go and give Bloc that good news sometime.'

'Captain Ron, I think we have a problem,' said John Styx, who was working at a nearby coms console.

Captain Ron turned to him. 'What is it, a leak?'

'No, a message from the Warden. I would have found it earlier but I was using this console to break into the ship's computer system.' Styx pointed towards the forward bridge windows. 'Yes, you can see it now.' He then pressed a touch-plate on the console, and the Warden's voice issued forth:

'Ebulan's spaceship, controlled by his now-adult first-child Vrell, is heading directly towards you. It is just submerged, and presently being attacked by drones and armoured Prador descending from the upper atmosphere. I do not know Vrell's intentions, but him being Prador I suspect they are not amicable.'

'Oh.' In the distance Ron could see objects silhouetted against the sky, like birds or bees, and amidst them flashes like distant lightning. 'Forlam, take us to port – quickly now.'

As the *Sable Keech* turned, Ron noticed dark objects in the sea immediately below the swarm of activity:

blockish columns of metal and rounded turrets, all generating wakes as they came towards the island and the
ship. Having watched Ebulan's ship crash, he instantly
recognized the upper weapons turrets of the Prador light
destroyer. Ron picked up a nearby monocular, held it to
an eye and kept knocking up the magnification. What he
saw confirmed everything the Warden had told him, but
gave him no explanation as to the *why* of it.

'Keep us turning. Have we got full power to those
engines?'

'We have, Captain,' replied the Hooper who was
operating the controls.

'Bugger.' Ron was still peering at the Prador ship,
now very much closer. It was turning as they turned,
remaining right on target. He lowered the monocular, no
longer needing it. Launched from one of the round turrets, missiles sped up into the sky and detonated high
above. EM blast – had to be. He looked around and
noted Styx stepping back from the coms console, whose
lights and screen had just blinked out. Squinting back at
the location of the recent blasts, he saw three objects
dropping from the sky: two war drones and one
armoured Prador, which he recognized even at this distance. With a bitter taste in his mouth he recollected
sights very like this from the first century of his life.

Then, as if in no time at all, weapons turrets were
passing on either side of the *Sable Keech* before slowing,
and it was as if a thunderstorm had enveloped the ship.
With a screaming crash, turquoise fire slashed up into
the sky. Launchers spun on one of the turrets, releasing
such a fusillade of missiles that they cut for the horizon
in a seemingly solid black line. Something detonated
nearby, scattering shrapnel across the ocean, and one

large fragment skimmed over the water and into the ship's side, with a low crump that shuddered through the deck. Then came a detonation above, and a wave of fire rolling across the sky. The ship dipped under the blast, throwing people off their feet. As a brief interval of quiet followed, Ron watched the turrets rising higher out of the sea, and heard that familiar grinding on the hull.

'Shut off the engines,' he calmly instructed. 'We'll only be going where this bastard wants to take us.'

He still called himself Vrell, no matter that his body was now made of metal and his brain was the flash-frozen tissue of a sibling. As he motored back underwater, towards his other self, his internal systems worked ceaselessly to repair the damage caused by the old Polity drone, and he refined deuterium oxide fuel from sea water for his fusion reactor, which in turn was charging up the depleted capacitors and laminar batteries powering his energy weapons. He was puzzled by his earlier actions, unable to fathom why he had not led his opponent within range of those weapons now devastating Vrost's forces in the air above him. His action had been allowed because the order for him to return to the spaceship took precedence over the one for him to destroy the old drone, but that did not wholly account for his own decision. Perhaps the bitterness of knowing his own chances of surviving this were little above zero lay behind his decision to let the old drone live?

Black shapes again streaked past him through the water. Some of the other drones and members of the King's guard had followed him into the sea, but they were no less at the mercy of the ship's weapons than those above. Reddish explosions detonated behind him and, over com frequencies, he could hear the sound of something dying. Then came contact from the *real* Vrell:

'Two drones and one King's guard have fallen into the sea *here*.' Vrell sent coordinates. 'All have been disabled by electromagnetic pulse. The guard's fusion device has not detonated. Destroy the two drones and retrieve the guard.'

'As you will.'

The Vrell drone obeyed – he could not do otherwise. However, he was still a copy of the original Vrell, and therefore not something loaded into a drone shell and programmed to military service from the moment he had hatched, so was capable of thinking about the reasoning behind that order.

The guard's armour having been disabled by EM and still containing a living occupant, the Prador drone's initial conjecture was that Vrell wanted a prisoner to interrogate, yet that did not really gel. There would not be enough time to break the guard's conditioning sufficiently to learn anything useful about Vrost's plans. The true Vrell might have sought to access systems in the armour so as to break into Vrost's com frequencies had it not been that the Prador above made little attempt to encode them. It seemed it did not matter what Vrell knew: from an utterly superior position, Vrost intended to obliterate them. Perhaps curiosity then, just that – Vrell wanting to know, or rather confirm, what that armour contained? Of course, such speculation was based on what the drone's own aims would have been. The real Vrell, however, had moved far beyond him. The drone could not, for example, see any possibility of repairing a surge-damaged U-space engine, yet his creator was obviously making plans to do so.

The water here was still murky from the first kinetic missile strike, and other clouds of silt and detritus were spreading out from the more recent explosions. The drone occasionally observed, deep down, turbul and smaller whelks snapping up animals damaged by an earlier blast. When he saw a molly carp cruising by in the distance, he felt an instant of fear caused by an emotional residue of his earlier self. Then anger took over and made him want to go after the creature to deliver some payback, but the real Vrell's orders did not allow for that. The drone watched the molly carp lashing out a tentacle to bludgeon a passing turbul, cutting it nearly in half before beginning to chomp it down. Boxies shoaled around the carp, like silver bubbles from its mouth, as like ship lice they scavenged scraps. But soon the molly carp was out of sight, and the drone approaching the coordinates Vrell had sent.

The drone immediately detected three metallic objects on the bottom, underneath a cloud of silt. Using his magnetometer, he identified one of the other drones, descended to it, then, from only metres away, extruded a thermic lance and began to bore a hole through its armour. Nothing came over com because the EM pulse had knocked out most of its systems, but doubtless its diagnostic and repair systems, being more hardened to such attacks, were still working, so it knew precisely what was happening to it.

The lance cut in slowly, for this exotic metal contained superconductive layers and had to be eroded away rather than burnt or melted. Finally the lance broke through. The drone switched it off, retracted it, then lined up his missile port to the hole and fired a torp inside his victim. A jet of fire and molten debris spewed from the cavity. The Vrell drone disposed of the next drone in exactly the same manner, then approached the King's guard.

The armoured Prador's internal repair systems were more advanced than those of a drone. It responded over com, threatening, promising, but never begging. It had seen what had happened to Vrost's two drones, and assumed itself in for the same treatment. When the Vrell drone noted the guard attempting to move some of its limbs, internally he checked the charge of some of his laminar batteries, then brought an emitter to bear and fired pulses of electromagnetic radiation at the areas containing the motor controls for the guard's armour. When the guard ceased moving, the Vrell drone clamped his own claw around the limp claw of the other and, blasting up clouds of silt with his turbines, hauled his captive off the bottom and continued back to the ship.

There were now two sailing ships for her to hunt. At first they moved slowly, and she could easily have caught one of them and pulled it down, but how they managed to sail against the wind puzzled her, so, after only a exploratory touch against one of the rudders, she held back. Slowly she began to understand the interaction of forces involved. The wind was blowing in one direction, the sails angled to catch it. Logic dictated that the wind should push the ship backwards. However, the hull was angled partially into the wind, which was trying to force it sideways through the water. The two forces – wind and water pressure – squeezed the ship between them, like a slippery stone between the opposing faces of a claw, so it shot out sideways, and thus the ship was actually travelling into the wind. This fascinated the giant whelk and, applying this new knowledge to the deep memories of her own life, her understanding of the way forces operated was increased greatly. But the fascination did not last long.

The giant whelk realized that, there now being two prey, she could catch one of them straight away and still have another to pursue, thus her quest could both succeed and continue. She was debating with herself which of them to take down when abruptly both vessels turned. Clearly she had been spotted. Surfacing for a moment, she observed the two ships speeding away, then she submerged again, deciding she would go for the second ship, not the primary target.

This pursuit lasted throughout the day and into the night. The moon gave the water a mercury sheen above her, and her happiness only increased upon encountering a turbul missing its tail and thus unable to escape. Forgetting the ships for a moment, she enjoyed a leisurely pursuit of the fish, before using her line to dice it into pieces which she easily gobbled down. Again moving after her original prey, she noticed a repetitive thumping from the sea bottom. It was a sound recalling unclear memories that elicited unexpected primal reactions in her body. The taste she then picked up in the water caused organs inside her to actually begin moving, rearranging themselves. But no, she was determined not to be distracted – that was all just instinct which would return her to the bottom and to a life abandoned. But then, for a moment, her instinct did override intellect, and she found herself banging a tentacle against her shell and releasing something into the water from glands located below her eyes. In reply, the sea-bottom thumping from the male whelk increased in frequency. She shuddered, took firmer control of herself, closed up the glands, and moved on.

17

Peartrunk Trees:
only the trunks of the younger trees are bulbous at the bottom
– i.e. pear-shaped. As these trees age and expand, they
develop splits that grow wider until the trunk resembles a
cage. The trunks are coated with a thick scaly bark that is the
preferred diet of land-dwelling heirodonts. The branches
spread out in a wide crown, each one of them terminating in
knotty tangles of black twigs from which sprout sparse green-
and-blue leaves. This plant produces no fruit or seeds, rather
sheds one or more of the twig knots, which then grows into a
new tree. Diversification is caused by the tree internally
shuffling the alleles in each twig knot. But the strangest thing
about the peartrunk tree is its symbiosis with the Spatterjay
leech. They, for reasons not clearly investigated, immediately
head straight for a peartrunk tree when they come ashore,
and roost in its branches. Occlusions through the wood of the
branches contain material similar to muscle. When a land
heirodont then begins tearing off the bark, the tree sends sig-
nals through a primitive nervous system to its branch muscles
which shake leeches down on the heirodont to drive it away.
Older trees are the most sensitive, and it takes only the pres-
ence of animal body heat anywhere near to the trunk to cause

this reaction. No one knows why, but older trees are populated exclusively by the permanent land leeches –

The blanks in the holding area were immobile, since most of their mental capacity was running the calculations Vrell needed to make for undertaking U-space engine repairs. Now that those calculations were nearly complete, he dropped four of the blanks out of the circuit. These were the ones who were still reliable, as they were not so badly suffering from the effects of starvation and from the havoc the Spatterjay virus was wreaking on them. He sent them trudging to the engine room, watching them closely through cameras in the corridors for signs of any unprogrammed movement. They appeared not to be doing anything outside of his control, but he knew they were fast approaching the time when they might reject their spider thralls. Satisfied at seeing them then begin the tasks he had programmed in – detaching all the optic and S-con cables in preparation for opening the engine casing – he turned his attention to his channel to the ship above.

The remaining blanks nearby, and those spaceship systems he had employed in the same mathematical task, should complete the calculations in a matter of hours. He did not really need the two minds of Aesop and Bones in the sailing ship above for that purpose, but another task had occurred to him.

Ebulan had died because of his perpetual underestimation of the opposition, and Vrell had no intention of being so arrogant and stupid. Above him lay a shipload of reifications and Hoopers, which Ebulan might have ignored as irrelevant but which Vrell considered a danger that must be either neutralized or otherwise distracted.

Vrell had already subtly manipulated Taylor Bloc into refusing to give Captain Ron access to the computer system, thus delaying the departure of the *Sable Keech* long enough for Vrell to get underneath it.

Bloc was the key, and now it was time for less subtle manipulation. That reif was full of bitterness and anger and, in human terms, not entirely sane. He possessed an overwhelming need to control which stemmed from a similarly overwhelming desire for adulation. At one stroke Vrell shut down Bloc's consciousness, causing the reif to slump from the edge of his bed to the floor. Then the Prador began making some alterations to Bloc's mind. Once he finished, Bloc would have to obey the Prador's orders, though he retained free will in everything else. Vrell watched through Bloc's eyes as the latter awoke and struggled to his feet.

'*Who are you? What are you?*'

Vrell did not deign to reply just then. He linked through the now-clear channels in Bloc's mind, and gazed through the eyes of Aesop and the visual receptors of Bones. After a moment, he returned to Bloc both his mobility and the reif's control of the others.

'*Secure your ship. Prevent any aboard from moving against me,*' Vrell finally ordered.

'*You are Prador.*' Bloc's observation contained something like yearning, and Vrell realized this stemmed from the reif's fanatical interest in Prador thrall technology – *control* technology. Ignoring the further flood of questions that ensued, he turned the bulk of his attention to another matter in hand.

Despite his present desperate circumstances, Vrell was determined to confirm his suspicions about the King's guard. The Warden had also obviously been as curious, hence Vrost's action in destroying the one who had drifted too close to one of the AI's satellite eyes. The armoured individual now in the drone cache had not detonated for one of two reasons. Either the EM that knocked it out of the sky had fused the relevant circuitry, or else Vrost somehow knew exactly the guard's location and was awaiting an opportune moment to send the destruction signal – probably when Vrell himself put in an appearance. There was only one real way to find out.

The Prador heaved himself up off the floor and, with his tool chest trailing along behind him, headed out of his sanctum. He noted, as he travelled the dank corridors of the ship, how the omnipresent lice remained somnolent on the wall, only shifting a little on sensing his presence. Lack of food again. He himself had not eaten for some time, and for longer there had been little for the lice to scavenge. Now suddenly aware of his own hunger, he summoned the two leech-headed blanks from where they had collapsed in the corridor outside the holding area. They joined him just as he reached the door to the cache, where he picked one of them up in a claw and began tearing it apart and feeding gobbets of its flesh into his maw. As he ate he noted how much longer his claws had now become, and how their colour was a translucent black like some kind of glass. Then he entered the cache itself.

Vrell first eyed what was left of the hooder, squirming over near the portal. It seemed more lively than before, looked longer and thinner, and gaps were growing between its segments. The Prador decided it might be quite a good idea to dump the thing outside sometime very soon, then turned his attention to his prisoner.

The King's guard was down on its belly with its legs

folded underneath and its claws stretched out slack on the floor before it. Its armour seemed to conform to the pear shape of a Prador first-child, but now, on closer examination, Vrell saw that it was just too big for that. A Prador of this size should be an adult, and therefore lacking some limbs. This one seemed to have all its legs and both its claws, and doubtless, underneath, all its manipulatory arms. Vrell speculated on the possibility that some of these limb casings might be empty of arms or legs, and instead wholly motor-driven. He would not know for sure until he took a look inside it.

After opening his tool chest, Vrell removed a powerful short-range microwave scanner, and began running it over the golden carapace before him. Soon ascertaining which areas of the armour shielded no vital systems, he summoned his drone over with a thought.

'Cut here,' he directed, stepping back.

The drone extended its thermic lance, which ignited with an arc-light flash. Soon the room was full of metallic smoke, and fans hidden in the ceiling began automatically drawing it away. The guard tried moving its claws and legs, but they only quivered a little. It would, in a moment, realize that there was only one way it might survive, and that would be without the encumbrance of dead armour. Vrell felt some satisfaction when he heard the sound of locks disengaging. He silently relayed another instruction to his drone, and moved further back.

The armour opened with a sucking crump, the entire upper carapace rising on silver rods, then hinging back. The ejection routine was fast, compressed air blowing the occupant's limbs from their casings. But not fast enough: as the grey and distorted Prador head lifted on a ribbed neck, and one claw and the legs on one side pulled free, the drone repositioned the lance and drove it straight into its grey body. The guard screamed, trying to bring to bear a short assassin-spec rail-gun. The drone snipped that manipulatory arm away, closed its claw on the creature's neck, and drove the thermic lance deeper into its body, searching out the major ganglions. The guard kept struggling and screaming for some time, green blood and smoke issuing in gushes from its mouth and over its grating mandibles. Eventually its struggles diminished, but never entirely ceased. Vrell knew that, unless this body was utterly destroyed, it would regenerate, though into what was open to speculation. After the drone dumped it down on the floor, beside its armour, Vrell moved over to investigate.

The Prador was almost the same size as himself, and its mutation quite similar, the only differences being its lighter colour, the saw-tooth edges on its legs and a thicker carapace around its neck. Was this what Vrell would eventually become? Next he turned his attention to the armour.

The fusion bomb was easy to locate and remove. It did not require disarming for the EM blast *had* completely fused its U-space receiver. It was also accessible to the armour's occupant, so clearly the latter was not expected to try shutting it off. This meant that these guards were utterly loyal to their chain of command, leading up to the King himself, which indicated pheromonal control. What then was this creature? What was Vrell himself? Were they adolescent or adult, or something else entirely?

Stepping back from the armour, Vrell studied it long and hard. He considered carefully all that its occupant implied – what it meant to the Kingdom and where he himself might fit in, if at all. Eventually he began to turn away, realizing at last the truth of his situation. He would not survive to leave Spatterjay in this ship, even with the U-space engine repaired.

He must die.

The Warden dispatched a recording of all recent events through an open link to Earth, and thereafter kept the leading AI up to date with current events. Earth Central could do nothing about what was happening here, except make promises of retribution.

'I am in contact with Oboron,' the Earth AI replied. 'Obviously there is more to this than we suspected.'

No shit, thought the Warden, privately.

As a result of five coil-gun projectiles obliterated by Vrell's particle cannons, incandescent gases billowed in high atmosphere. The blast from the second from last projectile, had it struck Vrell's spaceship, would also have smashed the *Sable Keech* into burning fragments and scattered them across kilometres of ocean. The last projectile would have left little of the ship but ash, since when it was fired its target was parked right underneath the sailing vessel. Both missiles would have resulted in a wave sweeping past the island to strike the two approaching Hooper ships with the force of a bullet.

There seemed little doubt: the moment Vrell's weapons were fully engaged defending himself from Vrost's troops, that coil-gun would fire again, and then again. The Warden could do nothing. By his actions, Vrost had called the AI's bluff.

Vrost, of course, could not resist commenting on this. 'I must assume then that you have decided not to use

your U-space weapons against me?' The translated voice
of the Prador was flatly devoid of emotion, but the sarcasm was implicit.

The Warden replied, 'I am consulting with Earth
Central on the matter, and EC is talking to your King.
I estimate it will take a few more hours before Vrell is
completely engaged with your forces, and therefore
before you can make an effective coil-gun strike. By then
I will have received my instructions.'

'I see,' said Vrost. 'I was beginning to think that perhaps your U-space weapons had malfunctioned.'

Screw you and the horse you rode in on.

The Warden felt brief disquiet at his own angry reaction, for that seemed very like something Sniper would
say, then assigned this pointless banter to a submind and
turned his attention to communication with Earth
Central.

'Oboron was apparently unaware of Vrost's actions
there, and is now attempting to open a communications
channel. But he is apparently experiencing some difficulties in that respect.' The Earth Central AI's sarcasm
was all too evident. 'I would suggest, however, that the
King is in constant com with Vrost. I am therefore about
to inform Oboron that Vrost's actions will not be tolerated. ECS beta-class dreadnoughts, though some distance from Spatterjay, are in a position to intercept
Vrost's spaceship upon its return to the Prador
Kingdom. I suggest you meanwhile raise the underlying
issue here with Vrost.'

The Warden acknowledged that, and returned his full
attention to communicating with the Prador captain.
His submind was saying, '. . . I am attempting to adjust
U-space targeting so as not to completely obliterate your

ship, but those adjustments are very finely—' The Warden absorbed the temporary mind in a microsecond, and in another microsecond scanned the previous exchange for anything of relevance. Word games: bluff from his submind and contempt from Vrost. Allowing a pause of some seconds the AI continued, 'It occurs to me, Vrost, that with your warriors and drones in the sky, and your ship in constant orbit, Vrell is unlikely to ever be leaving the planet. This being the case, I have to wonder at your anxiety. What is so dangerous about one post-adolescent Prador, that you need to kill it so quickly, despite risking the ire of Earth Central in doing so? We can surely wait until he attempts to leave, and destroy him once he is clear of the ocean and collateral damage minimized?'

A long pause ensued. Doubtless Vrost was speaking to Oboron and learning what lay in store for himself and his ship once he left Spatterjay. Clearly there was something Oboron did not want the Polity to learn about Vrell, but would the King want to sacrifice so large a ship as Vrost's to that end, or – the Warden now considered Vrost's destruction of that guard – allow that ship to be captured and its occupants studied?

After a few minutes the Warden detected the coil-gun powering down, then watched it fold back into Vrost's ship.

'Agreed,' said the Prador captain. 'I have finally managed to open a communication channel back to the Kingdom, and received instructions from Oboron. He has informed me that I must make this particular task my primary objective, rather than those other matters concerning me. My anxiety was due to my wish to quickly complete this chore.'

Other matters. Yeah.

'I appreciate your cooperation,' the Warden replied.

Then, utterly to the AI's surprise, he observed Vrost's other forces withdrawing out of range of Vrell's weapons. It seemed the storm had paused.

Erlin gazed down at the sea, eyeing the countless remains of marine denizens – most of them adolescent rhinoworms – floating on the surface. Clearly the under-water battle had been just as vicious as the one in the sky. Though it was night and Coram had yet to breach the horizon, she could see everything clearly. Even the ship's lights looked dim in the glare of the luminous clouds smeared across half the firmament. As she gripped the rail, her expression was stormy. She guessed at the cause of those clouds – the kind of weaponry recently employed from orbit, and fortunately negated – and how close they had all come to extinction. But now the dark weapons turrets of the Prador ship were still, and she could no longer hear the sound of distant thun-der. Perhaps they had made a truce, but it seemed more likely to her that they had run out of ammo.

Erlin knew her cynicism was due to weariness and frustration, though not necessarily unfounded. But she was busy – and that was important to her. She had spent many hours going from cabin to cabin, checking on the reifications. Though most of them could tell her if they needed help, a proportion of them possessing older reification hardware had been knocked out by the EM overspill from the surrounding battle. A steady stream of reifs had been going into the tanks, for their by-no-means-certain resurrection. One nanochanger had com-pletely dissolved a reif and filled that particular tank with a slimy mass of intestines. But that was the least of her problems.

She assessed all they thus far knew: Vrell was alive and well and parked directly beneath them in his father's spaceship; a larger vessel had then arrived from the Kingdom with the obvious intent of turning Vrell into Prador kebabs while the Warden had been trying to prevent collateral damage. Communication with the AI up on Coram had been intermittent at best, and even when they achieved it, the Warden did not have much to say. The AI probably felt that informing them they were about to die would only prolong the general anguish. The planetary server was also not doing so well and, what with the same EM interference that had done for the reifs, the *Sable Keech*'s com system was down too. But the attack had ceased, so what now?

'Thirteen!' Erlin bellowed.

Perhaps trying to find out more might be an unwise move. Really she should just head for her bunk, as had been her intention.

'Thirteen!' she bellowed again.

'I'm here.'

The seahorse drone rose up beside the ship and hovered before her, glinting in the light of the burning sky.

'I thought you'd gone,' said Erlin. 'This is not exactly the safest place to be at the moment.'

'It was safer here than trying to get to elsewhere. Even though I am small, Vrell's systems would still have detected me and shot me down.'

Erlin observed the water dripping from the drone's iron-coloured skin. 'You've been down to Vrell's ship.'

'Vrell's internal security is good, but not that good.'

'Anything to report?'

'I managed to slip inside through a damaged section of the hull. Vrell is in serious trouble. Not only does he have one of his relatives intent on obliterating him before he can leave the planet, but he cannot leave anyway.'

'Explain.'

'He has some of the *Vignette*'s crew working on the U-space engine. I scanned it. It's damaged and I very much doubt he possesses the facilities to repair it,' replied the drone succinctly.

'*Vignette?*' asked Erlin.

'Ah, you don't know,' said Thirteen, then explained.

Erlin contemplated the situation. Ron, having fought the Prador in that long-ago war, and being simply what he was, an Old Captain, would not be at all pleased. And certainly, knowing Hoopers were enslaved in the ship below him, he would want to act. She herself understood the horror of the situation, and realized that something must be done.

'The rest of the *Vignette* crew?' she asked.

'They are secured in a holding area, their thralls keeping them somnolent.'

'And Vrell himself?'

'As far as I can ascertain he is working in the drone cache. I avoided him completely – evading the spaceship's security systems was difficult enough.'

Erlin nodded. 'Why's the shooting stopped?'

'I do not know.'

'Then ask the Warden.'

The drone bobbed in the air, as if undecided, then agreed: 'Very well.' The delay before the drone's next utterance was brief. The voice, however, sounded different.

'Ah, Erlin, you seem well enough after your recent adventures.'

'Thank you so much, Warden. Now perhaps you can update me somewhat on current events?'

Still speaking through Thirteen, the Warden replied, 'Vrost, the Prador who recently turned this area into a war zone, has desisted for the moment. How long this will last is open to conjecture.'

'And what are we supposed to do, meanwhile?'

'Do you have by chance any religious inclinations?'

'None at all.'

'Then any suggestion that you pray would be wasted. I will let you know if there is any means I can use to get you out of this trap.'

The light advancing and retreating in its eyes, the drone jerked as the Warden suddenly withdrew.

To Thirteen, Erlin said, 'Wade tells me there's a submarine aboard. Maybe, with that, something can be organized to rescue at least some of the *Vignette*'s crew?'

'The hull of Vrell's ship is only three metres down,' the drone told her.

'Just breather gear or good lungs should do then.' She pointed to the dead creatures floating in the sea. 'It's not very lively down there at the moment. Tell Captain Ron I'll join him on the bridge shortly. I'm sure we can work something out between us.'

The drone drew back a little way, as if mulling over her suggestion. Erlin sniffed and wrinkled her nose. A putrid odour had infected the air. Somewhere close by was a virus-infected reif. Then Thirteen swivelled abruptly and bellowed, 'Watch out!'

Bony fingers closed around her throat, dragging Erlin back from the rail. Another skeletal hand opened before her face, extending blades from its fingertips. Then a blinding flash of ruby light cut the air, and she saw Thirteen fall from sight, canted to one side with steam pouring from it.

'Yes, let's join Captain Ron on the bridge,' said Taylor Bloc, from the shadows.

Aesop, clutching a laser carbine, stepped over to the rail and peered down into the sea.

'Fragile hardware,' he commented.

'Yes, Polity technology often is,' agreed Bloc, as he stepped hideously into view, five of his Kladites crowding behind him.

Erlin at once realized Bloc had not been looking after his physical condition. She also knew what it took to bring down a Polity drone like Thirteen. She remained silent about both matters.

Over a wide area, few creatures were moving. The underwater shock waves had ruptured leeches, prill and glisters; EM pulses had disrupted the senses of other bottom dwellers; and infrasound and ultrasound weapons had done for the remainder. However, right beside two downed Prador drones, a silvery eye extruded on a stalk from the settling mud.

Even though chameleonware had always been the form of concealment favoured by the Polity, Vrell, having installed such tech in his own drone, had expected no less from his Prador attackers and so had designed a defence to counter it. The attacking drones and armoured Prador *had* indeed used chameleonware, which was surprising to Sniper, but Vrell used EM pulses to disrupt the 'ware long enough for any attackers to be detected and destroyed, and the 'ware, not really being efficient in a medium like water, Vrell's torps had homed in on the *holes* it created. However, there remained one hole in Vrell's defence: conventional concealment.

Since his chameleonware would conceal him neither in the sky nor sea, approaching that way would have been suicidal. However, the mud beneath lay metres deep and, clinging to the rocky bottom below it, the old Polity drone had been able to drag himself, so far undetected, to within a few kilometres of Vrell's ship. Now it seemed the battle was over, there being no disrupting EM pulses coursing through the water. But Sniper was not fooled: the line of detectors might be a few kilometres behind him, but they would still pick up his *absence* in the water if he emerged from the mud and turned on his 'ware.

'What do you hope to achieve, Sniper?' enquired the Warden over U-space com.

Sniper paused and considered numerous foul responses. Instead he chose to be reasonable. 'If I can get to Vrell, this could all be over in the time it takes me to pull off his legs.'

After a pause, the Warden replied, 'Continue, then, and inform me the moment you are aboard his ship – should that remote possibility occur.'

Sniper retracted his eye and dragged himself onwards. Only another ten kilometres to cover.

The bar had no closing time. As rhinoworms were no longer trying to scramble aboard, and no local monsters seemed likely to try while the *Sable Keech* sat on a bloody great Prador spaceship, Janer decided there was nothing else for it but to enjoy a good drink or two then head for his bed.

'If Zephyr tries to leave now, Vrell's weapons would destroy him,' he observed to Wade, sitting opposite him at the table.

'This is true,' said the Golem.

'What was your plan then?' asked Janer. 'If our friend had not appeared below, and Zephyr did head off?'

'Follow him and try to dissuade him from his course, then if all else failed, destroy him.'

'It all sounds wonderfully simple, except for one problem. You can't fly.'

'Wrong, Mr Anders. I keep an AG harness in my cabin.'

Janer took another slug of rum. 'Just one?'

'Yes, just one.'

Janer liked Isis Wade and understood some of his motivations, but his trust of the Golem remained limited. Wade was here, apparently, to heal a rift in an ancient hive mind's personality and, failing that, to altruistically prevent a catastrophe which the other half of that personality might cause. That all sounded fine, but how close to the edge would Wade play it? Would he wait until Spatterjay and all its inhabitants were teetering on the edge of disaster? Would he wait too long and be unable to prevent Zephyr using the virus? Janer realized that if Zephyr flew and Wade pursued, he must somehow follow as well, but he was not sure how he could manage that.

Then other matters intruded. The ship's intercom gave an ersatz crackle and Ron began to speak. 'All passengers and crew must return to their cabins for the duration of the current crisis. This order comes direct from Taylor Bloc. Anyone seen on deck or in the ship's corridors will be shot on sight and tipped over the side . . . and that includes all you Hoopers out there. Go immediately to your cabins, and stay there or answer to me. Janer Cord Anders is to report to the bridge.'

'What the fuck?' murmured Janer, inevitably.

Reifications were getting up from the nearby tables. None of them could show much in the way of expression, but Janer guessed they must be scared. It seemed Bloc had finally gone completely power crazy, and the ancient expression *control freak* now occurred to him.

'So, what do we do?' he hissed to Wade.

The Hoopers were leaving as well. They could have quite easily dealt with any Kladites on deck and were probably not much concerned about anything else Bloc might do, but he knew that there were few Hoopers who dared risk Captain Ron's wrath.

'You will go to the bridge,' said Wade, his head tilted to one side as if he was listening to something. 'And you will do nothing with that nice little gun of yours, no matter how tempting that might seem.' Wade smiled tiredly. 'Of course, even Zephyr and myself have been experiencing problems after the recent EM emissions, so I very much doubt that any of the security systems are still operating below decks.'

'So?' said Janer.

Wade held out the flat of his palm. 'It won't be your concern, Janer.'

'What are you on about?'

'You had better go now. You've just half an hour, and the bridge is not that close.'

Janer swore, got out of his chair, and headed for the door.

Drooble and Shalen stood behind the Prador, handing it the tools it required. Orbus and Lannias stood back against the wall, out of the way but ready should Vrell summon them. Orbus blinked, comprehending the scene from inside the rigid Prador grip on his mind, like a glister wrapped in the tentacles of a giant whelk. When he managed to fix his mind on the contents of the engine casing, comprehension fled him for a moment, for there were things in there that twisted out of human perception, but it returned even stronger as his gaze fell away.

I'm beating the thrall, just like Captain Drum did, he realized.

Keeping his eyes averted he peered down at his hands and tried to move them. Nothing for a moment, then, as if his right forefinger suspended the full weight of a man, it slowly eased itself out from his thigh. He snapped it back down, his eyes facing forwards, when Vrell abruptly turned and himself selected from the tool chest something that seemed to bleed shadow. Orbus realized, by what feedback he could understand through the controlling link from the Prador, that the creature was not fully repairing the engine. He sensed the shifting of plot and counterplot in an incredibly complex mind, but could understand no more than that. Eventually, however, the Prador was satisfied. Hissing, it drew back from the compartment and its hinged upper half closed down on the incomprehensible components inside it. New orders then came through the Captain's thrall, and with Lannias he stepped forwards to go to work.

Orbus reached out, unhooked an optic cable from

where it had been tied to the framework above the U-space engine, and plugged it into the casing. Reaching for the collet that fully engaged the cable, he then paused for a moment. The itchy dug-in tic-like irritation at the back of his neck felt unbearable, but maybe now he could do something about it. With a huge effort he lifted his hand away from the casing. He found the further he moved it, the less effort he required, as he eroded the control over him. Finally, his hand poised at the back of his neck, he ground his nails in hard, scratching through skin and flesh down to the multi-legged cylindrical device beside his spine. The relief was immense – this was an itch he had been unable to scratch. Sighing, he glanced drunkenly round at his fellows, his mouth clamped shut to stop his leech tongue from escaping.

Their skin was dark blue, and they all possessed leech tongues, too. Lannias had a forehead now divided into segments, and Shalen's face jutted forwards as if turning into something bestial. But with robotic precision they all continued reattaching the optic and power feeds, and reinstalling the support equipment. Only Drooble, right next to him, showed any hesitation in his movements. And Orbus noticed a small scabby split had appeared in the back of the man's neck, over his thrall.

As he placed an optical amplifier against the casing and began pulling the clips across to hold it in place, Orbus considered his present situation. He had known something like this might happen, having heard Drum's story, but what now? He was only moments away from being able to pull the thrall from his own neck – its control of him now slipping away. Afterwards, he could continue with the job in hand without any noticeable interruption, as Vrell's instructions were firmly embedded in his memory rather than in the thrall itself. However, if the Prador at any time changed those instructions, or checked the thrall linkages, it would soon realize it no longer controlled him. Orbus wondered what would then happen. The thrall, once being rejected, could not be reattached. Vrell would either core him fully, or else kill and eat him. Not the most promising of choices.

He must escape, then, or die trying. He again glanced at these four members of his crew. He would free them of their thralls, as perhaps, despite their inclinations, they would realize what choices remained to them. Orbus reached up, stuck a finger into the wound in his neck, hooked it around the thrall's body, and pulled hard. The thing came out like a huge splinter, its wriggling legs coated with yellow pus. Reaching back to the tool chest, Orbus took out a large clamp, closed it on the thrall, then dropped both clamp and thrall underneath the engine casing. Had he destroyed it, Vrell might have been alerted. Now, with the heavy clamp on it, the thing would not be able to crawl away to alert the Prador. Drum had only got away with destroying his thrall because he had been enslaved to it by voice, not through a direct radio channel. Orbus then finished attaching the amplifier, before turning to Drooble, as he reached over for something on a work surface extending from one side of the tool chest. Orbus stabbed a finger into the opening wound at the back of the man's neck, and quickly hooked out his thrall.

'Oh, oh the bastard,' said Drooble.

'Keep working,' said Orbus, taking up another clamp.

Drooble gave him a wild look, the tip of his leech tongue questing around his chin, but he found enough sanity to obey his Captain. Orbus then moved around the engine casing, and positioned himself beside the next of his co-workers.

Kladites packed the foremast stair leading up to the enclosed bridge, which was also crowded. Including Ron and Forlam, there were five Hoopers here at the controls, besides John Styx and Santen Marcollian. Erlin was standing back against a wall, with Bones behind her, his bladed bony fingers at her throat. Two Kladites stood either side of the Captain, their weapons trained on him unwaveringly. A putrid smell permeated the air. Bloc, standing behind Aesop with his back to the forward window, was obviously the source of the stench.

Something was obviously going seriously wrong with Bloc's preservation routines. Rather than resembling a dried-out mummy, he now bore the appearance of a corpse that had lain rotting on a riverbed for some time. Some of his grey skin had slewed aside from the back of one hand and also from his neck, to reveal white flesh beneath. The transparent syntheskin on his skull had bulged up like a damaged fingernail, and the grey morass underneath it was veined with vivid yellow. His spectacle irrigator sprayed intermittently, and both his eyes wept constantly. When he moved, looking from side to side as if expecting attack at any moment, the exposed white flesh of his neck became beaded with yellow pus.

Janer realized Bloc was long overdue for going into a tank, since the Spatterjay virus, which in a living body fed upon dead tissue, was feeding on his entire body – rotting it away.

'Well, this is interesting,' said Janer. 'What are we doing here?'

Why had Bloc decided to do this?

'You – over there.' Bloc directed Janer to go and stand beside Erlin.

Janer did as instructed, turning to Erlin with, 'What's going on?'

Ron interjected bitterly, 'Seems Bloc doesn't want anyone trying to get to the Prador ship to rescue the crew of the *Vignette*.' The Captain ignored the two Kladites covering him, though his angry gaze never strayed from Bones. 'Now why is that, do you reckon?'

Vignette? Janer quickly put together the facts just made available to him, and came to the only conclusion possible: the Prador must have grabbed the crew, so they were human blanks now, slaves. That then was one source of Ron's anger. He remembered their conversation outside the Baitman when they had first encountered Wade. '*Never underestimate how Old Captains feel about that*,' Ron had said, referring back to thralldom and the Prador. The other source of his anger was the threat to Erlin, who all Old Captains now looked upon as something of an icon.

'It is not your right to speculate,' Bloc bubbled. 'You will all remain here, and everyone else must remain below decks.'

'Ah,' said Ron, 'that's to prevent anyone going over the rail to make that rescue attempt.' He finally now looked around.

'That is correct,' Bloc replied.

'What's *your* interest?' asked Janer.

Bloc glanced at him. 'You will all stay here,' he repeated.

'Why?' demanded Ron. 'I can understand you keeping some of us here, but what about the rest of them?' He pointed at John Styx, Santen Marcollian and the Hooper crew. 'This lot could cause you no more problems than those below decks, and it is a bit crowded in here.'

Bloc froze as if this was too much input to process, then after a moment said, 'Very well. You' – he pointed at Ron – 'will remain here along with Erlin and Janer.' He turned to John Styx. 'You too will remain.'

'Then I will stay too,' said Santen Marcollian.

Styx looked at her. 'Santen, please leave with the rest.'

Bloc seemed to have some trouble with this, since his eye irrigators were drenching his face again. 'You will *both* stay . . . as hostages.'

'There you go,' remarked Ron, looking towards Forlam, who was now heading for the door with some others. 'So you lot remember, no one is to go over the side and *submerse*.' While Forlam looked back at him he added, 'Anyway, there'll be no one to lead a rescue, what with that Polity drone, Thirteen, having been destroyed by laser.'

Janer winced at this flagrant hint, but it seemed to have shot straight over Bloc's putrefying head. The four Hoopers and the reif filed out of the bridge and headed below decks.

'What now?' Janer asked.

'We wait,' said Bloc. 'We wait until it's all over.'

The sun was due to rise at any time now, and was turning the sky into a rainbow maelstrom. Ambel thought about the battle they had witnessed the previous evening. He had recognized the glare of particle beams cutting the sky, laser flashes and the dull crump of explosions. But then it had all suddenly ceased, and only minutes later gold-armoured Prador and spherical war drones had been speeding overhead, to the sound of Captain Drum's curses as he waved his fist at the sky. Either Vrost had won the victory he sought, or for some other reason the Prador captain had recalled its forces. Ambel, though, now had more immediate concerns.

The island was visible; a dark mass poised between the psychedelic sky and its reflection in the ocean. Within a few hours they would be hitting the beach, and less than an hour after that, mayhem. He turned to Captain Drum, who now stood beside him on the foredeck.

'Maybe it won't touch the *Moby*,' he suggested.

'Maybe it'll tie a white flag to its tentacle and immediately surrender,' Drum replied.

He seemed a bit tetchy this morning, but Ambel felt this had less to do with rowing all night bringing across his crew, weapons and supplies from the *Moby*, and more to do with witnessing Prador up there in the sky, out of reach.

'Anyway,' Drum added, 'you better hope it does attack my ship.'

Ambel glanced down at the two crews standing ready on deck. They were all armed, and the harpoons from both ships were sharpened, their ropes attached. Ambel just hoped they would be able to find something to which those ropes could be tied. He harrumphed, raised his binoculars and gazed across at Drum's ship. The sail, Cloudskimmer, was doing an excellent job, controlling the *Moby*'s fabric sails and steering the ship with his jaws clamped on the helm. But inevitably the *Moby* was lagging behind.

'How much are you paying him?' Ambel asked.

'Twice his normal fee, plus he wants an aug like the

one you gave Galegrabber.' Drum gazed at Ambel esti-matingly. 'Supposing I can afford it.'

They had yet to settle who was to blame for all this. *Whelkus titanicus* had started out pursuing Ambel, and Drum had opined that had he himself sailed away, it would have left him alone. Ambel disputed this, adding that the creature's behaviour seemed very odd, and any-way it had not pursued him through any fault of his own. Drum then decided it was Erlin who would shortly be owing him a lot of Spatterjay New Skind.

Their pursuer surfaced occasionally, as if not wanting them to become complacent about it. Earlier, when they had necessarily run slightly athwart the wind and as a consequence slowed, it had drifted to one side, pulling away from the *Treader*, which was closer, to go after the *Moby* instead. It might have caught them otherwise. Ambel felt the whelk was enjoying the chase far too much.

'If there's shallows way out,' Ambel said loudly, 'we'll use both ship's boats to ferry everyone in. All the har-poons will have to take precedence in the boats. Without them we'll be running around this island till we all turn into skinners.'

'I doubt we'll get everyone ashore before it attacks,' murmured Drum.

'Let's hope for a steep beach,' Ambel murmured back.

As they drew closer to the island, the sun gilded the underside of distant cloud and now began washing colour from the sky. Meanwhile, the island's central vol-canic cone became distinct above thick foliage. A great swathe of peartrunk trees had been toppled, probably by the recent wave, but enough still stood for Ambel's pur-pose.

'Keep us straight,' Ambel told Boris, then bellowed, 'Peck, get forward and keep an eye out for shoals!'

His shotgun resting across his shoulder, Peck obeyed.

'The rest of you,' Ambel continued, 'load the boats. We want to launch as soon as we can, even if we can beach the ship.'

The crews began stowing harpoons and other items in the boats, which were hung like upside-down beetles' wings on davits either side of the ship. With Drum following, Ambel climbed down to the lower deck, then headed forwards to peer over the side. Even though the rising sun reflected off the water, he could see the occasional shape passing below the ship, and undulating masses that were the upper foliage of kelp trees.

'We need to get right in, and quick,' said Drum, pointing.

Ambel squinted in the direction indicated, noticing a mass of something floating on the surface. At first he thought he was seeing sargassum, then realized the mass was moving. Juvenile rhinoworms – the situation just got better and better.

'Starboard, two points!' Peck abruptly yelled.

The ship turned slightly, and Ambel observed a twisted mass of packetworm coral like some sunken temple sliding by to port. The ship shuddered as a grating vibration came up through the deck.

'Okay,' Peck muttered, 'three points.'

'Let's get that anchor chain up – we might be needing it,' said Drum.

The two Captains moved up behind Peck and began hauling heavy anchor chain out of the chain locker and coiling it on the deck.

Soon, over the side of the ship, the bottom became

clearly visible. Ambel estimated the depth to be four metres. Also visible down there were the pink anguine shapes of more juvenile rhinoworms. Nothing else was evident, but then anything else around here would have been eaten by now, no matter how solid its shell.

'I reckon we'll be able to pull her in,' stated Ambel.

'We'll need cover,' said Drum.

Ambel nodded and turned to the crew. 'Anne, Davy-bronte, and anyone with Polity weapons, let's have you up here!'

Anne stepped forwards screwing a new energy canister into her laser carbine, then came Davy-bronte, brandishing his QC laser. Ambel was glad to see that some of Drum's crew also carried the necessary weapons: one pulse gun, a laser carbine and a pulse rifle.

'Okay,' said the Captain, 'the rest of you with old guns, divide yourselves evenly between the two boats. That way you can cover us from either side if we have to haul the ship in.' Their various antiquated automatic weapons, rifles, six-guns and shotguns would not prove very effective against worms swimming under water, but were better than nothing.

When Ambel turned to face forward again, he observed Drum holding an apple-sized silver device with a small touch-pad connected to one end. 'I was saving this to shove up a Prador where the sun don't shine, but I guess I'll have to use it now.'

'Don't drop it too near the hull,' Ambel advised.

Drum snorted.

Now the bottom was only a few metres down, and the beach close. Ambel heaved up the anchor and moved beside Peck, gesturing him to stand back.

'It's reached her,' said Drum.

Looking back, Ambel saw Cloudskimmer taking wing from the *Moby*, which was canted to one side with its stern low in the water. A long white tentacle rose high out of the sea, reaching higher than the masts, then smashed down straight through the ship. Deck planking shot into the air and one mast began to topple.

'Fucking thing.' Drum faced forward and hurled his grenade into the shallows just before the beach. The *Treader* then began to shudder as its keel started to bite into the bottom. Another crash from behind, and the two halves of the *Moby* were sinking. A great fan of tentacles rose over it, a glittering mountainous shell visible behind.

'Get the boats in!' bellowed Ambel.

Rope hissed through the davit pulleys, the two ship's boats dropping to the sea. Crew not standing with Ambel and Drum began scrambling over the side and into them. From ahead there came a dull boom, followed by an explosion of spume and fire and snakish corpses. The force of the blast rode the ship up from the bottom for a moment, then it came down hard, shuddering to a halt and flinging some of the remaining crew into the sea. Ambel had no time to watch who might rescue those unfortunates.

'Get your heads down!' he bellowed, and, once his warning was heeded, began swinging the heavy anchor round and round above him on a length of its chain. He released it towards the beach and, towing out its chain with a rattling roar, it splashed down only metres from the shoreline. Drum jumped over the prow ahead of Ambel, who followed, submerging to his neck in the water, his feet just touching the bottom. Up again, and he swam after the other Captain, as pulse-gun and laser fire began hissing into the sea around him. On either side the boats came in, their crews also firing at writhing shapes in the water. When the water was only up to Ambel's waist, a rhinoworm – nearly out of adolescence, for it had dropped its forelegs – reared up beside him. He backhanded it up out of the sea and sent it flying back five metres through the air. Soon he joined Drum, who had lifted the anchor from the bottom. They took firm hold of one tine each.

'Well, here we go then,' said Ambel.

He knew that Polity citizens witnessing this sort of strength might be shocked, but for himself and Drum it was just something they accepted, as it increased over the centuries. At one time even he and Drum would have struggled to raise this anchor together, but now hauling on it to straighten out a tonne of chain behind was no big deal to them – it had taken the best part of a thousand years for them to become capable of this.

'Let's get her in, then,' growled Drum.

They began trudging ashore, pulling the *Treader* in behind them. Once they reached dry land, because of the combined weight being carried and the force they were exerting, they waded up to their knees in the sand. Reaching the head of the beach, they found an outcrop of volcanic stone, upon which they took a stand to continue pulling the chain, hand-over-hand, until the ship's prow was out of the water.

'Let's move it!' Ambel yelled, dropping the chain and gunshot-clapping his hands.

The crew were swiftly unloading the boats, hauling harpoons and other supplies up the beach. Nothing remained of the *Moby* but floating shards, and beyond the *Treader* a mobile hill was rapidly heading shorewards.

18

Turbul:
a billion years ago this creature was little different from any
Terran fish. It possessed a spine, the requisite internal organs,
gills, fins, a tail and teeth. However, the evolutionary pressure
of being fed upon by leeches for so long has wrought some
strange changes. The turbul still possesses all of the above, but
now in a configuration enabling it to survive leech attack. Its
fins stem directly from the spine, the muscles moving them
running inside its bones. Muscles also run down inside the
spine to the tail, and the jaw muscles are similarly encased –
just sufficient to keep it mobile and feeding. Its other internal
organs, contained in a bag attached to the spine itself, can
quickly regrow themselves. Outside all of this, with the fins
protruding through it, the turbul grows a dense cylinder of
nutritious flesh, which is nerveless and a prime target for
leeches. A turbul can lose all of this flesh and still survive. It
is as if, rather than evolve a thicker skin or a shell, the turbul
has accepted the inevitability of leech attack, abandoned its
defences, and retreated inside with its most vital parts. It thus
sacrifices its outer layer to keep its inner self alive. There are
many other fish forms to have done this, most notably the
boxy –

Forlam understood the oblique order he had been given by his Captain, also that others might deliberately misinterpret it in the hope of avoiding danger. Danger was not something that frightened him – only his own fascination with it did that.

'Go to your cabins; I'll handle this,' he said to the Hoopers accompanying him. 'I doubt more of us will be any help.'

'But that's where we're going anyhow,' said Dorleb.

Forlam sighed. It sometimes seemed to him that the fibres in the brains of many Hoopers strangled their thought processes. 'A laser won't bring down a Polity drone,' he explained. 'Captain Ron wants to free our mates below. He ordered me to go ahead and rescue them.'

'Huh?' came Dorleb's brilliant reply.

Now on the bridge stateroom deck, Forlam paused and looked around, then abruptly bellowed, 'Thirteen!' The others eyed him in a way he had become quite accustomed to. Let them think he was mad.

When they reached the door leading through to the crew cabins, one of the Hoopers stepped through immediately, while shaking her head and saying, 'Orbus . . . the *Vignette*.'

Two more Hoopers followed her. The two remaining just stood watching Forlam.

'You'll be needing our help,' said Dorleb.

'No, I won't,' said Forlam. 'More of us would just be easier to detect.'

Without further objection the last two headed off. Forlam soon reached the head of the ladder leading down into the bilge, but rather than descend he went into the nearby armoury. One crate remaining in the cage was still sealed. He tore it open and took out a laser carbine, then continued on down, finally reaching a walkway leading towards the submersible enclosure. He paused by the door, gave it a light push with the snout of his carbine, and watched it swing open. A floating shape was immediately visible, the moment he stepped inside. Thirteen was hovering in the middle of the enclosure.

'You've been expecting me,' Forlam suggested.

'I have not,' the seahorse drone replied.

Ahead of the submersible, the irised door abruptly opened in the hull to reveal a shimmer-shield and murky depths beyond. Movement to one side spun Forlam round, raising his weapon, then he relaxed on seeing Isis Wade emerging from the submersible.

'What happened up in the bridge?' Wade asked.

'Bloc sent away all those he didn't consider a danger to whatever plans he has. The Captain sort of ordered me here on a rescue mission.'

Wade smiled and pointed. 'Suits and breather gear are over in those cabinets.'

Just like that.

Forlam felt a surge of something unpleasant in his guts. He walked over to the glass-fronted cabinets and studied their contents. The suits were inset with chain-mesh. The breather gear consisted of full-faced masks from which pipes led to a haemolung that strapped on the wearer's back. The cabinet locks were coded touch panels, so he reached up to the top of the door before him and wrenched it off.

'I guess the designers of those cabinets didn't take Hoopers into account,' said Wade, stepping past Forlam.

'Or Golem.' He ripped off the next door and took out a suit.

'Why do *you* need a suit?' Forlam asked, as he began donning one.

'I can't be hurt by much out there,' Wade replied, 'but I could lose much of my syntheflesh.'

'What's the plan then?' Forlam asked.

'Thirteen can lead us to a place on the Prador ship's hull where we can gain access. We find the *Vignette*'s crew. If they've been fully cored we leave them and get out fast. If they're just controlled by spider thralls, we excise their thralls and lead them out.'

'Nice and simple then.' Forlam reached down and drew a ceramal diver's knife from where it was sheathed at his calf. 'What about the ship's security systems?'

'Where we are going, the security system is weak, and Thirteen can disable it undetected just so long as Vrell doesn't run a diagnostic check.'

'And if he does?'

'Then we're in trouble, and we may need our weapons.' Wade reached for his APW, which was resting against the door of the next cabinet.

Forlam eyed the footwear in the base of the cabinet, undecided on whether to wear flippers or the weighted boots. When he saw Wade choose boots he did the same. Soon they were ready and, hoisting a waterproof pack onto his shoulder, Wade led the way towards the shimmer-shield, where Thirteen was already pushing through into the ocean. On his turn, Forlam felt as if he was stepping through a wall of treacle. Once through, and dropping the few metres down to the Prador ship's hull, he felt a sudden horrible excitement. Few Hoopers learnt to swim, since no Hooper went into the sea as a matter of choice, fear of it being inculcated from birth. Forlam looked around, almost disappointed by the dead waters surrounding him. Then, clutching his carbine, he followed Wade across the spaceship's hull.

Thirteen led them out from the *Sable Keech* to the base of one of the weapons turrets. All about drifted the remains of juvenile rhinoworms, prill and glisters. This organic wreckage lay motionless, which for Spatterjay life forms was unusual because, even in pieces, they usually kept moving. This mess was, however, blurred around the edges and seemed to be dissolving. He realized that though the battle had killed most large animals in the area, the voracious plankton remained unaffected.

'Here,' came Thirteen's voice from a com button in the corner of Forlam's mask. He noticed that the hull nearby was very uneven where it curved down to the base of the weapons turret. Thirteen was poised over a metre-wide gap between the edge of the turret and the hull. Joining the other two, Forlam peered down into the dark cavity. The drone now descended, opening its seahorse mouth to emit a beam of light. Forlam immediately jumped after it, his boots dragging him down between narrow walls and landing him on a set of guide rollers for the turret. The light was now playing down by his feet. He stooped and peered into what might have been a crawl space for humans, so may well have been intended for human blanks. He ducked inside as Wade descended above him, more light spearing down from a torch the Golem held.

As he landed Wade said, 'The light, on your carbine,' and pointed with the torch he himself held. Unfamiliar with all of the controls but the trigger, Forlam groped about until Wade reached over and pressed a button on the stock. Now his weapon emitted laser light at the lowest setting and maximum diffusion.

'Thanks,' said Forlam, and wriggled after the drone.

Ten metres in, Thirteen tilted, manipulating something in the crawl-space ceiling with its forked tail. A hatch hinged down and the drone ascended. Forlam followed, standing up out of the water into a duct, then climbed up over the edge of it. As Wade clambered up behind him Forlam took off his mask. Somewhere he could hear fans operating, and a rank breeze blew in his face.

'Ventilation duct,' he decided.

'Even Prador have to breathe,' Wade observed, then turned to the hovering drone. 'Thirteen, your AG?'

'There are no gravitic detectors inside this ship,' the drone replied, moving on.

Now, half-crouching, they made their way on through hundreds of metres of ducts. Forlam realized that if he got separated from Thirteen and Wade he might not find his way out again. Finally they came to a heavy metal grating set in the floor.

'The holding area,' Thirteen announced. 'Do not shine a light in there as it will be detected.'

The drone descended tail first, turning slightly to fit through one of the diamond-shaped holes in the grating. Once Thirteen was out of sight there came a flickering of green light from below.

Lasers, Forlam realized.

Then, metallic clickings and scrapings ensued for a few minutes until Thirteen called, 'I have disabled the three cameras. They will show a previously recorded scene until I instruct them otherwise.'

Wade now shone his torch down inside, revealing the

scuttling of large lice. Directing his own light into the area below, Forlam discerned Hoopers sprawled on the floor. With a horrified thrill he realized that the lice were feeding on them.

'Where did you learn that trick?' Wade asked the drone.

'From an old Polity war drone who knows more about Prador security systems than the Prador would be comfortable with,' replied Thirteen.

Forlam grinned – he knew that old drone.

'Your carbine,' said Wade, holding out his hand.

Forlam handed it over, then shielded his eyes when the Golem knocked the weapon's setting back up and used it to cut their way in. It took some time; the bars were thick even though out of the prisoners' reach. When Wade had sliced along three sides, he used the beam only to heat the metal on the remaining side, before kicking the grating to bend it down.

'How do we get them out of there?' Forlam asked.

Wade opened his pack and took out an electric hoist and a webbing harness.

'Right.' Forlam snatched back his carbine and, jumping down into a mass of lice, began stamping on them. Wade landed lightly beside him, stepped over to the prostrate Hoopers, and began pulling off the lice still chewing on them. Soon the horrible creatures got the idea and began scuttling for cover. Forlam kicked one of the stragglers against the wall and leaned down to more closely inspect a woman lying at his feet just as Wade adjusted the setting on his torch so it became a lantern.

'They're gonna be trouble,' Forlam observed.

The female's clothing was ragged on her starveling dark-blue body; a leech tongue protruded over the unnatural jut of her lower jaw. The man next to her, he saw, had fingers twice as long as normal, had shed all his hair, and his nose had melded with his top lip.

'Evidently.' Wade placed his light on a stony slab jutting from the nearby wall. He then opened his pack and took out an injector – high dose Intertox.

Yeah, like that's going to work, thought Forlam.

He remembered back to when he had approached this state, and some of the things he had done at the time. He also recollected days spent in a reinforced straitjacket, being similarly dosed until he ceased to be a danger . . . to everyone. He hung his carbine from his shoulder by its strap, then reached down and turned the woman over onto her face. Drawing his ceramal knife he wondered where to cut . . . Then something lashed out beside him, snatching the knife from his hand.

'We cannot do that,' said Thirteen, now holding the knife in its forked tail.

'What's the problem?' asked Wade.

'I've been scanning,' said the drone. 'They have been converted into an adjunct to the ship's computer systems. If we remove their thralls now, Vrell will realize at once.'

'How strong is the signal?' asked Wade.

Thirteen turned in mid-air to face the Golem. 'I picked it up earlier on the *Sable Keech*, but could not identify it then. Some sort of high-level mathematical program is being run.'

'Then presumably,' Wade replied, 'their location won't be an issue?'

'This is so,' the drone replied.

'We move them, then,' said Wade, and turned away. 'Forlam,' he pointed to a large mass of cable mesh hang-

ing from the wall, 'cut lengths of that. We'll bind them
and take them out, one at a time.'

Forlam held out his hand to the drone, which
returned his knife. Reluctantly he resheathed it, then
with a sigh unshouldered his carbine. He had been looking forward to digging out those thralls, but really it
would be best if he did not derive his pleasures that way.

As he worked, Vrell noticed the requirement for
increased signal strength in order to stay in contact with
his blanks. Checking all other internal security systems
and encoded thrall channels, he immediately realized
what was happening. Two of the six in the holding area
had been removed from the spaceship and doubtless
those who had done the removing were still aboard, taking the others out, since there were many dead or suspicious areas in the security camera network. But it did
not matter all that much. The six were still thralled, so
he could continue to use their minds as processing space
whatever their location. Then he noticed that four who
had earlier helped him rework the U-space engine were
free of their thralls, though trapped in the engine room.
But even that no longer mattered.

Obtaining the nanochanger had been easy. A simple
instruction to Bloc, and the reif had been forced to toss
one over the sailing ship's side. Setting it working,
however, had not been so simple. Vrell quickly realized
that opening or scanning the device would destroy or
corrupt its delicate internal components. In the end he
instructed Bloc to next throw a reification cleansing unit
over the side. Now the changer was plugged into the
cleansing unit and working: injecting microscopic
nanofactories into the fluid Vrell was passing through

the cleanser. This fluid was then circulated through a vessel which took the place of a human body, and inside that the factories clung, just as they would attach inside human veins: little volcanic limpets pumping out masses of complex nanomachines. After hours of scanning these, Vrell selected one variety of machine particularly suited to his purposes.

Now, before Vrell, in the laboratory he had recently opened, antigravity containment suspended a mass of nanites cultured from his original selection, in a saturated solution of salts within a study pit. Vrell peered down at the watery lens-shaped mass. It was white but with a metallic hue, and shifted slightly as the nanite clumps inside it readjusted. While operating the pit through his control units, Vrell assessed a virtual representation of one of the nanites in his mind. The nanite came with its own toolkit, which could be programmed by radio. It was a supreme technological creation, and only by now using the system of ship's computers and human minds, earlier put together for U-space calculations, could Vrell fully interpret it, and change it.

The original nanites, on activation, replicated a millionfold before searching for bone. This they bored through in search of marrowbone stem cells. Their purpose was then to deliver this base genetic template to the other nano-builders throughout the human body. Stripped down to its skeleton, one of these nanites formed a perfect framework to take other molecular tools. However, its present tools could serve the Prador's purpose: the catalytic debonding molecule made to bore through bone could, with a small alteration, be changed to bore through Prador shell – merely a bonus, as Vrell expected them to gain access through the Prador lung.

Those tools which enabled the nanite to recognize marrowbone stem cells could be adjusted to detect genetic sequences Vrell had obtained from the dead Prador in the drone cache.

The tools that then enabled the nanite to locate other builder nanites and home in on them Vrell altered to locate certain potassium compounds found in Prador nerve tissue, and other tissues in the Prador lung. Upon finding a nerve, it then travelled along it until it hit a synapse, then it returned to its replication stage digesting surrounding tissue to build copies of itself. Finding lung tissue, it did the same. While dying, the victim would be breathing more nanites into the air.

Once the virtual shape was performing to Vrell's satisfaction, he loaded its parameters to the pit, before turning his attention to the delivery system. Some hours later he held a small wedge-shaped container that fitted perfectly between the faces of one claw. Gaseous dispersion. A few nanites settling on Prador shell or in the lung would be enough, for the right Prador.

With black amusement, Vrell well understood the King's need to destroy any Prador, outside his own family, potentially infected by the Spatterjay virus. Such a creature would undoubtedly make a lethal enemy.

Through omniscient senses from a commanding position Zephyr understood that Death – the enemy – took many forms and realized that he must defeat every one of them. The creatures that had died in the sea all around him were just the result of a concentration of Death's forces in this area; elsewhere in the ocean that was going on all the time. But then *creatures* did not count as life, so did their passing count as dying?

'*What about hornets?*' asked his other half, Isis Wade, from somewhere down below.

Zephyr shook his head, but the question would not go away. He smacked his head against the mast a couple of times, but that did not help either, only dented the mast.

'*Individual hornets are insentient, yet the whole can be ourselves,*' Wade persisted. '*You cannot make arbitrary distinctions like that.*'

'Then they died,' Zephyr replied out loud, 'and I must do what I must do.'

'*You can't fight Death, nor kill it. Death is an absence of life not the presence of a tangible something.*'

'I have the means of striking a blow here.' So saying, the Golem sail again cracked his head against the mast.

'*Assume that everything you say is correct,*' said Wade. '*Surely you see that by killing you serve Death, even if it is Death itself you kill.*'

Zephyr's head felt strange now, and that had nothing to do with its recent impact with the mast. The Golem sail looked up as shadows occluded the morning sky and both Huff and Puff came in to land on nearby spars.

'What's that about striking blows?' asked Puff.

'I will strike a blow against Death, my enemy,' Zephyr replied.

The two organic sails turned to look at each other. Huff shrugged, and Puff turned back to Zephyr. 'We've been hearing bits of your conversation with that Wade fella when he climbs up here. Death is an enemy of us all, I suppose.'

'Exactly,' said Zephyr.

'But it's not a thing you can kill,' Huff added. 'Without it there would be no life.' Huff pointed down to the roof of the midship deck cabin.

Zephyr peered down and observed a pile of meat – juvenile rhinoworms the two other sails had bitten into pieces.

Creatures . . . not alive . . . alive?

Zephyr felt a coil of angry buzzing inside himself. Hornets killed to find food for the hive. Was that wrong then? If hornets did not feed, the hive died, and so served Death. If hornets fed, then they killed, and again served Death. By living, all creatures served Death

'*You know, somewhere in your heart,*' interjected Wade, '*that your belief is paradoxical.*'

'But it is my belief!' Zephyr bellowed.

'You what?' asked Huff.

'*And thus we get to the heart of the issue,*' said Wade. '*I'll have to leave you for a moment – the damned winch just jammed.*'

Focusing on Huff, Zephyr shouted, 'If I don't believe I can kill Death, I will not be me! I will be only part of something!'

'You've lost me there,' replied Huff.

Extruding his silvery eye from a metre down in gritty mud, Sniper observed the spaceship, now visible through the settling murk. It extended out of sight to his right and left, and the side of it rose like a steel cliff before him. Having got this close he wondered *What next?* If he could get inside, there was no problem: what he would then do involved every missile left in his weapons carousel. The problem was penetrating that armour.

Sniper listened to the sea-bottom sounds at the lower end of the aural spectrum. Somewhere below him, the seismic activity of packetworms; a kilometre back he heard the scuttling of prill and glisters returning to the area, attracted by the organic detritus; and somewhere far to his left the whooshing and snapping sounds of a turbul shoal already feeding. Also, from somewhere above, there came rhythmic crumps as if someone were walking on the spaceship's upper hull. Now extruding one of his main spatula-ended tentacles, he activated the scanning devices it contained, modifying the emitted infrasound to mimic the other sounds around him. It took some minutes for him to clean up the return signals, in which time he also detected ultrasound and infrasound scans from the ship itself. In his mind he built up a fuller picture of what lay before him, and felt a sudden surge of excitement, though quickly curtailed.

It had to be a trap, he decided; there could be no other explanation. A major triangular port lay open in the hull – the kind that Prador disembarked from, or one for deploying large weapons. Sniper retracted his tentacle and eye, and began burrowing towards that port.

The mud here was increasingly laden with rubble and large shell fragments, so Sniper's progress slowed. In two hours he finally reached the ship's edge, below the port, and again extruded his eye up through the mud. It was much lighter than earlier, the sun well above the horizon and its light penetrating into the depths. For a long moment he studied a strange life form nearby. This segmented thing was long and wormish, and writhing slowly. One of its segments had detached and was inching away, and even as he watched another broke free. No record of this creature in his memory . . . but it was irrelevant. He again probed his tentacle into the sea, and listened. Eventually he realized he was detecting only echoes – signals of scans from the ship, bounced from ten metres behind him, probably emitted from some device above him. That meant he rested in a blind spot.

Has to be a trap, he told himself.

Sniper started his chameleonware generator, then slowly and carefully burrowed to the surface. Halfway out from the sea bottom – no reaction. Fully out – still nothing. Extending his tentacles ten metres up the ship's side, he grabbed the port's lower rim and hauled himself up.

Drone cache.

He scanned inside with a strong ultrasound analogue of glisters and prill fighting each other. No drones were evident, but he detected ten simple optic cameras, nailed them with ten indigo lasers and projected into them the image of what he had been seeing for the last few hours: mud. Still keeping the cameras targeted, he eased inside the cache, not yet daring to use any drives or AG. Now the complicated bit. Keeping the lasers on target, he groped around on the floor, spooning up silt with the end of one of his major tentacles. Closing its spatulate end around the mud, he injected the microscopic tubes he had used to sample the *Vignette* wreck's burnt timbers, but instead of sampling, used them to draw off the water. The silt, strained to the consistency of damp earth, he then injected with a slow-setting crash-foam mix. He then moved around the cache jamming the mixture into nine camera recesses. The tenth camera, still targeted by one laser beam, he decided he must try to subvert, as he could not go around sticking mud on every lens inside the ship.

It took him only minutes to remove this last camera from its recess and tap into the optic feed behind it. Using techniques learnt longer ago than he cared to remember and a programming worm stored from the same distant period, he accessed an optic amplifier and recording module behind the wall. In the module he found a clock and set it forward, then he linked recorded images into the real-time feed. The camera would now show this cache as it had been just before Sniper entered it.

Curious, the old drone copied to himself all the stored footage and, as he reinserted the camera in the wall and moved back, began studying it. What he saw was both fascinating and worrying. The life form outside had been in here, but that was not the most fascinating thing he registered. Sniper turned and gazed at a mound of remains lying to one side of the cache. He moved over and scraped away some of the silt, picking up a large piece of charred Prador carapace, then the remains of a claw. After delving for a little longer he uncovered half of a distinct visual turret, a head – something no Prador he had ever encountered had possessed. Abruptly his plans and intentions changed. He might be somewhat irascible, but he still worked for the Polity, and that organization might be served better by something other than the demolition job he intended. Turning towards the inner lock, he began sorting through his store of both physical tools and software for the right lock-picks.

The entity within the submerged vessel opened communication with the other Prador ship far above and asked, 'Why do you want to kill me?'

On the bank of hexagonal screens beside it, the entity observed all the safety programs come on as they restricted the communication to voice only, for Vrost had just tried to send a worm burrowing into the spaceship's systems. This probing continued for a few minutes, until the Prador captain admitted defeat and spoke.

'Because you are an enemy of our King,' Vrost replied.

'Under my father, Ebulan, I have always been a loyal subject of Oboron. Now my father is dead, why am I considered a threat?'

A long delay followed. This communication was open channel so that the Warden could listen in. The entity knew Vrost could not openly say why Vrell might be considered a threat without revealing what he himself was. The entity, itself called Vrell, had therefore decided to have at least a little fun before dying.

'All Prador adults are a threat, and only a greater threat keeps them in check,' Vrost replied.

'You mean Oboron, and his family, like yourself and the rest of the King's Guard?'

This was perhaps edging into dangerous territory, but this Vrell could not resist.

'It is by the rule of force and selection by power that the Kingdom survives. No Prador can remain unaligned.'

Vrell reflected on how Prador families that grew too powerful or made too many alliances were mercilessly crushed. In the Kingdom murder was a political tool. He now understood certain events that had meant nothing to him in the past: how many Prador families or individuals involved in biological research had been exterminated. Obviously they too had stumbled upon what he now knew.

'Let me align myself now. Let me swear loyalty to the King. You will then have no reason to kill me.'

'That seems reasonable,' interjected the Warden on the same frequency.

Vrost rebuked the AI: 'This is an internal Prador matter.'

'Yes, but one that has spilled over into the Polity domain,' the Warden countered.

Vrost had to be foaming at the mandibles by now. On a nearby screen Vrell observed an insistent signal from Vrost that they switch to a private channel. Doubtless the Prador captain wanted a one-to-one chat, and also to actually see Vrell – not because the bandwidth of a visual signal would allow a worm to be sent, but to confirm the truth of its suppositions one way or the other. That was not going to happen. And anyway Vrost would learn nothing by seeing *this* Vrell – who decided to play this game for a little longer before making the concession he had to make.

'There would have been no problem, Warden, if Vrost had not arrived here intent on causing an incident with the Polity, and an ecological disaster down here.'

'This is true,' the Warden replied. 'You too could have avoided an incident had you declared yourself to me. Under Polity law you are not culpable for anything you did whilst under the control of Ebulan's pheromones. Now, unfortunately, you have kidnapped some of the people of this planet, and killed one of them, and also endangered the lives of Polity citizens.'

Vrell felt a moment's chagrin at that. It had not even

occurred to him that the Polity would not automatically want to hunt him down and kill one of Ebulan's kin.

'I admit to endangering Polity citizens, but only so I could survive. Those citizens would have been in no danger were it not for Vrost's intemperate actions. I also admit to kidnapping citizens of this planet. The unfortunate death of one of them was due to a radiological accident aboard this ship. I will, however, release the others unharmed, should I be given the opportunity.'

Vrell knew that the blanks could recover from the changes they had undergone, but that to call them 'unharmed' was rather stretching the terminology. The lie about a radiological accident could be proven neither one way nor the other, but none of that really mattered. All that was needed was Vrost's belief in what was to follow.

'What then will be your actions?' asked Vrost.

'Obviously this situation cannot continue. Should you destroy me down here, that will result in diplomatic repercussions with the Polity, but I cannot remain down here forever.'

'This is so.'

'As I see it, I must prove my loyalty to the King. Allow me to leave this world and I will surrender myself to you. I will place this ship in a parking orbit, and come over to you in a suit only.'

More long minutes passed, then Vrost replied, 'That is acceptable.'

Vrell accessed the ship's systems and began to follow instructions.

Prador never showed mercy and never backed down. This Vrell knew that Vrost would allow him no closer than a hundred kilometres. He was going to die, and he was seriously annoyed about that.

Water, carried through the shimmer-shield in the folds of Forlam's suit, splashed onto the floor. He pulled off his mask, walked over to the submersible and shed his other load at the foot of it. Over many years he had incidentally met most of the *Vignette*'s permanent crew, and in latter years, before he went offworld with Ron, engineered encounters with them because he felt they well knew something he was only just beginning to learn. He did not recognize this crewman's features, but then they were no longer quite human. This one was a man and, judging by his clothing and the facial jewellery that seemed to be getting gradually sucked into his face, he was one of two Forlam had met earlier. The other might be one of the other two lying here. He turned round as a splashing sound alerted him to Wade stepping in through the shimmer-shield.

Wade trudged over and dumped the fourth crewman on the floor. He paused then tilted his head as if listening to something.

'Two more and we're out of there,' said the Golem, now focusing on his companion.

They could easily have carried more than two each – Wade being a Golem and Forlam being a middling old Hooper – but the difficulty lay in getting them through the ventilation ducts.

'There's still Orbus and the other three,' Forlam reminded him.

'I know, but Thirteen is having enough trouble with the security systems we have encountered. He says our chances of getting them out of the engine room are remote.'

Forlam contemplated that as they headed back towards the shield. He owed Orbus nothing, just as he owed these here nothing, and to endanger himself attempting to rescue the remaining four was near insane in its foolishness. If Wade was not up to it, he wondered if he could rely on Thirteen's continued help.

Again donning his mask, Forlam followed Wade back out into the ocean. Wade was just ahead of him, but rather than move on to the entrance beside the weapons turret, he turned to press a hand against Forlam's chest.

'Be still,' he instructed over com.

Forlam froze and watched a turbul shoal pass overhead. The urge to pull away from Wade and start jumping up and down was almost unbearable, but he managed to repress it. Abruptly he realized that the changes wrought in him over the years – which had been exacerbated by his problems on the Skinner's Island, when he had ended up looking something like those back inside – were going to kill him. But that was just an intellectual assessment: the prospect of danger and of death aroused in him a weird excitement.

'Come on,' said Wade, once the turbul were out of sight.

This time Forlam easily remembered the route through the ship. They dropped into the holding area where Thirteen, his AG shut off, clung to a wall ledge, then they stepped over to the last two of these crewmen.

'We have to hurry,' Wade said. 'I need to get back.'

'Why?' asked Forlam, dragging one of the two Hoopers over to the winch hook.

'It's complicated,' said Wade.

'What isn't?'

'Okay, I am presently in constant communication with someone above, trying to persuade that individual not to leave the *Sable Keech*. He's chewing on a spar at the moment, and I don't think the threat of the weapons on this ship' – Wade waved a hand about himself – 'will restrain him much longer.'

'You're talking about Zephyr.'

Wade looked at him oddly, then started the winch running with the remote control he held. Forlam grabbed the hook, over which he had slipped the cables binding the *Vignette* crewman's wrists, and rode the winch up with him. Up above he unhooked the man and dragged him to one side, then rode the winch down again.

'What makes you say that?' the Golem asked.

'Oh come on, we've all seen you climbing up that mast for your daily chat. I don't see why you do that though, if you can communicate with Zephyr from any-where.'

They hooked up the second man, and this time Wade rode up with him, and stayed up there to lower the hook back down for Forlam.

'Talking to him face to face, he cannot shut down communication, except by shoving me off a spar,' Wade explained.

'What's it all about?' Forlam asked, reluctant to reach out and grip the hook.

'Come on, we have to—'

Suddenly the Prador ship was vibrating. Thirteen shot away from the ledge to hover in the middle of the room, turning slowly, his tail lashing like an angry cat's.

'What is that?' Forlam asked.

'Turbines,' said the drone briefly.

'Come on!' shouted Wade.

Forlam addressed the drone. 'Can you open that door into here?'

'I can, but the ship's sensors would pick up anyone who moved beyond it.'

'Forlam, don't do this,' said the Golem.

From an earlier exchange, Forlam had learnt the location of the engine room: a hundred metres back down the main corridor then off to the left. If he was quick, he might be able to get it done before Vrell had time to react.

'Can you get those two out by yourself?' he asked Wade.

'I can't help you,' the Golem warned. 'What I have to do is too important.'

'Thirteen, open the door, would you.' As the drone drifted across the holding area, Forlam picked up his laser carbine and drew his ceramal knife from his boot.

The juvenile rhinoworms who had been sporting in the shallows, and occasionally venturing ashore until Ambel kicked them back, disappeared like fog in a gale. The giant whelk arose out of deeper water, and Ambel realized that seeing it out at sea, or attached to a leaping heirodont, gave no true impression of its scale. The creature was truly gigantic, and he began to feel some reservations about his plan. But there was nothing he could do about that now. He pulled back the twin hammers of his blunderbuss, brought the weapon up to his shoulder, and aimed at its eyes.

Coming athwart the *Treader*, it paused, one eye on the ship and one eye swinging towards him. It then snatched one of its huge white tentacles up out of the ocean and swept it across, tearing away the rear mast as easily as brushing cobwebs, then flicked the tangle of mast spar and rigging into the sea.

'Oh you bugger!' said Ambel, and pulled the trigger.

His gun boomed, kicking out a cloud of smoke, and its load of stones pocked the creature's lower body around one eye. It blinked, reached back with a smaller tentacle to rub at the base of that eye-stalk, then abruptly surged towards Ambel. The Captain turned and ran back into the forest of peartrunk trees. Behind him the whelk ploughed up the sand. He heard a sound as of some massive cork pulling out of a bottle, and glanced back to see a whole tree uprooted, then crashing down by the tideline. This did not bode well for the plan either. Finally he reached the spot he had designated and turned to face the monster.

The whelk's shell stood as high as the highest branches and, while scraping by, knocked showers of leeches down from them. He noticed how its stalked eyes now extended out sideways from its main mass as if triangulating on him. Its flesh skirt spread for many metres ahead of it, and extending from that its main two tentacles were nearly in reach of Ambel. Yet it hesitated.

'Come on! What are you waiting for!' the Captain bellowed.

The monster began to ease forward again, and Ambel began to move back. Then Drum stepped into view from the right, hefting a leech harpoon. He let out a growling shout and hurled the weapon, hard. The point of it struck the whelk's main body, but only penetrated deep enough for the barbs to engage. Behind Drum, Roach took up the rope and hauled it taut, while behind him two juniors wrapped the end of it twice around a peartrunk tree. The creature slapped its tentacle down, aiming for Drum, but clipped the rope instead. With a wrenching sound the tree tilted, and one of the juniors still clutching the rope was jerked hard against the trunk. He bounced once and landed limply on the ground.

'Over here!' shouted Anne from the other side and, firing her carbine, began to cut smoking lines across the monster's flesh. It swung towards her, further loosening the tree. Another crewman ran forward eagerly, swinging his machete at a nearby tentacle. The blade just bounced off it, and while the man stared with puzzlement at his weapon, the same tentacle shot up and hit him with a sound like a sledgehammer hitting a peach. He left the ground and disappeared into foliage, five metres up.

'Ready, lads,' said Ambel, taking up the harpoon at his feet. Pacing forwards, he threw this second weapon with all his might. It struck a soft spot just below shell, and penetrated deep. Behind the Captain, Silister and Davy-bronte took up the harpoon rope and wrapped it around a rocky outcrop. Ambel began running to the left, spying Drum heading to the right. The other Captain snatched up another harpoon.

'We need to get in closer!' Ambel shouted to him. 'We can't afford to have any of these come loose!'

On the other side of the creature from Drum, Boris carted his dismounted deck cannon out of cover. As he fired it, the recoil flung him over onto his back. Striking the whelk's shell, its projectiles exploded glittering shards all over Drum, who was now charging in with his harpoon held level. Peck, pumping cartridge after cartridge into his shotgun, covered Boris as he struggled to his feet and recovered the cannon. Drum struck, driving the harpoon half a metre in below the whelk's eye, then with a bellow and another massive shove, thrust it in a full metre. The whelk's bubbling squeal was painful to hear.

Another harpoon from Ambel, this time straight through the end of a major tentacle. A group of five hauling on the rope, trying to draw the limb down and immobilize it. Someone screaming on the other side, the ragged remains of a human thumping down onto the earth. Yet another harpoon from Drum, but snapped off before its rope could be secured. A peartrunk tree, ripped out of the ground, slammed down on two fleeing Hoopers. More harpoons. More ropes. Someone suspended high, crunched up like paper, discarded. Another Hooper dragged in to disappear underneath the fleshy skirt. Now came Ambel's tenth harpoon. He ran in while crew opposite him fired on the creature, again distracting it. He swore when one badly aimed shot thumped into his stomach, then drove the harpoon down hard into the base of a large tentacle, rested his full weight on it, and shoved again. The weapon went right through into the ground.

Ambel looked up to see one dinner-plate eye observing him from only a metre away, just as the tentacle twisted, smacking the harpoon haft hard against his shoulder. He felt his collarbone break, staggered back, then turned to run. He caught sight of Crewman Pillow struggling to tie off this latest rope, then a tentacle wrapped around Ambel's waist, jerked him to a halt, and lifted him off the ground.

The whelk now reared, exposing its serrated beak

and, on the ground below, what was left of a crewman it had grabbed earlier. The Hoopers kept firing on it from all sides as it drew Ambel in, champing that beak in anticipation. Some shots penetrated, most just bounced off. Black lines crisscrossed the tentacle holding Ambel, along with the glowing pockmarks of pulse-gun fire. Drum charged forwards with another harpoon, aiming for the same limb. He hurled it just as another tentacle swept his feet from under him, missed his target, but the harpoon struck and penetrated shell. Ambel heard a hissing, and smelt something rank.

'Fire at the shell!' he shouted. 'Fire at the shell!'

Anne was the first to transfer her aim, perhaps realizing Ambel's intent. And that was all it took, as her shots ignited the methane now hissing from the shell. There came a drawn-out roaring explosion, the shell splitting to spew out a sheet of flame that ignited the surrounding foliage. As the whelk screamed, Ambel found himself hurtling through the air above.

'Oh shit and buggeration,' he managed, before coiling himself into a ball as he crashed back down.

It was some hours later that Silister and Davybronte found him, and helped him back to join the others. He stood and observed the whelk, its shell still smoking, pinned tight by thirty harpoons securely roped down. One of its eyes was missing. The other blinked at him.

'Gulliver,' he muttered, pointing a shaky finger, but later found that his fellow Lilliputians had not done too well. Two of them were dead – sprine was administered to them because their head injuries were so bad that little remained inside their skulls. Seven others would be severely immobilized until their backbones healed; one was missing his legs, which were somewhere inside the whelk; and not one of them had come through this without broken bones.

'It could have been worse,' he said, finally.

He understood why Drum nearly ruptured himself with laughter.

19

Boxy:
this fishlike creature obtains its name from the cubic shape of its body. Like the turbul, the boxy carries a sacrificial outer layer of flesh but, due to its odd shape, is unlike the turbul in being slow-moving. That boxies manage to survive and prosper was originally put down to their breeding rate: after mating, one fully fleshed female will convert all her outer flesh into upwards of ten thousand eggs, and she can do this as often as eight times a year. The true reason for their flourishing remained misunderstood until their behaviour was studied by the Polity Warden's submind drones. Boxies habitually swim together in large shoals, and when an attack by leeches is unavoidable, they clump together to neatly form a large cubic mass. Those carrying the least outer flesh congregate towards the centre. Should an attack continue, this basic mass will rearrange, continuously positioning the more fleshy boxies to the outside. This is classic herd-like behaviour – putting the more vulnerable individuals to the centre. Some types of whelk have also evolved similar herding behaviour, specifically the frog whelk –

Bloc knew he could not hold it together for much longer. New error messages kept flashing up in his visual cortex every few minutes, and if he did not get himself into a tank soon, he would end up like Bones and have no body to resurrect. Also, since it was becoming evident that the Prador ship might soon be on the move, things were getting a bit tense here on the bridge.

'If it comes straight up, we're buggered,' announced Captain Ron. 'Let's start the engines so, if we get a chance, we can pull clear.'

Bloc stared down at his right hand, which was gripping his carbine. It was shaking, and that could not be due to the putrefaction of his body but to some deeper fault. He must not let anyone off this ship – that fact was hard-wired into his mind, had become his main purpose for being – but enforcing that order was now destroying his chance at resurrection. The longer he remained here in control, the more of his body would be eaten away. But once placed in a tank he would no longer be in control, and then would they even keep him there, after all he had done? He must remain totally in control to prevent anyone leaving the ship, but he . . . but . . . but . . . His thoughts spun round and round in circles, and for a moment he could not even find the will to speak.

'Bloc, let us start the engines,' Ron repeated.

'You will remain . . .' was all Bloc could manage.

'We'll all end up in the sea,' muttered Aesop.

Bloc immediately clamped down on him hard, but the effort of doing so resulted in displacement of the mess of software in his head, and he was mentally blinded by the mass of error messages scrolling up in his mind. As soon as he managed to turn them off, another flashed up:

MEMSPACE: 00018

He cleared that, and when he could finally see again, he found John Styx standing before him.

'Look.' Styx pointed outside.

Bloc turned his head to see one of the towering weapons turrets sinking. It was slowly being withdrawn into the Prador ship.

'It's preparing to leave,' explained Styx, 'and if it destroys our ship in the process, what then? All of us end up at the bottom of the sea, no Kladites to adore you, no power for you to exercise, no triumphant arrival at the Little Flint – your dream of the *Sable Keech* ended.'

Bloc felt a flash of anger. They were disrespecting him again, ignoring what he was and all he had done for them. He said to Styx, 'You . . . know too much.'

'What's to know? That you've deified a man who would have nothing but contempt for you. You crave worship as much as you crave control. Let us at least try to move the ship to safety.'

'Keech . . . would understand.' *Wouldn't he?* Everything was too confusing now.

Styx stepped forwards. 'You said I know too much. Would you like to know how? I know so much because I've known about you for a lot of years, Taylor Bloc. I knew all about the corruption and murder you instituted while you were alive, and how you used Cult power to obtain the industrial contracts that first made you rich.'

'Enough,' said Bloc, still trying to find some control in his own mind.

Styx continued relentlessly, 'I knew about your interest in Prador technology, for my interest was the same if not more than yours. I should have dealt with you back then, but I had more pressing concerns, and anyway I'd learnt that certain groups on Klader were sending friends Aesop and Bones after you, so thought that would be the last I'd hear of you. It wasn't until recently I learnt how you had been reified and were apparently served by two individuals called Aesop and Bones. Imagine my surprise. Imagine how little time it took me to figure out what you had done.'

'I said . . . enough . . .'

'You know,' said Styx, 'I actually thought about a change of career. But while there are shits like you running around, I've still got a job to do.'

MEMSPACE: 00007

'Of course I should have arrested you before you got this far, as here we are beyond Polity law, but it's surprising the power you have to fascinate. I should have acted. I should not have allowed you to establish power over the reifications on this ship.' He pulled from his jacket an aerosol canister of a kind Bloc immediately recognized, and held it up. 'I should not have allowed this.'

In a puzzled voice, Ron asked, 'What's that, then?'

Erlin, still restrained by Bones, replied, 'It's a hormone from a creature that grazes on fungus, and has a smell almost irresistible to hooders.'

Ron shrugged, then stepped over to one of the consoles.

'Stay were you are!' Bloc shrilled.

'I think we've had enough of this,' said Ron. With casual speed he reached out with his hands, grabbed both his Kladite guards and slammed them together so hard that their balm spattered the surrounding consoles. They stayed upright for a moment, then began to sag. Ron ignored them, pressing a button and stooping over the intercom microphone. 'Okay, Hoopers, time to come out and play. Take down these Kladite buggers.'

'Kill him!' Bloc screamed.

Ignoring the weapon in his own hands, Bloc sent an instruction to Aesop, who raised his carbine and fired it at Ron. The beam sliced into the Old Captain's arm, but briefly, for Janer was there in an instant, driving a thrust kick into Aesop's chest and slamming him back over a console and straight into one of the windows.

'That smarts.' Ron merely patted out his smoking limb, but when the two Kladites at the head of the stair-well started firing, he roared and charged straight across the bridge. Ignoring the holes being burnt into his body, he grabbed the two of them and slammed them together, before throwing them down amidst those try-ing to cram up the stairwell. Ramming the door shut on them, he spun the wheel and smashed his fist into the door's coded locking mechanism. By now the three remaining Kladites inside the bridge had also opened up on him. He ran at them, caught them, and one after the other tossed them out the gap where a window had been knocked out by the tsunami. They were nothing to him, the burns they inflicted were nothing to him. For the first time Bloc had some true intimation of what it meant to be an Old Captain.

Ron now headed over to another console and pressed a sequence of touch-plates. A new vibration thrilled through the ship as its engines started.

'Stop . . . or I kill her!' Bloc shouted, then shook his head, blinded again by error messages. He staggered back, waved his arm in front of himself. Chaotic vision returned. Through Aesop's eyes – Janer was pinning that reif to the floor – he saw himself waving his arm with rotten skin hanging off it in a sheet. He whimpered, fought for control, regained full vision.

'Stop the ship or I kill Erlin!' Bloc shouted.

'You forget,' said Erlin, 'I'm a Hooper.' She reached back, grabbed Bones and ducked down, throwing him. He landed near Ron and shot upright again. Ron backhanded him with such force he flew in a flat trajectory out of the window, after the Kladites. Erlin stood clutching a hand to her bloody throat. She spat some blood and grinned, exposing gory teeth.

The ship seemed to be tilting, then Bloc realized that no, it was turning. The Prador spaceship must have dropped down to pass under it, for to his left one of the low turrets was generating its own wake. What could he do now? The Prador had abandoned him, and now a void was opening in his consciousness. His attention swinging to Santen and Styx, he raised his carbine and fired. Santen stepped quickly in front of Styx, and staggered back gazing down at her burning chest, then up at Styx who had caught her.

'You think . . . I didn't guess,' she said to him, smoke issuing from her mouth.

MEMSPACE: 00005

Styx lowered her to the floor, her hardware obviously damaged for she showed no further signs of moving. Bloc swung his carbine from right to left, trying to cover everyone remaining in the bridge.

'All your dreams, Bloc.' Styx shook his head as he stood. 'I think, before you shoot me and Ron subsequently rips your head off, I'd like to tell you more about myself and my investigations.'

'What's . . . to know?' asked Bloc dismissively.

'Well, I'm a policeman,' said Styx.

'So? There is no law out here.'

'Yes.' Styx carefully held up his left hand and pulled back the sleeve to expose an antique watch. So as not to get anyone too excited he slowly reached out, pressed buttons on the side of it to change the display, then pressed his thumb against that display.

What now?

Travelling out from either side of the wristband, a fizzing light spread like embers on fuse paper, across John Styx's shrivelled skin. Behind this fire, his skin seemed to inflate, till it adopted the normal healthy texture of a living human being's. Though Bloc recognized some very sophisticated chameleonware effect, he could not understand the why of it.

The light fizzed to the tips of Styx's fingers and went out. It travelled up his arm and into his sleeve, lighting his clothing from inside as it spread all the way around his body. Eventually it reached his collar, travelled up his neck and over his face, revealing living human features.

Something familiar . . .

Bloc tried to dismiss the thought. Everyone knew that the longer you lived, the more readily your brain catalogued people by type, till everyone began to look familiar. Then it hit him so hard, the realization of who now faced him, that he lost his last shreds of control. He sank down on his knees.

'Well bugger me,' said Ron. '*That* policeman.'

The man stepped calmly forward, tugged the laser carbine from Bloc's limp grasp and turned the weapon to shove it against his chest. The carbine was pointed slightly to one side, precisely at where Bloc's crystal was located. It was all too much.

OUTPARAFUNCT: B.P. LOAD INC. 100%

WARN: EXTREMITY PROBES NIL BALM LA71–94, LH 34–67 . . .

WARN: ALL E-PROBES REG. VIRAL INFECT.

MEMSPACE: 00002

One after another, warning messages were now scrolling up before his inner vision and he seemed unable to shut them down. The next thing Bloc knew he was flat on his back staring through a flood of artificial tears at the roof of the bridge.

'How does it feel to have a ship named after you?' asked Captain Ron.

'Well, I'm honoured of course,' replied the man standing over Bloc.

MEMSPACE: 00000

OVERLOAD: CRYSTAL SAFETY MODE

Blackness.

The retracting weapons turret was closing the gap. Ignoring what injuries he might cause the two crewmen, Wade shoved them up through it then followed them. The spaceship was moving lower in the sea now, the blast of its turbines stirring up a great wall of silt specked with glittering shoals of boxies, whose cubic bodies seeming like pixel faults in a solid holographic display. The *Sable Keech* was now a few metres up, sliding over, driven by its own screws. The submersible port had to be some distance ahead of him, and there was no way he could swim to it encumbered with his present load. His APW strapped across his back, he quickly tore off his gloves, boots, then the syntheflesh coverings of his hands and feet revealing his skeletal metal fingers and toes. In his left hand he grabbed the cables binding the wrists of the two crewmen, squatted, then drove himself upwards off the Prador ship. Two metres up and the keel of the *Sable Keech* was speeding immediately over him. He closed his free hand on the keel's edge, sliding and tearing up splinters, drove his fingers in, then brought up his feet and drove in his toes. The current's drag threatened to dislodge him, until he released the crewmen, quickly stabbed his hand underneath the cable binding their wrists and slid it along his arm till the pair were dangling from its crook, then took a grip of the keel with his other hand. Now to climb.

Pulling free his right hand he reached up and drove it into the woodwork again, then one foot, then the other hand, the other foot. With painful slowness he began working his way out from the keel, across an upcurving ceiling of planking the size of a sports field. The two crewmen rode back along his arm until they were hanging from around his shoulder. Boxies zipped past as the ship accelerated, then a passing turbul closed its jaws on one crewman's foot and Wade had to drive his fingers deeper into timber to prevent himself being dragged from the hull. The creature finally separated from its prey, though it took the foot with it.

Wade could have moved very much faster without his burden, but even though needing to get aboard the ship with some urgency, he stubbornly held onto the two rescued Hoopers.

Zephyr, wait for me. There's something more you need to know.

It was a lie, but might be enough to delay the Golem sail, even though the threat of weapons fire from the Prador ship was growing less.

I have seen enough, said Zephyr. *Life is at constant war*

*with Death, and I will strike a blow in that campaign . . . It
is none of your concern.*

Wade realized, by that last comment, that Zephyr was
also conducting a conversation with the two living sails.
Perhaps *they* would delay the Golem sail. Now reaching
the steeper curve up to the side of the ship, Wade
observed white water above him. Not far to go now.
Then things began bumping against him in the water:
reddish-brown, swan-necked, with long flat bodies.

Oh, you have got to be kidding.

One of the leeches attached to his exposed ankle and,
with an electric screwdriver sound, reamed out a chunk
of his syntheflesh. The predator then fell away, writhing
like a blood worm, and spat out the unsavoury mouthful. Others attached to the two crewmen, taking out
chunks of them too, but unable to enjoy seconds as the
current swept them away. Wade concentrated on the task
in hand – talking to Zephyr just slowed him down. If he
did not get the pair of them out of the water soon, he
would be rescuing nothing more than what the Hoopers
called stripped-fish.

Finally reaching the surface he began hauling himself
up the sheer face of the hull. Twenty metres up he passed
one of the square windows, from which a female
reification observed him, perhaps with bemusement –
there was no way to tell. He saw her turn away and begin
punching touch-plates on her computer's console.
Meanwhile, to his right the remains of a laser turret projecting from the hull kept turning towards him, spraying
sparks as if in frustration. Finally, fifteen metres from the
rail, a face peered down at him. There came a bellowed
'Over here!' and shortly after a rope uncoiled down to
him. Once he grabbed it, he and his load were hauled

rapidly up the side. His supposition that some kind of winch was in use was proved wrong on discovering Captain Ron at the other end of the rope.

'That the lot of them?' The Captain eyed the two figures now lying prostrate on the deck.

'Four more down in our submersible enclosure,' Wade informed him.

'Forlam?'

'Still aboard the Prador ship, trying to free Orbus and three others.'

Ron winced.

'So how you gonna kill Death, then?' asked Huff.

'I told you . . . none of your concern.'

Zephyr swayed from side to side on the spar, glancing first over to where the Prador ship was surfacing half a kilometre away, then peering down at figures on the deck below. He had to leave soon. It had been a mistake his coming here to learn more about the enemy. What he had seen here only confused the issue, when in the beginning it had been so clear . . .

'Death will end,' said Zephyr firmly.

'But how?' Puff asked.

Before Zephyr could formulate a reply, Huff interjected, 'If nothing dies we'll be sitting neck-deep in leeches and prill, all eating each other and being eaten.' Huff shook his crocodilian head. 'Though admittedly things are not far off that around here.'

Zephyr observed Puff bow forward to catch Huff's eye, raise a spiderclaw up to the side of her head to scribe a little circle, then shake her muzzle. Zephyr did not recognize what this meant until digging deep into his database.

'I am not mad!' he yelled.

'Okay,' said Puff. 'Tell us exactly how you're gonna "strike a blow in this campaign". Or are your claims all piss and wind?'

Zephyr suddenly understood. Here he had encountered nothing but killers and the dying, because they were all the same. He had encountered nothing but argument for the same reason: they all served Death. That entity had put them here in his path to prevent him doing what he must do.

'I will kill sprine,' announced the Golem sail.

'What? You can't do that,' said Huff. 'How are you gonna do that?'

'You won't stop me, and you won't change my mind.' Zephyr began to spread his wings.

'Wait.' Huff reached out with his own wing, a few of his spiderclaws grabbing some of Zephyr's wing bones. 'You haven't explained—'

In any war there are casualties – this is unavoidable. Zephyr focused on Huff, his particle cannon coming online easy as blinking. The flash and the subsequent screech negated everything else, and what remained of Huff fell like a smoking comet.

'Huff! HUFF!'

Puff surged forwards, her jaws open wide, with a snarl beginning deep within her. Another flash, then more long-boned organic wreckage falling to the deck below.

Wings booming open, Zephyr launched himself from the mast. *You won't stop me*, he thought, but was unable to articulate more than a scream.

Isis Wade's words followed him into the sky: '*What have you done?*'

*

The corridor loomed as wide as a hangar and dank as a cave. Stepping out into it, Forlam immediately broke into a run. He glanced back to see Thirteen bobbing behind him, with a flicker of intense lasers all around as the drone attempted to flash out all the cameras around them. This time the drone certainly had no time to subvert them.

Foolish drone, thought Forlam. It should have fled while it had the chance. It could not know how little Forlam cared for his own life just at that moment.

Lice were now scuttling across the floor, probably shaken loose by the vibration of the ship's turbines. Leaping a pile of human bones, Forlam quickly came to the end of the corridor, blocked by huge sloped gratings. To his left was the door he sought. It was split diagonally and partially open. There came a hammering from inside, and he saw blue fingers tugging at the gap.

'Back off!' he shouted. 'I'll burn you out!'

'Whoo-is thaaat?' came a sibilant hiss from inside.

'Your rescuer. Move away from the door.'

'Whois whosss?'

It occurred to Forlam then that opening this door might not be such a bright idea – but, what the hell, he was here now.

'It's Forlam, from Captain Ron's crew.'

'Forlaam offworldss.'

'Well, I'm back now. Move away from the door!'

After a moment the fingers retreated and Forlam moved in close. He aimed his carbine waist-height just to the right of the diagonal gap, and fired. The dun metal surface glimmered under the laser, then suddenly grew painfully bright. There followed an intense flash, a smell like molten solder, and a wave of light and heat threw Forlam staggering back and down on his backside.

'Oh . . . buggerit,' was all he could think to say.

'Prador exotic metal,' said Thirteen, from somewhere to his side.

Forlam kept blinking, as his vision slowly returned in shades of grey. He finally noticed the drone hovering to one side of the door, its tail plugged into some kind of control pit.

'Are you really sure you want this door open?'

'Damnit, yes!' Forlam scrambled to his feet.

A grinding sound from the wall was followed by a thump, as some sort of hydraulic system caught up with how far the door had already been prised open by those inside. Its two halves then began to revolve away into the wall, till the gap was a metre wide. The first figure stepped through, and Forlam recognized Orbus by his bulk and his clothing – but that was all. As the others came out after the Captain, Forlam emitted a nervous giggle. They all looked to be transforming into skinners.

'Dronsesss!' Orbus hissed, turning to look down the corridor, then something snapped past through the air between him and Forlam and exploded against the nearby wall. As the blast hurled Forlam to the floor again, he saw Thirteen slam against the far wall. Forlam rolled aside, grabbing for his dropped carbine, but then saw it glow red, and hurled himself away as it exploded. Hot metal spattered his back and he rolled trying to extinguish his burning clothing. Then Orbus came down on him, leech tongue waving.

Oh hell . . .

Orbus spun him over on his face and pulled something searing from his back, then flipped him over again and, sitting on Forlam's stomach, held up a fragment of carbine.

'Theresss.'

The hot metal sizzled in the Captain's fingers, till after a moment he tossed it aside. Then, extruding his leech tongue again, he returned his attention directly to Forlam.

'If you'd just like to get off me now?' Forlam suggested.

There was no need, for another nearby explosion flung Orbus away from him. Forlam scrambled backwards, away from where the floor seemed to be burning. Then came a sound he recognized: the stuttering whoosh of a rail-gun firing. He turned just in time to see a huge Prador drone coming towards him, the space between him and it blackening with lines of projectiles. Then the projectiles struck something, igniting a translucent wall before him, bouncing off it and smashing into the corridor walls, floor and ceiling beyond. When the drone ceased firing, the wall blinked out.

Hard-field?

Forlam glanced behind to see Orbus and his three crewmen together moving crablike over to the corridor wall. Behind them a huge nautiloid drone hung in mid-air, with Thirteen clutched in one of its minor tentacles. Then it returned fire at the Prador drone.

Forlam just sat there thinking that now he was going to die. Abruptly it occurred to him that though such a process might have some fascination, it was only something you could go through once. He flung himself to the wall.

Another hard-field appeared, but this time the ricochets smashed around on Forlam's side of it. One projectile fragment just nicked his ear before slamming into the wall beside his head. One of Orbus's crewmen was flung away from his fellow by three successive hits. Orbus himself negligently pulled a projectile out of his chest and tossed it aside. It seemed a miracle that they had not all been chopped to pieces in this potential meat-grinder, then the firing abruptly ceased.

The safest place, Forlam decided, would be behind one of the drones, preferably the nautiloid one, which was probably Polity. He began edging along the wall in that direction, expecting the shooting between the two drones to start again at any moment. Strangely, nothing happened for long-drawn-out seconds, then suddenly the Prador drone was withdrawing, and a new vibration began shaking the ship.

'That is the sweet sound of a fusion engine test,' said the Polity drone. 'And now the ship's antigravity is coming online.'

'Erm,' was all Forlam managed.

A silver tentacle whipped out, wound around his waist, and hauled him in. He only realized the others had been grabbed when, drawn close to the drone's cold body, he found himself pressed against someone else's back. Luckily the woman could not turn her head or extend her tongue far enough, else Forlam felt sure he would have lost an eye to her.

Then the rescuing drone was moving very fast along the ship's corridors. A door disintegrated before it, another stretch of corridor, another door turned to fragments, then some kind of chamber opening to a triangular patch of sky. They shot out above a waterfall – sea water pouring from that chamber – then over the sea. Forlam glimpsed the Prador ship turning, like a city detached from the ground, till the drone turned sharply and accelerated across the ocean, cutting that view. He now spotted an island and, distantly, the *Sable Keech*. When the drone dipped down towards the island, Forlam prayed he would not be left there with Orbus and his merry crew. Before he could think to protest, he was released to drop onto a wooden deck. As immediately he scrambled away from the woman's horrible wriggling tongue, his back came to rest against a pair of solid legs.

'Well, that's a bugger – we ain't got no rope left,' said a familiar voice.

An equally familiar one added, 'Nor any harpoons.'

The news from one of the passengers, that she had seen some man climbing the side of the hull carrying two blue corpses on his back, had not attracted Janer's attention so much as watching the Prador ship rise from the ocean. Now the spaceship was just sitting motionless in the sky. It had not reacted to the Golem sail taking wing, nor had it reacted to a human figure with metal hands and feet departing the deck, suspended in an AG harness. Now he had missed out, for after committing murder the Golem sail was gone, and Isis Wade had gone after it.

'Here we are,' said Captain Ron, as they entered the submersible enclosure.

Janer stared at the four lying on the floor. Unlike the two he had earlier seen up on deck, these were struggling against their bonds, trying to chew through the cables binding their wrists, when their serpentine tongues did not get in the way. Seeing Janer and Ron with the six accompanying Hoopers, all four of them struggled to their feet and tried to make a break for it, issuing whooping hissing sounds as they ran around the enclosure. Ron stepped back and closed the door, resting his back against it. He folded his arms. 'Go get 'em, lads.'

The six Hoopers gave chase, quickly clubbing two of the four to the ground and binding their legs with reels of ducting tape. A third was tackled just before managing to throw himself out through the shimmer-shield. The fourth ran straight into Ron's fist and sat down abruptly with his eyes crossed. Janer looked down at the gun he had drawn and sighed. Then he looked around, realizing that here was his opportunity, for Wade had told him Zephyr's intended destination. Janer holstered his weapon.

'Ron, I have to leave,' he announced.

The Captain raised an eyebrow as, one-handed, he hoisted the stunned Hooper to his feet. 'Where?'

'Places to go, things to do.' Janer headed for the submersible, climbed the ladder and stepped into the conning tower. 'This is important. Don't try to stop me.'

Ron was showing no sign of doing any such thing. He waved a dismissive hand at Janer, then rapped his captive's head against the wall as the Hooper showed signs of regaining consciousness.

Janer dropped inside the submersible, sat down in the pilot's seat and studied the controls. Simple really. He turned on the screens giving him an outside view, waited until the Hooper currently between him and the shimmer-shield had dragged his captive aside, then hit the touch-plate labelled LAUNCH.

The acceleration flung him hard back into the seat. Then the shield rapidly approached, engulfed the sub, and he was hurtling through white water. He pulled safety straps down and clicked them into place, before taking hold of the joystick. It was standard simple format: you moved the stick in the direction you wanted to go, and the further you moved it in that direction the faster you got there. He pulled the stick up, heard the engine roar behind him, and felt the seat press up against his backside.

'Whooo! Hoo!'

The sub leapt from the ocean like a dolphin and came down in an explosion of spume. A further tinkering with the controls gave him a positional map. On that he located 'Olian's' clearly marked, experimentally shifted the stick from side to side so the submersible icon on the map turned, then finally got it directed towards that same location. He then pushed the stick forwards and the acceleration forced him back in his seat. Eyeing the many readouts before him, he wondered if he would recognize one warning him that the engine was overheating and burning out. Then he relaxed and thought about what he had learnt: how mistaken had been the young hive mind, and how more deadly were the intentions of one part of that ancient mind: Zephyr.

Hive minds were now unlikely to send their agents here to obtain sprine. Firstly, because with all that by now was known about this planet's life forms, right down to their genomes, any focused research would ascertain the poison's formula offworld. But, secondly and most importantly, because here was the only place it could be used and the Warden would not allow that. No, the agent of one half of the ancient hive mind had not come here for that purpose, since it already possessed the formula.

Wade had explained to him: 'Each separate part of

the mind can work on things without the other parts knowing. On the planet Hive, the Zephyr part of the mind synthesized sprine then, using the advanced genetic manipulation technologies known there, made a virus to destroy it.'

'But why do that?' Janer had asked.

'Because here sprine is Death, and Zephyr wants to *kill* Death.'

'You're saying Zephyr could release that virus at any moment? Do you realize what might happen? We have to stop him now!'

Wade shook his head. 'The small quantity Zephyr carries would be unlikely to survive long enough in this environment to propagate. Any leech infected by it would quickly die and be destroyed by all the other predators here. In such a situation the chances of it spreading planetwide are less than ten per cent.'

'Oh, that's okay then.'

'It is, admittedly, an appreciable risk.'

'How does Zephyr intend to up those odds?'

'The virus needs to be added to a very large quantity of sprine. With a sufficient food supply it can double its mass every few minutes, and it will then spread itself via a form of air- or water-borne sporulation.'

'A *large* quantity of sprine?'

Wade had nodded.

'Olian's,' realized Janer.

You waited too long, Wade.

Janer considered what might be the result of Zephyr's attempt to kill Death. The collapse of the present plane-tary economy, which was based on sprine, was the least significant worry. Through long and painful experience, humans had learnt how subtly balanced were all ecologies. The big leeches topped the food chain here, consuming whole other large creatures living in the ocean. Without them, therefore, their prey would just keep on growing and feeding, wiping out other species and causing a further cascade of imbalances. All the leeches would then die out, because it was only the large ones that procreated. Some might think that a good thing. It was not. If they were lucky, some new balance might be restored – in about ten thousand years or so. Quite possibly the entire biosphere would collapse into something almost Precambrian.

Janer tried forcing the joystick even further forward, but it was already at its limit.

With her single remaining eye, the giant whelk gazed behind herself and down towards the beach. Observing swarms of juvenile rhinoworms gradually venturing ashore, she again tested the ropes securing her, but found little give in them. There was even less give in the numerous harpoons embedded in her flesh, for it had healed around them, holding them firmer. She was now so exhausted and hungry she found it difficult to think. When she did manage to mull over what had happened, she felt hurt. It seemed almost like the betrayal of some contract in which she pursued the ships and they fled. They should not have stopped and ambushed her in this way. That was so unfair.

Turning her eye further, to study her shell, she observed that the split in it had nearly closed up. With luck it would be fully sealed before the rhinoworms started chewing pieces out of her, for if those things found their way in there, to her softer parts, it would all be quickly over. However, if she remained trapped here like this, she would still die. It might take them longer to munch away her harder extremities, but they would never give up. She struggled again, the harpoon wounds aching in her flesh and the trees around her shaking. Some of them did loosen a bit, but the taut ropes binding her to immovable outcrops of rock prevented her getting the leverage to pull the looser trees completely free. Then, vibrating through the ground from the ocean bed, she heard a familiar thumping.

The male whelk was out there. If she could attract him in he might be able to free her, but to do that she needed to free at least one tentacle. She struggled again, some of the ropes definitely slacker now, but every effort left her weaker. She focused her attention on one tentacle only: the one from which the fishing line depended. There was a harpoon driven right through it, a metre back from the tip of it. Folding that tip up, she could just touch the thick rope stretching taut from the harpoon's shaft to a nearby tree. That was all she could manage, but remembering how the fishing line had cut so easily through heirodont flesh and gristle, she now had an idea. Flipping the free extremity of tentacle, she whipped the line up from the sandy soil. It looped up and touched the rope, before dropping down again. After five attempts she got part of it up and over the rope, but it slid off again. On her fourteenth attempt it went over, and she finally caught hold of the line's loose end with her tentacle tip, wrapping it round securely. Just then pain messages began to register from some of her other tentacles. The rhinoworms were beginning to tentatively gnaw on her flesh.

Pulling on the line itself only tugged the rope down, making the harpoon tilt. It was only by accident, when her grip slipped for a moment and she drew the line across the rope, that she observed a few severed fibres spring up. Urgently, she began sawing the line back and forth.

By now some of the rhinoworms, finding she was not retaliating, were biting a lot harder, and the commotion they were making was attracting many more who were heading rapidly up from the beach.

Finally, the rope parted, and the giant whelk twisted her tentacle to snap off the harpoon haft. Then reaching over to snatch up the most persistent rhinoworm, she raised the writhing creature and used it like a rubber drumstick to beat a tattoo on her shell. The male whelk out at sea responded with an excited drumming. The rhinoworm, its skull now shattered, she fed under her skirt, to her beak, and quickly devoured. Now she reached round to tackle the next harpoon, trying to tug it out. But it was stuck solid and, with its rope still attached, she could not get enough leverage with just one tentacle to break the haft. At least there was less urgency now the rhinoworms had retreated a little way. Realizing that once she freed another tentacle things would get very much easier, she looped the line over another rope and again began to saw. She was about halfway through when the waiting rhinoworms began running for cover. A crusted shell had broken the ocean's surface and begun to head ashore.

Extending her remaining eye rearwards, the female giant whelk watched the male approach. She did not like the look of his shell for, encrusted like that, it looked untidy, and meant he spent most of his time on the bottom. He was smaller, as all males were, but it struck her that this one was particularly scrawny. He oozed

onto the sand, moved up to the edge of the clearing and
halted, focusing both eyes down to where a rope was tied
around a rocky outcrop. He tracked the rope up to the
harpoon embedded in her body, then his eyes swung
apart to take in the other ropes. She tugged briefly on a
couple of them to be sure he got the idea. He paused,
mulling the situation over, then reached out a tentacle
and plucked the nearest rope like a guitar string. She
wondered if he was particularly thick when he moved
aside and chose to slide towards her up the lane between
two ropes, careful to avoid dislodging any of them. When
he reached her and reared up, extruding the long, tubular, glassy corkscrew of his penis, she realized he had certainly assessed the situation here.

Angrily the giant female thrashed back at him with
her one free tentacle, which was larger and more powerful than any of his. But, having all his free, he caught
hold of it and held it down against her shell. His penis
partially unwound, probing under the back lip of her
shell. At this point, instinct took over in her, and she
extruded some of her softer body from underneath her
shell. His penis felt this, and snapped out straight, stabbing deep inside her. Feeling something that was both
pain and pleasure she emitted a hissing squeal. Letting
loose a series of whistling hoots, he began rocking back
and forth, his penis groping around between her internal
organs. One organ reacted, opening with a ripping feeling inside her, and he soon found it. She bucked hard in
reaction, and observed a couple of trees go crashing
down. His flailing about dislodged one rope so its
looped end snapped up free of the outcrop to which it
was secured. This constant rocking motion loosened a
harpoon embedded near his entry point, and the grow-

ing mass of slime there lubricated its progress out of her body. Then, with a final long-drawn-out hoot he filled her up, and with a gasp came to rest flat and limp against her. Screwing itself back out of her, his penis dropped flaccid into the sand.

The female felt strangely invigorated by this mating. Peering at the male, she observed his eyes blinking tiredly, and felt his grip slackening. Pulling her tentacle free, she snatched up the loose harpoon and drove it deep between his eyes. He squealed and retreated, becoming entangled in a fallen tree. Turning, she brought more trees crashing down and snapped two more ropes. Now with four tentacles unrestrained, she used them to snap harpoon shafts one after another, till finally breaking free. Her assailant meanwhile crushed his way over foliage and began heading back for the shore. She surged forward, picked up the relevant rope and waited. As the rope drew taut, he was jerked to a halt. Gradually she began to reel him in, clacking her beak the while. The reversal would have been lost on her: he'd had his way with her and now, dinner.

20

Lung Bird:
this creature seems to be an abortive attempt by the life of Spatterjay to get into the skies. They appear to be perpetually on the point of coming apart and possess a sparse covering of long oily feathers, between which is exposed purplish septic-looking flesh. Seen stationary on a branch, a lung bird looks like a half-plucked crow that has been dead for a week or more. But they are a fascinating oddity. On close inspection it can be seen that their beaks are extensions of a light cara-pace that entirely covers them, as are their feathers, for these birds have no internal skeleton. They are in fact closely related to the glisters, being crustaceans that took to the air. However, close inspection of lung birds is not something to be enjoyed by any human, and most investigation into these creatures is conducted by telefactor or by the planetary Warden, for the creature's body is heavily laden with putrescine, which comes from their main diet of putrephallus weeds −

Erlin gazed back at the Prador spaceship, hovering just out from the island which the *Sable Keech* was now rounding. It was itself a metal island, clouds forming around it as sea water boiled off hot cowlings then recondensed in the air.

What's it waiting for? she wondered, and as if in response to her silent query its fusion engines sputtered and sent the leviathan slowly drifting away. She pursed her lips. At least now, with every second that passed, the chances were reduced of them being caught in the middle of some bombardment from orbit.

'Look,' said Sable Keech himself, now standing beside her.

'I see it,' she replied.

Lowering his monocular, he caught her shoulder. 'No there.' He pointed towards the island shallows where a Hooper ship was making its way out to sea. Its progress was necessarily slow because its rear mast was missing and it was sailing under some temporary rig manipulated by its living sail. Erlin took the monocular Keech passed to her and studied the vessel. At first she did not recognize it, because of its current rig, then realization hit home.

'The *Treader*,' she breathed, then directed her attention to the deck. There seemed a lot of Hoopers aboard, and she wondered what Ambel had got himself into now.

'Why's it here?' Keech asked.

Abruptly Erlin felt guilty, understanding that the Old Captain may have come in pursuit of herself. There seemed no other explanation for him to be way out here, and she wondered if she deserved such concern.

'Perhaps we should tell . . .' she began, but there was no need. The *Sable Keech* was slowing and turning. 'Right,' she said. 'Right.' She turned and pushed back through the door leading into the Tank Rooms. She headed over to a nearby restraint table and rested her bottom against it. Looking mildly puzzled, Keech followed her in. She did not want to deal with what she was feeling at that moment, and did not want him asking her questions. Instead she eyed the new occupants of the restraint tables: six Hoopers – dosed up with Intertox but still fighting their bonds – and three others.

'Maybe we should just drop him over the side,' she suggested, eyeing the closest to her of the latter. That was not an acceptable Polity approach, but certainly how Captain Ron would like to deal with the problem.

Strapped naked to his table, Bloc showed no sign of movement. She studied his exposed injuries with belated interest, wondering what the hell had originally killed him. Aesop and Bones also lay immobile on tables nearby.

'Were I not an Earth Monitor, I would tend to agree,' said Keech. 'But I want to take him back with me. Would that be possible?'

'Aesop and Bones, too?' she asked.

'Certainly,' he replied. 'Tell me, why did Bloc just collapse like that?'

Erlin glanced at the status lights on Bloc's cleansing unit, which was positioned on a tray folded out from the restraint table. All showed red, and one of the pipes connecting into the reif's body was black with fouled balm. She then picked up a palm console, connected via an optic cable into the cleanser, and studied its readout.

'He seized up – not enough memory space for all the information he was processing.' She gestured at Aesop and Bones. 'Rather than use one unit to control one thrall, as do the Prador, his unit is partitioned. The readings I've been getting show three main partitions, and I've been able to assign two of these to Aesop and

Bones. The third one is wide-band, its channel operating twenty-seven thralls in parallel. I thought at first this was to control twenty-seven reifs, but that could not possibly work. Again, checking dates, I found that eleven of the thralls went offline while Bloc was on Mortuary Island, before I arrived. Then a further seven of them went offline at just about the time the hooder lost its head.'

Keech grimaced. 'The figure twenty-seven tells me all I need to know. The number of the beast, you might say – that's how many body segments a hooder possesses.'

'He obviously controlled it, though I'd question the extent of that control with him needing to use grazer pheromone to mark out its victims. Anyway, as those eighteen thralls were destroyed, they scrambled formatting in his memory space. Then the Prador somehow linked through the remaining hooder thralls, thereby controlling him. It also used him as a conduit for a while in order to run some sort of mathematical program in the minds of those other two. But that alone wasn't what pushed him to the limit. His viral infection was causing more and more diagnostic programs to run in his reification hardware, and as a result more error messages kept coming up, taking up more memory space. Then I think the sight of you pushed him over the edge.'

'Is that mathematical program actually running now?'

'It did shut down, but out of interest I recorded some of it. Now I'm running it cyclically with some strong memory he has retained, to keep him locked in a virtual loop.'

'How's his viral condition now?'

'Pretty far gone – at about the stage you were at when you resorted to using your nanochanger.' She gestured to the others. 'Aesop over there is nowhere near as bad.

In fact there are many in a worse state aboard this ship, and,' she gestured, 'already in these tanks.'

'Bones?' Keech asked.

'He's beyond infection. Take a look.'

Keech moved over to Bones and pulled back the reif's hood. A bare skull grinned up at him, its lensed eyes shuttered and the tip of a metallic tongue protruding between the teeth. He opened the reif's jacket for further confirmation, and eyed the bare ribcage exposed.

'He was called Bones when he was still alive,' Keech noted.

'Perhaps it amused Bloc to have him resemble his name. I wouldn't be surprised. So, what about Bloc? What do you want me to do with him?'

'Can you shut down his control unit? I'd rather he retained no control over these two.'

'Doubtful. I've had a look and it's closely interfaced with his memory crystal, so one mistake might wipe him out' – she shrugged – 'which would be no bother to me, but is obviously not what you want. How did you know about it anyway? Forlam said you already knew about the thralls.'

'Bloc was a student of esoteric or alien technologies even before he died. I found that out when I was researching him, just as I found out that some time back he had purchased spider thralls through an agent on Coram. That he had already used the technology seemed the only proper explanation to account for Aesop and Bones. Altering a Prador thrall to control memcrystal would have been no problem to him.' Keech walked back and stood looking down at Bloc again. 'Would our best option be him shutting down his own hardware?'

Erlin stared at Keech for a long moment, running her

fingers across the scar tissue on her neck. She frowned, then realization dawned.

'My recent problems must have scrambled my brain,' she said. 'It happened to you: the changer rebuilds the organic brain and then the program causes a complete download to it from the memcrystal before shutting the whole memplant down. Of course, this is presupposing the organic brain does get rebuilt fully.'

Keech shrugged. 'It is a risk, agreed.'

Erlin nodded, then unplugged the optic cable from Bloc's cleanser, wrapped it round her palm console, then put the console aside. From a table nearby on which she had piled Bloc's clothing prior to examining him, she retrieved his nanochanger. On pressing an inset button on top of Bloc's cleanser, a lid flipped up exposing a recess for the lozenge-shaped changer.

'Well, here goes.' Erlin pressed the changer into place, while Keech moved over to stand beside her. The lozenge clamped down and from all around its edges extruded small golden tubes which mated into sockets in the cleanser. The status lights then turned blue. 'Okay, let's get him into a tank and all connected up. He'll have to forgo his intended prior visit to the Little Flint.' She glanced around at the other tanks in use. 'He won't be alone, anyway.'

Half an hour later as Bloc was floating in his tank, autodoc clinging to him and optics plugged in through his suppurating flesh, the door banged open. Glancing past Keech while she wiped her hands, Erlin observed a crowd of Hoopers dragging in other Hoopers bound up squirming in sail cloth.

'Looks like my workload just increased,' she muttered.

*

The body of her rapist assuaged her hunger for a little while, but her insides processed his meat like a combined waste compactor and acid bath. Her guts bubbling and squirming, she crashed through the forest sending lung birds honking from their perches in the branches. Then, encountering a stand of putrephallus over which more of those horrible baggy birds squabbled, she turned and made her way down to the shore and into the sea. She could feel the organ he had penetrated expanding in slow pulses within her. Her ichor was thundering in her veins. Sometimes it became difficult to think.

Bloated and heavy she no longer floated, and had to push herself off the bottom again and again. Her hunger returned with confusing speed so, moving deeper, she began feeding upon negative-buoyant masses of young rhinoworm corpses. Then a hint of a taste permeated the water, and with it the slow return of vague memory. Yet it was a difficult memory to hold onto, since eating and that *growth* inside her now seemed so much more important. Bouncing aimlessly along the seabed she tried to regain her earlier sense of purpose, and to recall how it had felt to swim. It was only happenstance that took her to where that taste in the water grew stronger. And her intellect made another bid for freedom.

Something huge churned the water directly above her, as a shape, vaster than any heirodont, turned. Gazing up at the enormous hull, she tried to control her fear, her overpowering urge to return to feed in the island shallows and . . . something else. Then recognizing the smaller hull being dragged around in the wake of the larger one, she threw all her effort into launching herself from the bottom, using her skirt of blow-water jets to force herself higher. She was thirty metres down

from it when the smaller hull began to draw away. With
one more jet, she snaked out her longest tentacle and
snagged the ship's rudder. Then, her grip failing, she
pulled quickly closer and whipped out another tentacle.
Now the sea was roaring past her and she could not
understand how the ship could be pulling away with
such force. Another tentacle, then another two. Drawing
herself in, utterly exhausted, she clamped her skirt
around the hull and sucked down to stick there. In a
moment she would reach up to see what she could find.
In a moment though, after just a little rest . . .

Sniper observed that Vrell's ship was taking the slowest
route into orbit, climbing steadily around the planet
rather than going straight up. The Warden's sat-eyes were
everywhere above the ascending ship, and above them
Vrost maintained position. The ship came lumbering up
out of the well, its gravmotors continually going on and
off, sometimes dropping it back many kilometres, and
the fusion drive partially igniting then extinguishing.

'Does he think Vrost is going to believe that wounded
bird act for even a moment?' asked Thirteen. The little
drone had purposely fused itself into place on Sniper's
armour, and now resembled some baroque marine
encrustation.

'There's a double bluff here somewhere,' Sniper
replied. It was all an interesting game with ostensibly
only one outcome. Once clear of the planet, Vrell's
spaceship would be obliterated. Sniper, staying low over
the sea just behind the escort of drones and armoured
Prador surrounding the ship, was trying to fathom what
was really going on.

'Then perhaps he thinks he can manage a U-space

jump before Vrost gets a chance to smear him across the sky?' Thirteen suggested.

'Vrell's options are limited. More likely he hopes to ram Vrost's ship – to go down fighting. That's what an adolescent Prador would do,' said Sniper.

'But Vrell is an adult.'

'Take a look at this,' said Sniper, transmitting some image files across to Thirteen. The little drone fell silent, its coms shutting down as it applied its system space to study the images. Could Vrell properly be described as an adult, or even a Prador at all? Thirteen could decide that for itself after viewing what Sniper had obtained from the camera in the drone cache of Vrell's ship. Sniper felt the images indicated otherwise, just as they had for these armoured creatures ahead, for one of them had been driven from its armour in that cache. Sniper tried some more surreptitious scans, but again could not penetrate their defences. What was going to happen here seemed almost foregone, and it seemed his prime task now was to gather intelligence by whatever means.

'Sniper, what are you doing?' the Warden abruptly asked.

In reply Sniper sent the images to the AI as well.

After a pause the Warden replied, 'I see, you wish further confirmation. My own attempt to probe that Prador armour resulted in the destruction of both it and its occupant. What are you hoping to achieve here?'

Sniper now sent a snippet from a lecture he had recorded several centuries ago. 'During any conflict, combatants tend to drop their guard in matters not directly related to that same conflict.'

'Yes, Sniper, I have fifty thousand hours of recorded intelligence briefings available to me. Why do you think

I now have every one of my sat-eyes deployed in the area?'

'It's not just that,' the old drone finally replied. 'Something else is going on here. And when I've figured out what that fucking Vrell is up to, I might be able to find some further opening.'

'Very well. Keep me informed.' The Warden withdrew.

Sniper continued cruising behind the pack, trying every subtle scan he could manage. He began to wonder if, for the benefit of ECS Intelligence, he should bring one of those armoured Prador down once the shooting started, and squirrel it away for later examination. Analysing recorded events, however, he realized that was not viable. As well as the one indirectly caused by the Warden, similar minor fusion explosions had occurred both under the sea and in the air during the earlier attack upon Vrell's ship – doubtless the result of armoured individuals getting damaged beyond hope of recovery, and therefore self-destructing. Vrost would not be leaving any of his troops behind intact, not even as anything more than radioactive gas.

It was while he was running a narrow-beam microwave scan that Sniper incidentally noted a disturbance in the water below him. He peered down to see something speeding along underwater. At first he suspected a heirodont, but it was travelling too fast. Just as he redirected his microwave scan downwards, the object broke the surface, revealing itself as one of the armoured King's Guard. It had probably just self-repaired on the ocean bed and was now hastening to rejoin its comrades. Suddenly he realized that his scan was not being blocked, so redirected all his scanning gear downwards just as the Prador emerged from the ocean. Sniper found he was getting everything. The images from the camera in the drone cache had provided much information, but now scanning across the spectrum gave him so very much more. Momentarily shutting off his AG, he dropped down beside the armoured entity and probed deep, mapping the architecture of the armour and the entire external and internal anatomy contained within it. His recording of its brain structure would surely be invaluable to forensic Polity AIs. He then recognized scan returns similar to those obtained from Spatterjay wildlife. This Prador was infected by the virus, which had wrought its evident mutations.

Suddenly the Prador turned towards him, then like a woman realizing her blouse is undone, began buttoning up its screens. Too late. Sniper now knew the shape of the beast. And the physical sample he retained inside himself from the drone cache gave him its genetic blueprint. The secret was out.

It was only as the armoured Prador sped away that Sniper realized something else about that individual, and he began laughing to himself over the ether.

'What's so funny?' asked Thirteen, reopening com.

'Yes, do tell,' interjected the Warden, rather sharply.

'In good time,' said Sniper. 'In good time.' Then he locked the Warden out.

As she sat viewing the comscreen on her desk, Olian Tay felt more than pleased with her new incarnation as president of the Bank of Spatterjay. The huge wealth she was accumulating enabled her to pursue her life's work: her museum. It just kept on growing as new evidence of Hoop's rule here was unearthed. Items were also turning up on other worlds, for which mostly she was able to outbid the competition, and now, with the recent détente between the Polity and the Third Kingdom, she was able to purchase some things directly from the Prador themselves. Currently her bid for a man-skin coat once worn by Jay Hoop's wife, Rebecca Frisk – who was floating in her preserving cylinder just outside the door – was the highest. She was also very excited by the possibility of actually travelling to the Kingdom to view at first hand Frisk's erstwhile home on a Prador world. Everything was going wonderfully well. Till she heard the sawing explosions.

Olian stood up and walked around her desk. At that same moment the two skinless Golem currently serving out their Cybercorp indenture with her, and whom she had named Chrome, both of them, because she could not tell them apart, pushed themselves away from their normal stance at the walls.

'What was that?' she wondered.

'It sounded like the blast of an energy weapon,' one of the Golem replied succinctly.

'Then I suggest you both arm yourselves. We're closed to any withdrawals at present and I would like us to remain that way.'

One of them palmed the lock to a wall cabinet and opened it. He took out a riot gun and tossed it to his companion, then selected a Batian carbine for himself. As the two of them headed out into the foyer, Olian followed just in time to hear a hideous shrieking from beyond the twin doors accessing the museum. The Golem paused and glanced round at her; at her nod they opened the doors and went through. After a moment she stepped after them, then quickly to one side where she groped back to thumb the touch-plate right beside the pillar containing David Grenant. The lights came on.

The far doors into the museum were still closed, but there was obviously something wrong. By the statue of the Skinner loomed what appeared to be some metallic edifice, and the floor all around it was scattered with debris. She looked up and noted a large hole through the ceiling, then down again as that edifice screamed and extended wide metallic wings. Turquoise fire flashed between it and the statue. Olian threw herself to the floor as a boom resounded, followed by the sound of something collapsing.

Blinking to clear her vision, she looked up to see the Skinner statue was now a pile of smoking rubble. The other thing turned – and she now recognized the Golem sail whose arrival on Spatterjay had been the source of much speculation. One of her own Golem zipped back past her, and back into her office, returning with a heavy-duty laser of the kind normally mounted on a tripod.

'We may not be able to stop him,' the Golem warned, before darting off back into the museum.

At that point the other skeletal guard stepped out from his hiding place behind a thrall display case and started firing explosive shells at the Golem sail. Hitting one after another, his shots drove the sail gradually backwards but seemed to cause no damage. The intruder's eyes glowed and then a particle beam swept across the room, chopping off the Golem's legs before striking the display case. The Golem collapsed. Nothing happened to the display for a moment, but even tough chainglass could not withstand such abuse. It emitted a screeing sound escalating out of human hearing range, then flew apart in a glittering explosion. Olian quickly crawled backwards into the foyer, closing the doors behind her. Flinching at the sound of another case getting wrecked, she returned to her office and took a seat behind her desk.

Punching controls on her console she said, 'Warden, I seem to have a little problem here.' When there came no reply, she tried routing through the planetary server, then glared at the holding graphic on her screen. It meant the Warden was not answering calls.

From inside the museum, closer now, came the thrumming snap-crack of a laser firing. Olian closed her eyes and shook her head. This made no sense at all. What would a Golem sail want here? She began to stand up, then checked herself. If two Golem guards could do nothing, then there was nothing she could do either. Sitting down again, she grimaced upon hearing the foyer doors being ripped off their hinges, then ducked down as her own office door exploded inwards. She peered up over her desk just as the Golem sail loomed through, sat upright, flicking smouldering splinters from her jacket, then finally looked up.

'Yes, what can I do for you?'

The sail just stood there, half extending its wings, then drawing them back. Its mouth opened and closed as if it had lost the power of speech, and that dangerous glow advanced and retreated in its eyes.

'Olian Tay,' it finally said.

'Yes, I am. You do realize we are closed today?'

'Olian Tay . . . open the safe.'

Oh right, Olian thought, *a bank robbery.*

Erlin had learnt that the *Sable Keech*'s engines were steam-driven – the steam pumped directly from fusion-powered water purifiers – and, being Polity tech, could run at full speed almost indefinitely. The ship would therefore reach the Little Flint far ahead of schedule. Even so, she wondered if any of the reified passengers would survive to see that place.

Stooping over one tank, she observed its gross contents, studied readouts and sighed. Some of the reified passengers would never again inhabit their own bodies, and others were irretrievably dead. This one, for example, had just been turned into an organic broth by his nanochanger. Even his bones were gone. All that remained were his reification hardware and memcrystal, and even they were under attack.

Erlin keyed a certain sequence into her console, and watched as the opaque fluid began to swirl, then bubble. It was risky to just dump the contents of a tank like this, as though it was unlikely the nanites could survive in the surrounding environment – being specialized and with special requirements – some of them might. The liquid began to steam, the smell of it horribly like cooking stew. When she was finally satisfied, Erlin keyed in another instruction and the tank began to drain. But even now the liquid was still dangerous, which was why it drained into a purification plant in the bilge, where the water was evaporated off and the residue treated with diatomic acid.

Erlin had drained three similar tanks only this morning, and retrieved three memcrystals. The crystals themselves she externally flash-sterilized before scanning them for active nanites. One was corrupted – some mutation of the nanites from the individual's nanofactory eating into the crystal. Fifty-seven reifs had gone into the tanks, and thus far not one of them had attained resurrection. Fourteen in fact had been flushed into the purifier, and only nine of their memcrystals remained intact. Were she a reif herself, she would not think those good odds at all.

Erlin looked around. Forlam was still here – a Hooper with whom she felt a reluctant kinship – and she recognized Peck and one or two others of Ambel's crew scattered about the large room, carrying out tasks she had assigned to them. Still no sign of the Captain himself, though.

She walked over to Bloc's tank and peered inside. There was a lot of detritus floating around in the water, even more lying in a silty layer at the bottom, but she could see fresh new skin down one leg, where one large sludgy scab had fallen away, and a flexing pink hand. She checked the displays and confirmed that Bloc was undergoing download. He was near to resurrection now, and his memcrystal downloading to his organic brain. His control unit, attached to that crystal, was no longer within his mental compass. It seemed doubly ironic to Erlin that the one here most deserving to remain dead looked the most likely to live. Turning away she spotted a certain individual entering the Tank Room, and suddenly felt horribly guilty – a child knowing she has done wrong. He crossed the room and loomed beside her.

'An interesting and adventurous rescue attempt, I hear,' she managed, her mouth dry as she turned to him.

'It had its moments,' Ambel replied. He studied her closely. 'Did you need rescuing?'

'A sail performed that task when the danger was greatest to me.' She shrugged. 'Subsequent dangers were not so immediate. Bloc had no wish to harm me, just control me, and I doubt there was much even you could have done about giant waves and Prador spaceships.' She knew she was avoiding his implicit question.

'I asked you if you needed rescuing,' he said again.

She turned back to him. 'I don't think so.' She waved a hand at the chainglass tanks all around them. 'I am busy now, and will be busy for some time to come. Who can say what will happen then? As you once told me: I need to accumulate years.'

Ambel nodded thoughtfully. 'Ron tells me there's a nice bar just forard of here. You'll join me there later?'

'I will.' Erlin returned to her work and he moved away, calling out the occasional question to those of his crew who were scattered about the room. His implicit question had been, '*Do you want to die?*' She felt she did not, realizing that a giant whelk had taught her that lesson, and that her time here aboard the *Sable Keech* had only confirmed it. But she knew that such a feeling could be deceptive. Was her unconscious even now planning her next suicide attempt, or had she at last, having passed her quarter millennium, crossed some watershed?

Janer smiled to himself as he brought the submersible up against the jetty. Wade, moving slowly across the sky suspended from his grav-harness, must have been experiencing some difficulties for Janer to overtake him. That was good, for Janer could now do what he suspected Wade would not. Ahead, just before pulling in, he had observed Zephyr spiralling down to Olian's island. Now, staring at the screen, he registered expressions of confusion from Hoopers peering down at the vessel in search of its mooring ropes. He touched the anchor icon on the control screen, and heard the double thumps of four harpoons, trailing anchor wires, fired from the sub to the left and right, angled down into the seabed. Four reel icons then appeared, with an overlay of a top view of the submersible and the nearby jetty. He ignored the icons, touched the sub picture and dragged it across to the jetty. The anchor wires adjusted themselves accordingly, slackening on one side and pulling taut on the other, drawing the vessel up against the adjacent support beams. Janer then abandoned his seat and climbed out.

Now the Hoopers appeared to be less interested in finding mooring ropes than in something else that was happening inland. Others were emerging onto the decks of their ships to peer in the same direction.

As he stepped down onto the planking, Janer queried the nearest of them: 'What happened?'

The Hooper, a bulky woman who had lost all her hair and compensated for that with a white skull tattoo of writhing snakes, glanced at him. 'Explosion, back at Olian's.'

Janer immediately broke into a run.

'Wait a minute!' the woman called, but he ignored her and kept going.

Wade would be setting down on the island very soon, but what would the Golem do then? Zephyr had already killed two organic sails, and was now blowing things up. That meant the time for negotiation and metaphysical discussion was over. Janer did not want to bet Spatterjay's whole economy and biosphere on Wade's reluctance to act. Entering a street lined with stalls, he drew his gun. All around, Hoopers and a few Polity citizens were stepping outdoors to see what all the commotion was about. He dodged between them and soon caught sight of the entrance to Olian's museum. Hoopers were gathered there around the closed, and firmly bolted, doors. Janer ran up behind them and pushed through.

'Can you get in?' he asked of those Hoopers right next to the doors.

'I don't think so,' said a figure standing beside him – he smelt the pipe tobacco before he recognized Captain Sprage. 'These doors were made to keep out Hoopers, including even us Captains. Not very trusting, Olian.'

Two others stepped up beside Sprage. One, tall and long-limbed, bore a disconcerting similarity to the Skinner, the other was red as chilli pepper and built like a barrel.

Sprage introduced them: 'Captains Cormarel and Tranbit . . . I don't think you've met them, young Janer.'

Janer glanced at them, then around at the crowd. If he fired his weapon here, people could get hurt – and annoyed. And these were not the kind to have annoyed at you. 'I can't explain now – it would take too long. Sorry, but I have to get inside.'

He turned and hurried away, hearing the squat Tranbit say, 'Hasty lad, there.'

Janer pushed back through the crowd and around the corner of the museum. The ground here was covered with modified grass, greenish purple, stretching back a hundred metres towards the dingle. The long stone side-wall of the building was unrelieved by windows, and Janer ran along it to where it abutted Olian's bank itself. Stepping back five metres, he knocked his gun to its non-standard setting, pointed and fired.

A large section of stonework, all of three metres in circumference, disappeared with a screaming crash, then reappeared as an explosion of dust and compacted stone shrapnel. Janer hit the ground, hot flakes of stone dropping all over him. Then, with his ears ringing, he shoved himself up again and groped forward through the thick cloud to find the hole created. Visibility inside the museum was as bad, but at least he had some idea of the direction he must go. He stumbled on something, glimpsed a Golem metal skull amid the debris, and moved beyond it to a chainglass cylinder lying on the ground. Inside this he observed Rebecca Frisk writhing slowly and dragging her fingernails down the glass. He shivered and stepped over her towards the wrecked door.

Then suddenly a figure was standing beside him.

'This is not your concern,' said Isis Wade.

Janer turned abruptly, bringing his weapon to bear on the Golem. But he was far far too slow – Wade's hand snapped down, caught his wrist and squeezed. Janer yelled as his wrist bones ground together. As he dropped his gun, Wade kicked it clattering into the settling murk.

'I'm sorry,' the Golem murmured, then almost in an eyeblink, was gone.

'Fuck,' said Janer, rubbing his wrist. He stumbled off in search of the singun. Without it he could do nothing.

'Open the door or I will remove it,' demanded the Golem sail.

Olian decided it was pointless to pretend she could not get them inside. The wreckage behind her ably demonstrated the sail's lack of patience. She took a big iron key from her pocket, twisted it in the lock, and pushed the door open. The space beyond used to be her house's main living room. Now it was clear of all furnishings, which had been relocated to her new home built to one side of the museum. Stepping in, she glanced up at the security drone suspended from the ceiling, and quickly stepped aside.

'Intruder, identify yourself! Verbal permission not—'

The sail's eye's flashed, and the drone exploded into molten slag that spattered right to the far windows. Olian ducked, her arms over her head, as five more explosions ensued. When she looked up, she saw the five weapons pits in the walls had been turned into smoking cavities.

'Open the false wall,' the sail instructed.

Olian considered her rehearsed line: '*The security system has now put a five-hour lock-down on the safe. I cannot open it*' but she doubted this one would have any truck with that. The creature had just demonstrated a surprising knowledge of what this room contained.

'House computer, open false wall,' she murmured reluctantly.

The wall seemingly holding the two windows began to slide sideways. Their view of distant dingle blinked out, revealing them as screens. A large, utterly smooth, oval door came into view behind.

'Open the safe,' the Golem sail ordered.

Olian paused, remembering the last time she had been forced to do so – by Rebecca Frisk and her Batian mercenaries. On that occasion, Olian had duped them, managing to slip into the safe and close it again from the inside. Even so, one of the bitch's mercenaries had still managed to shoot her in the leg. And this Golem sail, with a particle cannon under its mental control, would possess reactions a hundred times faster, so attempting a similar ruse would be futile.

'House computer, cancel lock-down and open atmosphere safe,' she said flatly.

With a deep clonk and a clicking hiss, the door – a great bung of Prador exotic metal – swung open to reveal a highly polished spherical chamber. In here Olian had once kept her prized possession: David Grenant. Now it contained stacks of brushed-aluminium boxes.

'Aaah,' the sail hissed.

It advanced with its waddling sail gait and ducked its long neck inside the safe. After peering at the boxes for a moment, it struck down like a snake, catching the boxes in its teeth and ripping them open, and slinging them around the interior of the safe. Chainglass vials spilt out, their stoppers coming loose, till sprine spread over the floor like red sand.

What's this?

Olian backed away as far as she could get – breathing sprine dust could be fatal to her.

Satisfied with the chaos it had made, the sail backed out. Stretching out its wing like a cloak, it coughed up a small polished sphere and spat it into one of its spider-claws. It then swung round on Olian with its back to the safe. Dipping its head towards her, it blinked and said, 'You can go.' Then it turned to face the door through which they had entered. Olian got out of there just as fast as she could.

Aesop stared up at the pipework on the ceiling, and felt some species of joy. He was free, he could feel it: Bloc no longer controlled him. And he had survived: he had not been eaten by a hooder, nor destroyed in some mad scheme of Bloc's. Here, now, strapped to a table, he was freer than he had been in years. But what had happened?

Vaguely he recollected the fight in the bridge, then some kind of mad revelation and an overloading backlash from Bloc. He realized that his current vagueness about it all was because he could not connect his previous actions while under Bloc's control to the self he felt now. A face loomed over him, peering down.

'You're not too bad,' said the woman, Erlin. 'But, like them all, you're infected with the Spatterjay virus. What are we to do with you?'

Another face then appeared. It was familiar, but for the moment he could not place it.

'Under Polity law, no guilt attaches to him for everything he did while under Bloc's control,' said the man. 'But he and Bones probably killed Bloc before that.'

'Debatable,' said Erlin, turning to the man, 'what with Bloc coming back to life. Would the charge be assault?'

'They almost certainly killed others before Bloc.'

'Yes, I imagine they did,' Erlin replied. 'But you realize that you might not be allowed to take any of them back?'

'Yes, I understand that. Polity law is not the only law.'

Suddenly Aesop realized who the man was. It was Sable Keech. He felt a surge of some unidentifiable emotion, then wondered why. Such would be the reaction of a cultist, or one of Bloc's Kladites – but it was not for Aesop. He began thinking hard about his present situation. If Keech took them back, they would be AI-probed and all their crimes revealed. No possible plea would then prevent their complete erasure from existence.

'I won't cause any trouble,' he said to Erlin.

'And what about your friend?' she asked, looking to one side.

Aesop glanced over and saw Bones, also strapped down, watching them.

'He'll be fine,' he said. 'He'll do what I tell him.'

Erlin gazed down at him and gave a tight little smile he very much did not like. 'Neither of you will cause any trouble.' She turned aside and crooked her finger. Aesop raised his head in time to see four Hoopers approaching. He started to wonder if his earlier happiness had been a little premature. Then Erlin reached down and began undoing his restraints. Once she had released his hands, he began to free himself. While the Hoopers looked on, she walked over and began to detach the restraints from Bones, too. Keech did not look at all happy about this.

'Where's Bloc?' Aesop asked.

'Bloc is in a tank, and it looks likely he'll come out of it alive,' Keech replied. 'I'm confident he'll be coming back to the Polity with me to answer for his crimes.' He glanced at Erlin and grimaced. 'Old Captains permitting.'

'He could answer for them here.' Bones now sat up.

'We leave him,' Aesop said, studying his companion, though there was nothing to see. A skull could wear no expression.

'Why?' asked Bones.

Before anyone else could reply, Erlin interjected, 'There's no need for threats or for discussion.' She turned to one of the Hoopers. 'Forlam, you have your instructions?'

Forlam nodded.

'What are you going to do with us?' Aesop hurriedly took off his last restraints and removed himself from the table. He then glanced round at the other tables, most of whose occupants seemed to be Hoopers – there were just one or two who might be successful resurrectees. He knew that many had gone into tanks and that there had been many failures.

Erlin eyed Bones as he too stood up, then turned to Aesop. 'You'll be confined in Bloc's stateroom until some decision is made about you. If you attempt to leave that room, Forlam will then follow his Captain's instructions. What were they, Forlam?'

Forlam smiled. It was not a nice smile. 'Tear off their arms and legs and chuck them over the side.'

As two of the Hoopers took Aesop and Bones by the arms and led them to the door, Aesop experienced startlingly clear memories of the crimes committed by himself and his partner before their reification. Bloc's murder had been just one of many – but no one here knew that for certain. Keech might have some intimation, but as yet no proof. He and Bones were culpable of nothing they had done while under Bloc's control. If the Old Captains decided against them being extradited under Keech's custody, it was just possible they might survive this. Then he realized all his hopes were based on a simple premise: that, like Polity AIs, the Old Captains would consider them innocent of crimes committed while under Bloc's control. He glanced aside and tried to read the expressions of those Hoopers close around him – probably men whose companions had been killed by the hooder he himself had led into the encampment on Mortuary Island. Only Forlam showed any sign of emotion, and what Aesop read in his face was not at all reassuring.

*

'Who are you?'

The woman stumbling towards him he immediately identified as Olian Tay.

'I have come to stop this,' said Wade.

She eyed his APW, naturally coming to the wrong conclusion. That was a last resort for him. He and Zephyr could resolve this between them.

'But what are you stopping?' she asked, as he moved past her.

Wade winced on experiencing a sudden doubt. He was not sure if he knew.

Out at sea, he had opened his internal hivelink via the runcible back to the planet Hive, but had found no reassurance there, and no advice. He had sensed only deep confusion, fear, anger, with an undertow of fractured and contradictory instructions:

Destroy Zephyr – destroy yourself – flee – load to crystal – die – live.

Faced with this coming from the mind from which he had earlier been copied, Wade had become increasingly reluctant to face Zephyr, until at one point he found himself just hanging motionless in the sky. He realized that the conclusion to his and Zephyr's long-running debate might be no resolution for either of them. It was the sight of the submersible moving on ahead that had finally jerked Wade into motion again. That was Janer, almost certainly, and the man would have no reservations about using the weapon he carried. Arriving at Olian's and descending through the damaged roof, Wade had felt he might be too late, even though he could still hear the mad mutter of Zephyr's mind. Stopping Janer had been necessary – the man just did not grasp what was at stake, and would strike even though it might not be necessary.

The door into the vault room was open. Wade paused to one side of it and sent, '*I cannot allow you to do this.*' But no reply returned over the ether. Wade stepped round the door jamb, abruptly squatting and levelling his weapon. Sprine was scattered all around inside the open vault. Zephyr stood there, holding a pressure grenade certainly full of the virus – seemingly waiting for something? Obviously Zephyr wanted to be dissuaded from its present disastrous course. He opened his mind to the Golem sail, totally, and began transmitting all that he knew, all he had recently learned. He replayed all the arguments at high speed, created and then collapsed all the relevant logic structures, laying out his final case. This could bring about their resolution, in this moment of the sail's crisis. The surge of information would overwhelm its confused mind, and then it could do nothing but agree.

But the information he sent just seemed to drop into a black pit – and Wade recognized despair. He understood then just what his other half awaited: the enemy, Death. He increased the pressure on his weapon's trigger, but found he could not pull it back all the way, because then the irrevocable decision would have been made. The pause lasted only microseconds – but an age in Golem terms. Then Zephyr's agonized cry filled the room, and the Golem sail fired its particle cannon. The turquoise blast struck Wade in the chest, hammering him back against the wall.

I'm going to die, he realized, *I waited too long.*

On the planet Hive, up on its promontory, the building resembled a World War II concrete pillbox, with horizontal windows gazing slit-eyed across the lowlands. Beyond the bare and mounded earth surrounding it, which further lent the appearance of a recently installed machine-gun post, lay dying algae gathered in green and yellow drifts amidst the vines, wide-leafed rhubarbs and cycads. Snairls, ranging from the size of a man's head to creatures as large as a sheep, grazed on this abundance. The air immediately around the building seemed filled with smoke, but closer inspection revealed this to be clouds of hornets, killing each other.

Physically infiltrating the ancient mind's redoubt had been impossible at first, so the young mind's only means of access had been either by conventional inter-hive radio or by intercepting and interpreting spillover transmissions between individual hornets. The former means had slowly degraded – the ancient mind's communications becoming increasingly contradictory and opaque – and the latter was swiftly following the same course. The old mind was clearly fragmenting. But now that very fragmentation offered an opportunity to actually get inside both the redoubt and, by intercepting direct hornet-to-hornet transmissions, the ancient mind itself.

The six hornets did originally belong to the old mind, but the youngster had isolated them, shutting off their radio communication with the rest of the mind, then inside them installed transmitters tuned to his own mental coding, but also linked to their original transmitters. Such a ploy could never work on a guarded mind, for such minds constantly monitored their own function. The six of them flew into the swarm gathered around the redoubt, and through their faceted eyes the young mind observed hornets attacking each other in mid-air, chewing in with mandibles or stinging each other to death.

Now entering this swarm, the youngster began to pick up straight-line neuro-radio transmissions between hornets, and found that the mental coding of the old mind was beginning to vary. The young mind identified six variations: five still very close to the original, but one that was wildly astray. He lost four of his own six hornets to attacking insects before confirming that the attackers all used that disparate code. The old mind was now fully divided into two parts: one finite and hostile, the other in the process of breaking into yet another five. The surviving two spies finally entered the redoubt.

Inside it, paper nests grew like bracket fungi from the walls, layer upon layer of them, shelf upon shelf. In here the battle was horribly intense and the floor piled deep with dismembered hornet bodies. The young mind noticed that the hostile hornets were all issuing from one particular conglomeration of nests and, though they were the aggressors, they were losing because the defending nests contained five times their population. But the place contained not just paper nests and drifts of hornet corpses. Fluorescent nano-circuitry adorned the walls, linked to various machines scattered here and in the labyrinth of rooms beyond: furnaces, U-space transmitters, self-contained robotic laboratories and manufactories.

The young mind lost another of its two remaining spies, chopped to pieces by two attackers, that hornet's vision fading as its severed head fell to the crowded floor. The surviving one, settling on the curved cowling over a manufacturing unit for hornet crystorage boxes, he now fully opened to the surrounding neuro-radio traffic. Insane screaming fed through, along with a virus-like mental program aiming for division, for partition.

The youngster swiftly realized this program was no new creation, but in fact one older than the human race. Trying to hold his own sanity together, the young mind attempted to withdraw, tried to shut down the terrifying link. Underneath the screaming he detected a deep sadness – and a decision being made. From one of the slitted windows, a communication laser swivelled on gimbals and began firing. Also, an enclosed lens-shaped autofactory developed hot spots as contained furnaces were deliberately overloaded. Paper nests began to burn. The last com the young mind received from its spy in the bunker was the feeling of mandibles closing between its thorax and its tail, and a wall of flame falling towards it. Meanwhile, from other eyes at a distance, the young mind watched smoke and flame belch from the redoubt.

The old mind had chosen death rather than dissolution.

Wiping dust off his gun against his shirt, Janer tried to study its displays even as he ran. He passed Olian Tay, who was leaning against a wall and gazing back towards the vault room, raised a hand to her, then nearly fell flat on his face as Zephyr's particle-weapon fire lit up ahead of him. No time to pause. He reached the vault room door and stepped through, aiming his gun at Zephyr, looming upright with wings fully spread, turquoise flame blazing from its eyes. He glimpsed Wade over to one side, pressed up against the wall and burning. Then the fire suddenly ceased.

Janer pulled the trigger of his weapon; everything seeming to happen with nightmare slowness.

Too slow.

The Golem creature could move just as fast as Wade,

yet it chose not to. Zephyr's head was turned slightly towards Janer as the singularity generated, encompassing the sail in a collapsing sphere. Then, a light as bright as the sun, a wash of heat, and a blast that flung Janer back out into the corridor. He was slammed against the wall and began to slide down it but, his body already toughened by the Spatterjay virus, he remained conscious.

Why such a blast?

Then he realized: power supplies inside the Golem sail for itself and its weapons. He was lucky the explosion had not taken out the whole building. He lay there for a moment feeling dazed, then reached up tentatively to touch the burns on his face, and to check if there was still any hair on his head. Within the vault room he observed falling ash and gleaming fragments of ceramal scattered across the floor. One distorted claw, which had obviously been outside the sphere, now rested on a pile of charred sprine crystals. He was still staring at that when some blackened object dragged itself slowly around the door jamb.

'I should not have been fast enough,' Janer said. 'It was Golem.'

Wade was missing everything from below his sternum, and his metal bones still glowed at that severance point. His remaining syntheflesh was blackened to a crisp, and fell off in smoking chunks as he moved. He paused, made some clicking and buzzing sounds.

'You – should – not – havebeen,' Wade finally agreed, tiny embers glimmering in the air before his mouth, his skeletal jaw making chewing motions.

'Then why was I faster than a Golem?'

'Zephyr – wanted – todie.'

'Seemed reluctant to let you provide that service.'

'Icould – notkill – me.'

Janer absorbed that and let it go. He realized he was still holding his singun, which he pointed at Wade. 'Do *you* want to live?'

'I – haveto – thereis only – me.'

Janer supposed this was about as much sense as he was likely to get. He holstered his weapon and heaved himself to his feet.

21

Whelkus Titanicus:
this name applies to just one kind of deep-ocean-dwelling
whelk, and should not be confused with the adult forms of frog
and hammer whelks which, though large, do not grow to one
tenth the size of this behemoth. Titanicus can weigh more
than a hundred tons and stand twenty metres high. The preg-
nant female of this species gives birth to a brood of about a
hundred young, and guards them while they feed and grow in
the less inimical island shallows. When the youngsters reach a
weight of about half a ton, and their shells harden, the mother
leads them gradually into the depths. Only 10 per cent sur-
vive the journey down to the oceanic trenches. They there feed
upon anything available, but their main diet consists of giant
filter worms rooted up from the bottom. Virally infected as are
most of the other local fauna, the large adults are nearly
invulnerable, and it is speculated that specimens of this whelk
may be even older than some sails. It is also possible that their
survivability is enhanced by either conscious or unconscious
control of the viral fibres inside them. This theory was pro-
pounded upon the discovery of a small population of these
creatures growing the internal digestive systems of herbivo-
rous heirodonts. They did this in a part of the Lamarck

Trench recently denuded of fauna by an underwater eruption yet burgeoning with kelp trees thriving on the mineral output of that same eruption. But the adult Whelkus titanicus does not get things all its own way, for it is itself prey to an equally titanic ocean heirodont, and young adult whelks can even be broken open by the large adult hammer whelks –

Captain Orbus walked shakily from the Tank Room and leant on the ship's rail, staring out across the nighted ocean. After a moment he took hold of what remained of the manacle around his right wrist, pulled hard on it, squeezed and twisted. With a dull crack the ceramal shattered and dropped clattering to the deck. They had only managed to keep him restrained because he had not been in his right mind. Foolish of them to think such flimsy restraints could hold an Old Captain. But what now? Soon someone would notice he was gone and come looking for him, probably with weapons, or with something a bit more potent like Captains Ron, Ambel or Drum. Would he then fight? Would he seek his usual release in violence?

Orbus shook his head, feeling tired and dried up inside. He realized something in him had changed. He looked back upon his life – the long centuries of sadistic brutality and the pointless cyclic nature of it all – and saw it for what it was: a waste. Perhaps now he should end it, cash in his New Skind banknotes for their equivalent weight in sprine and the oblivion that would bring him.

No, no way.

Yes, his life had been a waste up until now. But it did not need to continue that way.

'Captain . . .'

Orbus looked round and recognized Silister and Davy-bronte further along the deck from him. They both carried Batian weapons, and both looked scared. Hearing pounding feet from behind, he glanced over that way and saw Forlam and other Hoopers approaching, but slowly enough for Ambel and Drum, coming along behind, to catch them up. He could fight now, then many of them would go over the side to the stripped-fish locker before they brought him down. What havoc and pain he could wreak.

'What can I do for you?' he asked.

'You broke your restraints,' said Silister.

'Feeling a lot better now,' said Orbus. 'I ate big lice on the Prador ship and they staved off the change, so I'm not going to hurt anyone.'

Davy-bronte snorted contemptuously, levelling his weapon at Orbus's head. The Captain stared at him for a long moment, then turned to the other two Old Captains as they approached. He nodded towards the Tank Room.

'The restraints in there won't hold me. Where do you want me?' he asked them.

'Where would everyone be safe from you?' asked Ambel, striding forwards.

Drum remained a few steps back, slapping a heavy iron club against the palm of his hand.

'I don't reckon you've anything that could hold me on this ship. But, if you like, I'll walk straight back in there' – Orbus again nodded towards the Tank Room – 'and Erlin can stick a nerve blocker on me, shutting down everything below my neck.'

Ambel frowned. 'Yes, that would seem a sensible course.'

'But I'll hurt no one if you let me remain free.'

Ambel stepped up close to Orbus and stared into his face. After a moment he said, 'Show me your tongue.'

Orbus stuck it out. The end of it was still hollow, and he could feel the hard bits inside it where plug-cutting teeth had started growing. But the Intertox and nutrients had worked quickly in him. After a moment he closed his mouth.

Ambel studied him for a long minute, then gave a sharp nod. 'Find yourself an empty cabin – there's plenty available.'

Silister and Davy-bronte and the other gathered Hoopers looked on doubtfully.

Orbus smiled tiredly and turned back to the rail. 'In a moment,' he said. 'I'll take the night air for a while.'

Like a swarm of golden bees, the drones and the armoured Prador were beginning to disperse from around Vrell's ship. This could only mean a strike was imminent.

'That's one big mother,' observed Thirteen dryly.

Vrost's ship was now plainly visible above the planetary horizon: a vast grey mass in the shape of a Prador's carapace, but a shape losing definition under additional blockish structures, engines, weapons arrays and other less easily identifiable components. It was slowly turning and tilting, so its massive coil-gun – like a city block of skyscrapers turned horizontal and lifted above the main vessel on a giant curved arm – was all too visible. Sniper was surprised at Vrost giving so clear a signal of intent, but doubtless the Prador captain was now certain of making a kill. This close to the planet, engaging the U-space drive would tear Vrell's ship apart, and no other drive would be fast enough to get it out of range. And his vessel now also represented little danger to those on the planet below, since anything left of it would burn up in atmosphere.

'Let's listen to what they're saying,' Sniper suggested. Cruising along ten kilometres behind, he snooped into the uncoded communications between the two Prador, and relayed it to the little drone.

'Why have you ordered your troops back?' the voice from the ship asked.

Vrost hesitated, perhaps wondering whether it was worth wasting energy on the soon-to-be-dead, but his curiosity won out. 'I have moved them back because I do not wish them to get damaged.'

'Coming to you as I have, I have demonstrated that I am no threat. Why should I then be a danger to them?'

They were both playing games, with layers of bluff and counter-bluff. Vrost and Vrell both knew the outcome of this encounter, and they both knew that the other knew, but Vrost had to be wondering if Vrell had accepted the inevitable and intended to go down fighting, or whether he had something else in mind.

'You do represent a small threat to them,' agreed Vrost. 'But the shock wave and flying debris will shortly be a greater danger to them.'

'I do not understand,' said that voice again – Vrell.

Sniper understood the reason for this pretence at ignorance, more than did Vrost, and very much more than Vrell himself would be comfortable with. Sniper could tell Vrost everything, which would immediately scupper Vrell's plans. But Sniper's equally apportioned dislike and distrust of all Prador was tempered by his rapport with the underdog. In this situation he felt on Vrell's side. Both of him.

Sniper interrupted. 'Listen, shithead, very shortly Vrost will be cutting you and your ship to pieces. It doesn't matter what you do now, you are dead. Down on the surface you managed to fend off some attacks, but only because Vrost could not employ the full power of his weapons without taking out half the planet. Up here he does not need to be so restrained.'

'My name is not shithead,' replied the voice.

'Whatever,' Sniper snapped. '*You make a very clear target against the sky.*'

A long pause ensued while the voice's owner processed that.

On a private channel Thirteen asked, 'Sniper, what are you up to?'

On the same channel Sniper replied, 'Just reminding someone of something.'

'Who is this?' asked Vrost meanwhile.

'Just an old Polity war drone who hasn't lost his taste for turning Prador into crab paste,' Sniper replied. 'I can't tell you how it gladdens my heart to see you two trying to kill each other.'

'The state of your emulated emotions is not my concern.'

'Bite me. *Vrell*, while you're getting fried up here, why don't you send out that war drone of yours for a rematch against me? I definitely owe it at least that. It doesn't matter what *you* do now – you're dead.'

'I don't get this,' said Thirteen.

'You will.'

Sniper wondered how long it would take for the underlying message to be understood. Then he was

answered when weapons turrets on Vrell's ship launched
a swarm of black missiles. Many of them began exploding – quickly picked off by Vrost's defensive lasers.
Sniper tracked the rest, then grinned inside when their
own drives ignited, turning them sharply towards the
nearest of Vrost's outside forces. A particle beam ignited
space with turquoise fire from Vrost's ship. It splashed
against a hard-field before reaching its target, but on
Vrell's ship an explosion blew wreckage into space, as
the relevant field projector overloaded. Then the coil-
gun fired, but the projectile was intercepted with a similar blast from the particle cannon on Vrell's ship. A wash
of candent gas streamed past the smaller ship. The
guards and drones were meanwhile occupied in either
dodging or shooting down those missiles.

More salvos launched from both ships. Again the coil-
gun, again the interception. EM explosions began to
screw up Sniper's reception, so he did not track the one
missile with an atomic warhead that detonated only a
kilometre from Vrell's ship. The vessel tilted, some of its
armour peeling away in the blast, then it righted and
continued firing. Vrost's ship was now accelerating. A
nuke detonated on it, blasting a glowing cavity. Sniper
realized the Prador captain was positioning his ship
where there was no chance of any of his coil-gun missiles
being deflected down towards the planet. Now came a
U-space signature, weirdly distorted. Endgame.

'There,' said Sniper to Thirteen.

Seeing Vrell's war drone blasting out into space,
Sniper accelerated. Perfectly timed. The coil-gun began
firing repeatedly. Four intercepted projectiles turned
vacuum to furnace air. Power low for the particle cannons, the next was intercepted by hard-fields. A line of

explosions cut down Vrell's ship as projectors exploded. The projectile impacted, substantially slowed, but still slapped its target like some god's hand. With fires burning inside it, a huge chunk of the ship fell away.

'He's mine!' Sniper sent to those of Vrost's forces who had spotted Vrell's drone and were hitting it from all sides. 'Vrost, pull them off!'

Just then, Vrost suddenly discovered more critical concerns. Again that distorted U-space signature. Vrell's ship juddered partially out of existence, shedding tonnes of armour like potato peelings. Then, with a screaming sound over every frequency, it flashed out of existence completely.

'Fuck me,' said Thirteen.

The ship reappeared a hundred kilometres closer to Vrost's vessel, only it no longer looked like a ship. Now it was a meteor-sized mass of glowing metal travelling at tens of thousands of kilometres per hour. Vrost's forces rapidly lost interest in chasing the drone, which was now falling into atmosphere, blackened and distorted and obviously without functional drives. Vrost himself kept firing every weapon available at what remained of Vrell's ship. Sniper gave a salute to the hugely accelerated wreck, turned on his fusion drive, and himself dropped into atmosphere. Long minutes later, he spread his tentacles wide and came down on the burnt Prador drone like a hammer.

Having routed control to a joystick and simpler console mounted in the conning tower, Janer motored on the ocean's surface under a starlit sky, only it was not just stars that lit the heavens. There had been some massive explosions up there, the glowing fallout from which was

now dropping behind the horizon like a false sunset.
Janer supposed Vrell had finally met his end at the claws
of his fellow creature in orbit. He would find out eventually, but now he just wanted to get back to the *Sable
Keech*, which was visible ahead of him, and there make
use of the cabin and bed provided for him.

The big ship was slowing and turning, at the end of
its journey, and had it been necessary for him to go in
manually Janer doubted he could manage it, but the
submersible possessed an automatic docking system.
Before returning inside to start that procedure, Janer
scanned the nearby ocean. On the console, the map
showed him to be almost on top of the Little Flint, but
he had yet to see it. Then, a few hundred metres out, he
spotted that dish of black stone protruding from the
ocean. This is what it had all been about: their voyage
here. He hoped Bloc was satisfied.

With the hatch closed, Janer took up the primary controls and submerged the little vessel then, hoping he had
got things right, he called up the docking icon, selected
it with a tap of his finger, and sat back. The sub immediately dropped deeper and accelerated. Outside the
water was dark, so he turned on the lights, just in time
to see a frog whelk tumbling past, perhaps dislodged
from the nearby flint. A few minutes later a massive wave
of white water was boiling past above him, and he
glimpsed the *Sable Keech*'s hull. The sub turned and
rose, turned again and accelerated, then abruptly decel-
erated and veered. This happened twice more. Janer
realized that the sub's automatics were having problems
compensating for the movement of the ship. On the
third occasion a warning flashed up on his screen: IRIS
DOOR CLOSED. He hit the nearby icon to open the iris

and this time there was no deceleration. Suddenly the eye of the shimmer-shield was before him, then he was through it, the sub dropping half a metre with a shuddering crash. Clamps engaged, motors whined. He watched the sub enclosure revolve around him as the vessel was turned to present its nose to the iris, which was now drawing closed again.

Stepping out of the submersible, Janer looked around. It occurred to him that he should present himself to Captain Ron, but he felt too tired. Anyway, there was probably some signal on the bridge to tell the Captain that the sub had returned. He left the enclosure, climbed the nearest ladder up to a mainmast stairwell, cut through the seemingly unpopulated reification stateroom deck, then continued up a mizzen stairwell to the crew's quarters. On his way he saw no one, and was grateful for that. It was with a feeling of relief that he closed his cabin door behind him.

Janer collapsed on his bed, allowing himself to just experience that moment of pure luxury – but something was niggling at his mind. He stood, pulled his backpack from a cupboard, opened it and removed his stasis case. Hinging open the hexagonal container, he observed two hornets ready in the transparent reservoir. That figured. He groped in his pocket and found his hivelink, stared at it for a moment, then returned it to his pocket. *Not now* – sleep seemed so much more important.

Taylor Bloc stood on his apartment balcony gazing out across Haldon, watching the sun rise over the city. He blew on his delicate porcelain cup of tea and took a sip, relishing its tobacco pungency. Imported all the way from Earth, China tea was a luxury others would not appreciate as did he, but then his tastes were somewhat more sophisticated. It was a pure thing, not some India tea adulterated with one of a thousand popular additives, not base coffee doped with stimulant enhancers. Bloc left such things to others, to the normals who lived in their millions all around him working through their drear dull lives. He shook his head and smiled, turning away from the sunrise just as mathematical formulae, in a language he had only just come to know, began sleeting down the sky behind the city. In some part of himself he knew this was all wrong, but that part was frozen in horrified fascination as it observed those elements of this scene it knew so very well.

Bloc walked back into his apartment, placed his cup down on a table whose top was made of a polished slice of Prador carapace, and dropped into an armchair beside it. He then picked up the spider thrall he had recently purchased. This was the sort of thing that fascinated him: baroque technologies, grotesqueries, the unusual. He supposed it almost inevitable that his interests had led him to greater and greater involvement with the Cult of Anubis Arisen. But thereby another of his needs was fulfilled: the acquisition of wealth. It was pointless possessing such sophisticated tastes if one could not gratify them. Bloc placed the thrall back down on the table underneath whose surface a six-dimensional shape – following the strictures of the formulae in the sky outside – was trying to turn itself inside out. He smiled again, his foot passing through Calabi-Yau space as he turned to glance to his left. The inversion, folding part of the room into a fifth dimension, impinged on him as little as the formulae in the sky and the shape under the table. Instead it was the two figures now standing in the room that caused him to gasp in shock.

'How—?'

The one on the right, a mild-looking man dressed in a slightly rumpled disposable suit, raised a short squat gun with a snout like a pepper pot. The weapon thwacked, and something more than the force of the micropellets entering Bloc's face flung him up out of his seat and across the table. He lay there quivering briefly, then quickly freezing up. The Calabi-Yau shape passed over above him like an interdimensional bat.

Neurotoxin, thought one part of his mind. *What the fuck?* thought another.

'Hi there,' said the mild man, gazing down on him. 'I'm Aesop, and my partner here is called Bones.'

Bloc's horror grew. Neither of them had bothered to cover their faces, and now they had revealed their names to him. Both faces and names could of course be false, but there was something else in their attitude. They were undoubtedly here to kill him. Deep inside himself, that other part of him already knew this, and it dreaded the *how* of it. That part now listened to well-remembered words as Bones, a slim fair-haired youth, dragged him off the table and deposited him in an antique rocking chair.

'You do of course understand how very annoyed with you are certain parties?' said Aesop, setting up a little tripod on the table on which in turn he mounted an old-fashioned holocam.

Bloc tried to utter a name, could not even open his mouth. He could, however, just move his eyes, and observed Bones opening a premillennial doctor's bag. These killers had style and panache but, even though he recognized this, neither that thought nor the neurotoxin prevented his bowel from emptying when Bones began taking out antique stainless steel pliers, forceps, scalpels, electric bone saw and cauterizer.

The holocam now perfectly set up and operational, Aesop took out an anosmic receptor and set that running. This device would continually sample molecules from the air, so that whoever viewed this recording, probably in VR, would miss nothing, not even the odours. Smelling the results of Bloc's incontinence, Aesop waved a hand under his nose. 'Playing to your audience, Bloc?'

Bloc managed to make a grunting sound, as the toxin was wearing off. Aesop glanced at his partner, who immediately walked over to the balcony and drew the doors closed, shutting out all sounds of the city beyond.

'Nicely insulated apartment this. I had considered taking you elsewhere until I studied the building specs. No one will hear you scream here and, of course, my clients want to hear you scream. They want you to suffer a great deal, Taylor Bloc. So, while that toxin wears off, I'll tell you exactly what we are going to do to you.'

Bloc screamed, his voice echoing off into unknown dimensions of a Calabi-Yau shape stretched as taut as his own skin as Bones peeled that away. He howled as they twisted out his nails and broke each of his finger joints, yet found himself bewildered by formulae writhing through the air behind his tormentors. Every aspect of his agony, every curve and angle of his surroundings, was redolent with mathematical meaning. Every movement and every change generated complex numbers. His skin represented in two dimensions the surface of space, and Bones shoving a finger through it, a gravity well. The bone saw flung up fragments of formulae that coalesced in the air, then spattered the floor as blood and vomit. There was direction to the calculation, as there was direction to Bloc's torture. Both ended with the enveloping comfort of death, and finally he sighed away into blackness.

Taylor Bloc stood on his apartment balcony gazing out across Haldon, watching the sun rise over the city. He blew on his delicate porcelain cup of tea and took a sip, relishing its tobacco pungency. Part of him, deep inside, began screaming immediately.

No, not again . . .

Then, almost like a light being turned on, he woke trying to scream, but only a hoarse cawing sound issued from his mouth. Thrashing from side to side, he opened his eyes. The morning sunshine hurt, stabbing sharply into his head, and tears began pouring from his eyes. Where were they? Where were his killers? *I escaped?* But no, he did not escape – he died a painful undignified death, screaming, then his death continued . . .

Aesop and Bones . . . I killed them and now they serve me. Only dreams.

The morning sunshine was glaring through the windows. Bloc felt terrible. His body felt as if it had been beaten from head to foot, his teeth ached, he was cold, and his skin felt so sensitive that every small touch to it was almost a pain.

Then, he suddenly realized: *I feel.*

A deep shiver of awe ran through him, and he turned his head from side to side, locating himself on one of the restraint tables. He was not restrained, so he withdrew a hand from under the heat-sheet covering him – the thin insulating monomer snaking over his skin in an avalanche of sensation – and held it up before his face. It was baby pink, and as soft. The nails were just small crescents at the quick of each finger.

I'm alive.

With slow careful movements Bloc sat upright, the sheet sliding down his chest. It was almost too much – too much feeling for him to process. He groaned and in an instant Erlin was standing next to him, watching him with careful contempt.

'You'll get no nerve-conflict with your cybermotors,' she said.

'Keech . . .' he managed.

'Keech was augmented and remained so after his resurrection – that's where his problems came from. You, however, are not augmented in any way.'

He turned to look at her, and while doing so tried to call up routines and diagnostics, access his control unit, open the channels to Aesop and Bones. Nothing.

'What have . . . you done?' It was a strange experience, breathing and speaking, and trying to arrange the two so they did not conflict.

'When you downloaded from crystal to your organic brain and it became plain you were going to come out of the tank alive, I used an autodoc on you. It pulled every single power supply you contained, and I also used the doc to remove this.' She held up something: a grey box that sat easily in the palm of her hand, with a hexagonal box affixed to the side of it, linked by a ring of sealed optics. Bloc recognized his memplant and the attached control unit.

'What gives you the right to do that?' he hissed. He was just a living man now.

'The right?' she asked, her voice incredulous. She

shook her head, pulled a comlink from her belt and spoke into it. 'You wanted to know – well, he's awake now.'

From the link Ron's voice replied, 'Perfect timing.'

As Erlin returned the link to her belt, Forlam came over. He tossed a disposable coverall in Bloc's lap. 'Get dressed.'

'You can't give me orders. This is my ship. You are under my command; your Captain is employed by me.'

Forlam shrugged. 'Naked or otherwise – don't bother me.'

What are they going to do?

Bloc slid the heat-sheet all the way off him and stared down at his body. He looked perfect: no scars, just pink skin. His pubic hair was just a shadow above his genitals, and while staring at what Bones had once cut from him – an event all too clear in his mind after repetition – he felt a sudden surge of sexual feeling. He dressed, quickly, the coverall cold and textured against his aching skin. Finally clothed, he looked over to Erlin again.

'*I* did this,' he said. 'It was because of me this ship was built. It is because of me that reifications will live. I own this ship and it is under my command.'

Erlin shook her head. 'Let me bring you up to date and back to reality. Windcheater has imposed a large fine for the use of this ship's engines, which in turn has caused a cost overrun on this voyage. Apparently, by your original agreement, Lineworld Developments now own this ship – not that it will profit them much.'

Bloc felt a tightness in his throat, and his eyes were watering again. Then a hand that felt as if made of rock closed on his biceps. Forlam marched him forwards.

'You can't do this!' Bloc found it even hurt to shout.

'I created all this! I did this! I am bringing my people to the Little Flint!'

Walking behind them, Erlin continued, 'Most of your people are either in tanks or have shut themselves down. They don't much like the odds, since successful resurrections are only one in seven thus far. Many of them are likely to end up like Bones, and the true cultists among them are angry at what you have brought them to.'

Bloc fell silent then, and allowed Forlam to lead him out on deck. They might think they had won, but they did not know him well enough. They would pay for this. How he would make them pay.

It was a long fall to the bottom and, heavy now, the giant whelk had landed hard. She gazed up at the shapes hovering on the ocean surface and felt an immediate protective fear. Large predators up there ready to attack her? She needed to get back to shallows where she could protect the mass inside her, and where food creatures were small enough to easily subdue. She began dragging herself along the bottom, heading instinctively upslope to shallower waters. Momentarily she felt a strange disquiet. She vaguely recalled there had been an easier way of travelling than this, and something important she had to do. But that thought faded under the exigencies of the present.

The slope ahead was scattered with broken shells and black rhinoworm bones. Wherever she disturbed the bottom, white chalky clouds gusted up around her. This was good, so she deliberately stirred up more for concealment. At one point she heaved herself over an outcrop of dark rock, which splintered into sharp flat flakes under her grip. The higher she got, the steeper became the gradient and the more such outcrops she encountered. On one of them she encountered a flock of hammer whelks, and instantly began snatching them up to smash their shells against the dark stone and chomp them down. She devoured half of them before the rest slid out of reach, but did not pursue. Higher still, and frog whelks diverged from her path, bounding downhill in slow motion.

There were more leeches evident here, and any that came close she snatched up and consumed. While thus engaged she spotted a line trailing from one of her tentacles, which stirred some memory but not enough to bring it into focus. In irritation she caught the line with another tentacle and tried to tear it free. The fact that this hurt only made her angrier. Eventually she succeeded in tearing the hook from her flesh, then watched the discarded tangle drift off and sink from view. There was some emotion then – some feeling of loss – but she resolutely turned away.

Now only hard dark flint lay before her – a cliff rising steeply from the slope. She hesitated as another vague memory hinted that this might not lead to island shallows, but instinct drove her on. She climbed, finding plenty of easy tentacle holds on chalky nodules or in dark crevices. If this turned out not to be the kind of place she wanted, then she would move on – her drive to do so was imperative.

Drawn out rattling crashes jerked Janer from uneasy slumber.

Anchor chains.

He sat upright and looked around blearily. Stumbling from his bed he then collected clean clothing from his pack and headed for the showers. Upon his return he stared at the stasis case still exposed in the top of his pack, took it out, hinged it open and pressed his fingertip to the touch-plate beside the reservoir. This opened, releasing two hornets into the air. Inured to the creatures now, he ignored their angry buzzing while pulling their carry case from his ash-stained trousers. Once it was in place on his shoulder the hornets landed beside it and crawled inside. Janer placed the hivelink in his earlobe.

'*The ancient hive mind is dead,*' the hive mind told him, then demanded, '*What is happening here?*'

'I would guess the *Sable Keech* has just anchored by the Little Flint,' Janer replied.

'*Tell me what has happened while I have been out of contact.*'

Janer considered the events of the voyage past, and knew he would be talking for quite some time. He also considered simply putting the hivelink back in his pocket, but then with a sigh stepped out of his cabin and began to relate the story. By the time he was halfway up a stairwell accessing the main deck, the hive mind interrupted to inform him, '*Vrell's ship has been destroyed and the other Prador ship is now departing. The Warden has now also informed me of the events at Olian Tay's bank.*'

Janer paused and peered at the two hornets. 'Did you want me to tell this or not?'

'*Please proceed.*'

'Oh, and knowing the events at Olian's you have of course authorized my bonus?'

'*Proceed with the story.*'

'Okay, but I'll be checking that later.' Janer continued upwards. 'Just as it seemed we might be getting things under control, Vrell moved his father's ship right up underneath us . . .'

The sun beaming on the deck, Janer observed that the anchors were indeed lowered but, by the noise of the chains being fed in and out of their lockers and by the intermittent sounds coming from the engines, he guessed the ship's position was being carefully adjusted. He glanced over the rail and saw they were in fact right next to the Little Flint – that place made holy by Sable Keech.

The hive mind once again interrupted his monologue. '*Windcheater warned of further punitive costs should the Little Flint be damaged in any way.*'

'He probably hoped they would crash into it then,' Janer muttered.

'*Now, from your point of view, tell me what happened when you reached Olian's.*'

Janer pointed along the deck to the crowd of Hoopers and reifications gathered amidships. 'You'll have to wait. Others will want to hear this.'

Keech had once told Janer that, to his recollection, his time here on the Little Flint had been no religious experience. Instead he'd had visions of some very *human* devils, tried to survive, then escaped from here to end up in a makeshift tank built by Janer, whilst Erlin had performed the midwife's task of delivering Keech into a new life.

Keech now stood back from the main crowd with Ron and Erlin. Janer approached them.

'What's happening?' Janer asked them.

'This is what this voyage was all about, apparently,' said Keech.

Erlin interjected, looking angry, 'Those reifs still

standing want to see the place – along with seven others who've survived the resurrection process.'

Ron turned and peered at the hornets on Janer's shoulder. 'That sail? Isis Wade?' he asked him.

'First I'll have to tell you who they were,' said Janer. He ignored the harrumph of protest from the hive mind and filled them in on *that* story, before proceeding to its ultimate outcome.

'Kill Death?' Shaking his head, Ron tapped his temple. 'That sail was all at sea without sails . . .'

'But Isis Wade has survived, I gather,' said Erlin. 'I'm glad about that.'

Ron took out his comlink and announced, 'All right boys; let it go.'

The deck began thrumming from the vibration of massive hydraulics, and Janer wondered for a moment what exactly was happening. He saw the nearby rail moving away from him, and the crowd back away from it as the movable section of the ship's hull began to fold down towards the sea, extending down with it the collapsible stair from under the main deck. Placing his comlink back into his belt Ron glanced round to where Forlam was escorting Bloc along the deck.

'What are you going to do with him?' Janer asked, expecting something nasty.

Ron merely shrugged, and gestured towards Keech.

Keech explained, 'He gets to walk on the Little Flint just this once, then I take him back to the Polity. Windcheater decided it would be better that way – for good relations.'

'You're not going to throw him in for a swim, then?'

'It would seem not.' Ron looked disgruntled.

The hull section slapped down onto the sea beside

the Little Flint, the stair from the main deck now fully extended. Hoopers scrambled down this to push out walkways leading onto that lonely piece of stone. After securing these, the Hoopers returned, and then the seven resurrectees walked down.

'I don't like this,' said Keech, moving up beside Ron.

'Seems only fair to let him set foot on the place,' replied the Captain. 'Why are you worried? You get him afterwards.'

'Still . . .' Keech looked round as Bloc finally approached.

Now, Janer spotted Captains Drum and Ambel stepping out from the nearby mainmast stairwell, propelling Aesop and Bones before them. When the four of them reached the edge of the ship, Ambel gazed over to eye his own ship, still trailing on its tow rope behind the *Sable Keech*.

'Not so low in the water, now,' he observed, glancing towards Ron.

The other Captain nodded, then, thumbing its volume down, held his comlink up against his ear.

'*I* did this, I brought them here. I brought them here to the Little Flint!' announced Bloc abruptly, as if that somehow gave him power in this situation.

The other seven resurrectees seemed bemused, and perhaps slightly disappointed. After wandering around on the surface of the Flint for a short time, they were already returning. Still-mobile reifications were now going down for a look around, too, some of them wearing the distinctive dress of Kladites. A few Hoopers joined them.

'The Little Flint,' said Bloc, triumphantly.

Janer eyed Ron, who was now muttering into his

comlink. He went up to stand beside the Captain, but only in time to see Ron thumb the link off.

'Y'know,' said the Captain, 'Convocation didn't agree with Windcheater.'

'Ron, what are you—?'

'Everybody get off there; we ain't got all day!' Ron bellowed, interrupting him. He turned to Bloc. 'I guess it's all right for you to go down for a look.' Indicating Aesop and Bones he added, 'Those two as well.'

Bloc placed his foot down on the Little Flint. He could feel it through the sole of his slipper. With all the obstacles *they* had thrown in his path, he had yet achieved this – no matter what they might think of him. He stooped down to touch the smooth stone, closed his eyes and absorbed the sensation. Standing up again, he glanced at Aesop and Bones, who had wandered off to the other side of Flint. They were conversing in low voices, and it seemed that, despite them having once been under his control, they now found themselves in the same straits as himself. He would make an alliance here. He straightened up and approached them.

'Aesop,' he said, 'Bones.'

'Bloc,' replied Aesop. Bones just licked out his metallic tongue.

'We're even now. You two tortured me to death, and I killed you and made you serve me. Perhaps now we should put our relationship on a financial footing.'

Bones emitted only a hissing titter.

Aesop remarked, 'Bones, even without benefit of flesh, is capable of expressing his amusement better than I can. Tell me, Bloc, what do you suggest?'

Bloc glanced over his shoulder to check the Old

Captains and the others were still back by the walkways. He did not know why they had come down to the foot of the stair. Did they expect him to try to escape?

'We have to retake the *Sable Keech*. More reifications will want to make this voyage here. I can offer you a percentage of the profits.'

As Aesop made a harsh hacking sound, Bloc realized the reif was trying to laugh.

'Oh Taylor Bloc,' he eventually said, 'and how do you think we would fare against three Old Captains? Or against reifications who now hate you because you've brought them here to final death? Or against the Hoopers – and against Sable Keech?'

'There is always a way.'

'It's over, Bloc. You wanted to come here to the Little Flint, because it was your mission, your calling, your destiny . . . whatever. So enjoy it – and remember it until that moment they wipe your mind.'

Bloc turned away to study the Old Captains standing on the stairway, along with Erlin, Janer and Keech.

'Anyway,' continued Aesop from behind him, '*you're* all alive again, and my, don't you look pink. We might as well have ourselves some fun here, as it'll make no difference to the sentence we receive back in the Polity. What do you think, Bones?'

The snicking sound as Bones extruded the blades from his finger ends was all too audible. Bloc turned, shuddering with horror at the memory of sharp blades cutting into his former flesh. He tried to back away, but Aesop's decaying hand closed firmly on the front of his coverall.

'No no . . . You don't understand,' he stammered.

'Too late now,' hissed Aesop.

Bloc heard a shout from behind, and glanced back to see Sable Keech running towards him. It was too late. Too late for all three of them. The other two had not seen the huge iridescent shell rising behind them, nor the dinner-plate eye, nor the enormous tentacles now reaching across the Little Flint.

Sniper closed his own tentacles around the Prador drone and began decelerating before they both burnt up on re-entry. He gripped tightly and kept his weapons systems online, just in case. They descended in a long arc that took them out of night into twilight, then towards daylight. As Sniper brought the drone down on an atoll just catching the rays of the morning sun, he once again opened communication with the Warden.

'What are you doing?' Thirteen asked meanwhile, detaching itself from Sniper's armour and swinging in a circuit around the Prador war drone.

'Repaying a favour.'

'And what was so funny earlier?' asked the little drone.

'You've not figured it out?'

'Knowing your humour, I suspect you somehow knew what Vrell intended to do to Vrost's ship. But how did you know?'

'It wasn't that,' the old drone replied. 'Vrost's ship is probably very badly damaged, but not enough to leave it unable to jump. I'd guess he's now recalling all his forces in preparation to pull out of the system.'

Sniper then concentrated on scanning the Prador drone. Its missile store was thoroughly depleted and its power so low it could not block his scans. Quite possibly the flash-frozen Prador brain inside there had been fried. Sniper began to go to work on the armour, worming his tentacles in through the weapons ports and connecting to some internal systems.

'So?' asked Thirteen, settling on his tail on top of the Prador drone.

'Was it sufficiently damaged for most of Vrost's security protocols to be knocked offline, do you think?' Sniper asked.

Sniper found the required system, short-circuited it, then injected power down one of his tentacles. A loud crump ensued as a triangular hatch opened in the drone's side and slowly hinged down, exposing the tightly packed components inside. Sniper noted the captive's remaining claw moving weakly, as if the drone was trying to reach up and close the hatch again.

'Why is that relevant?' asked the little drone.

'Tell me, Thirteen, don't you think Vrell has received rather shoddy treatment from his own kind?'

'This is how Prador generally treat each other. How they ever managed to organize a civilization beats me.'

'But who do you think is the better between Vrost and Vrell?'

'Neither; they're both monstrous.'

'Then, in conflict, which of them would you prefer to win?'

'Neither, if possible.'

'Please just answer.'

'As the Warden would put it, the one who causes the least collateral damage to Polity citizens.'

'What about internal conflict leading to a weakening of the Third Kingdom? Surely this would be a good thing for the Polity?'

'I guess so.'

Sniper transmitted the latest bit of data he had acquired. Thirteen shut down for a moment to digest it.

With cables and various components hanging about him like fruit-laden vines, Sniper finally found the main power conduits from the Prador drone's batteries. Only a trickle of current was getting through and, tracking back, Sniper found that the cables used to top up the batteries from the fusion reactor were severed, as were the cables providing a direct feed from the reactor into the drone's systems. He cut out some less essential S-con cables and used them to replace those necessary ones, then withdrew. With a cycling whine the drone began to charge up to power again. Eventually it spoke.

'You will get nothing from me,' announced the Prador war drone that was called Vrell.

'You don't have any information I want, anyway. I know about your other self's viral infection and what that infection caused, down to the last detail. I also know about the King's guard, and the orders you were given, and why.'

The Prador drone now lifted slightly, testing its AG. Sniper backed away and observed it drawing inside itself the components and cables he had pulled out. The drone's self-repair mechanisms, now under power, were taking over. The hatch closed, but the drone could not yet block any scan, so urgently was it engaged in diverting power to those batteries and accumulators mainly concerned with its energy weapons.

'Then what do you want?' it asked.

'To repay a favour – to save you.'

'Why?'

'Why didn't you let me fly into your master's defences?' Sniper countered.

'Because I was not ordered to.'

'Then the same answer will do. But tell me, what are your orders now?'

The drone paused, unable to readily supply an answer. It lifted higher into the air.

Sniper suggested, 'Your final order should have resulted in your destruction, so I doubt there are any further orders for you to follow.'

'I have no orders. What do I do?'

'Whatever you want,' Sniper replied.

The Prador drone dropped back down onto the stone surface. Sniper noted how it had reduced the power feed to its weapons and was now concentrating on self-repair. While it was mulling over its present circumstances, Thirteen came back online, having finished studying the data.

'I see,' the little drone said. 'Only one Vrell was aboard – this drone.'

'Exactly.'

'Shouldn't you tell the Warden?'

'Probably, but I'm not going to.'

A snaking tentacle looped around Bones and crushed him like a handful of straws, then discarded him. Aesop had Bloc down on the stone and was pummelling him. It seemed the reif had still not seen what was looming behind. Bloc had seen it, though. He was yelling incoherently and, under the onslaught, trying to crawl towards the walkways. The monstrous whelk finally heaved itself up onto the Little Flint's rim, as if it was reluctant to emerge fully from the sea.

Erlin felt an almost drunken hilarity inside her. Ambel rested a hand on her shoulder.

'Don't worry,' he said. Then, with Janer and the other Captains, he took off after Keech.

Reaching the two combatants, Keech caught Aesop hard with a kick under the stomach that lifted him off Bloc, then he drew and aimed a pulse gun. Ron reached them next, just in time for a tentacle to slam him down against the stone. Another tentacle flicked and Drum arced back through the air to land with a crash on the ship's stair. Erlin considered it a lucky fall – he could have gone into the sea – but Drum seemed in no hurry to get up again. Then she realized that, without thinking, she had moved right out onto one of the walkways.

Keech meanwhile hauled Bloc upright and began dragging him back towards the ship. As a tentacle poised over him, he turned and fired a constant stream of shots into it. The tentacle was snatched away, feeling the heat. Keech tossed Bloc onto the walkway adjacent to the one Erlin occupied, and she watched the newly alive man scramble back towards the ship. Ambel and Janer were now intent on freeing Ron, and the huge combined strength of the Old Captains was beginning to tell. But there were more tentacles to deal with; one snaked out to enfold Aesop and raise him high. As it flicked down again, Erlin flinched at the heavy thud against the side of the ship, and glimpsed Aesop stuck there for a moment before dropping into the sea. Looking down, she realized she now stood upon the Little Flint itself.

What the hell am I doing? Stupid question.

The single dinner-plate eye turned towards her, and the giant whelk rose up, exposing its clacking beak and extending its corkscrew tongue. It recognized her – she knew – and thus focused on her did not notice Janer step back and aim a weapon along the length of tentacle gripping Captain Ron. With a thunderclap, that length of that tentacle disappeared, then as suddenly reappeared in a confetti of white gobbets. The whelk screamed and slammed itself down again. Finally breaking free, Ron heaved himself upright and, leaning on Ambel, stumbled towards the walkways. For a moment the whelk hesitated, thrashing its tentacle stump against the stone, its eye turning to the sea then back towards Erlin, before tentatively stretching another tentacle towards her. Ambel and Ron reached the adjacent walkway, where Ambel paused as Janer moved past him and began helping Ron up the stair.

'Feeling mortal yet?' Ambel asked her.

Suddenly Erlin's body was drenched in cold sweat. Yes, she could walk on the boundary of oblivion, but the moment she stepped over it . . . nothing. And how easy would it be? If she ended up in the ocean, she could become a stripped-fish. If the whelk held onto her it would eat her alive. She turned and ran.

'Get this fucking ramp up!' Ron bellowed into his comlink.

The ramp stair was vibrating underneath Erlin as the tentacle smashed through the walkway behind her. Then the stair was collapsing even as she scrambled up it. Then it was folding back underneath the main deck, as she leapt the gap up onto the planking.

'Aargh, that smarts,' said Drum, holding his quite obviously broken arms away from his body. He had put them out ahead of him to break his fall – and they had. Erlin supposed she would soon be using one of her Hooper programs in an autodoc.

'Was that all part of some plan?' Janer asked Ron, still holding his gun as he peered over the rail.

Straight-faced, Ron replied, 'Not about that bugger.' He glanced over to where Keech had Bloc kneeling so as to face a cabin wall, the pulse gun pressed into the back of his neck. 'We reckoned those other two would do for him.'

Erlin wondered about that. She knew this ship had the facility to detect something the size of that whelk moving about below. And she remembered Ron's furtive use of his comlink. The problem was, being an Old Captain, he'd had plenty of time to practise lying, so she would probably never know for sure.

'Hooper justice,' stated Janer.

'Yeah,' said Ron, then called over to Keech, 'Why? Why save him?'

Keech looked round. 'I adhere to the laws I enforce.'

'You weren't so pernickity with Jay Hoop's gang,' Ron replied.

Keech grimaced, perhaps remembering his long and bloody pursuit of that gang. He said, 'Sentence was already passed on them in their absence. It was death in every case.'

Erlin did not listen to Ron's reply to that. The giant whelk was now wholly occupying the Little Flint, and she thought it still far too close. That single great eye remained focused on her and occasionally blinked. She wondered if she would have to leave Spatterjay to ever be free of pursuit by this monster.

'Not the right place for it, you see.' Ambel pointed. 'Needs island shallows to raise its young.'

Now, almost with disinterest, the whelk turned its eye away from Erlin and, sliding over the other edge of the Flint, it dropped titanically into the sea – and was gone.

*

Aesop made no attempt to swim, his body being so weighed down with internal hardware. Besides, his right arm was shattered, along with many other bones in his body.

Boxies came first, following the trail of balm he was leaving behind as he sank, then swinging round him in a cubic crowd. Soon they were darting in to snatch away loose flesh from his ruptured arm, and from where other bones protruded.

WARN: CELLULAR REPAIR REQ. SHUTTING BALM FLOW AB32 – 46, TORSO 65 – 70, LT (BOTH) 71 – 74 –

Yeah, right.

Aesop shut off all the error messages, which were irrelevant now that the leeches were approaching.

The first one, easily the size of a human leg, crunched into his midriff. Then, in a cloud of balm, it rolled away trailing two metres of carefully preserved intestine. Next a whole shoal of its arm-sized fellows began attaching and writhing round him until he could see nothing but feeding leeches. As this shoal began at last to thin out, he held up one hand stripped of flesh – all gleaming bone and nodular joint motors – and then observed the rapidly approaching bottom. He landed with a crump on a steep slope, and tumbled down it in a cloud of silt.

Eventually coming to rest against an outcrop of flint, he looked down at his ravaged body. Leeches writhed between his ribs. He considered pulling them out, but did not see the point. Others would come to finish the job, and he would rather sooner than later that the point be reached where there was no flesh on him to attract them. Standing up, he began making his way round the slope that ascended to the Little Flint. At one point he paused, looking up, and watched the *Sable Keech* depart.

By the time he found what remained of Bones, he was himself as skeletal as his companion had been. Bones, however, was now just a splintered ribcage with neck vertebrae and skull still attached to it.

Aesop picked him up. Now, where to go? He had no idea where the nearest shore might lie, and his power supply might give out before they reached it. This was, all things considered, the best he could hope for in the circumstances. At least he had a chance . . .

There were fires aboard Vrost's ship. From a distance they looked like small blazes on a floating island, but closer observation showed they burned at the bottom of huge chasms sliced into the very structure of the leviathan vessel. The coil-gun now tilted down against the hull, some missile or massive fragment of Vrell's vessel having cut through its supporting structure. Exposed girders glowed red, radiating into space. The ship turned as it fell away from Spatterjay, presenting its less damaged flank to the approaching swarm. Hundreds of triangular ports already stood open, into which the war drones zipped like bees returning to the hive. The com traffic was intense, since many safety and security protocols had been overridden to get all the troops back aboard and the ship safely away. Besides smoke from the fires wreathing the vessel, emissions of radioactive gas from fusion engines deliberately burning dirty, their flames shading from white to orange, helped provide it with further cover. Vrost did not want to allow the Warden time or opportunity to scan through damaged screening.

The Prador – designated by its armour's CPU as Cverl – had managed to ascertain its destination, even though its com-system had been damaged back on the planet, and it could apparently only send base code to the others. Taking its place in a swirling galaxy of golden-armoured individuals, it fell into line as they descended towards a port. When only two of its fellows were between itself and the opening, it got its first glimpse inside the craft and saw the armoured Prador preceding it land hard on the floor plates as the ship's gravity dragged it down. The long chamber lying beyond was crowded with others of its kind, since they would not be moving on further into the ship until the atmosphere door could be closed and air pressure restored. Air, of course, was vital, being the required fluid medium.

When its turn came, the Prador designated Cverl landed neatly, countering with its armour's AG and then scrambling on into the crowd. Five more came down behind it, then the outer door began to draw closed. With the slow return of atmosphere, the earlier silence was replaced by the incredible racket of heavily armoured Prador crashing around the metal floor.

Such a closely packed crowd was perfect. Only one thing more was required.

Ah . . .

Doors all along each side of the chamber began to open, and the armoured Prador started moving off to be about their assigned tasks. Cverl's own assignment was to collect a plasma torch and take it to a certain location to help clear wreckage. Vrell, now wearing that Prador's armour, crushed the wedge-shaped container he held in his claw, releasing the replicating nanite he had specially adjusted to destroy the nervous systems of Prador with a particular genetic code . . . like all these around him. Ostensibly about to proceed where he had been directed, he paused as a scream issued over com. Glancing back, he saw one armoured Prador collapse down on its belly, while another shot off on AG to crash straight into the ceiling.

Surprisingly fast . . .

Sighing with satisfaction, Vrell rechecked the ship's map in his armour's CPU, and turned to head for Vrost's sanctum.

Epilogue

The Warden viewed the recent report with some interest. It seemed Oboron had been bombarding the Polity with queries and threats for some time now. Apparently Vrost had broken his contact with the Third Kingdom as he took his ship out of the Spatterjay system, and had not been in communication since. The information Sniper had gathered was just part of the story. Obviously, like Oboron and all his kin, Vrell had been changed by the Spatterjay virus. But this report now put the final touch to the story.

'The real Vrell was not aboard his father's ship when it destructed,' the AI sent. 'He in fact boarded Vrost's ship in the guise of a King's guard.'

'Ding dong. Correct answer and zero points for effort.'

'What are you doing down there, Sniper?'

'Just introducing someone to an adapted version of "attitude",' the old drone replied.

'Sniper, I have one of my sat-eyes poised directly above you, and there is currently no cloud cover, so there is no point in you being disingenuous. Thirteen, if you would allow me visual access?'

After a delay, presumably during which the little drone and the old drone had some discussion or argument, the link established and the Warden gazed from Thirteen's eyes.

'Meet Vrell,' said Sniper, laconically.

The old drone and the Prador war drone were now cruising slowly above the ocean. Both of them were battered and scorched.

'What do you intend to do with your prisoner?' the AI asked.

'I just recruited him,' replied Sniper. 'You got a job for him?'

'I doubt a Prador war drone would best serve the interests of the Polity.'

'Oh, they ain't so different really. Scrap a bit of the conditioning, wipe standing orders, and in goes "attitude" – I think you'll find him useful.'

'And it has itself agreed to this?'

'Not really, but I established a programming link while I was repairing him.'

'Please route me through to that drone directly.'

As Sniper obliged, the Warden paused before asking, 'Vrell, do you wish to serve the Polity?'

'Yeah, fucking right!'

'And how best do you think you might serve the Polity?'

'Give me something to destroy!'

'Oops,' said Sniper, quickly breaking communication.

In its silicon heart the Warden sighed – and it would have shaken its head had it possessed one. The AI then turned its attention to one of its subminds. SM2, the metre-long iron turbot, was again working as a vending tray in the concourse of the Coram base, but this time at the Warden's behest.

Janer took his drink from the distinctly fishy floating tray, took a cautious sip, then eyed the tray as it drifted over to serve the sofa opposite.

Taking her own drink, Erlin asked, 'So what are your plans?'

'We will return to Hive,' said Isis Wade, who was seated on the sofa beside Janer. 'I am now the singular owner of some property there.'

Wade was now fully restored, in a physical sense, though there now seemed to Erlin a lack of the former surety in his speech. But it was open to conjecture whether that resulted from deliberate emulation or some more deep-rooted cause.

'But why are *you* going?' Erlin directed the question at Janer.

'I've been there before a couple of times, but only visited part of it, so there's a whole world still to see. You know,' Janer closed his free hand into a fist and bumped it against his temple, 'gotta keep busy.'

Erlin responded with a measured nod – indeed, how well she knew that.

'Shut the fuck up,' Janer muttered to the carry case affixed on his shoulder.

Erlin grinned, almost able to guess what the hive mind was saying to him – probably some sarcastic comment about Janer's 'busy-ness'. She then glanced beyond him towards a commotion on the other side of the concourse. 'Here they come.'

Janer and Wade turned simultaneously.

Even though the concourse was not particularly

crowded, the people occupying it moved sharply out of the approaching party's way. Erlin then noticed some of the Polity citizens groping in pockets for their holocams. Their fascination was understandable, as four Old Captains together in one place was not a common sight. It was certainly an impressive one.

Ambel, Ron, Drum and Orbus – they strolled along with leisurely power, appearing utterly dominant, as if they could rip this moon base apart with their bare hands. Forlam, not yet having attained such great age, just looked dangerous and edgy alongside them. Crewman Drooble still bore the smiling expression of the mildly demented. Keech alone seemed utterly normal and human amidst them, while his prisoner, Bloc, almost faded into insignificance. Even as this diverse bunch arrived at the bar, the turbot vending tray was returning laden with big mugs of seacane rum. Janer glanced at Wade and raised an eyebrow.

'Old Captains are always thirsty,' Wade explained, having summoned the tray by internal radio.

While the new arrivals gathered round them, only Keech held back.

'My slot is nearly due,' he announced. 'I should say my goodbyes now.'

'Then say them, lad,' said Ambel. 'Just give him to me.'

As Ambel grabbed Bloc's shoulder, the man stared up at him, terrified. Erlin considered what was in store for him: forensic examination and interrogation by AI, then inevitably mindwipe. But perhaps Bloc somehow thought he would escape that fate. However, there would be no such mercy if he remained here in the hands of the Old Captains.

'It's been as interesting as ever.' Keech shook hands all round. Then, eyeing Janer and Erlin, 'I will see you again, perhaps.'

Retrieving Bloc from Ambel's firm grasp he slapped that Old Captain on the shoulder. 'Stay well, Ambel.' Then he herded his prisoner off towards the runcible embarkation lounge.

'We should be moving as well.' Wade stood up.

'Yeah.' Janer quickly rose too.

The vending tray, now empty, abruptly swooped in on them. When Janer looked up, it was hovering only a metre in front of his face.

'Janer Cord Anders,' it announced, 'you seem to have forgotten something.'

'I beg your pardon?'

The tray opened two small laser ports situated on its underside.

'You're just no fun,' grumbled Janer. He removed the singun from his jacket and tossed it onto the tray. 'Can we go now?'

The tray floated higher. 'Of course.'

Janer said only brief goodbyes, until he came to Erlin.

'Will you ever come back here?' she asked him.

Grinning widely, he took hold of her chin and kissed her hard on the mouth.

'Oh definitely,' he said, and turned away.

Feeling slightly discomfited, Erlin watched them disappear after Keech and Bloc. Ambel sat down beside her, studying her with some amusement, before both turned their attention to Captain Ron, who was still standing, arms akimbo, conversing with Captain Orbus.

'Are you sure about this?' he asked.

'I'm sure,' Orbus growled, then glanced at Drooble.

'We've been on that ocean too long. We've got to do something new.'

'And can you?' asked Ron.

Orbus looked directly at Erlin as he said, 'The change, it twists you round. Mostly that's bad, but sometimes it twists you right.' Feeling further discomfiture, Erlin found she could not meet his gaze. Returning his attention to Ron, he continued, 'I've done some bad things in my life. But not any more.'

Ron nodded contemplatively, then slowly removed a palm console from a capacious pocket of his canvas trousers. He handed it to Orbus. 'It's all there: the manifest and the contract with the owners. They've no pilots out this way, so they're glad to have you on board. Their only real requirement is that you get the *Gurnard* back in one piece.'

Orbus accepted the console, grabbed Drooble by the shoulder and turned away, heading for the spaceport airlocks.

'How can Ron trust him?' Erlin muttered to Ambel.

Ambel smiled. 'We Captains, we're old – we know how to judge people.'

'Yes, I suppose.'

'What about you? Are you staying or leaving?' he asked.

'I'll stay – if you have the patience, and the time for me.'

'I've got plenty of both,' the Old Captain replied.